He continued to drop the photographs, one by one. Eventually, all the bodies were in the shallow pit and an earthmover was poised in one of the last photographs to cover them with the raw red earth. The dam project, the resort or whatever it was, had required the village to cease to exist: its inhabitants should have known better than to disagree. All that now remained of these people were these photographs, taken by a boy who was murdered just *because* he had taken them. Kumar was dead not because of Hyde or because of heroin or Straits Royal, but because he had seen and photographed a routine atrocity.

They'd killed a hundred, maybe more, in a site clearance – then killed Kumar because he had the evidence. Jesus Christ – it *always* appalled him, it was insanity.

Who had Kumar threatened to expose? Who was –

– a crash of glass from the passage. His chair clattered to the floor as he was startled to his feet. Then the table followed, spilling the snapshots as he overturned it to shield himself. Something rolled towards the door of the room, smouldering. Then it exploded –

Fire everywhere, blinding him, smoke suffocating him.

Also by Craig Thomas:

RAT TRAP
FIREFOX
WOLFSBANE
SNOW FALCON
EMERALD DECISION
SEA LEOPARD
JADE TIGER
FIREFOX DOWN
THE BEAR'S TEARS
WINTER HAWK
ALL THE GREY CATS
THE LAST RAVEN
A HOODED CROW
PLAYING WITH COBRAS
A WILD JUSTICE
A DIFFERENT WAR

Non-fiction

THERE TO HERE: IDEAS OF POLITICAL SOCIETY

CRAIG THOMAS

Slipping into Shadow

WARNER BOOKS

A *Warner* Book

First published in Great Britain in 1998 by Little, Brown UK
This edition published by Warner Books in 1999
Reprinted in 2000, 2001

Copyright © 1998 Craig Thomas & Associates

Lines from Aeschylus (*Agamemnon* and *The Eumenides*) are
reproduced by kind permission of Robert Fagles and Penguin Books
Copyright © 1966, 1967, 1975 by Robert Fagles

The moral right of the author has been asserted.

A CIP catalogue record for this book
is available from the British Library.

ISBN 0 7515 1808 5

Typeset by Solidus (Bristol) Ltd
Printed and bound in Great Britain by Clays Ltd, St Ives plc

Warner Books
A Division of
Little, Brown and Company (UK)
Brettenham House
Lancaster Place
London WC2E 7EN

www.littlebrown.co.uk

for

Daw Aung San Suu Kyi

and

The National League for Democracy

with admiration

PRELUDE

... the young are lost forever.
Yet someone hears on high ...
          Aeschylus, *Agamemnon*, 11.60–1

Across the river, the high-rise banks were like scorched, blackened trees against the sear of the lightning. Patrick Hyde flinched instinctively against the nuclear light of the glare, then at the tropical thunder which followed. The humid, hot night air smelt of ozone. Then the halo of light around the arrogant figure of the Raffles Statue died away, and he blinked and stretched the glare from his retinae and focused on the small group of men around the base of the statue.

The two Chinese were no more than bodyguards, one of them leaning on the railing, the river behind him, the second a shadow on the pavement twenty yards away. The river gleamed with the city's reflected neon and the strung-bead lights of tourist and restaurant junks. *His* man was half crouched in conversation with a Malay and a white man, between the statue and the river. The noise of the thunder rolled away towards the Malaysian mainland. He recognised the Malay as the usual supplier; the white man, the one this half-cock operation had been designed to draw out, was a stranger to Hyde.

The whispered, urgent conversation between the three men tickled in the earpiece of the surveillance equipment. The receiver and its tiny recorder were beneath his armpit. The harness was tight, sweatmaking, across his chest and back.

Hyde raised the SLR camera and its long, Minimodulux night-vision lens to his eye, resting the barrel of the telephoto lens on the parapet of the bridge. He adjusted the focus, and the features of Henderson, the crooked Sydney cop, appeared like a clear, sharp residue. The Malay was almost face-on to him; the white man was bending his profile obligingly into the frame. Hyde pressed the button noiselessly, and the film moved on silently. He took two more pictures. Their conversation had once more stuttered to a halt. Hyde could see black sweat stains on the armpits of Henderson's suit.

Lightning walked brutally along the edge of Singapore city, out near Changi airport, succeeded by deafening thunder. The humidity, having parted like an enveloping curtain for a second or two, pressed back around him. He listened in the returned silence to the hot, tense absence of words between the three men.

It was all too last-minute to allow any confidence. He had turned Henderson only a week earlier, photographing him handing over – out of the boot of his car, its number-plate sharply in focus in the shots – a consignment of Burmese heroin in Sydney's King's Cross district to a known dealer, a Vietnamese. Henderson, when confronted with the incriminating evidence, had crumbled, and agreed to force a meeting in Singapore with *someone higher up* than the Malay who usually supplied him. It had been an act of desperation, and unofficial. Australian Security and Intelligence, who had co-opted Hyde into the undercover team investigating police corruption and involvement in drug dealing, had been about to pull the plug on the operation. Just at the moment when it seemed to be widening and deepening. The politicians, in an election year, wanted only so much corruption, a show trial of the half-dozen crooked detectives they had exposed. Hyde, furious as a denied child, had wanted more.

So Henderson had been forced to arrange a meeting, ostensibly to try for an increase in supplies of Burmese heroin, and had to wear a microphone taped to his body. Be photographed. Provide enough evidence to force Sydney to allow the undercover operation to continue, to widen its brief. Six crooked cops didn't account for the hundreds of kilos of Burmese heroin flooding into Oz every year...

Henderson himself knew little, next to nothing. He and his corrupt cronies collected the heroin from various Chinese or Malay bagmen, in either Singapore or Macau – while staying free of charge at a five-star hotel or resort and playing the casinos with unlimited credit – then brought it into Oz by means of a brown-envelope job with two bent Customs officers at Kingsford Smith airport. The heroin would be in their hand-luggage, which was never X-rayed, never searched. It had been happening like that for three years. Sometimes Henderson or one of his mates took the heroin up to a Queensland resort, sometimes they passed it directly to Sydney dealers.

Hyde shivered into attentiveness as Henderson said:

'We *can* handle more, I tell you. It'll be no sweat, sport... We can guarantee the stuff can be got in – two, three times

as often, three or four times as much – in complete safety
. . .' He could hear Henderson's a rhythmic breathing,
stifled, harsh. Being wired turned everybody into a bad
actor.

The white man, tall and slim, grey-suited in the humid
night, seemed unimpressed. The long fingers of his right
hand stroked his narrow chin. Hyde could not avoid the
suspicion that he was assessing Henderson's performance. Did he suspect he was wired?

Again, Hyde cursed the electrics failure that had
delayed his flight from Sydney for eight hours. Cursed
more violently Medhev Kumar's scribbled note, left for
him at his hotel with the surveillance equipment he had
asked for. Something about his mother being ill . . . Kumar,
his invaluable local help, had bolted back to his
godforsaken Burmese village without even organising
local back-up for Hyde.

Although he had not told the Sydney cop, he was on his
own. If anything went wrong, he couldn't do a thing to
help Henderson.

'We're satisfied with present arrangements,' the white
man murmured. The accent was Australian, but ironed
out and cushioned by money or habitual authority. The
two Chinese remained posed in apparent unconcern, but
the Malay seemed to hover a step closer—

—lightning again, irradiating the group near the statue.
Startling Henderson, Hyde saw clearly through the
camera. In the moment before the thunder deafened him,
he heard the man's breathing leap, his heartbeat race in
the earpiece. Felt his own tension mount. The light died
behind the tall office blocks marshalled like glass and
concrete sentries on the opposite bank of the river. Then
the humid darkness returned with Singapore's nighttime
glow.

The Malay had moved still closer to Henderson, and the white man was bending towards him. Henderson didn't know the man, that much was obvious; and hugely disappointing.

'It wasn't necessary for me to be here,' he observed languidly, his words muffled by Henderson's rapid breathing. Hyde could see, through the camera lens, the sheen of sweat on Henderson's forehead. He looked as pale as a corpse. 'You asked for this meeting, Inspector, with someone who could authorise— You seem nervous?'

It had changed. The situation had teetered off-balance, and now it had stumbled.

'What's the matter, Henderson? What's wrong?' the white man asked.

It was like watching a very familiar movie, where Hyde already knew the next snatches of dialogue, the actors' expressions and movements. He watched, beginning to be appalled. It was going wrong, it was blown. Unless Henderson—

—lightning. Henderson's features crumbling into fear, the scene almost colourless through the night-vision lens, the tall banks standing out like mausoleums across the silvered water. The Malay moved closer to Henderson, the cop protested feebly, the light died away. The Malay exclaimed as his quick hands discovered that Henderson was wired—

—all noise drowned by the tropical thunder.

As the glare faded from Hyde's retinae, he made out a still, single form lying in the shadow of the Raffles Statue, other running shadows making for the long black limousine parked a hundred yards away on Parliament Lane. As the thunder retreated, he heard the car's engine catch and then accelerate away. A gleam of brake lights.

He lowered the camera from his eye and the scene

diminished, snatched away from him as certainly and violently as Henderson had been. Hyde pulled the silent earpiece from his ear and flung it away, glancing inside his cotton jacket at the webbing of the harness that held the receiver and recorder, as at some malignant tumour that moment confirmed.

'Shit,' he breathed. The humid air stifled other words.

He stood upright on the Cavanagh Bridge. At that distance, Raffles' statue was mansized and the prone shadow of Henderson's body was no larger than a patch of rainwater that hadn't yet dried. He banged his hands on the parapet, scenting the first food stalls beside the river, flaring with fires as small as pistol flames. Then he stared down at the sullen, light-flecked water flowing beneath the pedestrian bridge.

He wanted to blame Kumar, who had disappeared and left him stranded, unable to protect Henderson with local help. Knowing that it was really he himself who had got Henderson knifed to death. He'd become greedy for what he imagined Henderson could lead him to – new faces like that of the white man, connections with the hotel chain whose casinos *must* be laundering operations for the heroin profits . . . Hyde shook his head. Banged his palms once more on the parapet. He had wanted to stop the undercover operation being closed down, had wanted to see where it would lead . . . and had sacrificed Henderson, without authority, for the sake of his curiosity and anger. And a theory that ASIO and the Commissioner of Police didn't believe.

Dead end. There was nothing more, no other way of going on with it.

He unscrewed the lens from the camera and dropped them both into the sports bag at his feet. Took off his jacket and tugged at the velcro holding the harness tightly

8

around his sweating back and chest. Threw it all into the bag. Someone laughed on the deck of a tourist junk passing beneath the bridge. Lightning exposed the shape of Henderson's corpse. Then the returning darkness and the noise of thunder.

There'd be a show trial of the five surviving corrupt cops to reassure the public. The politicians and the businessmen would hear their heart rates subside, their breathing become easier. It was so bloody *big*, the Burmese heroin trade, that no one wanted to know the real truth.

Hyde picked up the shoulder bag. There was no point in going anywhere near the body and perhaps being seen. Henderson was dead.

He walked back across the bridge towards the tunnel of food stalls and Parliament House, not glancing once at the statue of Singapore's founder and the small stain of the body lying at its base.

Using her pencil with an angry weight, Marian Pyott scored through the man's name, amused by the image of castration that flitted through her imagination. Leaning back carefully in her chair to avoid aggravating the customary ache in her back and side, she lit another cigarette and blew smoke at the yellowing ceiling. The rain dribbled on the window of the constituency office like saliva on a geriatric chin. She shivered. Early October was already cold, and the central heating had not been serviced; the electric fire smelt of singed dust and was inadequate to the task of warming the big, drab room in which she held her Saturday-morning surgeries.

She snorted smoke at the memory of the man's telephone call. *Get me off this drink-driving charge, there's a good girl* ... When she had refused his threats

9

and bragging pleas, it had become a question of didn't know why he'd ever voted for her, wouldn't do it again, what else was she there for? The police had breathalysed him in a pub car park. His contributions to party funds, the use of his lawn to erect a tent for a fundraiser apparently had been enough to ensure her interference with the course of the law.

'I haven't time to help *you*,' she announced to the rain-smeared window.

There were constituents waiting in the outer room, silent but for the noises of a child playfully tormenting a dog. She looked down at her list. Four more cases. It was already eleven thirty. She had only the sketchiest details of whatever had interrupted their lives sufficiently for them to need their MP's help on a rainy morning in autumn when they would normally be shopping. She had already dealt with six cases. *Dealt?* Listened, soothed, upbraided, offered advice or assistance – but not solved. Most of them expected their problems to appear within the week on a televised Commons programme, at the heart of a ringing speech on justice, freedom and the rights of the individual; momentary celebrity where there was no real solution.

An old woman terrorised on a council estate abandoned by the police and social services to the depredations of muggers and burglars ... the wife whose vanished husband the CSA were too busy or incompetent to trace ... the MD of a local company swallowed by a conglomerate and whose workforce were now having their jobs exported to Mexico.

Her left leg ached as she shifted her weight in her chair. Must be the weather. She still walked with a slight limp. There was a neat scar behind her left ear and one on her neck; other and larger weals on her pelvis, stomach and arm – all of them tangible reminders that David Winterborne had tried to have her murdered in Brussels a year ago. Marian shivered at the recollection, then lit another cigarette and smoked it noisily. The child and the dog continued to bicker in the waiting room.

She had visited David once in prison – a large country house in Kent. In his first-floor room he had his hi-fi, his books and PC, and nothing but trust kept him within the prison grounds. He continued to run his business empire from what the Home Office was pleased to call his confinement. His father, Clive, had assumed non-executive chairmanship of Winterborne Holdings. She had gone there to show him she was walking, breathing, that the scars were covered by her hair and clothes... and to gloat, just a little. Instead, seeing his fax machine, his computer, the small bank of telephones, the deference of the prison officers, it had been she who had been outfaced and humiliated. David had laughed at her, sensing her motives and their disappointment.

In exchange for his pleading guilty to the misappropriation of European Union funds, the Crown Prosecution Service had dropped all other charges and abandoned their investigation into murder by proxy, the ruin of an American aircraft company, the sabotage of two airliners. The Home Office had refused to extradite him to face charges in the US. He would be free in another ten months *without a stain on his character*. The limp, the nightmares and the blinding headaches would all last longer than David's term of imprisonment.

Once more she snorted smoke at the ceiling. *Bugger David*, she decided savagely, grinding out the cigarette and pressing the buzzer to summon the next constituent on her list. Road-widening in a village on the edge of the constituency, where the city and its satellite market town

11

struggled out into Warwickshire. A farmer and a newcomer had joined forces to protest, the latter middle-class, articulate and Green. Whose car had they come in? she wondered, recovering her humour. Her dissatisfaction with David Winterborne's exposure and sentence was – she occasionally admitted – no more than a motif for a deeper vacancy and discontent; for something missing in her private world, a sense of empty space in her personal life.

She heard the woman's sharp voice raised in protest in the waiting room, then the farmer's bass lilt, and an Asian voice, young and female, that she recognised. The temperature of the voices was becoming that of a quarrel. Marian scowled and pushed back her chair, moving awkwardly, then more easily as the cramp in her left leg eased. Her agent's secretary must have popped out. She usually kept better order.

She opened the door.

Three actors and a small audience. The farmer and his Green conscience in her denims and Burberry waterproof. And Syeeda Lal, rain speckling the shoulders of her raincoat, water dripping on to the scuffed and worn carpet from her umbrella. All three turned to her as if on cue.

Marian held up her hands.

'Mrs Topping has popped out, I see. Please!' she insisted. 'One at a time.'

The Green conscience evidently felt that the Burberry conferred precedence. She was about to speak when Syeeda burst out:

'Please, Marian—! This is an emergency, really! I have to talk to you now!' Her huge eyes were stained beneath as if with kohl. Her quivering mouth seemed only able to approximate to her words and breathing. Marian could not ignore the hunted expression on her face.

Ostentatiously, she looked at her watch.

'*Five* minutes,' she announced. 'I'm sorry, Mrs Rainsford, I'm sure you understand—' She ushered Syeeda into the office and closed the door on the Rainsford female blustering at the offence to her importance and convictions.

Marian lost all interest in the traffic problems of a gentrified village. Syeeda looked like an escapee caught in a bright searchlight, frightened and bewildered.

'Syeeda – sit down,' she insisted. The young woman seemed rendered savage, unused to rooms and furniture, by whatever had happened to her. 'Please . . .'

She pulled the chair away from the desk and all but forced Syeeda Lal on to it, where she perched like a hunched, bedraggled bird, her hands twisting in her lap, the rain gleaming on her shoulders and sparkling in her black hair. Carefully, Marian regained her seat.

'What is it? What can I do?'

Syeeda looked up from her hands. The strap of her shoulder bag fell to rest in the crook of her arm. The umbrella stained the carpet. Her huge eyes filled with tears, which began to stream helplessly down her cheeks.

'He's – dead.' Utter bewilderment, the traumatic shock of a collision at high speed. 'Medhev . . . the police. They came to see me at the restaurant – to tell me. Medhev is dead . . .' Her suddenly husky voice seemed to be lost in her grief and despair.

'Now – today?' was all that Marian could offer.

She knew the boy. Medhev Kumar. She had been introduced to him some three or four months before, soon after he had arrived in the market town – from Burma, of all places. Syeeda managed the Jaipur restaurant for her father; the jewel in the crown of his small chain of Indian restaurants. Kumar was some kind of distant relative.

There was some concealed, even tragic reason for his leaving Burma.

'Today?' Marian repeated. 'How?'

Syeeda nodded fiercely, then abruptly the gesture changed to one of vehement denial. Tears and rain fell into her lap.

'They say – it was ... an overdose of *drugs*.' She swallowed with an ugly, gobbling sound. 'They asked me how long he had been an *addict* ... They asked me if I knew he was suspected of selling drugs!' It was as if she was a medium for the dead boy, protesting his innocence.

The rain was chilly on the fugged glass of the tall, eighteenth-century window. Even the framed photograph of the former Prime Minister and Tory leader, despite its egregious, smirking expression, seemed unsettled by Syeeda's outburst.

'They're saying that Medhev was ... a drug dealer? Surely they can't think that—?'

'They *do*!' The tears were gone and her eyes were darkly fierce. 'They thought his connections with Myanmar very interesting! They said they had been watching him for some time – even that his asylum claim might have been a lie to help him stay ...'

'Burma?'

Kumar was from Myanmar – she still thought of it as Burma – and so was a great deal of the heroin finding its way into the UK. He had come to work in one of Rabindur Lal's restaurants and had applied for political asylum. The grounds were his support for Aung San Suu Kyi and the democracy movement in Burma, and his opposition to the military junta. As far as Marian knew, his application was still being processed. Her few conversations with a junior Home Office minister on the subject had been reassuring. She had believed the boy's story, guided his application. Had it been nothing but lies . . . ?

She masked her expression of doubt behind cigarette smoke.

Kumar had, a month before, become engaged to Syeeda. If his application for asylum failed, he'd be able to stay as her husband. Syeeda's ever-indulgent parents had forgiven Kumar even his poverty, and had blessed the engagement.

There had been an aloofness about Kumar, a prickly secretiveness that was almost contempt for Marian's own protestations and articles in the cause of Burmese democracy. Almost as if he had regarded her as a complacent, bleeding-heart outsider. He had never discussed his tragic country with her. Was it her resentment of that that made it possible to believe ill of him now?

'Was it – heroin?'

'Yes!' Syeeda snapped back, as if she had read Marian's thoughts. 'Marian – Medhev did not take drugs. I trained as a *nurse*, I would *know* the signs! I know what addiction looks like.'

'You're certain . . . ? God, this is – terrible.'

He might have *dealt* in drugs, though. Marian, with a sharp, clear selfishness, did feel deceived. Syeeda's face was bent towards her hands. The rain beat against the window. She heard the hum of traffic, the noises of feet on the wet pavement. The dog and the child in the waiting room. Mrs Topping's over-loud, over-cheerful voice startled them both out of their long silence. Back from shopping, Marian thought, her mind eager to berth at some great distance from the knowledge of the boy's death and her suspicions of him.

Syeeda had been a nursing sister until the pressure of her parents' son-less marriage had squeezed her into the role of heiress to the restaurant chain. She *would* have known if Kumar had been an addict. Not necessarily known whether or not he was a dealer . . .

. . . The Union of Myanmar – Burma – was one angle of the Golden Triangle. Kumar had come from some obscure village in Shan state, in the north-east of the country, where the heroin trade was all-powerful, all-pervasive. Was he—?

She realised that Syeeda was shaking her head violently as she watched her intently. Her perm-frizzed hair swung as heavily as a cape about her small face.

'It's not true,' she said. 'You will help me find the *truth*, Marian – won't you?'

Then she seemed to subside, some spring in her broken. The Monet print on the far wall, the grey filing cabinets, the posters and lists, the dusty leather sofa and the scratched desk all reasserted their habitual impression that nothing as serious as this could happen amid those surroundings.

Yes, she would ring the local police, a detective inspector she knew quite well. Perhaps even the Chief Constable. The matter could, at least, be clarified. She hesitated, then asked:

'Did – did the police say they found drugs? On Medhev, at his—?'

Syeeda nodded angrily.

'They say there was heroin hidden in his flat. Under the mattress on which he was . . . found—' The words vanished into a tunnel of grief, her features collapsing into anguish. Marian glanced aside from the desperation in her eyes and picked up the telephone. Then Syeeda recovered her voice. 'I hadn't seen him for twenty-four hours . . . He rang in to say he couldn't come to the restaurant, that he wasn't feeling well – yesterday. Then, this morning' – surprisingly, she looked at her watch – 'an hour ago, the police came. I'd

16

just got back from the market and they were waiting for me ...' She was no longer speaking to Marian but to herself.

Marian dialled the police number. Kumar – Burma – heroin ... Syeeda's beloved fiancé an addict and a dealer ... ?

PART ONE

The Golden River

A keen hound, this stranger.
Trailing murder, and murder she will find.
                    Aeschylus, *Agamemnon*, 11.1093–4

The Buddhist concept of law is based on *dhamma*,
righteousness or virtue, not on the power to
impose harsh and inflexible rules on a
defenceless people.
                    Aung San Suu Kyi (1989)

CHAPTER ONE

The Lotus Eater

The pleasure of Ros' mood increased as she entered the house that looked down from Sydney's North Shore towards the Bridge and the Opera House – until she saw him standing at the open windows of the lounge, hands in the pockets of his Armani suit, shoulders slightly hunched, staring abstractedly down at the Harbour and the city. The Bridge was already a necklace of vehicle lights, though the spring day lingered in the soft air beyond the balcony.

Evidently flung angrily aside, a newspaper lay on the thick carpet near the window. Its front page blared the first day of the trial on corruption and drug charges of five officers of the Sydney police force. The set of Hyde's body, back still towards her, was that of sullen, even baffled defiance. When he turned to her, his expression was grim, his disappointment obvious.

'OK?' he asked without any real interest, nodding at the briefcase and the big artist's folder that she dropped on to the *chaise-longue.*

'Fine!' she returned, still hoping that his mood would evaporate. 'Great!' The words fell between them like unfilled balloons. 'You're ready early,' she added, brushing her hair away from her cheeks.

The distant hum of traffic from rush-hour homegoing reached her through the open windows. Hands still in his pockets, he seemed to study her and the context of the room as if he had that moment awoken in a strange place.

Ros took the tumbler of gin and tonic from the housekeeper and raised it towards him. The room's occasional tables and other polished surfaces were suitably littered with trays of canapés, bowls of nibbles for people to peck at. In the dining room beyond the lounge, the William IV table was laden with glasses and a cold buffet. She had glanced in and been satisfied.

'Here's to a good day's work. Cheers, Hyde.'

'I'm glad,' he responded without enthusiasm. 'You swung the contract, then.'

She shook her head, confidence undimmed by admission.

'Not yet. But close—'

He followed her on to the balcony. The big house seemed to lean out over the water like a poised, confident diver. Sails speckled the Harbour, most of them as small as wave-flecks. She smelt the early evening's first barbecue, heard the murmur of voices from a neighbour's garden. She breathed deeply.

When she spoke, her tone was one of parental cajoling.

'Never mind, you did well, there's no need to be upset.' The trouble with Hyde was, the whole business had become an obsession. 'Can't you just forget it for this evening. Please—?' She held his arm and squeezed it.

'Ros, for Christ's sake—!'

'Hyde! What's the bloody matter with you?'

'The Commissioner, what do you think?'

'You got in to see him, then?'

'Him and the bloody Director of ASIO – after banging on every door I could find for the last four months, someone heard me knocking!' He walked away from her to the far end of the balcony. 'They told me to piss off. The Commissioner thought my theories were *more than a little fanciful, Mr Hyde. We're grateful for your help, of course...*'

Ros burst into laughter at his wickedly accurate impersonation of the Commissioner of Police. Hyde disgorged a tired grin in response.

'You did your best, Hyde. Bugger the powers-that-be if they don't want to listen ... They don't need the hassle. Having five blokes in the dock is enough for them. It reassures the public that the people they vote for are looking after them. I did—'

'Warn me? Darling, you did.' He raised his arms above his head in bafflement. 'You even told me I was barking up the wrong gum, that my theories were crap. The first stages of paranoia.' His impersonation of her was just as cuttingly accurate.

Behind them, the caterers moved as if on castors through the well-lit rooms, their voices whispers, their movements a reminder to Ros that she was a rich businesswoman, a charitable hostess, an arts patroness. That evening, after a brief cocktail reception at the house, a column of limousines would take them and their guests to a charity première of *Don Giovanni* at the Opera House. Supper would follow, back at the house.

'I'm sorry.' Her impatience bubbled despite her

sympathy. Hyde was looking for something; his motive was dissatisfaction. 'But you've come back here carrying the banner with the strange device, Hyde. On a crusade to clean up the whole bloody country.' She moved closer to him and again squeezed his arm. He tossed his head in reluctant admission. She finished her gin and tonic, the ice clinking against her teeth. 'I need a shower – and I've got ten minutes!' she blurted, looking at her watch. Her plump hand patted his arm. 'You'll be all right – this evening, I mean?'

'Just pissed off – I'll be OK. I won't misbehave.'

'Ta. Anyway, now that you've signed off, you can come to Singapore with me next week. Or go and do Aubrey's little errand first, and I'll met you in Penang. We'll have a bit of a holiday—?'

'OK. Sure – distraction's OK, Ros.'

'You can't take this any further, Hyde.'

'No, I bloody can't, can I?' he sulked. Then he smiled and raised his hands. 'OK. They've blown full-time. I promise.'

'Good.'

Ros, prepared to be easily satisfied, retreated from the balcony, at once calling out to the housekeeper and the caterers something about the time, the number of guests, the table setting.

Hyde continued to watch the flecks of the sails on the slowly darkening water of the Parramatta. Across the Harbour, the city went about tidying its glittering business day and anticipating its evening. Insects had begun to detonate against cold blue lights along the balcony and those scattered like mines over the terraced gardens below.

Ros was right, of course and as always. He knew he must acknowledge failure, four months after Henderson had been killed in Singapore. In reality, that had been the door closing; he just hadn't heard the slamming noise. Since then, everything had been abortive, time-wasting – all the trips to Queensland, Singapore, Macau, the bank accounts of the arrested police officers, the hotel records that demonstrated that they had always forgotten to pay their bills, that they had been allowed unlimited credit in hotel casinos on their jaunts to collect the heroin ... Everything growing bigger and cloudier all the time, and more messy. The political joes didn't like that. Ros was right again. They just wanted a nice *little* show trial and the votes it brought.

The Commissioner of Police and the Director of ASIO – who had flown up from Canberra for the meeting – had read his palm for him. *Bugger off and leave this alone*, was the unmistakable message. *You're becoming a nuisance.* He'd stormed out like a tragedy queen, of course.

It *had* become an obsession. Nice two-year-old by boredom out of displacement. The dirty weekend with Dangerwoman was over, it was Monday morning ...

Ros had flourished in Oz while he had quietly wilted. She'd inherited her uncle's cattle stations and property interests, sold the former, invested wisely, bought up companies as if by whim rather than design, and Midas-touched them, for the most part. The interior design agency she'd acquired had become a passion. Ros was having fun, discovering a talent for business, design, fundraising. She was utterly at home in Australia ...

... while he was merely resident here. London was no longer home, while Oz, which he had left as a child, remained somehow alien and unreal; a holiday destination he had forgotten to leave before his airline booking was past its sell-by date. He wore the country like his Armani suit, as a disguise, an apparent identity, but without meaning. His sense of somehow being on a desert island like a lotus eater rarely left him. He was tied to London only by the unsold house in Earls Court and the cats, who he refused to collect and bring out to Oz. They remained in Earls Court, half adopted by Max, the ground-floor tenant.

Ros was fixed now, as surely as any Ten-Pound Pom who'd come out in the fifties or sixties. He, too, was quartered safe in Sydney's best suburb. There was no going from here. He could never leave Ros, ought to be content.

Wasn't ... *Othello's occupation's gone*, Ros had quoted at him. The mockery hadn't worked. The undercover operation had been work, while it lasted. Something in the job centre for his peculiar talents. And it remained out there, unfinished ...

... five crooked cops didn't account for the heroin flooding into Oz from Burma. Straits Royal Group hotels *had* to be involved, otherwise why the free holidays for the cops and the unlimited credit in their casinos? Perhaps if Kumar hadn't buggered off when he had, Henderson might have led them on, further into the maze ... ? Kumar had gone to England, working in a curry shop in the Midlands. No explanation in his one letter as to why he'd dropped everything and gone running back to Burma. Just hints that he was on to something big ... daydreaming like Hyde himself while he adjusted to dull normality, in all probability. He hadn't replied to the letter.

He shook his head, then rubbed his curling hair angrily, as if rubbing out ideas, regrets. Then he stretched in the evening warmth. His ribs hardly even ached now from a beating he'd taken in the King's Cross district from two of the suspect coppers and a dealer's minder ... Within an inch at that point—

He grinned. Sniffed loudly, as if scenting something on

the breeze other than cooking smells and the perfume of flowers and shrubs. In a dark, wet, filthy alley, getting his lights punched out, the shit kicked out of him – who'd want that, after all?

He clapped his hands, startling a hovering member of the catering staff. The young man waggled a bottle of chardonnay and Hyde nodded. Tonight the Opera House, not the dark alley. He took the proffered glass and sipped the chilled wine.

Straits Royal Group had to be a vast laundering machine, with its five-star hotels, casinos and resorts scattered across Australia and South-East Asia. Moving into America and Europe, too. A perfect means of distributing Burmese heroin and recycling and washing the profits. He was convinced of it. He hadn't a shred of proof, no one believed it, and even Ros laughed at the whole idea. It was no more than a gut feeling, instinct. Or *was* it paranoia? He must try to make it not matter to him. He sipped at the wine. He was like someone at the door with an unwelcome revelation. A Mormon in a secular climate. He must opt for the holiday in Penang, where Aubrey, the old fart, had some crony who claimed he was being frightened off his property and feared for his life. Scudamore – part of Aubrey's past, not his. *As a favour to me, Patrick*, Aubrey had written in the familiar, loved-and-loathed, neat handwriting. It was hardly any effort, so why not . . . ?

He suppressed the niggle of pointlessness.

'Cheers, Hyde,' he murmured, staring down at the city he had been asked to adopt as home.

'Thank you, Roger – I'm glad you returned my call.' Marian stared at the sunset beyond the lounge window as if at a painting, but unseeingly. 'It all seems pretty conclusive – sorry to say.' She cleared her throat. 'I'll try to soften the blow—'

'Sorry my lads barged in in quite that way, Marian.' The local detective chief inspector shared her distaste for his information, even understood her difficulty. *How to tell Syeeda?* She quailed at the idea. 'But it was all pretty cut-and-dried. As I said, the West Midlands Drugs Squad had had him under surveillance for a few weeks because of some rather suspicious friends he'd recently acquired – known dealers. And they found a stash of money at his flat, along with a serious amount of heroin. The pathologist's report confirms it was an overdose . . . Doesn't make your mission of mercy any easier, Marian. Sorry—'

'Thanks, Roger.' She wanted to be done with the call now. The constituency flat seemed to crowd around her. Syeeda would be working in the Jaipur by this time in the evening. It was only hundreds of yards down the street, beyond the minster pool. The sense of the girl's proximity made her cowardly; and angry that she had been placed in such an invidious position. 'I owe you a pint.'

'When do you get your driving licence back?' the policeman asked, in a clumsy attempt to lighten their shared awkwardness of mood.

'Another three months.'

'Thank God you weren't doing a hundred and fifteen on *my* patch – *very* embarrassing!'

'I'll try not to!' then: 'Bye, Roger.'

She put down the receiver and lit a cigarette, her feet stretched out on a pouffe, the lounge thick with smoke. The sunset burned along the horizon like a stubble fire, turning the minster pool into a brazen shield.

Damn, damn, *damn* . . . Kumar *was* a heroin dealer. She felt angry at having been deceived by the young man. Angry at Syeeda, too, who had plunged her into this like a hand into boiling water. Damn, damn, *damn*! She expelled smoke furiously at the ceiling, then struggled to her feet and poured more malt whisky into her glass. Afraid, she realised. Afraid to shatter all Syeeda's illusions, squash out love like the life of a beetle.

Tomorrow, she thought, sharply aware of the past two days, during which she'd postponed any contact with Syeeda. Nevertheless, wait until tomorrow to tell her, she determined. Use the phone – the coward's method of bearing bad news ...

'Bugger,' she breathed. 'What a bloody *mess*!'

His first-floor room looked out over the grounds of Cheveney Park. Late blackbirds still skittered and squabbled on the lawns in front of the house, near the fountain or beneath the yew hedges. The high-ceilinged, ornately plastered room was west-facing, and the setting sun glowed in the room and made him narrow his eyes as he looked from the window. A gardener in overalls pushed his wheelbarrow towards the tumble of outbuildings, and a prison officer idled on the terrace before grinding out his cigarette on the gravel.

David Winterborne turned away from the view, his right hand cupping his narrow chin, his left arm folded across his chest. The room was furnished with a few of his own pieces from the Eaton Square house, and his own bed. The thick, pale-green carpet had been the choice of his predecessor, a City fraudster who had gone directly from the open prison to Heathrow and luxurious retirement in the Bahamas.

The room was confining, of course, but sufficiently spacious to accommodate his desk, the telephones, a fax machine, his books and filing cabinets. It was adequate for the remainder of his sentence.

His stomach rumbled softly. In ten minutes or so, his usual officer, Reg, would be bringing his evening meal. He had ordered smoked salmon to start and beef to follow. The restaurant in the village, half a mile away, knew how rare he liked it. He had not, even with mockery, invited Ralph Lau to share dinner with him. Ralph's car – *his* Rolls, to be precise – had vanished along the drive only minutes earlier.

Ralph was a problem, increasingly so; but still to be tolerated for the brief period of his incarceration. His cousin was drawing back the scope and energies of Winterborne Holdings to their Singapore and South-East Asian roots, even as he wished to increase his penetration of Europe and America. Ralph was a necessary evil, a counterweight to the mild moral crusade being waged on behalf of the conglomerate by his father, Clive. After the exposure of the EU fraud, Clive had become non-executive chairman, and had at once withdrawn Winterborne Holdings from the Urban Regeneration Project, Aero UK and any other company in any way tainted by the fraud – as if he wished to hand back to his son an exorcised multinational, something that had had a great deal of holy water sprinkled on it. Poor Clive . . .

The Asian operation had, meanwhile and unbeknown to Clive, infected the European and American businesses. The banks had Winterborne Holdings on a kind of probation. No one had wanted to lend after his imprisonment. Ralph had provided the increasingly necessary – the desperately needed – injections of cash, through the hotel chain subsidiary, Straits Royal Group. Massive funds had been needed and had grown like mushrooms in a dark cellar. *Investment by other means*, Ralph Lau had called it soon after David had appointed him as CEO of Winterborne Holdings.

There was a polite knock at the door.

'Come in, Reg.'

The prison officer, small, rotund and cheerful, placed a tray on the table, put the main course in the portable oven beneath it, pulled out David's chair, and left. His idolised daughter apparently disliked her new private school, but Reg was adamant she must take advantage of David's demonstrable generosity. He had merely continued the payment of fees inaugurated by his predecessor in the room.

Winterborne sat down and uncovered the smoked salmon and buttered brown bread. He eschewed wine. There were lengthy phone calls to be made later in the evening.

Straits Royal had doubled in size and profits in two years. It had, to his dislike but also admiration, become the engine room of the entire conglomerate. It funded his US expansion like a rich uncle providing an unlimited allowance. His only reservations were epitomised in an image of Straits Royal Group dandling the whole of Winterborne Holdings on its knee like a dependent child.

He studied a sheaf of faxes as he ate. Pondered Ralph Lau's briefing and the sense he sometimes had of himself in Ralph's company as no more than some kind of risk-assessment consultant to his own empire. *That* would change on his release. Lau's second-stage scenario for Burma was, ultimately, so tempting he did not think he would oppose it. Much depended on Lau's meeting at the Myanmar Embassy, of course. If the Mekong River project provided sufficient profits, it would help make Winterborne Holdings once again unassailable; dominant in the US, as powerful as before in Europe. It would rebuild his damaged, uncertain empire.

He finished his smoked salmon and, bending beside the

table, removed his beef and fresh vegetables from the portable oven. The last of the sunlight was orange on the wall. The beef was as rare as he'd demanded, inducing complacency. Perhaps a single glass of wine ...? The room adjusted to his illusion of it as his office rather than his cell.

The man Hyde ... an *Aubrey* man. He had concealed from Lau the momentary shiver of nerves the information had brought on. Was Aubrey poking his old nose into the affairs of Winterborne Holdings once more – or was this Australian ex-spy merely frustrated at the containment of the potential disaster in Sydney? He did not know, and he could not offer a hostage to fortune. Lau had wanted his permission for the elimination of Hyde, and he had, after some thought, given it. *Use my people*, he had said. *They're less likely to make a mistake*. Lau had flinched, his cheekbones pinkened by anger, at those words.

Marian was another matter, of course. Ralph had been surprised at his lack of reaction to the news that that most persistent of Furies-who-were-really-flies had brushed up against their web. The Kumar business had been handled properly, but the girlfriend had intrigued *dear* Marian. Lau had thought he would be alarmed into action by the news. Eventually, he must do something about Marian. If she took a greater interest, came closer, then he would have to overcome his almost spiritual fear of her.

The beef palled. Marian – damnable Marian – had done that to his appetite ... He pushed his plate away from him. He must have a *sufficient* reason to have Marian put down. He could not dismiss her, even now, with the ease with which he consigned the man Hyde to the dark. Superstitiously, he remained linked to her from child-hood, a sometime affection that was almost a need. She was still in his head, still part of him.

He had attempted to have her killed once, and she had survived. He had been able to countenance the act only when she was of the utmost danger to him. She must threaten him in a very real way before he could again think of her murder.

Kenneth Aubrey felt himself drained and exhausted. Yet the cause was not simply the long evening of sitting through Aeschylus' trilogy; rather it was the tumultuous experience of sharing the encounter with Marian, seated beside him in the warm darkness of the National Theatre's main Olivier auditorium. Her absorption, as she perched on the edge of her seat, was like being too near a flame that burned too intensely. The energy that she seemed to give to the performance of the *Oresteia* was reciprocated by the power she drew from it. It was all too intense, too wearying, for a comfortable old man. Little wonder that Giles, her father, had passed his own ticket to Aubrey. He had known what to expect from his daughter, his shining girl.

The actors and the chorus left the undecorated stage, the barbarism of the *Agamemnon* over, the horrors of the *Libation-Bearers* behind them. The Furies had been tamed. Marian's eyes remained possessed of a rapt gleam as the audience became preoccupied with late suppers and last trains rather than with Athens and justice. She exhaled slowly, as if fearful of losing some savour of the drama. Then, turning to Aubrey, she asked with quizzical irony:

'Well, Kenneth, did you survive?'

'Mm – yes.'

'But once in a lifetime is enough?'

'I think it might be – for me. Thank you, however. I would not have missed it . . . though I'm not certain what good it may have done me, at my age.'

Marian took his thin arm as they reached the aisle and began descending to the exit. Aubrey leaned as if breathless on his stick. To continue the lightening of the mood, after the chain of murders, the dark night of the soul, that had been the matter of most of the trilogy, he murmured:

'I don't expect to be presented with such fundamental choices at the few board meetings I attend, or at the Club.' He sensed his complacency knitting itself together with reassuring ease after the nakedness of Aeschylus' tragic poetry.

'Even though you faced such choices, decade after decade?' Marian mocked gently. 'You have retired, after all.' Then, abashed, she added: 'I suppose I do take it all a bit seriously, don't I?'

The crowd, murmuring of disappointment that the director had not drawn the most obvious parallels with Bosnia and Chechnya, seemed to hem them in as they made their way downstairs. Aubrey experienced all the vulnerability of the old surrounded by a crowd, and clung to Marian's arm. She seemed to enjoy the sensation of his dependence.

'Just like the Kumar business,' she murmured into his ear. 'I was too serious there, too. I'm sorry I bothered you with it – when all there was to be discovered was that the young man was a drug dealer and *I*'d been completely fooled by him!'

Aubrey smiled and patted the hand that held his arm. A scarf being flung around a collar flicked his cheek. People pushed impatiently past them as Marian halted, distracted.

'Marian—! I caught sight of you during the second intermission. I just wanted to say hi.' An American accent.

The man was handsome in that sense that was not quite

real, as if he had been flatteringly photographed and the portrait itself placed before them amid the last dwindlings of the audience. Aubrey felt the tremor that ran through Marian's arm, and her response was a teasing clue that led him to recognise the American. His companion he knew well enough by sight; a member of the Club, an Opposition spokesman on trade and foreign affairs – Peter Grainger.

'Robbie,' Marian murmured, turning at once to Aubrey to introduce them out of what was either embarrassment or a momentary inability to return the man's ingratiating smile with an equal amnesia.

'Good evening, Congressman Alder,' Aubrey muttered, nodding.

'Sir Kenneth – of course!' the American returned, thrusting his hand forward. Aubrey shook it briefly. 'A real surprise – an accidental meeting . . .' More intimately, he added to Marian: 'A great and good surprise . . . When Peter here asked me to the theatre – for Greek tragedy, too! – I didn't expect the evening to turn out like this.' He nodded back up the stairs. 'Some performance, uh?'

'Indeed,' Aubrey concurred drily. 'A long evening.' Something like Giles's antipathy seemed to be flowing in his old veins. He felt an unconscionable objection, even aversion, to the American's reappearance in Marian's life.

'I – um, I had to talk to you, Marian. Couldn't let the chance go by.'

'No,' she replied throatily. She still held Aubrey's arm. He remembered she had had *two* affairs with this man. He suddenly wanted to utter her father's reaction, which would have been that Alder still only had to crook his little finger in her direction and she would come running. Marian shook her hair back and added: 'It's nice to see you again, Robbie.'

How long was it since their second affair had dwindled?

Three years? Alder had returned to America, resigning his State Department posting to Grosvenor Square at the siren call of politics in an election year. He had been elected for his home state to the lower house of Congress and put his foot on the first rung of the tall ladder to the White House. He was populist, comfortably radical, exhaled charm with every breath. Marian had been torn – and desperately unhappy – but had chosen her own political career over Alder and his. She had not, as he had invited her to do, followed him to Washington. It was a decision that Aubrey sensed she had always regretted.

Alder, touted like a dozen others as a future President, was not inheritedly rich, but a lawyer by profession. Looking at him now, Aubrey thought aciduously that the man had the hair and the teeth for the highest office. Perhaps, he added with the jealousy of a much younger man, it was those attributes that still exercised a sway over Marian; he was her undoubted intellectual inferior and of a shallower composition altogether.

I have borrowed more than your ticket, old friend, he told himself, imagining Giles.

'Look, can I buy both of you a coffee, some sort of drink – dinner?' Alder proffered. Then, including Grainger as well as Aubrey, he added: 'Maybe it's not too late for supper—?'

'I have a speech to work on,' Grainger offered brightly. 'Though I would like your advice, Sir Kenneth, on the situation in Russia – permission to pick your brains, so to speak.' His smile was large and persistent. 'I think the government's not half tough enough regarding loan repayments, checks on where funds are ending up . . .' He had already drawn Aubrey aside from Alder and Marian and was escorting him in the direction of the door.

'My dear young man, you flatter me!' Aubrey announced. 'However, if you will see me to a taxi, I'll attempt an answer to any questions you might have. Good night, Marian!' He knew he couldn't interfere in Marian's personal life, even though he wished to.

He waved at them. Alder's head was slightly turned to display his best profile. He presented an elegant, tanned portrait of a man of forty, his hair determinedly older than his years in colour, but thick and wavy. An etched jawline, clear blue eyes. Marian's beauty was quieter, more serious; lit now, he realised, with a resurrected passion.

'Bye, Kenneth!' she called gaily. The mood of the trilogy, even of their conversation, had been replaced by something blithe, recklessly of the moment.

'Enjoy yourself, my dear,' he murmured, sounding even to himself like some member of the chorus of the drama he had just endured.

The first moment in a strange place. The interior of the car was stifling and Hyde wound down the windows even before throwing his only luggage, a sports bag, on to the rear seat. The smell of plastic and dust. Cloud was already gathering across the narrow strip of sea between Penang and mainland Malaysia and had begun to hide the hills to the north of the airport. It was the monsoon season.

Ros had arranged to fly up to Penang for a long weekend after she finished her business in Singapore in a few days' time. She was close to getting the commission for the complex in Burma.

He leant away from the hot metal of the car's flank, waiting for the interior to cool. Dark palms attempted slow, grave semaphore in the slight, hot breeze. The rental company compound near the main terminal flashed and seared with sun-reflecting windscreens and chrome. He was grubby and tired from the flight, but exhilarated, and could not stifle the grin that had begun at the Hertz counter. Around him, the airport-without-nationality submerged itself, becoming a fragment of a strange country.

Hyde sighed comfortably. An old man was afraid that someone wanted him dead.

The sea glittered between the island and the mainland, the morning light brighter even than in Sydney. On the mainland, the jungle climbed the mountains towards the massing cloud. He clambered into the car, spreading the map on the passenger seat before starting the engine. Then he steered the car towards the compound's exit. The breeze ruffled his hair, cooled his forehead as he turned on to the main road running north along the coast. He sniffed the air as eagerly as a dog.

A Buddhist temple, a colonial façade, the flash of parrots from one tree to another. Another bright, smaller bird flew ahead of him towards the suburbs of Georgetown. A muddle of huts, stilted houses, shacks, bungalows and shops gathered at the roadside like spectators of the high-rise buildings that rose ahead of the car. The modern centre of Georgetown scorned the jungle that surrounded it.

He vaguely felt the hangover of the Opera House, the charity gala, the fundraising buffet, money and art, Ros' and his mutual dependence all clear from his head. There was little traffic. A green Nissan kept station and pace behind him ...

... on the north-western outskirts of the town, it was still in the driving mirror, he realised, vaguely unnerved. He had been careless; he had no idea when the Nissan had first appeared behind him. Had had no expectation that anyone would be interested in his arrival or would even know of it. He pressed the accelerator smoothly, following a band of the coast road that suddenly threw an expanse of dazzling, blue-dyed sea across the windscreen, and a vista of tall white resorts. In the mirrors, the green car accelerated, then, as if exposed, dropped back to its original speed as the road straightened once more. He slowed the Ford and the Nissan echoed the deceleration, keeping the same distance behind him.

The hotels passed in line astern, great commercial ships in a leisure fleet. Batu Ferringhi, stuffed with tourists even in the monsoon season. The windscreen of the Nissan was tinted and he could not make out the faces behind it. It was as if it was pushing him ahead of it towards Scudamore's bungalow.

After the fleet of hotels, where the monsoon rain only lasted the length of three or four cocktails, there were small bays and coves, with the hills tumbled against the roadside, the green jungle speckled with clearings and *kampongs*. Then the beginning of a landscape of monsoon-lush gardens neat with rose borders and bedding plants. The expatriates reclaiming the place for suburbia, or just hanging on by their fingernails. The car was tailing *him*. The game appeared more interesting than a reluctant visit to an old stranger; he was being invited to play.

Why? Because of Sydney . . . ? He'd been turned off, put out to pasture. Did he still *worry* them?

He glanced more frequently at the map and at the names on the white fences. He slowed the car as the road nudged up towards a headland. The crystal sea was littered with windsurfers as he pulled the car to a halt beside the fenced garden of Scudamore's bungalow and waited—

—for the Nissan to overtake him. He watched it as it passed the bungalow and, without slowing, turned out of sight beyond the headland. He repeated the registration to himself. It was probably hired, but you never knew ... certainty and numbers produced carelessness. Then he got out of the Ford into the damp, clinging heat.

A Malay in a white shirt and bright tartan *sarung* opened the door, his black velvet *songkok* cap nodding in greeting. Immediately, there was a bellow from the rear of the house.

'I told you not to open the bloody door without checking, Rahim!' The accent was Lancastrian, the voice thick with drink.

'Mr Scudamore's at home?' Hyde asked. 'Tell him I'm the messenger boy and ask him if he'll see me. I've come from Aubrey *tuan*—'

A shadow loomed between Rahim the servant and the glimpse of sea and rock beyond the patio doors that were visible from the door. It moved unsteadily towards the teak-panelled hallway from what must have been the bungalow's lounge. Hyde could see a large green and white umbrella flicking in the breeze, and cane patio furniture. Then Scudamore's bulk cancelled the scene. Hyde scented drink and fear in equal measure.

The old man remained at the far end of the hall, a glass in his hand, his heavily jowled features and sharply bright eyes weighing Hyde with the stare of a wounded bull. A fat old Englishman, reefed and castaway. Hyde was aware of his disappointment. The man's untidy, drunken bulk erased the small, feeble anticipation with which he had travelled. Though there was the tail car ...

'Who are you?' Scudamore blustered.

'Can I come in?'

'Not yet.'

The suspicion was chronic, but also habitual. The man was a hulk, but the wreckage was of a former Special Branch officer.

'Aubrey asked me to—'

'Couldn't be bothered to come himself, could he?' Scudamore sneered, shaking his head as if to clear it and taking a single step towards the front door. Rahim remained as still as something stolen from a temple. 'Old fart,' Scudamore grumbled.

Hyde grinned.

'You're speaking of my former employer — I'm Hyde. Can I come in now?'

Unalarmingly, he glanced up the road towards the headland, as if reassuring himself that he had locked the Ford. The green Nissan's nose and blind windscreen were nudged like the features of a spy around the bend of the road. Scudamore had not been the one under surveillance; it was Hyde himself who interested them. Then his memory glimpsed hardly digested, unexamined impressions... A car behind him on the road to the airport in Sydney, a man near the check-in desk ... someone at Kuala Lumpur International while he waited for a change of flight ... ? He'd been sloppy.

Scudamore did not answer him but backed away down the hall as if he had surrendered all interest in his visitor, lumbering through the lounge towards the open patio doors. Rahim gestured Hyde inside. Awareness of the green Nissan remained as tangible as a fresh tattoo between his shoulder blades.

'Something to drink, *tuan*?'

Hyde paused, and then said: 'Coffee. Thanks.'

He wandered through the patchily furnished house. It gave the impression of a place belonging to people who had just begun living together, or of someone without any real interest in possessions or reminders of the past. The furniture was old, shabby, utilitarian, as if Scudamore was merely camped in the place, expecting orders to move on at any moment. He thrust his hands into the pockets of the baggy trousers of his cream suit – Bruce Oz rather than Oldfield, Ros had remarked when he bought it – and leaned against the frame of the patio doors.

Scudamore had already regained his cane chair, which squeezed and moulded him like a child's inexpert fingers into shapeless grey dough. His tight shirt was open, and hair sprouted at the throat and waistband, curling on his stomach. The man's face was red with sun and alcohol, his eyes a rat's colour and moving as quickly and expertly as that animal's in inspecting Hyde.

'You don't look much.'

'You look a lot less.'

Scudamore's laugh was a hard, barking noise that caused him to cough. Eventually, he announced:

'You might as well sit down now you're here.' His hand shook as he temporarily and reluctantly released his tumbler. Whisky slopped. Scudamore must have been drinking for most of the night and all morning . . . and for days now, days and nights. He was deeply, unmistakably frightened. The spots of whisky, which at once attracted a long-legged insect, were signals almost of terror.

'What is it you want from Aubrey?' Hyde asked.

'I want – I want that old bugger to take me *seriously!*' Scudamore blurted, the cane chair protesting his angry agitation, squawking like one of the parrots on the headland.

There was a curve of beach below the cliff on which the bungalow was perched, blue water held in the space between the thumb of the headland and the forefinger of gentler rocks like a glass in a hand. The beach was empty. Presumably it was the one Scudamore owned and which he was in the process of selling to Straits Royal Group, who wanted to build a new resort hotel and casino.

Scudamore is not a man to be frightened of shadows,
Aubrey had told him. And Straits Royal were, according
to Scudamore, employing strong-arm methods to lower
the asking price.

'He sent me. He thinks that's serious enough.' Hyde
lounged in a chair on the other side of the white-painted,
wrought-iron table. 'Serious enough for you, anyway,' he
added with pleasurable malice.

Scudamore glared at him before his eyes returned to
the vista of the headland and the beach below it. The
scene was inspected with the fervour evoked by lost
valuables rather than as a source of danger. A motor
yacht glided possessively across the water, a windsurfer
fell sideways as a passing jet-ski's wave unbalanced him.

Scudamore said into his tumbler, once more safely
clenched in a fist as big as a boxing glove: 'You can see I'm
scared, right?'

'I can see that.'

He disliked the wreckage of Scudamore, despite
Aubrey's assertions that he had once been a good copper
– and that he owed him his life. He had spoken with
warmth of the lumpen, drunken oaf opposite Hyde.

'Want to know why I'm shit-scared?' Scudamore
challenged.

'How much do you expect to get for this place?'

'Half a million,' Scudamore replied as if confessing to a
minor offence, then adding almost volcanically: 'Their
bar takings in the first six months'll more than cover the
price!'

'What are they offering?'

'Forty per cent of that.'

'And you wonder why they're leaning on you?' Hyde
scoffed.

The tumbler banged on to the table. Scudamore's wrists

glistened with spilt whisky, like his knuckles.

'You fucking smartarse!' he roared. 'Straits Royal Group are trying to cheat me, the buggers! You want to see how serious they are?' He lurched upright, blocking the sun and most of the headland, then he charged at the open doors as if breaking into someone else's property. 'Come in here and see the price of building land!' he roared over his shoulder.

Hyde shrugged and followed Scudamore into the lounge. The fat old man was on his knees in front of the television set, his breathing stertorous as he inserted a cassette into the VCR beneath the large Japanese set. He looked up at Hyde, his eyes filled with knowledge and cunning.

'I know about you, you fucking Aussie!' he snarled. 'Aubrey's long-lost son, his favourite boy! You've got some pretty weird ideas about Straits Royal Group yourself, haven't you?' He waggled his hand at Hyde's surprised expression. 'Aubrey told me, I'm not psychic. When he did, I thought the idea that those buggers had it in for me, too, might bring you up here on the run!'

He staggered upright, grabbed the remote control from the arm of a shabby settee, into which he noisily lumped himself, and flicked on the TV and the video recorder. His breathing was as violent as that of someone fighting for his life.

The video image flickered on. A dusty Mercedes saloon, not new, was driving along a road that might have been the one Hyde had travelled from Georgetown. It moved towards the camera and then past it. The camera tracked it, and he caught a glimpse of a headland and white-painted bungalows. The fat man was gripping the arm of the settee with a hand closed in terror. On the screen, a shadowy figure appeared beside the road and flicked something like a matador's cape towards the bulling car. It was one of those spike-studded carpets the police used to slow fleeing cars. Tyres burst, and the car lurched wildly towards the edge of the cliff—

—the film had been edited so that now the camera was suddenly at the bottom of a high cliff and was filming the flying car as it hurtled downwards, to burst into spectacular, movie-like fire as it hit the rocks.

Hyde looked cautiously at Scudamore, whose loose jowls quivered and whose vast body was attempting to hunch away from the images. When he spoke, his voice was hoarse.

'Two days ago, that happened to *my* car. A bloody miracle *I* didn't drive over the cliff—!' A shaking hand pointed to the image of the burning wreck. 'Same colour, same model. It was a last fucking warning! I've been waiting a fortnight for it to happen, and two days ago it did!'

Hyde got up and went outside. He filled Scudamore's tumbler with whisky. There was more monsoon cloud out to sea now, masking the mainland mountains. Fewer windsurfers and small boats. He returned to the lounge and handed the old man the glass. Loose lips swallowed greedily. Scudamore whined plaintively:

'I want to die in Bournemouth, not here!'

'You want to die with half a million quid in the building society, you mean.'

'Why not?' Scudamore snapped. His huge linen jacket hung over his stomach like a poor, thin curtain. His Panama hat was a battered caricature. A washed-out, washed-up expat with a drink problem and arthritis, by the look of his knuckles, wanting to get back to the suburbs and the National Health and decent programmes on the telly. 'Why not . . . ?' he repeated.

Why not, indeed? Straits Royal Group could certainly afford half a million.

Hyde sat down opposite Scudamore, leaning forward like a priest hearing confession. Rahim entered with coffee and set it on a low table. He glanced in disapproval at the tumbler in his master's hand, then left the room. Hyde poured his coffee and sipped it. Then he said:

'Who have you been negotiating with? Anyone important in Straits Royal?'

'Interested, are we? I wonder why,' Scudamore mocked. 'You think they want a casino here to launder drug money, is that it?'

'They only have one casino in the whole of the Malay Peninsula, in the Genting Highlands—'

'I know that.'

'And I realise Aubrey trusted you with a lot of background on what I've been doing.'

'The old fart told me you were as mad as a nymphomaniac in solitary confinement when they chucked you out. *And* that he didn't believe a word of it, your fancy conspiracy theory,' Scudamore added maliciously.

Hyde smiled. 'You're right. Just as I was. Malaysia's an Asian Tiger economy. Big tourist trade. Just what the doctor ordered as far as Straits Royal are concerned . . . A dozen new casino and resort hotels could wash a lot of money. More than they can pass through casinos in Laos and Cambodia, places where Westerners don't want to go in large numbers. Mm?'

'Christ, what bullshit! Is that the best you can do? Besides, I thought you were supposed to be helping me,' Scudamore sneered. But his attention was caught. Hyde was diminishing Straits Royal for him, making them crooks, the kind of people he had locked away in the course of picking up his salary cheques. 'I agree they're spreading like a plague, all round the Pacific Rim.' His smile was indistinguishable from a snarl. 'Your country's full up with their bloody casinos and hotels. I still don't believe it.'

'Malaysia doesn't like gambling. The government—'

'There'll be plenty in it for them. They're facing the facts. Gambling casinos attract tourists, so they'll have casinos and resort complexes coming out of the country's ears in five years' time.'

'All owned by Straits Royal? Including the one on your bit of beach?'

'It's big enough for a resort – with the adjoining plots. They've already sold up – *without* the frighteners.'

'And you thought that made your patch practically priceless? Greedy old bugger, aren't you?'

'Sod off.' There was no rancour in the words. 'They could build villas, have a private beach, huge casino, health club, the lot. They can afford to pay me what I'm asking.'

'Who's the most senior bloke you've met during these negotiations?'

'Another bloody Aussie – posher accent than yours, though. Name's Pearson. Bruce Pearson ... are you *all* called Bruce?'

'No, there's a bloke named Shane in Melbourne. Or so I heard.' Hyde suppressed his excitement as he drew an envelope from his breast pocket and shuffled through the photographic enlargements it contained. He handed one of them to Scudamore. 'Sorry it's at night and from a distance. Is that Pearson, on the left? The bloke on the right is dead. He had about four minutes left when I took that.'

Scudamore looked up at him, his eyes narrowed in anxiety. His huge frame shuddered, the flesh as loose as if merely a garment.

'No,' he said with relief. 'Never seen that bloke.'

Hyde's disappointment was intense. Another blank. This was a wild-goose chase, coming up to Penang in the hope that Scudamore could finger the man who'd had Henderson killed.

'Pity.'

Get a life, Hyde. Ros' words. Why *was* he still digging? To hang on to the old life by his fingernails? He shook his head, silently instructing himself – sort this old fart out and get back to Oz.

'What about my problem?'

'Your problem. OK – I promised Aubrey, so I'll help if I can. You arrange a meeting with Pearson for tomorrow. Allow me to size up the opposition, take some pictures. What we need is proof – a confession from one of the foot-soldiers would be enough to get us into the blackmail game. OK?'

CHAPTER TWO

Kali's Dancers

Scudamore's repaired, conspicuously valeted Mercedes idled past him along Penang Road towards the KOMTAR tower complex, where his solicitor maintained his expensive, impressing offices. The morning retained the memory of freshness, and Hyde wound down the window of the Ford. He was parked opposite the Odeon cinema, a couple of hundred yards from the drab, anonymous hotel in which he had spent the night. The Malay meal they had served was still on his tongue and the roof of his mouth.

The sun had already bullied itself above the mainland hills; shadows receded, became harder. He had told Scudamore to be early, so that he could approach the tower complex on foot, and pick up any surveillance on the fat man. His hands tensed on the steering wheel. The green Nissan had followed him back to Georgetown from Scudamore's bungalow, but he had lost it in rush-hour traffic long before he reached his hotel. They needed to find him again. It required nimble footwork. The simplest option was to pick up one of the surveillance team and sweat something out of him that incriminated Pearson and Straits Royal; then trade the information for Scudamore's money. Anything more complex required a team to carry it out.

He turned the Ford into the traffic, tailing Scudamore's Mercedes. No one seemed to be tailing Scudamore. An early trishaw trundled beside him for a moment, the straw-hatted, ancient Chinese bent over his handlebars as if engaged in a desperate attempt to keep pace with him. Hyde pulled up at the next set of lights. A bazaar threw scents, noise, the glare of bright cloth at him. Cheap jewellery glinted and a garish blue and red dragon glared at him from the entrance of a tiny Chinese temple.

Green. He accelerated, and crossed the next set of lights only one car behind Scudamore. He would rid Scudamore of his demons. But Scudamore couldn't lead him further into the Straits Royal maze . . .

The Mercedes dipped its nose like a bull about to charge as it entered the underground garage beneath the KOMTAR. Hyde drew the Ford into a gap at the kerb. As he switched off the engine, a shopkeeper slid up his grille with a sudden noise, alarming Hyde's alert nerves. There didn't seem to be anyone interested in Scudamore's car. A Malay, lighting a cigarette, leaned unconcernedly against a grey Lexus fifty yards ahead. Commuters debouched from fume-belching buses, cars clotted at each set of traffic lights. Hyde got out of the car and locked it. He'd scout the KOMTAR's environs, watch the entrance to the tower that Scudamore decided Pearson was likely to use. There was no sign of a green Nissan, or of any interest in himself.

He walked beside old shop fronts, glancing into dim interiors like any tourist. A parrot squawked beside one spice-laden, shadowy doorway, and rattled the mesh of its bell-shaped cage. He passed a tiny Buddhist *stupa*, the small, gold-leafed statue of the Siddhartha in meditative posture, peeling and melancholy. A window filled with TVs, another offering sex videos and the kind of female underwear he had ceased to dream of at fifteen. He drew level with the Lexus and the unconcerned Malay. The car's passenger window slid down.

Hyde was shocked into stillness, recognising the face that was revealed. An ex-agent he knew. Jessop. Who knew him. His nerves came alive in a moment; the same moment in which surprise became pleasure and certainty on Jessop's features. An overloaded electrical wire seemed to be stretched between them.

'Hyde—' Jessop blurted. Estuary English. Malice in the tone.

'Jessop . . .'

Hyde's hands remained in the pockets of his baggy trousers. He could see Jessop's expression rummaging for a mask of innocent surprise. Jessop's skill was elimination, the wet end of the intelligence trade. The man was a complete shit – and, in the private sector, pricey to employ. He *couldn't* be in Penang just to frighten an old man into dropping the asking price on his bungalow . . . Hyde was aware the Malay's posture had become awkwardly unrelaxed against the flank of the car.

He experienced a disorientation, a desperate exhilaration, too, as he watched Jessop's thoughts circling him like dark crows. He had stumbled on a tripwire. It had to be *him*, not Scudamore, who interested Jessop. It must be. Straits Royal employing Jessop . . . because of heroin—

Jessop glanced up at the now alert Malay. There was a

Chinese driver, another Chinese in the rear of the Lexus. The passenger door began to open—

—running. At last he was running, dragging his feet out of the mud of shock as Jessop's body began to straighten and his mouth opened, as his hand reached into his jacket. He heard:

'Tan - *him!*' Jessop's next words were mere noise, urgent and threatening, startling people as much as his own flight. 'Hyde!' he did hear, and glanced behind him.

The Malay was already in pursuit and Jessop was directing the two Chinese after him. Hyde lurched his heated body into an alleyway, at the end of which the morning gleamed. He skipped aside from a thin dog and its enquiries into a heap of vegetable rubbish. He reached into his armpit for a gun he did not have. He heard the Malay's running footsteps, the yelp of the dog as it was kicked out of the way. Jessop - for Christ's sake, that psychopath. His thoughts burned and whirled as he staggered into the glaring sunlight, colliding with a small Malay woman in a business suit. Her designer sunglasses flew away from her face as it opened in a smeared, sudden terror.

He pushed her aside and ran on, the smells of spices, petrol, dust clogging his senses. Glanced back. The Malay and one of the Chinese were no more than thirty yards behind him. Jalan Dr Lim was crowded with cars, trishaws, trucks and buses belching fumes. The rush hour. He was brushed against by the hurrying crowd and almost enveloped until, like a swimmer remembering an efficient stroke, he began burrowing through the crowds. He glanced back once more and was unable to see either of his pursuers.

A bus debouched its passengers into his path, but now he was familiar with the element in which he moved, confident. In his wake, the Chinese and the Malay must be struggling, pausing continually to catch sight of him, treading the water of the crowds. Traffic halted once more. Hyde slid between cars, in front of a truck, bewildering the pedaller of a trishaw. On the other side of Jalan Dr Lim he took stock, out of breath yet exhilarated by nerves and adrenalin. The Malay was struggling against the tide of people moving towards the KOMTAR tower, hurrying from buses and taxis. He would not be able to recognise the Chinese at any distance.

Hyde slipped into the first narrow street which offered itself. The buildings at once aged around him, becoming bent, stunted, poorer. Cafés, eating shops, grocery stores, the smells of spices and vegetables. Rattan baskets and chairs were suspended from unneeded awnings in the shadowy side street. He began to hear his own breathing. No one was moving with any urgency behind him. He passed a bookshop, then the strange, sprouting plant of an elephant's foot filled with polished canes. The scent of coffee made him immediately hungry. Sculptured stone lions protected a temple dedicated to the goddess of mercy; they glowered at money-changers' shops across the narrow street, but no more malevolently than at a Hindu temple where images of Shiva and Parvati united in stone sexual congress. Then he passed a chaste mosque a hundred yards further down the street.

He halted, dragging in gulps of fetid air, his hands on his hips, the jacket of his cream suit stained with perspiration. He did not dare go near Scudamore now – yet he had to. The old man was in danger from Jessop, could be used to lead them to himself. He needed a gun . . .

Jessop was a psychopath. He'd been working with Fraser, but Fraser was dead, killed somewhere god-forsaken in the States. Tony Godwin had gone to the funeral and sent him a postcard to keep him up to date ... *Had to make sure the bastard was really in his box*, Godwin had postscripted.

But Jessop was alive and in Penang, and his target had to be Hyde himself. Straits Royal Group believed he was still coming after them. To them, he had walked off the job with a grudge, and he had a background and a reputation, and they knew he would continue to cause trouble.

He had to get to Scudamore quickly. No doubt the meeting with Pearson would be cancelled. He'd told Scudamore where to meet him, but he couldn't just walk in there now ...

Hyde rubbed his hands through his curling hair. His desire for a gun was a metaphor for his excitement – and his nervousness.

Jessop dialled the number furiously on the car phone. The weariness of the long-haul flight from London scratched at his nerves, the jet-lag reawoken by Hyde's escape. The Malay and the Chink had lost him in the crowd. But the old bastard was still in his solicitor's office in the KOMTAR tower. He'd lead them to Hyde—

'Sir, it's Jessop—' They liked deference. Pearson remained still with affront beside him. 'I think Hyde has become interested in Mr Pearson. You and Mr Winterborne were right to—'

'Where is Hyde now?'

'Disappeared – for the moment, sir, only for the moment. We have the old man he contacted under surveillance—'

'You haven't disposed of Hyde.' Ralph Lau's voice was crystalline, coming from halfway round the planet. Jessop rubbed his chin with a nervous anger. Pearson's hand demanded the car phone. 'They were your orders,

Jessop.' There was noise behind Lau's voice, a gale of conversation and throbbing music. 'Is there likely to be difficulty?'

'No, sir. The reason I'm calling you is Mr Pearson. I'd like him on the first plane back to Singapore, out of Hyde's way—'

'Why is this man interested in Pearson? Does he *know* Pearson? How?'

'I suggest you don't underestimate Hyde—'

'Yes. David seems unduly upset, like you, about his connection with Aubrey. That isn't important – not if you get rid of him.'

Pearson was becoming impatient, as if his seniority had been usurped by Jessop.

'Sir, will you advise Mr Pearson to leave Penang?'

'If it's necessary. He – very well, put him on.'

Jessop handed the car phone to Pearson. The immaculate grey suit was belied by the hot fluster on Pearson's features, the sense of shock. His limousine had drawn to the kerb outside the KOMTAR and, like a mugger, Jessop had bullied his way into it and sat beside him, blurting some story about the man Hyde being in Penang and certainly being aware of his presence there. He resented being given orders by someone only a single rank above the louts he had employed to frighten Scudamore into lowering his price.

'Sir – Pearson. This situation seems containable, at least to me. There's no reason why I can't attend the meeting with Scudamore and close the deal—'

'I told you,' Jessop insisted beside him. 'Not with Hyde this close to you.'

Angered by the man's contempt, Pearson forgot Lau and deference, and snapped:

'How can Hyde have any interest in *me*?'

'Bruce,' Lau insisted silkily in his ear, 'Jessop's is the professional assessment in the present circumstances. Do as he suggests and go back to Singapore until this matter is cleared up. Now, put Jessop back on.'

Affronted, and aware that Jessop was luxuriating in his treatment by Lau, Pearson handed him the car phone.

'Sir?'

'Get rid of Hyde – quickly. Do *not* harm the old man. At least, not until this deal is completed.'

'Sir.'

'Today.'

Lau broke the connection. He must have answered his mobile in some club or disco. Jessop carefully excluded contempt from his expression as he turned to Pearson.

'Sorry, Mr Pearson,' he said with exaggerated politeness. 'You couldn't have known. Twenty-four hours and you can return to Penang to close the deal.'

'He gave you today,' Pearson observed, smiling for the first time. 'I'd get moving if I were you – sport.'

Even as she inserted her key into the door of the flat, Marian reaffirmed her determination that, this time, she would accept the limitations and difficulties of a transatlantic affair, if Alder offered nothing more. She ushered him into the flat like an obsequious servant, to mask the seriousness of desire. He grinned at her and passed into the top-floor apartment overlooking the Chelsea Physic Garden at the rear, the Embankment and the river from its front windows. Flicking on the lights for him, she felt her home invaded by a friendly power.

Alder was at his ease in the hall, then the lounge almost immediately, though he had never seen this flat before. She'd been living in college rooms, still a junior history don and he a Rhodes Scholar, when they had first met, then in a small flat in Maida Vale when their affair had briefly reflowered. She had known him, she realised sharply at that moment, for almost a decade. No, nearer twelve years. He had returned to the States the first time to become a career diplomat in the State Department, having decided after a brief spell in a London set of Chambers that he disliked all law, and English law in particular. The second bout of intimacy and mutual dependence had occurred after she had entered Parliament, when he had been posted to the US Embassy in Grosvenor Square. Three years ago. He had returned to America at the invitation of powerful and wealthy backers who wanted him to run for Congress. He had asked her to go with him. The Commons had been – then – a more persuasive, seductive lover, and she had stayed in London.

Now . . . ? His assurance, his ease of occupation of her home, unmasked a hope that he would stay the night. Stay longer, be in her life again . . . She recognised her need, and was shocked at it, almost as at an illness.

She drew the heavy curtains, unhooking their floral extravagance from the tiebacks and closing them on the flaring sodium lamps along the river. She hesitated for a moment, her back to him, afraid to face him as she sensed her own desire, once more finding it inextricably identified with love. With Robbie Alder, she had never known where desire ended and love began, or even if the one was ever a signpost on the road to the other.

When she turned, his gaze was intent, inquisitive, half amused; eager, too.

'I like the apartment. How long have you—?'

'Almost three years,' she blurted immediately.

'I like it. The colour scheme, the escritoire . . . being here,' he added with a gravity that would have seemed comic to an observer. Which she was not ... Except that she was painfully aware of the bookshelves, the hi-fi and the racks of discs that seemed to intrude themselves on her attention. It all looked too much like a stage set designed to suggest an unfulfilled life. 'Yes,' he sighed, clasping his hands behind his head as he stretched himself on the sofa. 'So – you're happy here, right?'

She nodded too quickly, too emphatically, as if she resented his intimacy, his perception. His invasion of the room was complete, and she sensed the first assault on her life had begun.

And unable to resist it. Her few and occasional lovers before and since Alder had never been able to diminish or obscure her capacity to detach herself, to become the observer, in the way he did.

'Coffee?' she asked, her voice husky.

She experienced a momentary dislike of her eagerness, her immature desire. A lamp threw his shadow into profile on one wall as he inspected the bookshelves. Even in silhouette, he was familiar, desirable.

'Sure.'

His ambition required an *American* wife, she tried to remind herself, out of duty rather than instinct. The recent past gave her a sense of her independence; the farther past, containing their two brief affairs, moved around and over that independence like a swollen river, eroding it. He might have to wait another fifteen years and collect a score and more of rich supporters before he could make a bid for the White House. She had known his ambition when he left and had sworn that that was the end of it. It had been a solemn oath.

She cut off the memory. In the three days since they'd met at the theatre, she'd felt so alive.

'I'll just boil a kettle—' She shivered, wrapping her arms

across her breasts, crushing the silk of her blouse in her nervousness, tasting the dinner they had enjoyed together. I want him to stay – please, she thought, propitiating her own past decisions like household gods.

Her answerphone sat squarely on a kitchen worktop. There were four messages waiting for her. She ignored them and filled the kettle. Alder had shone – and she had gleamed in a reflected light – at the Embassy cocktail party to which he had taken her. He had been fêted by staff and guests alike. Marian had been able to measure the distance he had travelled towards his ambitions. He had left Grosvenor Square a minor functionary in the Embassy and returned the subject of in-depth profiles, a member of powerful Congressional committees, an inspirational politician.

He was back in London at the behest of the Congressional Foreign Trade Committee. To be briefed by the Foreign Office and the DTI on South-East Asia, particularly Myanmar. There was a softening in US attitudes to trade with Burma, matching that of London, Bonn, Paris.

She switched off the kettle and spooned coffee into the cafetière, pouring on the water distractedly. She realised she was shocked at her lack of mockery, the absence of opposition in herself at the reception to his bland assurances over Burma, his lack of any insight into or concern for her opinion. She had been mesmerised by his coronational progress through the reception, and his proximity.

She was hardly even angry at herself. The answerphone caught her eye but, though she had not the least desire to check her messages, her fastidious orderliness made her switch on the machine.

Giles's voice. She felt her cheeks heat, as if her father

had suddenly walked into the room and she and Alder, teenage fumblers, had had to rapidly readjust disarranged clothing. She smiled at the image. Lunch with her father tomorrow, as arranged. No, Daddy, I hadn't forgotten. The second call was from her researcher, Rose, to forewarn her that the Deputy Chief Whip was seeking her scalp because of a Commons question she had put down regarding the DTI trade mission to Burma. The Opposition was siding with the new government, evidently. God, she really *ought* to disagree with Alder—! The third was her constituency agent, and the fourth was from Syeeda Lal.

Marian blushed guiltily as she recognised the grief-laden voice. The young woman was still waiting for the call that Marian dreaded making. There was no avenue of escape from it, no possibility that Kumar had not been a drug dealer. Syeeda had been mistaken in her lover—

'What is this?' he asked at the door of the kitchen.

'What—? Oh, a constituent. Her boyfriend's just died – gone to the bad before that, I'm afraid. I have to tell her, somehow – just routine, but awkward.' She shrugged as the message ended and the tape rewound.

His hand was on her shoulder and she darted her cheek against it. The touch was familiar, as if there had been no interruption of their intimacy. His hand squeezed her shoulder, encouraged by her eagerness. In turn, it encouraged her to lift her mouth to his and thankfully forget Syeeda Lal. She wanted him now, fiercely, remembering their last lovemaking, years before.

Oil tankers slid through the deep blue water between Georgetown and the mainland. The mid-morning traffic was light along Lebuh Farquhar and the white colonial buildings dazzled in the sun. Rainbowed arms of water, whirling slow as windmills, were thrown up by sprinkler systems that reinvigorated an empire's lawns. Scudamore had entered the Eastern & Oriental Hotel ten minutes earlier, and by now he'd be camped in the bar. One of the two Chinese who had tailed him, presumably all the way from the KOMTAR, had gone in after him. The other remained on the hotel steps, reading a newspaper.

Hyde had seen neither Jessop nor the Malay. He was sitting at the smeared window of a coffee shop, a two-day-old copy of *The Times* open on the narrow table. The place was noisy with Chinese and Malay voices, a television set sat behind the counter and the punctuating screech of a parrot came from somewhere deep in the shadows at the back of the shop. On the pavement outside, the food stalls were being primed, their stained awnings stretched over clouds of acrid smoke.

He couldn't go near Scudamore. He checked the hotel number in the dog-eared guidebook he drew from his pocket. He had to talk to him, however ... There was no way he could pick him up outside the hotel, not with the Chinese standing there and his oppo coming out behind Scudamore and ready for anything. Would they allow Scudamore enough space and time? He got up and wandered to the public phone.

He dialled the number and asked for the bar, leaning against the cracked plaster and watching a spider near the low ceiling and the scene beyond the dirty window. A Malay voice.

'Mr Scudamore is in your bar. I'd like to talk to him.' The Malay protested the privacy of the extension, his own preoccupation. 'It's urgent. I'm his lawyer.'

In a few moments, after dimly heard recitations of his name, he heard Scudamore's voice, cunning and nervous.

'Yes?'

'Hyde.'

'Where the bloody hell have you been? You said to meet you—'

'Listen to me. There's a Chinese on you—'

'Even I noticed *him*, Hyde!'

'There are others. One of them I know.'

'One of your old lot?'

'Exactly. But I don't think he's here because of you – he must want to take care of me.'

After a breathy silence, Scudamore said: 'I'd better stay well away from you then, hadn't I? What bloody happened, anyway – why didn't that bugger Pearson turn up? He just bloody cancelled – or do you already know?'

'I know. I was – spotted.' It was an admission of failure, of stupidity.

'Where are you?'

'Across the street. Keeping watch.'

'And you think they're after *you*? I'm safe, then?'

'No. They think you can lead them to me. They're bound to think that . . .'

He heard an indrawn breath, then a swallowing noise. Finally, a firmer voice.

'How do we work it? Can you collect me outside?'

'No. There's another Chinese on the steps, and a car that's too obviously parked.'

'Will they give us any room?'

'We'll have to hope so. Take your time, but leave soon and head for the Esplanade . . .' He was studying one of the guidebook's maps. 'Near the old fort, OK? Look out for a blue Ford and don't hang about when I open the passenger door. Got that?'

'Where do we go – afterwards?' Scudamore asked with heavy irony.

'I thought supper and a nightclub – suit you?'

Scudamore snorted. The man was not unamused, his nerve was holding; to Hyde's surprise and admiration. There *was* a younger self inside that huge sack of loose flesh. 'OK, come out in five minutes and make for Fort Cornwallis.'

'Five minutes. Right.' Then he added: 'You stupid pillock,' as he put down the receiver.

Hyde put the phone back on its rest and returned to his table. Trishaws and taxis idled past between the window and the strip of English lawn that bordered the sea. He was aware of Jessop's unseen proximity and, primarily, that he was himself unarmed.

He folded the newspaper, got up and threw change on to the table. Then he walked out under the awning of the coffee shop and immediately turned into the narrow street in which he had left the car he had hired a half-hour before to replace the Hertz car he dare not return to, still parked on Penang Road. He unlocked it, got in, started the engine and strolled the Ford to the corner of Lebuh Farquhar. The red Citroën of which he had become suspicious remained parked on the opposite side of the road; the Chinese was still reading his newspaper on the hotel steps. Another minute—

Scudamore emerged from the hotel, stepping out from the shadow of the portico into the hard sunlight. He paused exaggeratedly, ignoring the Chinese, and then turned left along Lebuh Farquhar towards the Esplanade. Five seconds later, the other Chinese emerged, consulted his pal, then they both began to tail Scudamore.

Hyde waited in sudden tension, watching two people who might have been a drug pusher and his customer, a trishaw that halted near them, a BMW that stopped at the traffic lights. The red Citroën moved out behind the BMW, then, as the lights changed and he turned the Ford out on to Farquhar, the BMW slowed beside the two Chinese while the Citroën kept pace behind Scudamore, hugging the kerb. The Chinese were talking to someone in the BMW, then after only moments they continued their pursuit of the old man. Hyde remained two vehicles behind the BMW as it accelerated.

Scudamore reached the junction with Jalan Penang. The Citroën had moved ahead of him, towards the green of the *padang*, then it slowed and moved into the kerb once more. The manoeuvre was evident. Scudamore would be picked up by whoever was in the Citroën, the two Chinese would help bundle his bulk into its rear. Jessop was probably in the BMW, which maintained its kerb-crawler's pace. If they started watching the driving mirror, they'd see he was doing the same, know who was—

Scudamore had reached the *padang*, its palm trees and white wedding cakes of colonial buildings clustered as if to watch cricket or a military parade. He was a large dot amid tourists and townspeople. The BMW began accelerating. The passenger door of the Citroën opened—

Hyde accelerated across the junction with Lebuh Light, overtaking the BMW, dodging two cars, a truck, avoiding a trishaw. There were no more than moments before—

Scudamore, oblivious, continued to stroll towards the Citroën, passing beneath the piebald shadows of palm trees against a background of imperial splendour and bright *sarungs*. The Chinese were closing on him as Scudamore reached wrought-iron railings before turning towards the fort. Hyde's body felt hot as he raced past the Clock Tower. They'd finished pissing about; Scudamore was about to go into the bag. The Citroën's door remained open; the two Chinese were only yards behind Scudamore.

Hyde screeched the brakes and savagely turned the

Ford into the kerb behind the Citroën. He flung open the passenger door.

'Get in, you stupid bugger – come on!' he yelled at Scudamore's startled, unmoving bulk. In the mirror, the BMW was closing; one of the Chinese was reaching into his jacket. '*Get in!*' he screamed.

Scudamore moved towards the Ford. A small, flat, cracking noise – twice. Scudamore staggered and collapsed into the passenger seat, bright blood on his shirt and jacket. Hyde accelerated with a scream of tyres, lurching the car out into traffic, the door slamming shut as it grazed the flank of the Citroën. Two thudding noises into the boot of the Ford. Scudamore was groaning, clutching his side. Another shot shattered the rear window. The BMW was no more than thirty yards behind them; the Citroën was pulling violently away from the kerb.

He slewed the Ford across the road between the Esplanade and the sea wall, then back again, accelerating wildly. Jumped one set of red lights, then a second, before turning left past the façade of the Library. He had no idea how much back-up Penang could offer, even whether they would respond if he called on it. They had to. No police, no local involvement. The lights were green as he crossed Lebuh Light then Farquhar into Love Lane. He didn't know if Scudamore was bleeding to death. There was a lot of blood on his shirt and his face was clay-grey. The BMW wasn't in the mirrors—

—was now. He swallowed drily, momentarily inspecting Scudamore's putty-coloured face, listening to his ragged, stertorous breathing. His bloodstained hand was on his side, clutching hard to hold life in. The BMW was still behind.

Cheap hotels and small shops pressed around the car, food stalls and barrows crowded the pavements. A temple dog roared stonily at the corner of eyesight before he screeched left into a narrow alley, scattering two youths on a scooter and someone wheeling a long trader's barrow heaped with bright spices. They flew in a rainbow cloud in the mirrors.

Left again, then right, then right again, as if following a narrowing perspective into darker, tighter alleyways. Then, suddenly, he stopped, almost throwing Scudamore against the windscreen. The old man groaned. In the mirrors, the BMW flashed past the end of the alley, heading for Lebuh Carnarvon. Breathing deeply, slowly, Hyde backed the Ford out of the alley.

The guidebook told him where to find the British Representative; the nearest Penang boasted to a commission or an embassy was in the UMBC building on Lebuh Pantai, where the banks and the moneychangers congregated, two blocks from the harbour. The Representative had his offices on the fifth floor, within the Price Waterhouse offices ... HMG working out of the offices of bloody *accountants*. The Foreign Office where it should be, after all – part of the financial services sector.

'We're going to see my accountants,' Hyde announced. Scudamore glared at him with wet-eyed pain.

In no more than five minutes, he turned the car into the first street after the UMBC building, parked and switched off the engine. Shiva, Parvati and their elephant-headed son were the only figures who remarked his actions from a small Hindu temple, crushed between the bulk of the Bank of Malaysia and the lowering presence of the Hong Kong & Shanghai Bank. The dwarfed gods maintained a curious, detached dignity. Ganesh's elephant head seemed to be smiling through its gold leaf and blue paint.

'It's only a short walk.' He opened the passenger door and pulled gently at Scudamore's reluctant bulk. The old man groaned. 'Come on – get you patched up.' They must have a first-aid kit, even a nurse to attend to the hangovers at Price Waterhouse. He got the old man out of the car and rested him like an awkward parcel against it. The upholstery was dyed with blood. *Don't* pass out on me now ... Scudamore leant his great weight against Hyde's small frame. 'Let's go—' Hyde grunted.

He staggered under the total, inert weight, stumbling along the narrow street, Scudamore's breathing wet on his cheek, his blood staining the light suit. The sunlight on Lebuh Pantai fell like a hammer blow. Pedestrians stopped in shock and surprise. Hyde waved them away. There was, anyway, something repellent and sinister about the wound and the two men locked together in a drunken progress. People hastily stepped aside, opening a channel for them.

He lurched Scudamore against the blank, aquamarine-tinted windows of the UMBC building. *Fifth floor*. Then he pushed him through the revolving doors, ignoring the uniformed commissionaire who made to move towards them, as did the security guard.

'Stay away!' they forced him to bellow at them. 'Understand? *Stay away!*'

It worked for long enough for them to reach the elevators. One set of doors was open and he bundled Scudamore inside. The cabinet of the lift rattled with his impact against the far wall. Hyde closed the door on curiosity, half-decision, the growing sense that the police should be called. *Fifth floor*. Price-Bloody-Waterhouse ... Scudamore lolled against him with the lift's silent, imperceptible acceleration. The doors opened. Two shirtsleeved young men wearing thick, multicoloured braces, and a young woman in a vivid blouse and brief skirt half stepped into the compartment before surprise halted them. Hyde jammed his leg against the door to prevent it from closing and grabbed the arm of one of the two men in a hard grip.

'The British Representative – where?'

The doors at either end of the short corridor were black, unpolished wood, brass-handled and with security number pads to one side of them.

'You use the intercom.' He pointed. 'You're let in.'

'*You* let me in. *Now.*'

A moment of defiance, then the man shrugged, moved to the door and punched in his number. The door buzzed and he nudged it open. Hyde hefted Scudamore against him and hurried him through.

'Where?'

'First offices – on the left. Is he—?'

'Thanks—' Hyde murmured.

He pushed open a dark-wood door plaqued with the name and title of Her Britannic Majesty's Representative. Scudamore blundered through it, startling the occupants and untidying the neat suite of rooms. A middle-aged woman moved at once to him and knelt beside him as Hyde lowered him to the carpet. Beyond glass, the Representative had risen uncertainly from his desk. He was at once puzzled, even threatened, as he came from behind the glass screen.

'Does this door lock?' Hyde asked, then saw the key in one of the locks and turned it.

'What is this?' The Representative was perhaps thirty-five, slender and of medium height. His face possessed a blank, inexperienced kindliness now overcast by a sense of his office and his timidity. 'Who are you? Why have you brought—?'

'Is this a gunshot wound?' the middle-aged woman asked in a Scottish accent. Green, intelligent eyes. 'What happened?'

'Can you patch him up, temporarily?'

She nodded, getting to her feet.

'I'll get the first-aid kit. But he needs a hospital.'

'Later. I need to talk to KL, to the High Commission.'

'Why?' the Representative asked. 'Who *are* you?' There was a frisson of excited curiosity, that of a child confronting strange animals in a zoo.

'You're Fuller?' His name was on the door-plaque. The man nodded, brushing his hand uncertainly through his hair. 'Good. Look – this isn't a game, but it also isn't happening. Not officially.' Fuller was studying him as if he had been reminded of someone he had once seen in an old photograph.

'You're—?'

'Was. I don't know exactly what this is,' Hyde lied, 'but he needs protection. You know the people in KL? Good. Is Evans still posted to the Commission?'

'Evans? Oh, *that* Evans. Yes, he's on drug surveillance now—'

'Get him for me.'

'I – he was ... were *you*? One of Aubrey's people?' He shrugged. There was the vicarious excitement of a movie about the situation for him. In another ten minutes, Fuller would probably become bored, even fractious, unless Hyde satisfied his celluloid image of Intelligence.

'Yes. *Was*. Get Evans – please. No, before you do that, call the security man at the front desk and tell him you're in control, there's nothing to worry about. Just a nasty accident to a British citizen. *Quickly!*'

'Marjorie, be careful,' Fuller said as the Scotswoman returned from an inner room and tore away Scudamore's shirt. Hyde heard her indrawn breath as she saw the gape of the exit wound. Only one of the shots had hit him, Hyde thought. There was blood on the peach-coloured carpet.

Fuller was already behind his glass screen, speaking reassuringly to the security man. His acceptance of responsibility seemed to affect him like dyspepsia. Then he dialled again and began speaking to the High Commission in Kuala Lumpur. Hyde moved towards his desk. Eventually, Fuller held out the receiver, wincing as Scudamore groaned. Hyde glanced into the outer office. Marjorie was winding a bandage around Scudamore's huge stomach while holding a lump of gauze against his side. Her salt-speckled red hair had flopped against her cheek. She looked up, noticed his attention, and announced:

'The bullet went in and came out.'

Hyde took the receiver.

'Evans – it's Hyde.'

'Christ – a rave from the grave! I wondered which one of the old lot it was. Should have guessed it was you – dragging in wounded old men off the street, like. The boy there sounds a bit put out. Mind you, faced with you, most of them would be—'

'Listen, you Welsh windbag,' Hyde interrupted without malice, even with amusement; a sense of welcoming back the comfortably familiar. Like running into someone from school years later, in a warm pub. 'You know I'm not on the payroll. As for the wounded man, Jessop, of dubious renown, was behind the shooting. It's me he wants.'

'Jessop? That pal of Fraser? Is he out here, then? Christ, boy, I opened a bottle of champagne when Tony Godwin faxed me Fraser had copped it!'

'Naturally.'

'How about the victim? Is he dead? Who is he?'

'No, he's not dead. And he's just a bystander – a pal of the old man. He needs protection, and *I* need getting out.'

'Where to? Back to Sydney?'

Without conscious deliberation, Hyde said: 'No,

London. I want to talk to the old bugger about it.'

'OK.' The excitement in Evans' voice was feverish; like the thought of sex goading a man coming out of prison, Hyde reflected. 'You *sure* you don't know what it is?'

'There was – something in Oz. This has to be connected. Whoever employs Jessop thinks it's time I walked the plank.'

'It must be shitty if Jessop's in it, boy. I heard he'd been moving around a lot in the private sector. Top-class clients only, mind. Usually with that even bigger bastard Fraser – doing this and that. Doing 'em in, more like! Look, I'll fly up myself – can't miss the chance of seeing your ugly mug again. We'll look after you. Put Fuller back on. By the way, he's not a fool, just a bit inexperienced in the black arts – OK? I'll give him instructions to look after you there until I arrive. And take care—'

'Sure.'

It was eight in the morning. There was a bright, cold sky beyond the bedroom window. She turned to Alder with the afterglow of passion. The bed beside her was empty, and she felt a chill of shock. She had wanted to reach out and touch his shoulder, his neck and profile, his lips that had been on hers, on her breasts, everywhere. Then she heard, with a flush of relief that she might have despised in a cheap novel's prose, small noises from the kitchen. He hadn't left.

She lay back in the bed, stretching luxuriously. He was evidently making coffee for them. *Toujours la politesse...* It had only been as he was undressing her that she had become conscious of the scars of the car accident. And that the bedroom lights were still on. He had been shocked but uninterrupted at seeing the weals on her flesh. Later, he had been gentler, more enquiring. She had explained the accident, but not that it was her first sex since then. She had wanted him very much. Wanted *them*.

Expectations had been fulfilled, she observed drily to herself, as if signing a student's assessment. Beside him, afterwards, slowly, luxuriatingly falling into sleep, the past had become something spotlit by their affairs; a montage of rooms in which they had made love, a sequence of images of their bodies and their tenderness together. *My bikini days are over, though*, she had managed to joke of her scars. *You always preferred the museum to the beach*, he had replied.

The telephone shook her out of recollected sensation.

'Marian Pyott,' she answered, her voice still cloudy with passion.

'Marian – Deputy Chief Whip's office here.' She recognised the smooth tones. Bill Marriner, a junior Opposition Whip. 'Sorry to trouble you at this early hour ...' Which meant it was deliberate. It was the Whips' equivalent of the four-o'clock-in-the-morning knock on the door, their attempt at making the party a police state. She smiled to herself, hoisting her body into a sitting position against the headboard. If you could only see me now, Bill ...

'Yes, Bill?' she replied gaily.

'Ten thirty suit you, Marian? George would very much like to have a word.' Just as Rose had warned her on the answerphone last night. The Whips were angry. They wished her Commons question withdrawn. With the Foreign Secretary claiming the DTI junket was a moral challenge to the junta in Rangoon, and the PM telling the Burmese junta they could either board the democracy train or it would leave without them, the trade mission to Burma was a cross-party jolly good thing. No rocking of boats.

She did not relish a meeting with George Theobald, the Deputy Chief Whip, but she could not refuse.

'Fine. Will you be there to mop up the blood?'

Marriner attempted a snicker, then murmured: 'Thanks, Marian.'

She put down the receiver, at once attempting to recapture her previous mood, to dismiss the political. She could not, despite the nakedness of her breasts, the sense that Alder would be bringing coffee in a moment, that he would sense her abandon, desire her ... Damn Bill Marriner. She got up quickly and tied her wrap around her, politics having swept passion away. She wandered into the hall, and then towards the kitchen.

Alder followed her. Enjoying the sensation of his nearness, she asked, 'And what are *your* plans for today, my errant and returned love?'

'I have to be at the Department of Trade at eleven. Meet with some British businessmen who are investing in Burma. Get the feeling *they* have – see if it agrees with my own.'

'Which is?' she bridled.

'That Suu Kyi is wrong to oppose investment and tourism. So is the White House, and . . . so are you, my love. So are you. It's the only way – prosperity will bring about what Suu Kyi wants quicker than talking to the converted over her garden wall!'

She opened her mouth to speak, and then closed her lips tightly until they were able to smile. She was prepared, she realised, to stifle all opposition, become totalitarian with her own dissent, in order to avoid quarrelling with him; spoiling what there was. Passion is a police state, she observed to herself, undeterred.

'I'm glad you're back.'

'So am I. I missed you, Marian, I really did. Even if I didn't realise it until last night!'

'Thank you, kind sir . . .' she began, but her voice faltered on hope and sudden passion. She kissed him fiercely.

CHAPTER THREE

Insolence of Office

The taxi dropped her near the Members' Entrance to the Commons. A stiff, chill breeze scuttled around the cobbled yard, distressing her blonde hair and blanching the cheeks of the policeman beside his glass-fronted security post. She paid the driver, standing in the wind, struggling with her long scarf, her full skirt pressed against her or billowing like a cloak. High white clouds were tugged across the sun in a quick succession of unsuccessful disguises. The policeman grinned in response to her smile as she passed into the building.

A government Member, as Euro-mistrustful as herself, though less vocal, passed her in the corridor, pipe in mouth.

'Morning, Tony.'

'... Levellers' Association dinner next month,' she heard as she passed on, unfolding her scarf, her briefcase banging against her breasts as she did so, her handbag encumbering her movements. 'Will you be coming, Marian?'

She waved her hand airily without turning round.

'Put me down for that, Tony!' she called out.

'Enjoyed your article the other day,' the erstwhile peer called back with a chuckle.

'Thanks!'

Her article on the government's new policy towards Burma had appeared in the *Telegraph* the previous week. Its title had been 'Sleeping with the Enemy'. In it, she had excoriated a Labour government for being wooed by business, seduced by the City and the EU, and heeding the siren calls of the generals in Rangoon. She had poured especial scorn on the claimed moral position of the government, and on the blandishments of the Burmese junta regarding greater freedom for Suu Kyi and her supporters. The article's peroration had been suitably ringing, if a little pompous, was her own judgement. She described the present Cabinet as *yet another garage extension with staff accommodation for the Foreign Office*.

Her father had rung as she was hurriedly dressing, made late by their lovemaking, to inform her that Clive Winterborne would be joining them for lunch. She had countered, as in a chess game, with Alder. Bearding the lion in its den, confronting her darling father's disapproval – which was inevitable – that Alder was back in her life. She had hurriedly put the receiver down on Giles's response.

She passed into Central Lobby, more populated with tourists and their shepherding guides than by Honourable Members, and almost collided with Peter Grainger beneath the Churchill Arch. The habitual and practised disdain of his expression, one befitting a senior Opposition spokesman, softened as he recognised her.

'Hello, my dear.' She did not bridle. Peter Grainger patronised all women, however distant their orbit from himself. It was said to be the reason why he found it necessary to continually change wives and mistresses; they tired of the condescension.

'Peter.' She beamed at him. After all, Grainger had been Alder's companion at the National, had perhaps effected their reintroduction. She could afford to be generous. 'How nice.'

'I hear,' he began lubriciously, grinning, 'that all is well with you?' He raised his eyebrows as archly as any bad actor playing a Victorian seducer.

'I hope my American friend is maintaining his discretion, Peter?'

'Oh, certainly! I expect to hear absolutely *no* lurid details when we meet in half an hour! I'm just on my way to the DTI. Robert *will* be there, I take it?'

'Before you insinuate it, Peter – yes. He is still capable of volition without collapsing into exhaustion. A shame, considering the purpose of your mutual visit to the DTI.'

Grainger's features darkened around the ruddiness of his good, uxorious health. He frequented the Commons gym with a tinge of fanaticism, a health club in Chelsea, and a number of beds scattered across the more salubrious postal districts of the capital. His fitness was not in doubt.

'Your appearance on *Newsnight* the other evening was *not* helpful, my dear girl,' he murmured. 'You know the party's attitude – support for the government for the trade mission to Burma. Banging on about the moral high ground and what that angelic-looking woman Suu Kyi would prefer the West to do *does not assist*–' He paused as she patted his arm.

'No need to remonstrate, Peter. George Theobald has me in his sights already. The Exterminator does these things with more effect.'

'Oh—' He evidently was not party to her imminent dressing-down. 'Can't say I'm surprised – but one wouldn't wish George Theobald on one's worst political enemy.' The fleshy, contented grin was back. 'Good luck. I'll pass on your undying affection to Rob Alder, shall I? Or have you pledged that already this morning?' His eyes sparkled knowingly.

She was smiling as he said: 'Even young Alder' – Grainger had recently celebrated his fiftieth birthday and seemed to consider it incumbent upon him to adopt a patrician seniority of years and wisdom – 'thinks a great deal of the criticism of the junta is propaganda and we shouldn't swallow it wholesale, but look on the bright side. They're *coming round*, Marian!' It was the hushed, expectant tone of a prime minister finding a less awful opinion poll rating than anticipated. *God's in his Heaven, all's right with the world*! she all but quoted aloud. 'We're making them see their future more clearly, the *benefits* that tourism and investment can bring . . . and what they need to do in exchange—'

'Stop locking people up without trial or shooting them for exercising freedom of speech – that kind of minor misdemeanour. Is that what you mean, Peter?' She smiled with all the innocence that ever Kenneth Aubrey had mustered. Grainger's features became empurpled, and he snapped:

'I foresee some domestic altercations in the very near future, my dear girl, if you exercise your sixth-form humour on young Alder – and your sixth-former's bleeding heart!' She laughed, and his features softened. 'You're impossible, Marian!' he announced, shaking his head. 'Impossible ...' His tone was tinged with sexual regret.

'... and impervious,' she teased, then exclaimed: 'Must get on – my execution, you know.' She waved and left him standing beneath the Churchill Arch, and strode down the corridor away from the subdued hubbub of Central Lobby, her smile still pleasurably in place.

Rose, her researcher, was about to open the door as Marian entered her office.

'Oh, I'm just popping out for half an hour. That OK?' Marian suspected the younger woman was having an affair with a junior minister in the last government, a married man sternly in favour of family values. She smiled complaisantly.

'Off you go!'

'I've left your mail on the desk. The Whips' Office has been on the phone – twice.' Rose adopted her most lugubrious expression.

Marian looked at her watch. She had time to read the mail ... compose herself, more like, she admitted.

'Are you out or in?' Rose asked.

'Out to lunch, then back – and off to the constituency on the four-ten.'

'Oh – almost forgot! That girl – Syeeda? – has been on again. I – not my business, Marian, but she really could do with a call...' Rose shrugged apologetically and vanished through the door. 'See you,' drifted behind her.

The young MP with whom she shared her office – one of the few remaining backbench MPs within the Palace of Westminster – had won a by-election against predictions before the last government's popularity had terminally plummeted. He nodded at her and smiled appealingly. His ambition was as brash and shiny as the chrome on an American car in the fifties. The loss of office by the party had daunted him. He had acquired consultancies since the general election almost like bandages for his wounded, delayed ambitions. She glanced at his crowded desk. The smile had been a plea for assistance. He was trawling through sheets of statistics on the Common Fisheries Policy issued by the EU, and emitting grunting, puzzled noises at regular intervals. His was a fishing constituency and his lack of a head for figures was complemented by his urban upbringing, both of which rendered him at a loss in dealing with plainspoken, demanding men who manned trawlers.

Normally she would have helped him, and he knew it, but her appointment with the Deputy Chief Whip of her party allowed her no more energy than that required to flick idly through her constituency correspondence. Syeeda – and Rose's plea on her behalf – loomed in her guilty conscience like reprimanding shadows. She was struck, too, by the clarity with which she had registered Westminster and its occupants; afraid that it was somehow valedictory, and that she had begun to think the unthinkable . . . of leaving. Going to America – if he should ask her. Did she *really* intend . . . ?

She snatched up the phone as if inviting distraction, and sombrely dialled Syeeda Lal's number. The young MP at the other desk was puffing like a steam engine in a vain attempt to attract her attention and assistance. She owed Syeeda at least one consolatory telephone call—

'Syeeda – it's Marian. How are you?' There was an inten-sity in the silence of the connection, then Syeeda said:

'I've been to his flat . . .' It was like a confession to a crime. Marian felt her own reluctance return. 'Sorting things – you know . . .'

'Yes,' Marian murmured. The quiet voice seemed to

come faintly from a lightless tunnel. Marian was struck by the empathy she felt for Syeeda; by her own sense of something valuable that might be lost to her. 'I – there's nothing I can say, Syeeda, that will make any difference, I know.' Now she was irritated by the facial grimaces and pleading glances of her companion. 'You – got my fax? It wasn't ... I mean, I thought I could explain it better in writing ...' She had outlined, in clear, minimally compassionate prose, the police evidence, the views of everyone to whom she had talked. Hated doing it, and the cowardice that had made it necessary.

'Yes. I got it.' From her tone, there had been nothing at the boy's flat that had helped her, no spar among the wreckage to which she could cling. 'There wasn't much – at the flat. But I knew that. Just reminders—' She broke off, her voice engulfed by a choking, sobbing noise. Marian felt it scrape her nerves, like the magnified soundtrack of something being devoured.

'Yes ...' She was angry at her helplessness; angry, too, that she had made the call before seeing Theobald. She didn't need it, not this, not now —

'I forgot to tell you – of Medhev's excitement, the evening before he disappeared' she heard. 'I told you he wasn't around for twenty-four hours before ... There was a cutting in the flat, folded in his diary. Nothing to explain it, that day he wasn't ...' She teetered at every sentence on the brink of a fall into incoherent grief. 'It was from the local rag. Medhev had cut out a photograph and the caption. It was of Sir Clive – your godfather, you know—?' Was this the spar, in some incomprehensible way? Syeeda seemed to cling to it as if it were. She knew Clive. Marian had taken him to the Jaipur, introduced him to the Lals. 'I only remembered, when I saw the photograph, that Medhev had been excited when he was looking through the newspaper. He asked if he could take it home. I don't know why he wanted it,' she concluded. 'Sir Clive was at a charity lunch. The caption said who he was, where he lived – you know. Why did he cut it out and keep it? He never met him.'

'I don't know, Syeeda,' Marian eventually replied. 'I shouldn't think it means anything. Would you? Perhaps you told Medhev you'd met Sir Clive . . .'

'Yes. Probably.' There was a loud, determined sniffing noise. 'Thanks for ringing, Marian. I understand why you sent the fax instead – I understand. Will I see you soon?'

'Yes. I'll call in—'

She was on the point of settling herself with a sense of relief more comfortably in her chair when the door opened and the bulk of the Deputy Chief Whip appeared, his stomach preceding the rest of him into the room.

'Must go, Syeeda – sorry. Bye—'

George Theobald's gait possessed a rolling awkwardness that was nevertheless filled with the most obvious, bullying menace. Marian put down the receiver. This was an old trick of his, to storm into an MP's office when that unfortunate was consoling his or her nerves with the thought that there was another ten minutes before the fateful encounter. She should have expected him.

Her companion, the innumerate young MP, was at once as white and startled as a rabbit in headlights, and he bolted from his desk to the door at a vicious nodding motion of the Whip's bull-like head. The door shut behind him.

This minor exercise of power, and the visible evidence of fear it evoked, seemed to satisfy Theobald. With summoned menace, he leant across Marian's desk, the broad knuckles of both hands pressing down on her correspondence and her in-tray.

'Ah, George – I see you're going to help me with my constituency letters. And with your usual signature,' she added, nodding at the position of his clenched knuckles. It was, of course, all too easy to mock George Theobald; his humourless dimness was as evident as his bulk. It did, however, require nerve. Built like an elephant, his memory possessed the same retentiveness where insults were concerned.

Theobald stared down at his hands and the joke became obvious. His small eyes, folded like raisins in creases of doughlike fat, glinted with animosity.

'Not interrupting you, am I?'

'I'm quite ready for you, George. Is it important?'

'Just a cautionary word – Marian.' He made her name sound like an atrocity committed in a distant war and still associated with infamy. 'Your appearance on *Newsnight*. Not to mention your latest article. Quite the celebrity. We're used to you banging the Europe drum, but now it's Burma you seem to have taken under your wing. The Chief Whip asked me if you could provide him with a list of the lame dogs we can expect you to adopt over the coming months ... or a list of those causes you *won't* be taking up, if that's shorter.'

'George – what a long sentence! And all the words in the correct order.' As his features compressed into a rocklike solidity and became suffused with crimson, she added: 'Sorry. But I didn't say anything to Jeremy that would embarrass the party, only the government. And, as you pointed out, the article was mostly old hat. Why the fuss?'

'I expect it's the *accumulation* of lost causes that worried the leader and the Chief Whip.' He leant further towards her. 'I would have thought the trouble you're having from local bigwigs in your constituency might have encouraged a bit of restraint, if not a period of helpful silence? Or is Sir Clive's protection irremovable?'

The threat was evident, as much as if he had drawn a weapon. Central Office was stirring up the landed and not-so-landed gentry in the constituency in an effort to have her deselected.

Despite herself, Marian felt her cheeks becoming heated, her body language more submissive. The fat, vulgar bully with the saurian brain was *effective*. His invariable technique of falling like a rock on errant MPs and crushing them might produce no more than a winded sensation in people as experienced in his tactics as herself, but the sensation was, nevertheless, very real.

'I can understand your dislike of my opinions on the European Union, George – even the futility of revenge ... But why are you so interested in my attitude to Burma?'

'We are not here to embarrass business. Do I make myself clear? Shooting off your mouth about the DTI's junket to Burma is not good news. You can try keeping your bleeding heart in your breast pocket. We're in agreement with the government that trade links with Burma are *important*. Very important. So drop it.'

'Or ... ?' she was forced to challenge.

'Would you be at all interested in resuming your academic career, Marian? In the near future? If not, keep your lips as tightly together as they say you keep your knees, and give us all a rest! You're a bloody nuisance, Marian, and we want you to keep quiet! Otherwise, Sir Clive Winterborne may be prevailed upon to see you in a different and less doting light. Understood – *Marian*?'

In the end, it had been the easiest of matters, the airline tickets, the passport, the change of clothing; so much so that it evoked nostalgia rather than tension. Evans had simply reinvented old skills and training. He was on the

plane to Kuala Lumpur, then a Singapore Airlines flight to
Heathrow, in business class, complete with hand luggage,
laptop computer, mobile phone and expense account.

Hyde rubbed his face as if massaging potter's clay into
the features of the mask he was at present wearing. The
airport in Penang had been easy to monitor; Evans's team
had encountered no surveillance. Which meant that
Jessop realised he would have called in help. The half-
time whistle had blown in the match. Perhaps Jessop had
anticipated his aroused interest in him, even guessed that
it would be Aubrey he would want to consult. Whatever
the reason, they had been prepared to let him fly out –
probably expecting him to make for London.

The stewardess, in the bright wrapping of a silk sari,
neat as a gift from an expensive boutique, paused long
enough to deposit another glass of champagne on the arm
of his seat, her smile flickering from side to side of the 747's
aisle like a small torch. Hyde sipped the cold bubbles and
glanced through the window, down towards a night-
enveloped India, speckled with the lights of cities and
towns that seemed lost in the vast darkness of the
continent; as if they were the first explorers, carrying
lamps through a great wilderness. He was another six or
seven hours from Heathrow and Aubrey.

Scudamore's features had still been the colour of clay as
the ambulance door closed on them and his grunts of
renewed pain. The old man was safe now, from Jessop . . .
the expert, the ex-agent hired to eliminate someone who
continued to tread on the toes of Straits Royal Group.
Hyde's proximity had been enough for them to suspect a
trap for Pearson. Evans had discovered that he had flown
out of Penang for Singapore only two hours after
Scudamore had been shot.

A large city passed beneath the aircraft's wing like an

electrical circuit board of lights. He'd called Ros to rearrange their rendezvous in Singapore. She had been suspiciously angry at his return to London, but that couldn't be helped. She had an insight into the tangible pleasure he felt at the thought of London, the flat in Earls Court, the cats, Max the dentist.

There was a greater, more earnest tickle of anticipation in the certainty that Jessop, too, would be heading for London. He had no doubt that the man would turn up. He had a contract to fulfil. He glimpsed his immediate future with anticipation which twisted in his stomach like a worm. Jessop would be the way into the maze. He'd know who he was working for. He could be made to tell—

Her father rarely, if ever, invited her to lunch at the Club, out of deference to what he believed was her feminist dislike of its air of masculine exclusivity. In fact, she enjoyed the Club. *Madame Tussaud's with moving effigies*, she often called it, to Giles Pyott's amusement, or *the Palace of Westminster's drawing room*. Because of Giles' over-zealous sensitivity, they were seated in the kind of fashionable Charlotte Street restaurant that did not serve vegetables with the main course and which made her father and Clive Winterborne feel superannuatedly uncomfortable amid the expense-account clientele. Alder, on the other hand, seemed at ease, sipping the water that he refused to turn into wine. For him, the restaurant must be shinily intimate after the hangarlike spaces that Washington and New York offered for power lunches and overpowering dinners.

They moved, by mutual consent, from the main course directly to coffee.

'Thank you, Daddy,' Marian said, toasting him with the remaining white wine in her glass. Someone at another table was smoking – good. One could never be certain when a non-smoking *diktat* would be issued in restaurants. She lit a cigarette. Alder glanced at her, for an instant disapproving before regaining his smile and continuing to engage her father in conversation. 'Good of you,' she added, not referring to lunch.

'Pleasure, my girl,' Giles replied. There was a small sense of relief on Clive Winterborne's aquiline features.

Her father had acquiesced in Alder's reappearance in her life, and acceptance had turned to a reserved warmth between the *hors d'oeuvres* and the entrée. Clive, who knew Alder via politics as well as through Marian, seemed altogether more delighted, without reservations.

'Are you attending the bash tonight, Robert?' he asked, waving Marian's cigarette smoke good-humouredly away from his face. He looked at her meaningfully.

'Yes, I've invited him. He wouldn't dare not come.' She smiled teasingly, then said to Giles: 'Daddy, why don't you break your date?' Some regimental business. She was teasing. He detested charity galas where thousands were spent on food and wine, detested even more most of the people, whether politicians, the rich, the momentarily famous, who attended such things . . . and would probably not wish to test his new complaisance towards Alder any further than lunch.

'Clive – something I almost forgot. I know this is going to sound ridiculous, but you didn't know a young man by the name of Kumar at all, did you?'

'Kumar . . . ?' Clive Winterborne pronounced the boy's name very slowly, as if searching his memory, even though not recognising the name. 'I – don't think so . . .'

Alder murmured: 'Sir, you got that call – while I was at Uffingham. A week ago – a little less? You told me about it . . . A young man with an Indian name, was it Kumar—?'

Clive clicked his fingers.

'Yes – strange call …' He turned to Marian, smiling. 'Sorry, my dear. I make the connection now. The young man who died of an overdose. Yes, I did have a weekend call, Robert, you're right. Couldn't make head nor tail of it. Rather garbled, excited conversation. Wanted to see me. I – put him off, I'm afraid. Politely, of course. But firmly.'

'Good job too,' Giles offered, 'from what I've heard from Marian. Wouldn't do your social standing in the county much good, associating with drug addicts.' There was an exchange of complacent smiles between her father and godfather. Marian felt a hot resentment on behalf of Syeeda, even the dead boy.

'Oh, that was all,' she murmured.

'What did you expect?' her father remarked, still smiling. 'Clive was going to mourn him as a long-lost son?' His irritation was slight but evident. She felt it was disguisedly directed at herself, its real target being Alder.

'So, you've been in the country longer than you let on?' she asked him archly.

Flushing slightly, Alder mumbled: 'I – I wanted to consult Clive over this Burma thing. Winterborne Holdings has interests there, all over the Far East. And—'

'Yes. Quite,' Clive intervened, embarrassed. David, she realised. Alder had known David for a number of years. And David was not in any position to offer *respectable* advice at present. Alder had evidently gone to Clive instead.

'I did think of inviting you that same weekend,' Clive whispered, leaning towards her, his liver-spotted hand on hers, 'and thought better of it.' His eyes indicated Giles. 'Nevertheless, I'm very pleased the way things have turned out.' His smile was warm, genuine.

'So am I,' she whispered back, aware that her father was

smoothing all intuitive censure from his expression as Alder once more engaged him in conversation. 'So am I, Clive.'

The cats followed him from the hall into the flat's mustiness as if into a new and dangerous environment, frequently pausing, sniffing enquiringly at everything, as they gradually reinstated themselves, in imitation of himself, into a former home. The tortoiseshell hesitated, then glided on to the armchair that had been its habitual bed for years. Hyde looked at the bug in the palm of his hand which he had removed from the telephone. He closed his fingers on it, as ferally aware of strangers having been there as were the cats. The Burmese was, indeed, sniffing the carpet near the telephone lead. Someone had knelt there, recently.

Max, the dentist who leased the ground-floor flat of the Philbeach Gardens house, had told him that the gas board had called that morning. Later, he would check Ros' flat for similar bugs. He inspected it once more, opening his hand. It had been left as earnestly as a bouquet of flowers, welcoming him back. Then he placed it on the carpet and ground it beneath his shoe, scooping up the shards of metal and plastic and placing them in a bowl of woodshavings that had long lost their fragrance.

Max had surrendered the cats with the easy certainty that they would soon be back with him and the latest of a succession of partners; a pleasant, open-faced young woman with a Yorkshire accent who worked in the City.

The Burmese was sniffing his legs, almost failing to recognise him in the suit Evans had supplied. He stroked its face and head and was identified.

He sat on the sofa and the cat rose on to his lap as he dialled Aubrey. There were no more bugs in the lounge.

'Yes?' The old man sounded breathless. Probably his age.

'It's me. Someone called before I got back.'

'Safe now?'

'Safe.'

The Earls Court evening glowed over the darkness of the rear garden of the house. He could smell Max's cooking, hear the young woman's narrative of her crowded day.

As if exasperated at being interrupted at a meal, Aubrey snapped: 'What is this you find yourself in, Patrick?'

'I've told you the tale before – you didn't believe me. Told me I was barking up the wrong tree, indulging in flights of fancy . . . I seem to remember. But it isn't anything to do with Scudamore – that was just negotiation by means of the heavy mob. This is something a lot more important.'

Aubrey remained silent for some time, then he murmured: 'It does seem somewhat excessive to employ someone with Jessop's peculiar skills, not to mention his psychological profile, to frighten one old man off his property. That far, I agree with you.'

'I'm nobody – no danger to anyone. I haven't been connected with *anything* for a couple of years. Except the work I was doing in Oz. Which was obviously more important than a handful of crooked cops enjoying free holidays!'

'I simply can't see that a company like Straits Royal Group would be involved. You still have no proof – none whatsoever. Have you?'

'None,' Hyde admitted angrily. 'But people like Straits Royal would be the sort to employ a *white* ex-professional. The expected heavies, if it was something local, something second-grade, would be Malays, Chinese. But *not* Jessop.'

'Perhaps . . .'

'I must talk to you tonight.'

'This evening? I have a gala supper to attend, in aid of Covent Garden. It's difficult—'

'Where is it?'

'Grosvenor House, but—'

'I'll be there.'

He hung up, amusement dispelling his frustrated anger. He stood up and the cat leapt from his lap, snagging his suit with its needle-like claws. Hyde went into the kitchen to open the tin of cat food Max had supplied. Both cats appeared at once. He dished the food on to a saucer and put it down on the tiles for them.

He should call Ros . . .

. . . the lounge was folding around him as warmly and familiarly as a favoured garment. Faint noises of the cats chewing, the traffic outside, the clicking of long-unused central-heating pipes and radiators. The flat was bespoke, made for him, unlike the house on Sydney's North Shore. There, he had always been accompanied by the sensation of clinging to the edge of something, as if after an accident at sea. The spars of his sunken life had floated past him occasionally, but nothing else of it had been left . . . until now.

He walked into the unlit bedroom and looked out of the window down towards the curve of the street and the gardens, where yellow light from the streetlamps fell on already sparsely leaved trees. A familiar, if rusty excitement stirred in his frame and there was little or no sense of jet-lag. The Burmese entered the room, trotting towards him before jumping on to the windowsill. Outside, a figure in a raincoat paused at the window of a parked car before glancing up at the window of his flat.

Hello, old friend . . . First the bug, now the surveillance.

The pieces were falling into satisfying place and pattern. They'd followed him, Jessop had given them their orders. The game was still on. His fingers itched, as with the mildest of electrical shocks, as the figure on foot moved away from the parked car and resumed his patrol. He felt as alert as the cat.

They wanted him stopped, regardless of time and place. They were in a hurry and whatever he did and whoever he talked to were of interest to them. Money, manpower, resources, all now focused on him, and money was no object. They wanted him *tidied away*.

He returned to the lounge, leaving the cat to continue its observation of the surveillance team. Time for a shower and a shave, then he'd take the team of watchers on the town, all the way to Park Lane. They'd learn nothing. He expected to learn a great deal.

Hyde grinned, stretching his arms. Life again possessed interest, an edge of darkness.

Someone in the rear of the big Rover stirred as if in embarrassment. The rustle of a heavy, uniform mackin- tosh. The noise caused Cobb's smile to broaden.

He half turned in the passenger seat. Neon and streetlighting fell wearily into the car, blotching the occupants with birthmarks and palsied skin on their hands. The town's evening traffic passed, swishing in the rain and glaring with brakelights. The Rover was parked at the corner of a pedestrianised shopping street. His driver was smoking, something which seemed to offend at least one of the back-seat occupants. Light caught the silver of the uniform collar and buttons. Cobb yawned and studied his watch. These provincial Plods were the most boring company on earth – though that was what one had to take in exchange for their incredible stupidity. A couple of prearranged phone calls, Special Branch ID, and they were rolling over like dogs to have their stomachs tickled.

'Your man's inside.' It was not a question. 'We'll give him another ten minutes.'

He stared through the streaked side window, craning to see the sign outside the Jaipur, a little way down the pedestrianised street. It was Lal's best Indian restaurant. Mentioned in Egon Ronay and the *Good Food Guide*. They'd seen Lal himself enter the building an hour before – it was the night for his office work – and the girl, Syeeda, was supervising, even waiting on table. The restaurant was full, just the ticket for the little drama they were about to play out. The gourmet lager trade was out in force.

He wondered whether Jessop's flight from Singapore had reached Heathrow yet. Pity he'd been delayed, because it meant that he, Cobb, had had to field the phone call from Ralph Lau. Winterborne wanted something done to shut the girl up. She'd been on local TV, in one of the regional papers, protesting her dead boyfriend hadn't been an addict or a dealer. People were beginning to wonder . . . Maybe even the Plods in the car with him were wondering. They'd swallowed without hesitation the whole story about Kumar. The legend he and Jessop had created for the boy had been watertight. Except the bloody girl kept banging on and on about his innocence, keeping the story alive . . .

. . . and *she* wouldn't just roll over and keep her mouth shut. She might even reawaken the interest of that bitch of an MP. As it was, she was pestering the local Plods to reopen the investigation.

'I – don't wish to question your authority, Mr Cobb,' the senior policeman in the back of the car began in a voice gruff with discomfort, 'but I simply see no need for my presence here.'

'They're your men, sir. Local Branch men really do need local supervision.' Beside Cobb, the driver grinned, lowering his window and throwing his cigarette end into the rainy night. 'You can see that, sir.'

There was a throat-clearing noise, then: 'Very well. You assure me that this is all tied in with the death of that drug dealer of yours – I accept that. But I want it understood that you'd better be right about Mr Lal and the use to which he puts his restaurants.' It was the bombast of the impotent.

Cobb turned and glared at him.

'*Sir!*' he snapped warningly. 'We're here to obey orders, not *question* them.'

'Very well.'

Cobb offered sweetly: 'I accept the operation's a little unorthodox, but we really do need to get this Lal inside for a while, to ask him the questions we want answered. And we don't have enough to hold him at the moment. Hence the little sting we're pulling here.'

Frighten the bloody wog off for good. To get out from under the mound of ordure with which they would cover him, Lal would promise anything. He'd stop his stupid tart of a daughter talking to the papers and TV before the nationals picked up the story. The whole family would go deaf, dumb and blind.

The senior officer behind him subsided into the shallow sleep of obedience, where conscience and curiosity worked only like fragments of dream and memory. Cobb turned to the other occupant of the rear seat. Young, casually dressed, almost louche, hair fashionably slicked back.

'You're clear on your part, are you? Just make the exchange and we'll arrest you and your pal inside. What's-his-name – Peel, is it?' The young man nodded. 'Peel and you will be bundled into the other car, then it's back to the station. I'll talk to Mr Lal and his daughter. You, Tate,' he added to the driver, 'half an hour, then you bring me the bad news. Then we'll have Mr Lal down at the station to join the party.'

The young Special Branch officer was nodding with excitement and ambition. A yellow-brick road stretched away from this piddling little business all the way to the Met and higher rank. The senior officer's mackintosh demurred with slurring, creaking noises, but the man said nothing.

'OK, a few more minutes.' He grinned. 'Think Lal will offer us something from the menu while we're questioning him?'

'David, I have that business under control,' Ralph Lau asserted, at once angry that he had employed such an ingratiating expression, the vocabulary of an underling. 'There are no real leads and there won't be. That man of yours, Jessop, may have missed his opportunity in Penang, but' – he smiled sarcastically – 'I suppose I can assume his competence?' Then he added: 'The Indians will say nothing more.' He was puzzled by the fleeting disappointment he glimpsed on Winterborne's features.

Lau realised that he was very deliberately aware of David's situation, of the room that was his cell. It was as if his cousin's incarceration was a painting. It allowed him to remain relaxed, controlling the situation.

'Marian is beginning to interfere in my life again!' Winterborne snapped back at him with a malice that still surprised. The window was a frame of darkness behind him as he sat, like a raptor with clipped wings and a calming hood, on the edge of his chair.

'She is *convinced* Kumar was dealing in drugs. What

more do you want?' On an inspirational insight, Lau added: 'You *want* her interference, as you call it, don't you? At least, part of you does—'

'Nonsense! I'm worried that the man Hyde is now in London. As an old associate of the damnable Kenneth Aubrey, he may talk to Marian. Resurrect her suspicions. *That* is my concern.'

'Then Hyde must be disposed of before he has a chance to infect your childhood friend, mustn't he?' Lau shrugged, spreading his hands. 'If that's all you needed – reassurance – then I've wasted my time answering your summons!' His tone was one of waspish spleen. Winterborne's nostrils narrowed. The light of a table lamp revealed the heightened colour of his cheeks.

Lau was dressed in a casual Armani suit, a vivid silk shirt, loafers. He had been interrupted, his couture suggested, in his pleasures. For what good reason? his appearance seemed to demand. Winterborne watched him much as he might have watched the progress of disease in a loved child; both of them understood the manner and the inevitability of the rivalry between them.

'I wanted you here to ask you about the Czechoslovakian telecommunications contract – *and* about your trip to the States that you keep postponing.' His cousin had shrunk, Lau decided, become institutionalised. However lax and luxurious, this *was* a prison. Winterborne, to his gratification, seemed already to feel the reins of Winterborne Holdings slipping from his hands. He waved his hand in airy, angering dismissal.

'Czechoslovakia? The sums are good – but not that good. I'm still looking into it. It *will* proceed, though I think it's more hobby-sized than it is real business. And I *will* get across the Pond in the next couple of weeks. I'm

not neglecting the company, David.' There was a sharp
little switchblade of mockery in his tone.

'That Czechoslovakian contract is for their entire
telephone system, Ralph,' Winterborne flung back. 'And
it leads us to every other country in eastern Europe. Can't
you grasp that? Why is Asia still *everything* to you?'

'Because countries like Myanmar, Laos, Cambodia are
prepared to surrender their whole economies to people
with the wisdom to expand them. We can grow the
economies of whole countries, David, not just install
telephones!' Lau leant forward in his chair. 'The Tiger
economies have suffered badly in the past couple of
years. It's given us great leverage. We have power and a
fair wind. When those economies recover, we'll be more
powerful in Asia than ever before.' He seemed like a large
dog about to pounce. 'My meeting at the Myanmar
Embassy in a couple of days. It's not just to put my
signature on the contract for the resort complex. There
are microprocessor plants in the offing, heavy industry,
the dam project, railway construction. *We* – Winterborne
Holdings – has all the companies, all the expertise, to take
a great deal of this on single-handed ...' He at once
became irritated, and added: 'Come on, David, think *big*,
just as you used to.'

'My plans focus on America!'

'*Our* new world isn't across the Atlantic, it's in Asia. The
profits, the power and influence will all be so much
greater—'

'Even if the financial base is rotten? Even if we're tied to
the devil in the meanwhile?'

'You *needed* money, David. *I* have kept Winterborne
Holdings afloat – after *you* nearly brought the whole edifice
crashing down! Why else are you here, for God's sake?
And when you appeared at the Old Bailey, what banks

wanted to lend, who wasn't calling in their loans, who'd *invest?*' Both men were breathing like struggling wrestlers, crouched on the edges of their chairs, facing one another. 'You needed millions – *billions.* I got them for you.'

Lau sat back in his chair and very consciously inspected his cloudily grey fingernails, enjoying David's discomfiture; enjoying, too, the charged, naked atmosphere in which they had finally unmasked themselves and declared their mutual enmity. To David, of course, it must seem as if he was the victim of a swift, rapacious dawn raid by a rival. *Sharper than a serpent's tooth*, an ungrateful cousin ... He smiled with dazzling, compassionate innocence.

'Winterborne Holdings has recovered almost all the ground it lost. Clive's patrician honesty helps me, of course. We are poised to move on, grow—'

'Unless you attend successfully to small matters like Hyde, there will be nothing left for you to pocket, Ralph – not even Straits Royal Group. Make certain you bury him – and all interest in that Kumar boy. It will bring us all down more certainly than anything I've done. Do you understand that? What happened to Kumar and our involvement must never see the light of day!'

Red and gold wallpaper, the swordlike leaves of tropical plants, a tank of small, bright fish, crowded tables and waiters moving with the speeded-up grace of a Chaplin film. It was a luxurious parody of every Indian restaurant Cobb had ever seen, out of which the greater formality and the seriousness of good food emerged.

He recognised Syeeda Lal from her photograph. She was serving food two tables away from the young copper and his dark-spectacled, leather-jacketed companion, Peel. Cobb signalled to two other police officers at a table near the door, then they began the pantomime.

He brushed past Syeeda waving a warrant card and confronted Peel, who melodramatically got to his feet, his movements uncertain but guiltily quick. The other young copper's face wore surprise and guilt in vivid colours as Cobb grabbed his wrist and shook from his hand a small polythene bag of powder. It lay on the crisp, pink tablecloth, the size and bulk of a condom packet. Cobb pushed Peel back into his chair.

'You're nicked, son!' he bellowed for the benefit of the clientele and the charade, distracting the customers from their food towards the impromptu cabaret.

'What d'you fucking mean, nicked?' Peel protested.

'These two – take 'em away,' Cobb ordered Tate and the two other officers, all of whom now produced warrant cards, handcuffs. 'Don't even think about it, son. Let's do it the easy way, eh? You too,' he added, clamping his hand on the shoulder of the young copper who had sat in the back of the Rover. 'You can tell us your stories down at the—'

'What is the matter here, Officer?' Syeeda asked, puzzled but somehow affronted. Cobb saw the dark, sleepless stains beneath her eyes, the tired sense of a blank perspective in her gaze.

'Drugs, miss,' Cobb replied earnestly. 'I'm afraid your restaurant is being used for the sale of Class A illegal substances . . .' He held up the small packet and its white powder. 'We've been watching *him*' – he indicated a subdued, sullen Peel – 'and this place for weeks. Just waiting to catch him in the act.'

'Rubbish!' Syeeda snapped, her privately educated English accent irritating Cobb. The young woman's huge, dark eyes challenged him, then inspected Peel. 'I've never seen him in the Jaipur before tonight. How long did you say you'd been watching the restaurant?'

'Weeks. Is your father in, miss? I believe he's the owner? We'd like a word with him – in private. *Here*, for the moment. Later, who knows—?'

The quiet hubbub of gossip, speculation, excitement seemed to unnerve the young woman. The veneer of Englishness was stripped in a moment and, to Cobb, she became just another immigrant. She seemed smaller, more uncertain, beginning to be afraid. Much better—

CHAPTER FOUR

Charitable and Uncharitable

From his surveillance point on the balcony, Hyde watched the self-conscious glitter beneath the chandeliers of the Grosvenor House ballroom. Aubrey was a shrunken, disconcerting figure with a walking stick, on which he leaned more heavily than in the past, hemmed in by bright gowns and dinner jackets. Groups surged or darted, swaying like penguins or bright seaweed in the currents of money, art, gossip, power; politics, commerce and the arts mingled like streams of dye entering a river. Beside the old man, supporting his light weight, was the taller figure of Marian Pyott, her free arm waving in emphasis or greeting, blonde hair to her shoulders, silver-gowned. Her posture suggested ease, even intimacy with the tall American on her other side. Hyde had recognised Alder immediately.

The Minister for Culture, a self-revealed philistine,

appeared to be being jostled by a coterie of administra-
tors and patrons of the Royal Opera House, while the
Foreign Secretary, bearded and impish, hovered as if he
suspected that the culture minister might at any moment
require the services of a translator. He nodded ironically
to Marian as she passed him, and seemed to recognise
Aubrey in the slight way that someone half recognises a
distant cousin in a sepia photograph. Marian's smile
dazzled in return. Alder appeared ingratiating.

Marian Pyott knew Ros quite well. Hyde had met her a
handful of times. Now he re-encountered his reluctant
admiration. She was one of the very few politicians, and
almost the only Tory, for whom he could feel any
admiration, however grudging. Besides which, he liked
her father, Aubrey's oldest friend. Old ... That was
Aubrey. The old man couldn't help it, but he disappointed,
ushered as he was now between his two tall, handsome
escorts with the speed and care they might have offered
an invalid. Hyde lounged against his pillar, no longer
uncomfortable amid worn and spoken money, sophistica-
tion. His time in Sydney with Ros had cured him of that, if
of nothing else in his past. Which was why, he supposed,
Aubrey's snail-like progress was so deeply irritating.
Outside the hotel, his flat was being bugged, he was under
surveillance, events were accelerating.

Heavily padded men and slim women squeezed past
him at the top of the staircase as if they sensed he was an
intruder. Scraps of their conversation whirled like sparks
from their display of conscience, cultivation and self-
satisfaction. Aubrey's head and then the rest of him
appeared, laboriously climbing the last of the stairs.
Despite his misgivings, Hyde grinned and moved at once
towards him.

'Patrick!' the old blue eyes were still sharp. It was

painfully obvious that he was surprised and relieved by Hyde's white dinner jacket and red bow tie. Then his appraisal was over and he shook Hyde's hand warmly, almost clingingly. 'You're looking well,' he murmured, then: 'Marian you already know—' Hyde nodded a small, amused greeting. Marian's mouth smiled while her eyes studied him. 'This is Congressman Robert Alder—'

The tall American, head turned slightly to display his best profile, nodded and smiled without interest. Marian shook Hyde's extended hand.

'How is Ros?' she asked. 'I owe her a letter—'

'Fine.' He sensed the habitual anaesthesia she employed whenever she had been in his company in the past. It was as if she were shutting out the shadowy stereotype that always stood at his shoulder – his role as one of Aubrey's field agents, someone who killed other people. He appreciated the effort she always made. 'Business is booming . . .' He added to Aubrey: 'There's a room we can use along the corridor.' Then, with evident mischief: 'What time do they serve tucker?'

'We've time,' Aubrey replied. 'I – Marian has an interest in matters Burmese. Do you mind if she hears your story?' It was evident that the pressure for her inclusion came from the woman herself, not from Aubrey.

'OK.'

At the door of the small conference suite, Hyde turned after ushering Marian and Aubrey into its subdued lighting, and shook his head at Alder.

'Hey, I'm with the lady.'

'Not at the moment you're not, sport.'

'What is this? Marian—?'

She seemed to expect Alder's inclusion, an attitude that obscurely denigrated the significance of the meeting.

'A private function. Sorry.' Alder made as if to push

Hyde aside, then relaxed as Hyde added: 'We won't be ten minutes – go and talk opera to somebody.'

As he turned back into the room and closed the doors, he witnessed a vivid dislike on Marian's face, her scarlet lipstick like an accusing wound. He shrugged and offered:

'I don't know him.'

'He knows a great deal about Burma!' she snapped back.

'I still don't know him.' He leant back against the closed doors to prevent intrusion.

Marian lit a cigarette and Aubrey lowered himself on to a reproduction dining chair. The long table in the middle of the room was covered with a blue baize cloth and was neat with ashtrays and carafes of water. An easel for flipcharts stood at one end of the room, a coffee machine rested on a side table, next to a tray of bottles.

'OK,' Hyde announced. 'I need to know who Jessop's employer is. *Exactly* who.'

'Firstly, Patrick – this Scudamore business. You are certain that you were the target?' Hyde nodded. 'Very well,' Aubrey sighed, 'then – Jessop. I'm afraid I must agree with your analysis. Someone important, with much at stake, is employing him.' His gnarled knuckles rested on the head of his walking stick.

Marian perched herself on the edge of the table, near Aubrey's chair. Her whole posture suggested no more than the briefest interruption of her evening and her priorities.

'It's Straits Royal Group – and drugs. Has to be. They don't want me stumbling around in the dark. I might bump into something I shouldn't.' He shrugged. 'I want it stopped. To do that, I have to go after Jessop. I need something to trade, promise silence *about* something.'

'Yes, of course.' There was a new animation about

Aubrey's expression and posture. Recalled to life? Hyde wondered. His own satisfaction was evident to him, even in the neutral, innocent surroundings. 'It was supposed to be complete, rounded off, by those arrests in Sydney? Is that your theory?' Hyde nodded. 'But your reputation goes before you. They would not expect you to be satisfied. Penang would have seemed a sufficiently out-of-the-way venue for your demise. This needs careful—'

He was interrupted by a faint trilling noise from Marian's handbag, beside him on the table. Irritation clouded his features. Marian snatched the purse from the table and opened it.

'Sorry – forgot to switch off the mobile,' she stammered, her cheeks flushed. 'Marian Pyott,' she announced into the phone. Her tone was one of irritation, but he heard in the voice at the other end an evident, distraught panic. Then Marian's expression became one of growing disbelief as she moved away from the table towards the night-dark window. Hyde felt the tension of the communicated excitement. Then Marian exclaimed:

'Of course your father's arrest is a mistake, Syeeda! Yes, of course I will . . . No, do *nothing* for the moment. Just try to assist these people . . . that's all I can suggest for tonight. No, I *will* look into it in the morning—!'

She closed the mouthpiece of the phone and turned angrily to them, her cheeks still flushed and her shoulders hunched belligerently. She was angry not at the caller, but at what she had heard.

'What is it?' he asked.

'Oh – just a constituent. You could call her a friend. She's having a bad time at the moment. Her father's about to be charged with using his restaurant as a venue for the sale of Class A prohibited substances! Special Branch are interested in him, for heaven's sake! Absolute nonsense . . .

and on top of the death of her fiancé, the Kumar boy. The one I asked you, Kenneth, to—'

'Kumar?' Hyde asked, his voice cold and intrusive. His tone affronted Marian and she glowered at him. 'Sorry,' he murmured. 'Coincidence—'

'Is your restaurateur a drug dealer, like the dead young man?' Aubrey's tone was lofty. 'I take it we are talking of Mr Lal?'

Marian nodded, puffing furiously at her cigarette, her expression one of emphatic outrage.

'It's absolute rubbish!'

'But the boy was certainly a dealer, this Medhev Kumar—'

'*Who*?' Hyde snapped. 'Did you say *Medhev* Kumar? Was he *English*-Indian?' he asked Marian.

'No. As a matter of fact, he was from Burma ... Why?'

'How did he die?' Hyde's voice was remote, without emotion.

'An overdose of heroin. He was an addict and the police are certain he was also dealing ...' Her voice tailed off in obedience to the furious, continued shaking of Hyde's head.

'Medhev Kumar didn't do drugs.'

'How can *you* be sure of that?'

'How long has he been in England – a few months? Less than six? Do you know how long?'

'Less than six. The Lal family are—'

'—distant relations,' Hyde concluded. 'They're from Burma, too. I *know* him.' He turned to Aubrey. 'He was my inside man, working in one of the hotel casinos in Singapore. He even spent a bit of time in Macau. I couldn't do it, I wasn't the right colour ...' He wiped a forefinger across the line of cold perspiration below his hairline. 'I found Medhev working on a radical freesheet in

Singapore, full of righteous indignation and only just escaped from Myanmar. The Burmese generals didn't like his opinions. He did good work for me – good work . . .' The explanation wound down like the voice of a speaking toy that had come to the end of its vocabulary. 'When did he die?'

'A few days ago,' Marian answered in an absorbed whisper. 'He *wasn't* an addict?'

'He grew up on the edge of the Golden Triangle, in Shan state. He loathed the drug economy as much as he hated the regime in Rangoon – and as much as he adored the Lady. She was his Hindu goddess. He skipped Burma when the army arrested hundreds of Aung San Suu Kyi's supporters to try and stop her last big political rally. Didn't fancy the idea of being tortured. They were looking for him . . .' As if unused to such admissions, he added: 'I'm sorry he's dead. But it wouldn't have been an overdose.'

'Then what was it?' Marian demanded breathily.

'Murder.'

'God—' she breathed. Her arms and hands rose to her face, as if she were trying to protect herself, even ward off some attack. Hyde's world was palpable in the room.

'The generals in Rangoon?' Aubrey asked into the hot silence.

'He wasn't *that* irritating to the junta – a biting insect, not a disease. He wasn't even close to the Lady. They've tried to kill me, and Medhev's been murdered. What was he doing in England? Was he investigating drugs?'

Marian shrugged. 'I can't see how, but it could be the same story . . .'

'But why *here*? Marian – you've no idea what he was doing?'

'Sorry, Kenneth. I really – don't know a lot about him.'

'You said Special Branch arrested this Lal?' Marian

nodded. 'Where were the local drugs squad? Why the Branch? Was the girl mistaken?'

'She says they showed her Special Branch warrant cards.'

Clearing his throat, Aubrey murmured: 'I very much doubt if they were genuine, Marian. I can check, but I doubt it—'

'The Branch doesn't descend to drugs sales in Indian restaurants. Or Chinese takeaways. They'd just tip off the local Plods if the information happened to come their way.'

'But—?'

'Who are they if they're not Branch? I think we'd better find out – don't you, sir?'

Aubrey looked up at him with a narrowed, sharpened expression that was almost suspicious. Hyde grinned. He *knew* it was Jessop and the people behind Jessop. Straits Royal Group—

'You said that Straits Royal Group were involved?' Marian asked, surprising him as much as if she were telepathic.

'Yes . . .'

'They're a wholly owned subsidiary of Winterborne Holdings,' she replied, and when Hyde appeared bemused, she added: 'David.' It seemed to her to explain everything.

'David's in prison, Marian!' Aubrey snapped, but it was the tone of a parent seeing a child's hand nearing a fire. Hyde saw a gleam of determination in Marian's eyes. 'There can be *no* connection with David.'

Hyde resented something in her manner, as if she had committed some swift and violent appropriation. There was a dangerous, greedy excitement about her that somehow matched his own.

'When can I talk to this girl – Syeeda?' he asked abruptly, wrenching back the volition of the conversation.

'I – er ... tomorrow? I'm back in the constituency tomorrow. I could—'

'Arrange it. Please. I want to know everything she knows.'

Aubrey seemed alarmed, like a nanny whose charges have run off, courting danger.

'Tomorrow, then. Your place in the constituency ...' Hyde turned to Aubrey. 'I need to know where Jessop hangs out, how big the army is, that kind of thing. I'll do that tomorrow. Impersonating Special Branch is—'

'—an old ploy,' Aubrey added with a weariness that was half-pretence, half-excitement. Turning to Marian he explained, as if to someone unaware of the rules of a secret, archaic game: 'People like Patrick, in SIS, used a Special Branch cover whenever they were required to operate within the United Kingdom.' He smiled with wintry affection, but at something in his mind's eye. 'Such operations were, of course, entirely illegal.'

Marian felt distanced by her distaste. Hyde had brought back Aubrey's past to him, and somehow brought him alive in a way that was rare in his old age.

'It could well be Jessop,' Aubrey continued. 'Yes, find him. Since the execrable Fraser's demise, he will have changed the headed notepaper and his address, but it shouldn't be too difficult. Getting any closer than that will be.'

'If they killed Kumar?'

'Then that could well be the key—'

Marian rubbed her naked arms as if cold. The cigarette smoke ascended like puffing signals of distress as her hand moved. 'I'll arrange for Syeeda to be at my flat tomorrow, late evening. Will that suit?'

'Fine.'

'Then have we finished? Shall we return to the supper, Kenneth?'

She wasn't afraid, Hyde realised. He watched her brush her hair aside from her face and noticed a scar behind her ear of which her fingers appeared to be conscious. *She's after Winterborne ...* He vaguely remembered something that Ros had told him, reading a letter from Marian Pyott. A car accident, the Winterborne fraud, a connection between the two things...?

She still wanted some kind of justice against David Winterborne ... *He* should have remembered the man was a crook.

Even so, that composed only the surface of the thing. This had become an environment in which people were easily disposed of, as if they came and existed in bin-liners. People as mere cartons for junk food. Kumar had been done away with as easily as that...

... but *carefully*, too. The disguise of his murder demonstrated the level at which it had been ordered, and the expertise of the murderers.

Why had Kumar left Singapore? He had come to England, so why had he left the note for Hyde that said his mother was ill? Kumar would not have run away, been scared off. If that had been the case, he would still be alive. But he had ended up working in a Midlands curry shop, his death made to appear like an overdose of heroin. Kumar had been *special* enough to merit a disguised murder; something which would stop any further investigation.

The why of his murder might be the way in – and his one way to safety. Kumar had stepped on a landmine in the Midlands ...and he could easily do the same, because it was even bigger than he had thought, more widespread...

He watched Marian gather Aubrey up and guide him towards the doors. There was an instant in which he thought of demanding her discretion ... except that his own need to know more pressed his lips together.

He gestured Marian and the old man through the doors after opening them wide on the hot, thronging noises of the charity supper. He was out of place here, as Jessop would have been. David Winterborne, unimprisoned, would have been near the top of the guest list.

'I mean, Marian – just what did that guy *want*? Hyde or whoever he was ... Something happened in there. You've gotten more prickles than a porcupine since you went into the huddle with him and Sir Kenneth. What were you talking about to produce that much effect?'

She switched on the lights in the lounge as he followed her into the room. He went directly to the drinks tray on the breakfast sideboard and poured himself a large measure of the bourbon she had especially bought. He swallowed at it angrily, as if determined to intoxicate himself. His cheeks were flushed. Then he challenged:

'Your mood had just – changed, somehow, when you came out of that room ...' He was shaking his head in what might have been disappointment as much as mystification. 'Like you'd heard some really bad news – about me or yourself. Something personal—?'

'I – oh, Robbie, I'm sorry about this evening. I don't want to bother you with it ...' Her hands were making little fending-off gestures, as if she were worried by wasps. He moved closer but she retreated slightly, angering him further.

'What the hell is going on, Marian? Don't I have the *right* to know, if it affects you like this? Without crowding your space or anything like that?' She reached a hand to the lapel of his dinner jacket, then slid into the embrace he offered. 'What is it?' he murmured into her hair.

'That – that constituent, on the answerphone ... Her dead fiancé – Hyde thinks he was murdered. He's certain of it.' She lifted her face to his, eyes dazzled by tears. 'It's awful. Hyde *knew* him, knew he wasn't a drug addict or a dealer. He was murdered ... How do I tell Syeeda *that*?'

He lowered her on to the settee and poured her a cognac. Handing it to her, he soothed:

'Drink this.' Then he added: 'How can this guy be so certain?' He clicked his fingers. 'He was one of Aubrey's people, right? An agent?' Marian nodded, chuckling on tears and the cognac, then clearing her throat.

'Yes. Kenneth's favourite – his best, probably.'

'Why was he with the old man?' Alder asked sharply, then added disarmingly: 'I mean, Sir Kenneth's long retired, right? Is this guy Hyde still working for him?'

'No. It was something originating in Australia – drugs. Hyde believes he's in danger. He wanted to talk to Kenneth. Father to son, as it were.'

'Drugs?' Alder asked after a moment. 'Hell, the whole of the industrialised world is awash with drugs. Does this guy think his discoveries are something new? Are the Australian cops employing him, or is it their intelligence outfit?'

'Cops, I think. The case is closed anyway. Hyde's theory sounded pretty fantastic. He thinks that the Straits Royal Group is involved—'

'*David*? The guy's in prison, Marian, for *fraud*, not murder, not drug dealing—' He seemed surprised by the shiver that ran through her frame. 'What is it?'

'Nothing. Someone walked over my grave, I expect.' She smiled, wiping away the half-formed tears.

'You have to start forgetting this vendetta you have

against David,' Alder murmured, sitting beside her after refilling his glass. 'I know you went head to head over the fraud. You told me, other people have told me ... But, drugs? How? *Why*? You've noticed David's companies short of money recently?' He grinned. 'Look, I'm not defending the guy, just because I know him and his father. But you shouldn't see him behind someone's crazy account of international gangsterism! Deal?'

She nodded vigorously, sniffing.

'Deal. No, it wasn't really that that struck home; it was the idea that Medhev Kumar had been murdered – and having to tell Syeeda.'

'Why tell her anything? You can't prove he was murdered, nor can this guy Hyde, whoever he is. Just keep it to yourself. Uh?' He stared at her, his desire evident. Her own was at once awoken.

'Just let me check my messages,' she murmured, slipping away from his embrace. 'I won't be a minute, I promise.' She went into the study, where she'd now put the answerphone. Alder followed, hovering at the door, watching her hair fall across her cheek in the soft light from the desk lamp. She was aware, flattered and aroused by his hot inspection of her.

There was just one call, from Jakarta. Gerry Mountford. A former graduate student of hers at Oxford, reading for his doctorate in international politics and modern history. At thirty-two, he was still indulging a passion for distant and preferably unstable parts of the world. He funded his desires by means of a succession of posts on small-circulation, expensive newsletters for an audience of politicians, businessmen, diplomats. At that moment, he was working for one to which she subscribed, the *South-East Asia Newsbrief*. Two hundred pounds per annum for a monthly eight-page pamphlet. She smiled at the thought, and at the familiar, cocky cheeriness of Gerry Mountford's voice.

'... something in the post for you, my darling tutor. Concerning your childhood friend currently enjoying Her Majesty's hospitality for a while...' She glanced at Alder guiltily, as if he had surprised her in an embrace with Mountford. 'Can't put it in the *Newsbrief* at the moment, it's not hard enough. Seems your old playmate's companies are simply *cleaning up* in Burma, Laos, Cambodia and all points east. They must be doing some *big* favours for someone. Anyway, you'll see my deathless prose in a couple of days – I'm off up to Phnom Penh post-haste for more info – love and kisses. Bye.'

She realised that Alder was standing next to her, staring at the answerphone as its tape rewound. When he spoke, it was with a contemptuous growl.

'Just like your Bob Dylan records, Marian – you're still playing student politics!' His tone was acid, hurtful.

'What is it?' she challenged.

'You *believe* stuff like that?' He gestured at the answerphone. 'You really believe it? You and that guy Hyde, you're as gullible as each other.'

Angered, she snapped back: 'And you want to make things comfortable, don't you, Robbie? Democrats in uniform who don't know they're really liberal-minded – is that how you see the generals in Rangoon and the government in Indonesia? Washington is torn between principle and profit and you want to tip the scales in favour of profit?'

'Hey, come on—' he protested.

'Sorry, sorry...'

He held out his arms. 'Forgive me?' His expression was winningly apologetic. She burst into exasperated laughter, and said:

'Just about... Come on, let's finish our drinks.'

She put the answerphone message aside. She'd carried her Dylan albums through university, Parliament, love affairs. Alder had mocked them before. They belonged to every period of her life – even if, she admitted ruefully, she had purchased the earliest recordings retrospectively. She had been no more than six or seven when Dylan had first announced that the times were a-changing. By the time she had been captured, the outlaw was middle-aged and seeking his shelter from the storm and trying to revive his career. Speaking to an America that had long lost Kennedy and was still facing the idiot wind of Vietnam – and no longer wanted to change the world but simply to acquire it for hard cash.

'I'm sorry,' he whispered, catching her from behind and folding her in his arms. She pressed her cheek against his shoulder. 'Why don't you get yourself on this junket to Burma, huh? They've invited me along and I was going to suggest it anyway. See for yourself, Marian – please? Don't take my word or anyone else's.'

'You want to make a *holiday* out of—?' she began, twisting in his arms so that she could face him. Then, immediately, she pressed her lips shut, cutting off the accusation. It was so bloody stupid to argue!

She'd done it before. During their two previous affairs. Perhaps too much. Had she driven him away? *You can keep him this time if you learn to keep quiet*, she told herself. She did not want to be alone again ... The car accident had done that. It had changed her, that brush with her own mortality. She had wanted to rekindle the affair with Alder. She was afraid of loneliness; she needed something more than her work, her career.

She kissed him quickly, fiercely, opening her lips to receive his eager tongue, feeling her own immediate arousal. *Don't lose him—*

***

Hyde took the car keys from the garage mechanic, and the young man got out of the Ford into the fine morning drizzle and crossed the car park towards the main portico of Waterloo station. The shoulders of his overalls were speckled with the misty rain. Hyde flicked the wind-screen wipers, and the black Mercedes that he had trailed around central London for the last two hours emerged from the swept-aside water. One of the surveillance team was already inside the station, looking for him, and another had just emerged from the Merc and wandered towards the Vauxhall they had seen him hire. He moved slowly, turning up the collar of his raincoat against the rain's insinuation. They were beginning to worry that they had lost him.

It hadn't been really difficult. Taken long enough, though, he told his sense of smug satisfaction. Two hours or more. The garage from which he had habitually hired cars – in a previous life, it almost seemed – had welcomed him back with conspiratorial interest. He'd booked the Vauxhall, while he had been watched from across the street, and arranged for the Ford to be delivered to Waterloo. Simple stuff . . . so long as they led him back to wherever they came from and whoever was in charge.

The man in the raincoat inspected the Vauxhall, then gave a thumbs-down gesture towards the black Merc. They *loved* black limos, it made tail-men feel like business executives. He had recognised neither of the men who had got out of the car. They were Caucasian, though, not Chinese or Asian.

The Merc's driver got out and waved the raincoated man towards the station concourse, almost shooing him into urgency. An angry, pinched young face, its expression running into frustration, suspicion. The man on foot hurried into the station. Eventually, they'd probably leave both men at Waterloo and be called back for a bollocking, lunch, or a rethink. Just so long as they didn't think it clever to return to Philbeach Gardens and remount their stakeout . . . Patience, patience.

The knowledge that Ros would have reached Singapore by now niggled at him. He had to call her, even though he knew that she would remain unabashed at his concern. He ought to pull her out, to be absolutely safe, but she wouldn't agree – *I'm here on business, Hyde* – just laugh and claim she was as safe as houses and he was being paranoid. Even though it needed only one pair of eyes to recognise her and connect her with him.

He couldn't control that part of it. *Patience . . .*

. . . is a virtue. It was after twelve before they gave up the search of Waterloo. It had involved all four of them, and angered them all. They'd lost him. Then the driver positioned the man in the raincoat and the fourth man beneath the station portico, watching the Vauxhall, before returning to the Merc. The wiper flicked its rear window clear for a moment. Hyde wondered if the driver was on the car phone. Then the Merc pulled away in the direction of Waterloo Bridge. He started the Ford's engine and slid unsuspiciously out of the car park. The two men were oblivious. He slipped into the lunchtime traffic on Waterloo Road half a dozen vehicles behind the black limousine. Somerset House and the Savoy ahead, across the river. He sensed a small, persistent nerve become calm. He had wondered whether they might not head for Vauxhall Cross . . . that they might be *official* after some fashion or other. They weren't

He turned the Ford on to the Victoria Embankment. Now across the river, the stained concrete of the South Bank complex, ugly and suited to a lowering sky and rain.

The Mercedes was in no hurry ... Blackfriars Bridge, Southwark Bridge, London Bridge ... Hyde settled into the city as if exploring a loved, long-lost countenance. St Magnus Martyr, the Custom House, Lower Thames Street. He felt a slight qualm of guilty betrayal towards Ros as London worked mistresslike on him, promising excitement, fulfilment.

The black limousine reached Tower Hill. Tower Bridge ...? No, St Katherine's Way, towards the redeveloped St Katherine's Dock area. A bistro lunch? Docklands offices? Where else for upwardly mobile ex-agents like Jessop? The Mercedes drew into the kerb and came to a halt beside a converted warehouse, opposite a hotel.

Tinted glass glowered in Georgian window frames. Boutiques and chintzed pubs peered from beneath the heavy pillars of colonnades. Tower Bridge had been rendered a Disney component of the refurbished scene; historical ships were set-dressing in a marooned marina. The two men got out of the Merc. He saw the hazard lights flicker twice as the alarm was set. On the river, yachts and long-stay barges were moored. Hyde watched the two men pass beneath a colonnade and enter one of the refurbished warehouses, then got out of the Ford, locked it and casually crossed the street towards the Thomas Telford façade.

He passed a shop whose doorway and pavement were heaped with terracotta pots and reproduction garden ornaments, another that was vivid and veldtlike with dried flower arrangements; a pub's tables and chairs beside the water, parked BMWs and Porsches. He paused at brass plates beside a dark-green, heavy door. The ground floor of the warehouse defied him with black glass. It was all offices ... a music agency, interior designer, art gallery, film production company, ad agency ...

International Security Consultants Ltd. – a Winterborne Company. Well, well, Marian Pyott could be right after all. Was this Jessop's place of work?

Hands in his pockets, he meandered back to the Ford, climbed into the driving seat and slid to comfort in it. The shoulders of his jacket were damp, but the rainclouds seemed to be retiring southwards. The river was gun-metal in colour now, not grey-black. He could see the door of the security company offices from where he was parked. Anticipated seeing Jessop come through or use his keycode to get in. Twelve forty. International Security Consultants Ltd. – a Winterborne Company. The notion of the size of the thing no longer troubled him. This was pure gold. Bull's-eye.

'No, Marian, he's already been released. I've just checked with the local station inspector. False alarm, apologies offered and so forth ...' The Chief Constable's tone was blithely reassuring. 'As to your other question, regarding the bona fides of the Special Branch officers who conducted the interview with Mr Lal – I'm sure you're on the wrong track there!'

Marian raised her eyes to the ceiling of her office in the Commons. Alistair evidently considered the incident closed. An initial instant of lost nerve when she had announced her suspicions – *Hyde's* suspicions, and those of Kenneth – regarding the men who had arrested Rabindur Lal had been replaced by a blanket of re-assurance and inactivity. The Chief Constable's portrait, alongside those of a plethora of local notables, including herself, hung on the walls of the Jaipur. Lal would be mollified, the incident smoothed over.

'Thank you, Alistair – for looking into it. I'll be in touch. Bye.'

She put down the receiver and lit a cigarette. For the moment it was wise to leave matters unresolved. Pending further information. She dialled Syeeda's number and waited. When the girl answered, Marian said carefully: 'I'm glad to hear that your father has been released without charge, Syeeda. Is he all right?'

There was, in the silence that followed, an intrusive sense of reserve, even reluctance. Then Syeeda murmured: 'He's very angry ... Look, Marian—' she blurted, as if prodded by someone at her shoulder. 'My father was very frightened. He – he doesn't want the subject brought up again. He thinks I should have no more to do with Medhev's death ...' It was probably imagination, but it was almost as if her Indian accent had become stronger as she submitted to her father's injunction. Damn—

'Syeeda – about that ... the death, I mean. There's someone, someone I'd like you to talk to. He wants to know—'

'Father says I mustn't—!'

'Just one conversation, Syeeda. This person *knew* Medhev, in Singapore. He wants you to talk to him about Medhev ...' It was the cheapest kind of emotional blackmail, she realised. But Syeeda was slipping away from her into filial obedience. Lal had been frightened off, had promised whoever those bogus Special Branch men were that there would be no more fuss about Kumar's death. '*Please*, Syeeda? This evening, at my flat? He was Medhev's friend.'

Gulping noises, the first small wavelets of returning grief. Marian felt wretchedly guilty.

'Yes,' Syeeda breathed. 'I will see him.'

'About nine, then. It won't take long, I promise. Thanks, Syeeda—'

The girl had already put down her receiver, as if

realising that she had engaged in a small betrayal. Marian, relieved, blew smoke at the ceiling. For the moment, and thankfully in the circumstances, she was alone in the office. Rose was at lunch – or making the beast with two backs with the family-values espouser – and her fellow MP was industriously lobbying on behalf of a haulage contractor in his constituency who wanted to acquire the grounds of a listed building in order to expand his truck park. Good luck there. The listed building was little more than a shell, but the environment and heritage mafia were powerful opponents. She smiled, then plucked her lower lip. Almost time for lunch with Robbie. Lobbying—?

She crossed to the overstuffed, untidy bookcase and drew out the Register of Members' Interests. Returning to her desk, she began to thumb its pages, running her finger down the alphabetical lists of MPs. *Grainger, Peter John*. Beneath his name were all the directorships and con- sultancies he held, as well as details of his other extra- parliamentary remunerations. *Straits Royal Group (UK) Plc*, she read, sighing with satisfaction. Grainger was a non-executive director. Lobbying had been the clue. She had vaguely remembered Grainger's parliamentary lobbying and local arm-twisting on behalf of a foreign hotel chain ... and it *was* Straits Royal. Hyde would be as interested as she was.

Grainger was a barrister by training and profession. Robbie Alder had been attached to the same chambers – this memory was less vague – in some student capacity during the first of their previous affairs. He had thought to remain in England with her – and then had been seduced back to the State Department in Washington. Grainger, she reminded herself, was also a radio personality dis- pensing legal advice on two or three different consumer programmes. His constituency bordered her own, though it contained a greater number of leafy suburbs as well as a slice of the city centre. Straits Royal, she recalled, had built the first of a new chain of wooded, weekend-break resorts on the leafiest edge of his constituency.

Peter Grainger knew a lot about Straits Royal *and* about Burma. She should – *really* should – have a chat with Peter about both subjects.

Smiling with regained composure, all memory of the first and unfruitful affair with Alder dismissed, she picked up the telephone.

'Kenneth, my dear – how sweet of you to invite me to lunch!' Alex Davenhill pecked lightly at each of Aubrey's cheeks in turn, ignoring his proffered hand. The library of the Club, where they were both members, had long become accustomed to Davenhill's homosexual bravado. His tall, elegant figure, curled, greying hair and square, handsome features saved the exaggeration from straying into campness; as Alex well understood.

They sat down opposite one another in creaking leather armchairs. At once, there was a steward at Aubrey's elbow. Glancing at the whisky and soda before Davenhill, Aubrey murmured:

'Dry sherry, Albert.'

'Very good, Sir Kenneth. I'll leave these—' and he placed menus and the wine list on the table.

Davenhill's smile was one of genuine, long affection. At fifty-four, he was the third most senior civil servant in the Foreign & Commonwealth Office. Despite his Eton and Oxford background, it was the conventional wisdom of Whitehall that he had done extremely well to become a Deputy Under-Secretary, having for years been tainted, as the expression was, by his association with the Secret Intelligence Service. His friendship with Aubrey, and his continuing loyalty to and admiration of the old man, was disliked by many of his colleagues and political masters. His homosexuality had always erred on the comfortable side of the discreetly overt.

Aubrey's sherry arrived and Davenhill raised his tumbler.

'Cheers, old dear. Your continued good health.' Aubrey sipped like a maiden aunt at his sherry and Davenhill startled him by asking: 'This is *not* a reunion between a former Director of SIS and his Foreign Office Special Adviser, I take it, my darling?'

'No, Alex, it isn't. Are you in something of a rush, having no time for five minutes of the niceties?'

Davenhill's laugh startled a junior minister and his African guests. When the Minister of State recognised Davenhill, he turned quickly away from the designed embarrassment of Alex's exaggerated wave.

'Poor young man. I don't think he's quite sure about his proclivities. I seem to frighten him.'

'Alex, you're incorrigible,' Aubrey chuckled.

'And about to be interrogated?'

Aubrey leaned forward.

'I know Burma and South-East Asia are not your especial brief, Alex—'

'No, that dreadful man Salter concerns himself with such distant parts.' Davenhill sighed. 'Unfortunately, I have to constantly mingle with cultures I admire and envy and people I detest. Europe, in short. But I mustn't waste your time polishing my *bon mots* on you, my dear. What do you want to know?'

'Burma, particularly. The general background.'

'*Not* HMG's current attitude to?'

'Is there one?'

'Of the what-can-we-get-away-with kind, yes . . . Unless

you prefer Janus's other face, how much can we ignore? The horns of a very phantom dilemma, Kenneth. Go on.'

'The DTI seem to be taking a less vague view. Aren't your colleagues in agreement with them?'

'Absolutely – but don't quote me, as they say. Toe in the water, test the temperature of the baby's milk. Ever since the Asian economies hit the buffers, the West has been rushing there, to invest, buy out, own while things were still bad – and *cheap*.' He shook his head mockingly. 'Burma is even cheaper to buy into – or buy up. Hence everybody is simply just dying to love Burma, Kenneth – the country's like a very ugly duckling who's turning into a beautiful, swanlike young man—' Davenhill smiled with theatrical lasciviousness. 'Since Deng's death, the Americans are very keen on a Presidential initiative to maintain close relations with China – very cosy – and China is acting in part as guarantor and character referee for Burma. There's not to be talk of human rights in relation to China – that's *very* official policy – and that moratorium extends to China's friends and client states such as Burma. Politically, all the murders, beatings and imprisonments are rather exaggerated or have miraculously ceased.'

He smiled, almost sadly, at Aubrey as the old man shook his head. 'There's a notion doing the rounds, rather like a 'flu bug, that democracy means something quite different for Asian countries. We should admire them for their economic successes and their sense of *order*.' He sipped at his whisky and added: 'Order and prosperity are the watchwords, and everyone's sure it will all work out beautifully!' He laughed ringingly and silently toasted Aubrey. 'Anyway, that's how the FO and the DTI are able to appear so publicly keen on doing business with Burma and the ruling State Peace and Development Council – the same generals as before . . . Marian still refers to them as the SLORC because it makes them seem more Orwellian: *Law and Order Restoration Council*. She's behind the times in that, as with everything else!' Then, with amusement rather than malice, he added: 'By the way, how is Myanmar Marian these days? Hanoi Jane without the benefit of a flying visit, mm? She's gone a little quiet – for her – on the subject of Burma, hasn't she? Dear old Giles told her off, has he?'

'No. But we will trade – sooner rather than later? Despite the junta's record on human rights – and Marian?'

'If the Yanks do, we will. Can't afford not to.'

'Will they?'

'If young Alder – isn't he pretty? – can persuade Congress and the President. Rumour has it that they want only a go-ahead to change policy. Someone to take the fall if it goes wrong – Alder would do – and they'll be in like a shot. I say, didn't I hear that Marian and Alder were – I believe the current argot is – an item? I'd like to hear *their* pillow talk when the subject of Burma comes up!' He roared with laughter once more, waking a dozing novelist of patrician appearance, great age, and small *oeuvre*. The old man seemed startled into an unfamiliar world.

'So, Alex . . . trade is uppermost?'

'Despite the magical Lady, Aung Sang Suu Kyi. Do you know, Kenneth, I swoon over her as some of my gender swoon over Shirley Bassey or an operatic diva . . . But we have all persuaded ourselves that, beautiful and brave as she is, she is wrong about trade and tourism. So – bugger her, as they say.' He shrugged. There was an angry gleam in his brown eyes for a moment, and a quick, dismissive gesture as his hand wiped at his hair. Then he was at once his persona again. 'Continue, sweet torturer,' he murmured.

'Very well, to the point – David Winterborne and his cousin and Burma?' Aubrey asked lightly.

Davenhill pretended shock.

'Surely David is in the Bridewell and can be involved in nothing so vulgar as trade?'

'Perhaps.'

'May I read my menu, Kenneth?'

'Of course.'

'In which case—' He picked up the leather folder from the table. 'Ah. Let me see . . .' He flicked half-glasses from his pocket and donned them. 'Ralph Lau is, they say, the more *astute* businessman of the two cousins.' He did not look up from his menu. 'His early years – like those of so many of us – seem to be shrouded in mystery. Presumably he was attending *all* the best business schools, which would account for the sudden, even meteoric success of his hotel group. Its expansion has been breathtaking . . . I think the smoked salmon to start, and I'd prefer you to order a good Alsace wine with that, my dear . . . Cynics – among whom there are very few in the FCO – have been heard to wonder what Mr Lau is doing in return for the favourable treatment he has been receiving in the Republic of Myanmar, in Laos, Cambodia . . . And the lamb to continue. Too late for fresh peas, alas . . . I'll leave the red wine to your choice, Kenneth . . . The appalling Salter, of course, is definitely not a cynic and is often heard to speak admiringly on the subject of Straits Royal Group.'

'You don't share his golden opinion?'

Davenhill looked up, closing his menu.

'A selection of fresh vegetables, I think, Kenneth,' he responded. 'What are you up to – or shouldn't I know?'

'I think not. Is Mr Lau in any way, by any stretch of the imagination, engaged in substance abuse, do you think?'

'I should hope not, Kenneth my dear. Much egg on many

faces, were that to be the case.' He shrugged. 'I prefer not to speculate. I advise you *not* to follow suit. Mm?' He smiled, removing his spectacles. 'It *is* good to see you, my dear!' he announced brightly.

'And you, my dear. You're intimating, then, that I should follow my nose.'

'It has rarely failed you, Kenneth.'

'What scents should it expect?'

'Some of the contracts. There was a dam project, won by AsiaConstruct, a nuclear power station being built in co-operation with the Russians ... A railway line, new roads. Some of the tenders would be unlikely to show a profit . . . and yet, profits there are.'

'And AsiaConstruct is a wholly owned subsidiary of—'

'Exactly. There are all sorts of truffles buried out there that a good snout should unearth. Have you such?'

'Patrick Hyde is in London at the moment.'

'A holiday? Dear Patrick! I should say you may well have just the snout to find the truffles. In company with your own infallible organ, Kenneth.'

'All these projects are in Burma?' Davenhill nodded, toying with his tumbler. Aubrey summoned a steward and ordered another whisky, refusing a second drink for himself. 'Mm. Quid pro quo truffles, then. What could be more profitable than—?'

'Exactly.'

Jessop parked the black Mercedes, got out and locked it. The hazard lights blinked. Hyde watched him cross Eaton Square towards David Winterborne's house. Occupied for the duration, so Aubrey had told him, by Ralph Lau. Jessop rang the doorbell and hovered on the steps, between the cream-painted columns. Hyde had managed to park the Ford less than fifty yards away. Weak, watery sunlight fell on the gardens of the square, on fallen leaves and tired, damp grass. The roses were blown, skeletal.

Jessop leaned to speak into the video entryphone, then pushed at the heavy black door and disappeared into the house. Jessop. Hyde sighed. Jessop and Ralph Lau. Straits Royal Group. Neat as a parcel, but much better wrapped than the ancient aunts who had brought him up had ever managed for his few Christmas presents. He chewed on the remains of the sandwich he had forced from its plastic container.

He glanced at his watch. Four ten. There was little point in hanging around Eaton Square just to watch Jessop come out again, or make certain that Lau was in the house. The connections had already been made. He had to be in the Midlands by nine, so Marian Pyott had informed him on the mobile, to meet Kumar's fiancée. Had Jessop personally executed Kumar, he wondered, just before flying out to Penang to do *him* in . . . ?

Give it another ten minutes, then start fighting the traffic out of London towards the M40 . . . The thought was barely completed when the door of Winterborne's house opened again. Summary dismissal of—

—it wasn't Jessop. Shockingly, unexpectedly, he recognised the tall figure who paused for a moment on the wide pavement, as if expecting photographers. Hyde's hand picked up the camera from the passenger seat and his eye was squinting into it. He focused the telephoto lens. Smile, you're on *Candid Camera* . . . Congressman Alder.

Robert Alder . . . Jessop . . . Ralph Lau. Alder had been visiting Lau—

CHAPTER FIVE

Local Crime Statistics

There were more people in the large, high-ceilinged room than Ralph Lau had anticipated. Above all, there were more Chinese faces than he had expected, all turning to him like incurious dolls as he was ushered in by the High Commissioner. The Chinese appeared misplaced beneath the ceiling's ornate plasterwork and the gilded cornicing of the eighteenth-century drawing room. Their suits were grey, functional, shiny, their shirts white, ties subdued. There were two who seemed distanced from the others; both men were strangers to him.

There were three Burmese, including the High Commissioner who had greeted them on the stairs, hurrying towards him with an eager deference. The others were generals from Rangoon, one the Minister for Hotels and Tourism, the other the minister whose portfolio was Burma's borders. There were three Chinese he knew – two of them, brothers of the old Communist Party of Burma and now the men who controlled the Burmese heroin, its growth as the poppy, the refineries, the transport of the heroin out of Burma. They were the men with whom he habitually dealt, just as he did the Chinese middleman from Mandalay. Advisers and secretaries were ranged behind the chairs, even though he had been asked to come alone.

The Minister for Hotels and Tourism rose from his chair, to come forward to greet him; *after*, Lau realised, he had glanced at the two Chinese who were strangers, as if seeking permission. He shook the soldier's hand.

'Mung Thant,' Lau murmured, controlling the quiver of edgy suspicion he sensed in his hand and arm. 'I – the size of the meeting is something of a surprise . . .' There was an implied criticism, a distancing, in his tone.

'I will introduce you to those you do not know.'

'We are meeting to open discussions on the dam project, are we not?' he asked with a forced lightness and a dismissive gesture of his arm towards the table. 'The oil and gas contracts? I understand why some of—'

'Mr Lau,' Major General Mung Thant murmured in a whisper, his long-fingered brown hand patting the sleeve of Lau's silk jacket. Curiously, Lau did not resent or interrupt the familiarity, but permitted it. 'I will introduce you to the guests who are strangers to you.'

As the State Peace and Development Council minister turned towards the room, Lau sensed the stirrings of the aides, advisers and secretaries, like that of flies that had been disturbed on a sunlit windowsill. They had been dismissed without a gesture; almost as if by thought. The men at the table remained seated, still, as carved as the chairs they occupied, as expressionless as the reflections of their faces in the high polish of the mahogany. Lau's next intuition unnerved him; he sensed the room's power centre. The two Chinese. As the aides and secretaries drifted past him and seemed to take the High Commissioner with them as if they were a tide and he a poor swimmer, Lau was more easily able to recognise the ungestured, silent deference of the two drug smugglers and the Malay middleman.

He saw that the two Chinese were studying him, their cigarettes and the smoke from their exhalations employed as cleverly as ladies' fans to mask their interest in him. One of them must be at least sixty, the other younger, perhaps not even fifty. There was control about them, authority ... and the sense that they commanded obedience from others, even from military men like Mung Thant and the other Burmese minister. The deference was that of soldiers to those more senior than themselves. These two were People's Liberation Army, and high-ranking.

He disguised his own excitement, but they seemed to apprehend and even disdain his enthusiasm.

'My fellow minister you know ... Mr Lim from Mandalay, of course. You and he have done business in the past.' Lim nodded, but his eyes, too, darted at the two Chinese. 'And other acquaintances of yours, Mr Lau, from northern Burma ...' He gestured at the two brothers, the oldest men in the room. Lau bowed almost formally. Mung Thant introduced a Laotian and a Cambodian, both government ministers, and again Lau nodded in formal greeting. He had been shunted closer to the two Chinese at the end of the long table almost like a camera on a track, moving into revealing but sinister close-up. 'Our principal guests are from Yunnan Province, from Kunming—' Lau realised that he *did* know one of the two men. His inexpressive face and short, tubby frame had lingered like a mote at the corner of eyesight, a speck that

had become more and more irritating and distracting.
The man had hovered, said nothing except in whispers to
other Chinese who were deferential towards him, but had
been there ... Then, as now, a magnetic field, a power
centre. Lau had dismissed the memory of him and all
recollection of the meeting in Kunming in August. It had
been a wasted opportunity, a sequence of full meetings
and futile lobbying. But the same Chinese was here, now,
in the Burmese Embassy in Berkeley Square ... why?

The meeting in Kunming, in China's most backward
province and the region which bordered northern
Burma, had been called by the Greater Mekong Sub-
region, an organisation established by Beijing as a
counterweight to the Asian Development Bank and the
Association of South-East Asian Nations. It envisaged the
development of the Mekong River along its two-and-a-
half-thousand-mile length and its journey through six
Asian countries. A hundred grandiose and priority
projects had been identified and costed. Forty billion
dollars was the conservative estimate to turn the Mekong
into Asia's Danube. Roads, dams, bridges, railways, a
fibre-optic telecoms loop through the whole region – all to
turn the sub-region into a massive new power centre for
South-East Asia to rival Japanese industrial power.

Was *he*, the Chinese general, here now to broach the
subject of the Mekong? It would help explain the presence
of the Laotian and the Cambodian.

Mung Thant's hand gestured towards the two men at
the head of the table, and his expression seemed to seek
for a form of address. There was a nod as slight as a facial
tic from the man Lau remembered from Kunming, and
the Burmese minister at once announced:

'Generals Wang Wei and Feng of Yunnan Province. You
are no doubt surprised, Mr Lau—?'

There was, Lau realised, a large map folder in front of Wei. His hands played with it, as enticed as if they had encountered a woman's clothing, or gold. Beyond the tall windows, Berkeley Square was retreating into dusk. Lau felt as if it was Wei's presence that distanced the traffic, the people.

'Lau Yen-Chih, we meet once more – though at our previous encounter, we were not introduced.' Wei addressed him using his Chinese name. It implied knowingness, a file on him, familiarity and possession. The words came from a ruined heavy smoker's throat.

'General Wang Wei, General Feng,' Lau replied in his correct, even bookish Mandarin; his exactitude amused Wei. His laugh became a dry, croaking cough. 'I am perhaps a little surprised. And honoured ...'

The two drug lords of the old Communist Party of Burma seemed as much elements of an audience as did the Burmese who were present, and the Laotian and Cambodian. He was aware of their subordination in the presence of Wei and Feng. Who *were* they ... ? *What* were they? The relationship of ease, familiarity and even trust he had enjoyed with the drug lords was unsettled, subtly altered. The two men controlled more than sixty per cent of the heroin production of Burma; they were backed by an army of more than five thousand fighters, and responsible for forty per cent of the heroin smuggled into the United States ...

... and yet they were *not* the power centre of the room, even though Lau would have given his solemn word that Mung Thant and another half-dozen of the Burmese generals were in their pockets. Until that moment, he had never doubted that they *controlled* northern Burma.

Now they sat, hands clasped on the table in front of them, like junior members of some Politburo.

Wei said croakily: 'Lau Yen-Chih, you left Kunming empty-handed.' Cigarette smoke curled around his leathery, waxed features, and he narrowed his eyes into the fierce slits of a medieval warrior's helmet. 'You and your many advisers and business associates.' He glanced in the direction of the drug lords, who had been themselves shadowy presences at the Kunming conference. The Mekong River flowed along the border between China and northern Burma. A golden river for them. 'You departed in anger.' It was almost an accusation, as if Wei addressed a barbarian from the West, a European or American with no decorum, no politeness, merely greed and haste. 'You were mistaken.'

'I was?' It was both question and apology.

'You may sit. There.' Wei pointed to a vacant chair beside the younger of the two drug lords. Lau was precisely placed, defined.

'Thank you, General Wei. Gentlemen . . .' He sat down.

His cousin, David, half-English as he was, would not have been able to deal with the stifling Oriental politeness, the constant shifting of the masks of threat, subordination, deference. Nor would a racial purist such as he suspected Wei to be have agreed to deal with a half-barbarian like David.

'You show Western impatience, Lau Yen-Chih.' It was the tone of a grandfather as well as a warlord; archaic and powerful as a temple.

'I did not think the conference went well,' Lau replied. 'There was much to do. The time was wasted with words of doubt, small-mindedness.' Wei nodded, stubbing out one cigarette and at once lighting another. 'The transformation of the Mekong Sub-region is a great project – it deserved better words, greater imagination.'

'Such as yours?'

'Respectfully, yes.' Who *were* they?

As if telepathic, Feng broke the silence that was immediately tense.

'The numbers nine-nine-nine. You understand their meaning?'

Carefully and without surprise – his hands were, thankfully, not on the table – Lau nodded.

'Nine-Nine-Nine Enterprise Group. I have seen the neon signs throughout Guandong Province, even in Hong Kong.'

'Good,' was all Feng offered in response.

Wei and Feng were People's Liberation Army generals, and a great deal besides. Lau breathed calmly, his features devoid of expression. The power centre was explained, their magnetic force, the natural subordination of the others. The 999 Enterprise Group was the largest and most active business conglomerate controlled by the army. In one province of China alone, it controlled three thousand factories, two thousand farms, property, clothing, car manufacture and even investment trusts; hospitals, universities, scientific research centres, high-technology companies ... Altogether, Western experts estimated its size at around forty corporations or conglomerates controlling at least twenty thousand companies. Some were arms factories, some were restaurants. The 999 Enterprise Group was tentacular and everywhere, in every strand of commercial life in China.

He ought to have realised that Wei and Feng were the representatives of the 999 Group in Yunnan Province ... and that 999 controlled the heroin. It was obvious to him now.

In a small sense, they controlled *him*, too ... What *was* true was that the conglomerate that the group controlled dwarfed Winterborne Holdings and all its interests, whether in Asia, Europe or America. David and he were pygmies; these two diminutive, cheap-suited Chinese generals were giants. He felt a coldness inside him that doused the excitement of the prospects opening ahead of him. They controlled Yunnan Province, and therefore its heroin refineries, and the drug traffic across the border and, no doubt, the distribution of heroin to the rest of China. He had been using Straits Royal Group and the huge construction company, AsiaCon, which was building new hotels, casinos, factories, small towns, dams all over the region, to launder *their* drug profits.

'This is, then, with respect, a continuation of the discussions in Kunming in August? The agenda comprises the Greater Mekong Sub-region?'

'Perhaps,' Feng admitted. He removed a file from the battered briefcase he lifted from beside his chair and opened it in front of him. He was a caricature of modesty, impoverishment, humility, Lau realised; the old briefcase, the cheap suit, the wire-framed glasses he now donned. 'The problem of security,' he announced, startling Lau as he very theatrically consulted the open file, 'has not been resolved. We understand that the man Hyde has not yet been eliminated.' He looked up. Wei remained wreathed in smoke, like a small buddha enveloped in incense. 'Such details are not unimportant. The Kumar situation was handled efficiently, but not this one. Why not, Lau Yen-Chih?' The politeness of the final sentence was insultingly overdone.

'It *is* in hand.' The words came from a throat tight with rage and affront. It was only with the greatest effort that he was able to keep his hatred from his features.

Wei, with further patronage, grumbled: 'These are matters that can be left – for now. We have more important business.' He placed his hand against the large map folder and thrust it along the polished surface of the table towards Lau. It came to rest in front of him. 'Read that.'

Their condescension writhed in him like a poison he had drunk. He reached with a forcedly calm hand for the folder and opened it. He glimpsed a blue, winding streak across a folded map – the Mekong – but was evidently intended to read the single page of close typing that lay above the maps. It took him no more than moments to absorb its contents, which were little more than a digest of his own proposals, and those of the Chinese delegation, at the Kunming conference.

'I am – honoured,' he murmured. 'I was listened to well, General Wei—'

'Though you did not think so at the time,' Wei laughed. 'It is the privilege of wisdom to be heard.'

'Sometimes.'

He let the page drop from his fingertips back on top of the map of the Mekong region. The digest of the proposals to make the Mekong into Asia's Danube lay before him as a supreme temptation; and, like all temptations of cosmic proportions, it echoed his own imaginings and was couched in what might have been his own words. He experienced both a dizzy breathlessness at what was in prospect and the sense of being winded by a blow because of the price he would have to pay. The ageing general from Yunnan Province had taken him to the high place and shown him all the kingdoms of the earth ... Winterborne Holdings, Winterborne Straits, AsiaCon – *every* business in the conglomerate – could swamp the Mekong region like an invading army, on virtually monopoly terms ...

... and, in return, Straits Royal Group, AsiaCon, then the rest of Winterborne Holdings would become one gigantic laundering operation for the profits from the heroin, and one vast means of distributing it in Europe and America. In effect, Winterborne Holdings would be *paid* in heroin; its *business* would be heroin.

'You retain your own counsel, Lau Yen-Chih?'

This was not, in reality, a business negotiation or a board meeting; it was the first formal discussion of a takeover. If he engaged the conglomerate with them, he would be their creature . . . He *was* their creature already. They could expose Straits Royal Group and himself tomorrow, even if that set their distribution and laundering operation back eighteen months or two years. They'd find another way. He'd be incarcerated like his cousin, but for much longer.

With Chinese subtlety, Wei and Feng were being generous, and, as Chinese, they expected him not to insult that generosity but to accept it and show gratitude.

He forced back another welling-up of rage, acid as nausea in his throat. He would be angry *later*, when he could afford to be.

He looked up at Wei.

'I am – surprised,' he offered. Wei nodded. The oblique gratitude was acceptable. 'There is a very great, and risky, investment here, and a preoccupation for Winterborne Holdings over the next decade—'

'At least.'

'At least,' Lau agreed. He sensed the greedier, more alert interest of the other men around the table, satisfaction clouding the polished surface like the heat from their hands. 'We would require' – he excised the word *guarantee*, since it would insult needlessly – 'a proportion of the priority projects outlined in the Asian Development Bank's study of not less than—'

'—ten per cent,' murmured Feng.

'Twenty per cent, General Wei,' he concluded. Eight,

perhaps, ten *billion* dollars ... That was the investment, most of which would be met by the laundered heroin profits. The eventual proceeds from such a share of the hydro-electric schemes, the roads, railways, factories and the exploitation of natural resources would be three or four times as much. Maybe forty billion dollars.

It would be the equivalent, per annum, of the 999 Enterprise Group's profits for the last fiscal year. According to the CIA. He wondered whether Wei had already done the same sums as himself—

—then Wei laughed, and Lau knew that he had. The takeover might, if properly managed, become almost a partnership. Lau responded with a small, polite, self-deprecating smile.

'Thanks for returning my call, Peter.'

Marian, her sports bag and briefcase resting against her shin, bent down as she inserted the key into the deadlock of her street door. Her handbag dangled from her shoulder. She listened as Grainger offered her a brief conversation the following afternoon.

'—around three suit?'

'Your place or mine?' she joked.

'Your office, I think, Marian. On the terrace if the weather's fine?'

'And in the church hall if it rains! Bye—'

She dropped the mobile phone into her handbag, glancing back down the narrow street which led up from the town to the cathedral close. The lights of waterside lamps reflected from the minster pool, and the shadow of the market town's cathedral was illuminated. The Dean and Chapter must have come into a small legacy ... The three spires thrust up bravely against cloud that was made a dull orange by the lights of the distant conurbation, the edge of which was within her constituency. The cathedral was massively deposited on rising ground, as if to keep at bay the market town that had recently tried to swell itself, like a mate-seeking frog, into something bigger, more modern.

Marian removed the key from the deadlock, then used the Yale to finally open the street door, poised for her habitual and unnecessary dash to the burglar alarm keypad. There was a momentary sense of panic, something that now came to her every time she returned to her constituency flat. It was the memory of the fire and the intent to kill her ... More than a year ago now. The whole place had been refurbished since then. The door opened and she heaved her bags through it—

—into silence. The sharp, whistling tone of the alarm was absent. She stood in the narrow passageway of the Georgian terraced house, bemused, almost fearful. *Idiot – you forgot to set it* ... Not for the first time, either. The house was empty, the ground-floor flat temporarily abandoned by the young couple who lived in it. They were enjoying a safari in an Africa that owed more to Meryl Streep and Robert Redford than to David Attenborough or *National Geographic*. They were a bland, pleasant couple with a year-old BMW and up-to-the-minute pretensions. They hardly ever offended her sensibilities, but they, too, sometimes forgot to set the alarm.

She began climbing the stairs, rattling a plant pot on a delicate old table in the hall. And somehow the silence of the old house pressed around her. She shook off the impression and climbed the last few stairs to her own territory. There were no dual entrances, no sense of separateness between the two floors of the house. Light from streetlamps glowed through the landing window, making the broad leaves of an aspidistra look like small, waving arms signalling distress. She heard her own breathing and watched the lights of a passing car slide from one side of the ceiling to the other . . .

. . . saw the light beneath the door of her lounge, a narrow bright strip like a brass rod. Heard her bag and briefcase drop as slow as stones through amber with a deep, underwater sound. Saw the door open, the crack of light become a glare, outlining the man's tall, heavy shape, realised he was wearing a mask—

—she felt the material of his anorak under her fingers, felt the muscles of his forearm and shoulders. Felt the blow as something struck her forehead and temple. Pain, lights, her vision blurring. Her nails scraped at something that might have been skin. The window leaned tiredly sideways, as if the building had been bombed. More pain from the downstroke of a black-clothed arm. She lurched towards the open doorway to see the wreckage of her furniture and papers and an overturned jardinière, its dark soil like clots of blood on the pale-green carpet.

She saw everything through throbbing light, through a wetness that dazzled . . . then the room retreated into a cloud of darkness that enlarged to envelope everything. Darkness—

'You all right?' Hyde asked. The evening wind swept across the airfield-like surroundings of the motorway service station. His own voice was muffled by the last of a sandwich as he stood beside the Ford in the car park. He was speaking to Ros in Singapore. 'Having a nice time? How's the jet-lag?'

'I'm *fine*, Hyde.' It was the impatience of a child on holiday with a parent worrying at home. 'No one's tried to rob me, kidnap me or do me in – even though I'm in foreign parts!' She laughed mockingly. 'Sometimes you are a bloody old woman, Hyde ... Look, I have a breakfast meeting in half an hour. Sorry to rush and all that, but I'm *fine*, honestly.'

Hyde could say nothing to her. Staring into the wind, watching the flow of headlights on the M40, he felt both helpless and agitated, but also dismissive. The chance of anyone making a connection between himself and the woman who ran the interior design company in Sydney was unlikely ... *Had* to be.

'Listen, we'll all be flying up to the resort site itself, later today. See for ourselves. Good – eh?'

He wanted to offer a further warning, but she would only become more mocking.

'Fine ...'

'Look, Hyde, I've had the inoculations, there are *four* of us – and John's a rugby player, for Christ's sake! — and we're here on business. It's not your world, lover!'

'OK, sorry. Just—'

'Keep in touch? Course ... Anyway, Hyde, what are *you* doing?'

There was, in her voice, the suspicion of a foreboding. That perennial sense he so detested that one fine day he would waltz off and leave her — that most of his waking hours were spent planning his escape. It was part of the reason she disliked, with such intensity, the idea of his returning to London; as if he were visiting the city where his mistress lived.

'Not much. Aubrey's not a lot of help, frankly—'

'So you'll be back soon?'

'Should think so.' He could not tell her he was a target. 'I can't see it being too long ... I'm getting fed up with it anyway,' he confessed.

'Right.' Her tone was immediately brighter. 'Listen, I've

really got to dash – love you.' Ros always offered that assurance as if half expecting a rebuff, or a silence at the other end of the line.

'Love you. Cheer-oh.'

He flicked off the mobile. How could he caution Ros without revealing his own danger, panicking her? Their relationship – or so it sometimes seemed, especially since they had moved back to Oz – was like a series of tiptoed steps on rocks that jutted out of a river known to be inhabited by crocs. So long as he remained with her, so long as he was usefully but not especially dangerously occupied, the river was filled only with flowing water. Separation, moods, her awareness of his boredom and frustration – all were gaping, teeth-lined mouths. He had never concealed his whereabouts from her, what operation he was engaged in, how dangerous his circumstances. Now he had done – because he could not be certain of her response. And, in hiding his own danger, he could not warn her of her own.

Angrily, in the dusty wind blowing across the hard-lit expanse of bare concrete, he dialled Aubrey's number. His revived anxieties, for Ros and for himself, reminded him of Marian Pyott and of Alder emerging from Ralph Lau's house in Eaton Square. Marian, too, would be endangered, but if he told her, she would rebuff his fears, see matters only by daylight, not the dusk things seemed to be slipping into. She'd ask Alder outright, be told it was a coincidence, unwittingly give information to him.

'Aubrey.'

'Me.' He attempted calm. 'How did your lunch go?'

Aubrey chuckled, infuriating Hyde.

'Alex sends his undying love.'

'What did the old shirt-lifter have to say?' Hyde snapped. He liked, respected Davenhill. The man was almost as clever as Aubrey. But not just *now!*

'What he offered was mostly background, I'm afraid. Very general . . . Winterborne companies in Asia making large profits where none should be, gaining many and vast infrastructure projects in Burma. Favoured status, large returns. It would mean a great deal of laundering, perhaps a great deal of smuggling . . . ? He had no hard evidence of misdeeds, I'm—'

'All that's just background! What do I *do*—?' He sensed the nerves in his voice, knew Aubrey would be aware of them. Monitoring his tone carefully, he asked: 'How do I get leverage on this thing? Something as *big* as this?'

He was febrilely unsettled; a small emotional step away from a foreboding that somehow he would not escape his situation, would not survive it. He shook his head like an angry, wounded dog. In Eaton Square it had been all right, satisfying; he had been the observer, the one in control. After talking to Ros, reaction had set in.

'Jessop is linked to Ralph Lau,' he announced. 'I tailed Jessop from St Katherine's Dock to Eaton Square. There's a security firm there that belongs to—'

'—Winterborne Holdings. Yes, the appalling Fraser was part of that little operation. Jessop too, mm? It all does tend to lead us back to Straits Royal Group, I'm afraid.'

'It proves the reason they want me out of the picture. Doesn't it?'

'Yes . . .' Aubrey sighed.

'I don't like a canvas this big. Not without back-up, intelligence. How do I get it?'

'You must turn *against* Jessop, Patrick. Would *he* have been involved in the death of the Kumar boy? It would seem likely. Jessop must be your leverage—'

'He'd better be! I've got no one else I can touch.'

'Enough on Jessop, or from him, would suffice. The Lal

girl will talk to you, won't she?' Hyde climbed into the car and switched on the engine. Struggled with his seatbelt, still holding the mobile phone against his ear. 'You're on your way there, I take it?'

'About another forty minutes or so.'

'Concentrate on Kumar's movements immediately prior to his death. His contacts, who he knew, where he went. But keep your main attention on the twenty-four hours Marian says he was out of touch.'

'You think there's something?'

'*That* would have been when Jessop appeared on the scene. If he ever did. Reconstruct the boy's last hours, if you possibly can.'

'OK. What will you do?'

'More background. On Jessop, his associates, his ... *connections*. If we can find a casual link between Jessop and Lau – an order given and received – then you will be safe, Patrick.'

'And until that happens, I won't be. Right?'

'I'm afraid so, Patrick, yes.'

Hyde had reached the slip road on to the motorway. He thrust the Ford out into the middle lane.

'OK. I'll just check with Marian that she's sure the girl's going to show – will she be there by now?'

The hidden towns on either side of the motorway stained the dark sky dull orange. Headlights glared towards him on the southbound carriageway, an endless, rushing rope of light.

'Definitely. She caught a late-afternoon train. At least, that's what her researcher told me—'

'OK, I'll ring her. See you—'

He dialled Marian Pyott's flat. It would be a very irritating, even dangerous, waste of time if the Indian girl decided not to show. She had to talk to him. He glanced at the dashboard clock as the phone continued to ring out. Almost eight. She'd have been at her flat for an hour or more by now ... *Ton-up Marian*. In one of her very occasional letters, Marian had sent Ros a newspaper cutting with that headline. Front page of the *Sun* – some sort of record, a front-page story in Murdoch's rag devoid of any sexual element, as he had observed to Ros. Marian had been booked three times in six months for speeding on this same motorway, hence the driving ban and the train journey back to her constituency. The mobile continued to ring out—

—unnervingly. Either she'd been delayed, or she wasn't answering. There was nothing more to it. The answerphone cut in and he heard her recorded voice. It was the worst main line in the country for delays, after all. He switched off his phone and threw it on the seat beside him, obscurely concerned. Alder's image. He distrusted all accident.

He pushed the speed of the Ford up to ninety, then ninety-five. Another thirty minutes or so and he'd be there—

As David's Rolls Royce reached the gates of Cheveney Park and turned out on to the minor road towards London, Ralph Lau looked back at the grand country house looming against the clouds that scudded across a sliver of moon and distant stars. He experienced a fierce, heady delight; an exultation. He had left David Winterborne, in his first-floor cell in the open prison, almost demented with baffled and impotent rage. Features twisted, hands clawed, as if David had been acting some villain in a Victorian melodrama. There had been no considered reasoning, just the clichéd responses. David was beaten and knew it. Then, as if he, too, had become engaged in the same melodrama, Lau had swept from the tall-ceilinged room in his moment of triumph, not even glancing back at his defeated cousin and enemy.

You can't refuse, David. You have to do it my way. He'd said that to David, after he had outlined the Golden River file – his hand patted the folder as it rested on his lap – and David had rejected it out of hand.

It had simply been a matter of convincing David that the Chinese would do it – expose them all, ruin Winterborne Holdings irrevocably – if David didn't capitulate. The silence had seemed to go on forever, the muscular control he had had to demand of himself had been like supporting a great crushing weight that threatened to fall on him. Then David had broken, his collapse coming with the sound and fury of an edifice crashing down. Rage, fury, threats, a tantrum of monstrous proportions upon which Lau had fed like a voyeur.

Then he had abruptly left his cousin to wallow in the futility of his rage, because now he had work to do. Quickly. Clive Winterborne, as chairman, would comply simply because he was entirely ignorant of the heroin.

He glanced, as if to reassure himself, at the soundproof glass that separated him from the chauffeur, then picked up the car phone, placing the file on the leather seat beside him. *Golden River* – the Mekong. He had drawn up the material in the file before his abortive trip to Kunming in August, long before. He had felt himself like a putative author hawking a manuscript which had no possibility of publication. Now, it was only David who refused it.

He smoothed the material of his suit as he waited for the call to be answered. He had instructed his two principal aides, those who had helped to create the file that was now reactivated, to convene an emergency meeting of the Golden River team at Eaton Square by the time of his return. He expected the preliminary meeting to extend through the night and into the following day. He smiled. David, maddened as if by a plague of flies ... That had been very satisfying.

'Lau.'

'Sir, almost everyone is already here – very excited. Do you want to speak to—?'

'Put Ludwig Fischer on ...' He hesitated, as if one of the insects plaguing David had somehow got into the back of the Rolls and was hovering about his face. 'No, wait a moment. I'll ring again. I have – other calls.' He slapped down the car phone, and his hand was shivery, slightly clammy, as he released the receiver.

The Rolls turned on to the main road. A road sign displaying the distance to the M20 flashed beside the window. Orange light flooded into the interior of the limousine. Traffic flowed past. The headlights seemed to inspect him, almost jeer. An image of the meeting at the Burmese Embassy, from which he had hurried to see David, had returned. The features of General Wei, wreathed in cigarette smoke, eyes hooded by heavy lids, croaking, ravenlike voice reminding him of the continued existence of the man Hyde ... as if he had been prompting a servant to clear up dog-mess from the Embassy steps! He was *forced* to attend to that piddling matter as if it was of greater significance than the whole of the Mekong project! By a Chinese general in a cheap suit, his remaining hair cut as brutally as that of the rawest recruit in the People's Liberation Army ... staring at him along the table as if daring him to demur. A squat, unblinking little buddha, his cigarette smoke like incense rising around smug, unchanging features.

Lau's hand continued to hover over the car phone, set in the armrest. Until he got rid of Hyde, he would remain no better than Wei's manservant. He realised he was knead-ing his knuckled hand against his jawline. Damn Jessop, he should have eliminated Hyde by now. He snatched up the receiver as if to rip out its wiring. Dialled Jessop's number.

Immediately he snapped: 'Don't bother to tell me where you are and what you're doing. Get rid of the man Hyde tonight – do you understand? Tonight! *Don't* make another mistake!'

He slapped the receiver back into the armrest and almost lay back in his seat. The motorway's overhead lights, as they flashed by at the top corner of the window, gradually calmed him. His thoughts were able, at last, to concentrate on the banks, the joint-venture companies, the individuals and governments, the meetings, the phone calls, the loans and the investments ... He would need Winterborne Holdings' UK companies and US operations in order to borrow sufficiently, spread the risk. The resort complexes, the casinos, the construction projects in Europe would swallow the dirty money and clean it effectively half a world away ...

He was soothed, even satiated, as if after sex. He allowed the tableau of Golden River to parade itself in his imagination. There was no longer any awareness of Hyde. That matter had been taken care of.

'No, she's all right ...' Hyde sat cross-legged on the carpet as if tidied into a corner of the neatened room as part of her obsessive removal of the signs of the intruder's invasion. He watched Marian intently as he spoke to Aubrey. 'Yes, there were things missing ... No, it wasn't casual labour.' Marian was shaking her head violently, kneeling on the carpet, rubbing at the stains left by the spilt soil from the jardinière. 'Yes, I'm certain,' he added.

'No, I won't ... The girl's not here yet. She's expected any minute. Right - bye.' He put down the telephone and placed his hands on his knees like an image of the Siddhartha. Marian continued cleaning the dark patches, her hair hanging forward on her lowered face, masking the reddened skin, the cut lip. She had changed into a cream silk blouse and black slacks because blood had stained her sweater. Her breathing was effortful with suppressed outrage.

'He's relieved,' Hyde offered. 'But he has no idea why anyone would be interested in you at the moment.'

The doctor had been, a languid Scot with an engaging manner. He had accepted Marian's assurances that she would inform the police, had talked of Europe and the NHS with her, and then left. Mr Plod had not been informed - it wasn't the local CID's sort of thing, was it, after all?

'I don't *see*,' she began with heavy emphasis, pressing a towel into the carpet to soak up the excess water she had used with such enthusiasm, 'how you can be *sure* it wasn't just a burglary. Such things do happen in the real world, you know.' She did not once look up at him.

'It wasn't accidental or opportunistic. Look at what's been stolen, for starters—'

'They pinch laptops all the time!' Marian snapped. 'You're not very up to date in your view of petty crime, are you?'

'And the telly and the video have gone, too,' he sighed with amusement. 'I know what it *looks* like. Except that your floppies have gone as well. All your records.'

'They are re-usable ...' She seemed to falter in her confidence. Or perhaps it was just the machine running out of fuel. He noticed a quiver in her arms as she pressed the towel down. Delayed shock.

'Try to realise ... you've been hijacked, taken over the

border into a different country. The one where *I* live.'

She looked up at him and brushed her hair away from her watering eye. Naturally, there was nothing professional about the superficial damage that had been done to her. Had there been, he might have found her stiffening body on the floor, instead of a dazed, frightened, very angry woman.

'I refuse to believe you.' Gingerly, she turned to sit on the carpet, her back against the sofa. 'I haven't anything to do with your situation,' she concluded.

Hyde shrugged.

'You're still across the border,' he murmured. 'You've taken an interest in Kumar's death. That's enough to set off their alarm. Look, I don't *like* the fact that you've aroused their interest, but you have.'

'I don't have anything here on Kumar,' she retorted. 'I don't *know* anything about Kumar!'

'Why don't you just poke out your tongue and complete your impersonation of a defiant kid?' he asked, grinning and rubbing his hands through his hair. 'The old man believes me, *I* believe me – why don't you?' Wrong question, he realised, and immediately added: 'You're the most stubborn woman I've ever met – apart from Ros.'

'What do they want? Why—' She faltered, and the expression in her eyes confirmed that she had stumbled over his world like a stone in her path. Her hands clasped at her upper arms as they were tightly crossed over her breasts. She was visibly shivering, almost with the violence of an addict suffering from withdrawal symptoms. She seemed to be staring at something just about his head, a sign on the wall, and be terrified of it.

The mood lasted for perhaps ten seconds, and then she announced, clearing her throat: 'Sorry about that. Just an old nightmare.'

'Because of who might be involved?'

She nodded repeatedly, admitting: 'Yes. Or delayed shock. The doc did mention it might creep up on me.'

'OK – shock.' It was not good. What had always been an accident in Brussels had, according to Aubrey, been David Winterborne's attempt to murder her. Old ghosts were stirring. He looked at his watch. 'Nine, you told her?'

'Yes ... Sorry.' She seemed to wish to confide, but he recognised on her features that occasional disdain with which she regarded him whenever his world was a little too close. She had always preferred meeting him when Ros was present, bringing the normal and ordinary with her like a chaperone. 'It *is* them, though, isn't it?' she all but forced herself to ask. 'All that effort to frighten Rabindur Lal – he can't be important to anyone, surely?'

'His daughter is. Or might be.'

'Is she in danger?'

'If she tells me everything she knows and something I can use – no. So long as she keeps away from you – you from her. OK?' She nodded. Then suddenly she was shaking her head, as if to loosen from it the thoughts that crowded her imagination. 'Good,' he continued, ignoring her turmoil. 'Is she bringing a curry with her? I'm starving.'

A watery smile, a loud sniff.

'She offered. I accepted.'

'Great.'

'What do you need from her?'

'A key. Something that I can use.' He spread his hands in front of him as if to inspect whether or not they quivered. 'It has to be a trade-off, mutual tolerance. Blackmail.'

'If you could hurt them, they'll leave you – *us* – alone?'

'Yes.' He smiled. 'We're not going to hurt each other, are we? You know the sort of thing. It's just like politics—'

The doorbell rang in the hall, startling Marian as much

as if she had heard a terrible screeching of tyres outside.

'Syeeda—!' she blurted, hurrying to her feet. 'Don't say anything about—' She indicated the room. Hyde shook his head, climbing to his feet. 'Oh, and put the oven on, would you – and try not to look so daunting!' She moved brightly from the room and he heard her open the door. 'Syeeda! Come in – ah, that smells superb!' It was the role-playing of a consummate politician. 'Oh – no, we've had a burglar. I stumbled in on him. No, nothing serious – I just need more make-up!'

Hyde re-entered the lounge as Marian ushered the Indian woman into it. He thought Syeeda Lal looked at the small signals of intrusion and damage as if seeing Kumar's dead body. There was immense strain, in the erosion of grief beneath her eyes, and in the stranded slump of her posture, as if she had become unused to the ordinary.

He went forward and took the polythene bags from her unresisting hands.

'I'm Patrick Hyde,' he murmured. 'I'll just keep these hot.'

He wandered back into the small, new kitchen, its aluminium saucepans openly displayed on self-consciously simple shelving. Placed the foil-topped cartons in the oven, listening as he did so to Marian's bright, birdlike cooing. Syeeda Lal might just be approachable in a straightforward, semi-official manner, simple question-and-answer. Marian was attempting to soften her, create intimacy where the awkwardness of strangers seemed to predominate. From the kitchen door, he asked:

'Can I get anyone a drink?' The Indian girl seemed nervous of his presence, flinching as at a blow, or her own guilt. She shook her head.

'There's a bottle of chardonnay in the fridge,' Marian responded. 'Corkscrew in the drawer to your left.'

He brought two filled glasses back into the lounge, hesitated for a moment, then said:

'I'm very sorry about Medhev, Miss Lal. Marian's told you I knew him quite well ... I'm so sorry.'

The woman's huge dark eyes welled with tears, before she rose jerkily from the sofa and announced:

'I'll just dish up, Marian – no, don't worry, I know where everything is!'

She hurried into the kitchen. Hyde handed a glass to Marian and shrugged. Plates clattered in the kitchen.

'How is your father, Syeeda?'

'Very angry,' came the reply. 'Angry with Medhev,' followed in a hoarse, guilty whisper. Then, raising her voice, she continued: 'He's really very frightened – as if he was some kind of illegal immigrant the police had caught!' She was outraged for him and for herself. 'I shouldn't be here.' Marian had risen and was laying the mahogany table that occupied most of the lounge's small alcove. 'I promised him I would not mention Medhev again in his presence. He – he's never been so angry with me, ever ...'

Hyde felt guilty at the rumbling of his stomach in response to the scents of the curry. Syeeda's features were as bright and empty as those of a waitress as she brought the plates and bowls into the lounge and arranged them on the table. They sat down in silence and she served them efficiently, distantly. Hyde poured more wine, filling the glass Marian had set for Syeeda. They ate in silence for more than five minutes, then Syeeda suddenly asked:

'Are you another policeman, Mr Hyde?'

'Kumar – Medhev – didn't mention me?' She shook her head. 'Well, not really. Nothing to do with the police your father's been dealing with. Can you describe them to me, the men who questioned him?'

She seemed surprised, but began speaking at once.

There had been two of them, neither of them Jessop by the descriptions. Their *manner* – arrogance, secret amusement, a pleasure in subordination – made them known if not recognisable. Jessop's people.

'Thank you – Syeeda?' She did not resent his use of her name. 'Good. Can you . . . talk about Medhev? He'd been in England for some months. You fell in love—' Marian appeared disapproving of his bluntness, but he knew he could tap the memory beneath her immediate sense of loss.

'He was not a drug addict!'

'No, I know that, Syeeda.' He felt himself burdened with her desire and outrage. Later, he would have to talk to her about Kumar during the time he had known him. 'What possible reasons could they have had for thinking he was? Have you any idea how they could have been so wrong?'

Syeeda shook her head violently.

'They made a mistake!' she blurted.

'I know. It was murder.' Marian's intaken breath sounded loudly in the silence of the room. Hyde continued eating the biriani as if he had remarked on nothing more significant than the weather, allowing his words to be absorbed. Marian's pale hand lay on that of the girl. He listened to her sobbing, the punctuating, angry breathing of Marian.

'Thank you,' he heard eventually, and looked up.

'I am sorry. There's no other explanation.'

'Who . . . *Why?*'

Slowly, almost glamorously, Hyde described Kumar's role in the investigation in Singapore. When he mentioned his suspicions of Straits Royal, the hotel chain's name stung her like a slap.

'The New Midland—!' she blurted.

'I'd forgotten,' Marian added. 'There's a new Straits

Royal hotel just opened in the city – ten miles away. What about it, Syeeda?'

'Medhev had friends there – others from Burma.' She hesitated, as if frightened at the intensity of Hyde's interest. He lowered his eyes to his plate. 'Any seconds?' he asked, then added: 'Go on. Friends, you said . . .'

'Yes . . . Would you know any of their names – from Singapore?'

'It's probably coincidence,' he murmured. 'Have you got any names?'

'I think there was one called Win. I never met any of his friends. Win worked at the New Midland, in the kitchens. Washing up, cleaning.'

'OK. It's a start. Why was he at home, Syeeda? The day he died, and the day before that? He was ill, right?'

'He telephoned to say that. I don't know . . .' The tears welled again, as if she had failed Kumar in some way; or she had suddenly sensed a distance between them before he died. A quarrel?

He continued: 'That time needs explaining . . . There's something else. You visited his flat. Did you bring anything away with you?'

'A few personal things,' she replied, challenging him to ask for them. He gestured pacifically with his fork. 'The cutting I told Marian about—'

'There's nothing in that,' Marian intervened defensively. 'I asked Clive. He couldn't explain it. He had a phone call, but Medhev didn't explain why he wanted to see—'

'Clive Winterborne?'

'There was a photograph in the local rag,' Syeeda explained, picking up her handbag from the floor beside her chair and dipping her long fingers into it. 'I brought it – together with the keys to the flat.'

'Thanks.' He took the keys and the cutting. It had been

folded and refolded and already appeared old and worn, an items of news from the distant past. He opened it, pocketing the keys with a carefully suppressed excitement.

Charity lunch, Clive Winterborne aristocratically cajoling money for worthy causes out of men in suits and women in posh frocks. Some of the faces at the top table included a broad, beaming figure wearing some chain of office, a woman beneath a Byzantine coiffure ... and Alder. Congressman Robert Alder.

'I see your American friend was in attendance,' he observed drily.

'Yes. Good-looking, isn't he?' At once, she was embarrassed at her own joke in front of Syeeda. 'He was Clive's guest. He'd have been a help, charming money out of some of the deeper pockets there.'

'They know each other well, then,' he observed as he refolded the cutting and handed it back to Syeeda. 'The keys are what I need. Where is the flat, by the way?'

'About five miles away. I'll show you, if you have an A to Z or something—?'

'I'll get mine,' Marian offered. 'And make some coffee. You two can talk ...'

'Sure.' Syeeda was already leaning towards him, her eyes hungry, demanding. 'About Medhev ...' It seemed to act on her like the promise of sexual gratification. Hyde glanced surreptitiously at his watch as his arm rested on the table. It was ten fifteen. He shut off the excitement he felt growing in the pit of his stomach. The girl deserved a few warm memories. She had nothing else. And it was as if this was some last meeting between the two lovers, before she submitted to her father's injunction. 'When I met him in Singapore, he was working on a radical freesheet,' he began, and heard Marian, who might have been awaiting her cue, begin to prepare the coffee. 'What I remember most is how *angry* he was about Burma ...'

The curry shop was closed and blinded with a solid steel grille, halfway along a row of lock-up shops, most of them empty and boarded up. Weeds grew in the concrete, the slabs were uneven and in disrepair. A sign rattled somewhere – then he saw it, blowing in the wind; it advertised the city's daily newspaper and was scrawled with graffiti. Concrete walkways and underpasses echoed with the wind in a kind of insincere lament for the dilapidation of the sixties shopping centre that the banks, building societies and retail chains had long deserted. Their blazons remaining only as shadows – Tesco, Lloyds Bank, the Midland Bank, the Britannia.

He was startled by the barking of a dog somewhere in the distance. There was the noise of a radio or ghetto-blaster, faint yells from the last of the homegoing, drunken yobs. The distant shattering of glass.

Rabindur Lal, Syeeda's father, had started his business here soon after he had left Burma, in a time when a curry takeaway had been rather beneath the area, a lowering of the tone. He had prospered, moved on like the banks and Tesco, leaving this first shop to be operated by any new management possibility he employed. A sort of school certificate, Syeeda had explained. Make a success here and you could go on to manage one of Lal's better restaurants in the city. Medhev Kumar had been allowed to occupy, rent-free, the flat above the shop.

Hyde stood outside, hands on his hips, surveying the stained concrete and blind windows above the grille. To his amusement *A Rabindur Lal Restaurant* appeared pretentiously beneath *The Bengal Takeaway* on the shop's hoarding. At the end of the open tunnel of rundown shops, waste ground was bathed in moonlight, as were the façades of a shabby Victorian terrace. A few old cars, the occasional van, illuminated as much by the moon as by the few, fitful streetlamps. He tossed his head, recognising his childhood in the East End where two maiden aunts had brought up a lonely, introverted orphan from the age of ten. A child from the other side of the world they had never seen until he was brought off the boat by a purser who held his hand down the gangway. He saw, and still resented, the same poverty, lack of hope, grimness, the atmosphere of failure and crime.

Not *petty* crime, though, he reminded himself. Not *here*, not now. This was something altogether different.

He had left Syeeda with Marian, having exhausted his recollections of Kumar. The woman had been reluctant to let him leave, almost envious of his visit to Kumar's flat. As Marian supplanted him, began to soothe, he had watched Syeeda beginning to accommodate herself to her future, making her conscious decision that Kumar constituted her past.

He had no great expectations of a search of the flat. The police would have done that thoroughly, looking for heroin, and it would have been searched again since, by Jessop or his people. More than once, possibly. He was the last man at the jumble sale and there wouldn't be anything of value, no bargains left. He shrugged in the cold wind. Live in hope—

He walked the length of the row of dingy shops until he reached the concrete staircase to the passageway that ran along the rear and allowed access to the first-floor flats. The wind blew dry grit in his face, together with the smells of cooking, damp, grime. There were still a few lights showing as he paused and looked over the parapet of the passageway. The inner-city district struggled away from the shopping centre, towards where the streetlights became stronger, banded together like a swelling defensive force. It was like a map of affluence rather than places that he was seeing, an affluence that had drained away from this place out towards smarter, new suburbs, gentrified villages, private estates. The district had been left beached by the tide of money and concern that had retreated from it.

He continued along the passageway until he reached the door of the flat above the curry shop. It consisted of starred glass above and below the panel which contained the letter box. The glass had been reinforced by pieces of plywood. Beside the door, *Fucking Pakis Out* had been spray-painted, and *NF Rules OK* was daubed on the parapet. Pakis? An Indian from Burma? He sniffed in amused contempt. After fifty years of immigration, they had the right to expect racial prejudices to be better informed. He turned the key in the lock, after glancing back down the empty passageway. Then he shut out the surroundings, the noise of the wind and the fading cries of the yobs, and entered the flat.

It smelt of stale curry and spices, mildewed carpet, old paint. He closed the door behind him and searched the greasy wall for the light switch. It illuminated, shadelessly, a narrow, grubby passage with three doors leading off it. The one directly ahead of him was slightly ajar. He assumed it led to the living room and the kitchen. He heard a small, scurrying sound and ignored the mouse or rat. To work, he prompted himself, hearing faint noises from the adjoining flat; someone shouting in a foreign language above the noise of a television set. His aunts' decrepit back-to-back had been much cleaner, smelling strongly of soap. It was dark, after Australia, for which he had cried incessantly, more than for his dead mother in

Woollongong. Sydney's North Shore seemed, at that moment, as distant as his memories of his childhood.

One in the morning. He opened the door of the living room.

A few scraps of old, worn furniture, some casual clothes – denims and a couple of sweatshirts draped over an armchair – a sports bag in one corner. The light possessed a shade, but the wattage was low, giving the cramped room an added dinginess that stultified, depressed. A TV and video remained unmolested in one corner. He began his search methodically, routinely, pushing away the thought that too many expert searchers had preceded him . . .

. . . one thirty-seven . . . one fifty . . .

The bedroom, eventually. The wardrobe. It was taped to the underside, invisible unless one crouched and inspected by touch. A brown envelope with the name *Kumar*. It had been easy to miss. They'd had the floorboards up, the drawers out of the other furniture, the underside of the sofa ripped away, but they hadn't found it. He had. Because he'd shown the boy how to hide things . . . So why has it taken you nearly an hour? he added in his complacent pleasure as he sat down at the rickety kitchen table and opened the envelope. Two folders of snapshots. A slim notebook, one or two letters. The separate, and older, photograph of a middle-aged Indian woman staring into a hot sun, squinting but smiling.

The scent of curry that pervaded the flat from the shop below soured the aftertaste of his supper. Or was that sensation caused by what he held in his hands, the link with the dead boy? The chair creaked as he leaned back on it, away from the scarred, unpolished table. He pushed the notebook aside and opened the first of the two folders, spreading the pictures like playing cards in front of him.

A jungle or forest clearing, machinery, red earth; a Burmese village? The boy's own village? He had left Singapore in a hurry because of his mother, risking arrest by going home. Why the urgency? Just illness ... ? He glanced at the features of the woman in the large snapshot. She could have been Kumar's mother. He saw protestors with banners confronting and being dwarfed by an earthmover in one shot. Hyde yawned, admitting his weariness. The red earth again, newly gouged, the landscape re-created in many of the snapshots; the impression of a remote, jungle-enclosed Burmese village encountering the late twentieth century. It must be the village from which Kumar came and whose name he did not even know. In one shot there was the flash of a blurred parrot against the darkness of trees in the foreground, and the distant, toylike figures of cranes, diggers, trucks ... the curve of an embryonic dam wall. Then the swathes of raw earth where jungle had been in a previous shot, mountains in the distance in one direction, a spreading plain in another. Mountains to the north or north-east, the plain to the south, if the shadows did not lie. He flicked on, encountering a series of close-up photographs of the village and its people – like watching a documentary on Channel Four, he thought sourly.

He opened the second folder and spread the bulk of glossy prints like a new hand of cards he had dealt himself. The village again, the dam in the background more nearly complete and identifiable, the jungle seemingly more sparse ... There was the recognisable concrete strip and skeletal buildings of a new airport in another shot, and the outline of the kind of structure that would eventually metamorphose into a huge hotel. Some kind of resort development such as were springing up all over South-East Asia.

Uniforms...? The shot was not quite in focus. A group of figures crowded together – and being approached by men in uniform. In the succeeding picture, there were bodies prone on the raw earth. In the next, more bodies, and burning huts. Then the sequence continued and Hyde stared, appalled, as he dealt each card afresh, dropping one after the other into a neat, awful little heap on the surface of the table. A line of bodies in the hard sunlight, men, women, children... The photographs were all taken from the same position, from some hilltop or other promontory, looking down. The village burned to ashes at one edge of the photographs, the dam's curve mirage-like at the other edge... Some of the bodies had disappeared in the succeeding picture, more from the one that followed. Armed soldiers watched, other uniformed men were spilling the bodies into a pit. Orange firelight was weakened by the strong daylight, visible only because of the remaining jungle's dark greenery. Flame, fire, soldiers, bodies...

He realised he was shaking his head. It was just that it was so familiar. So *routine* in its awfulness. The late twentieth century, any one of dozens of places on the planet. For someone like himself, with his past, it possessed the repetition of an old movie shown every Christmas holiday. You *expected* it – *this*. Burning stilted houses, soldiers with automatic weapons, dead bodies.

This was why Kumar had gone home, this was what he had feared or what his mother had warned him was about to happen. This was the Burmese equivalent of a compulsory purchase order.

He continued to drop the photographs, one by one. Eventually, all the bodies were in the shallow pit and an earthmover was poised in one of the last photographs to cover them with the raw red earth. The dam project, the

162

resort, or whatever it was, had required the village to cease to exist; its inhabitants should have known better than to disagree. All that now remained of these people were these photographs, taken by a boy who was murdered just *because* he had taken them. Kumar was dead not because of Hyde or because of heroin or Straits Royal, but because he had seen and photographed a routine atrocity.

They'd killed a hundred, maybe more, in a site clearance - then killed Kumar because he had the evidence. Jesus Christ - it *always* appalled him, it was insanity.

Who had Kumar threatened to expose? Who was—

—a crash of glass from the passage. His chair clattered to the floor as he was startled to his feet, then the table followed, spilling the snapshots as he overturned it to shield himself. Something rolled towards the door of the room, smouldering. Then it exploded—

Fire everywhere, blinding him, smoke suffocating him.

PART TWO

The Points of the Compass

At last!
The clear trail of the man. After it, silent
but it tracks his guilt to light.
        Aeschylus, *The Eumenides*, 11.242–5

The words 'law and order' have so frequently
been misused as an excuse for oppression that
the very phrase has become suspect in countries
which have known authoritarian rule.
        Aung San Suu Kyi (1989)

CHAPTER SIX

A Place on the Map

A second petrol bomb exploded, making livid scars of damp-stains and the room a harsh negative on his retinae as he crouched behind the kitchen table, blinded. Automatically, his hand scrabbled for the spilt photographs, and slipped as many as he could find into his pockets. He felt blindly for the slim notebook and rescued it. Even in the traumatic shock of the attack, he continued to see the images of the atrocity in Burma.

The heat seemed to search for him as his vision began to clear. The smell of petrol was close enough to be on his clothes. The wall was against his back, hemming him in the kitchen as the fire caught. He turned to the window, and made out, slowly, a shadow below, then a second. They were waiting for him to be driven out like a rat by the fire. The entire flat would be matchwood in minutes. Two shadows flitting on the windy concrete below him, and one more at least on the concrete walkway outside. Probably four men in total. He squinted against the glare, his throat retching against the fumes. There was one other door in the kitchen and he tugged it open. A smell of damp and dirt for an instant. Something scuttled towards the spreading fire then away, squeaking in panic. It was a narrow store cupboard, windowless and with its shelving almost empty. The scent of the fire swallowed the aroma of omnipresent spices.

He glanced behind him for a moment. The passage to the front door was engulfed, the other rooms off it bright with flame. He was trapped in the kitchen. The wind, coming through the shattered glass door, was fanning the fire . . .

. . . he could still get through the flames – *just* – with a wet towel around his face. And get himself shot as he reached the front door. He could smash the kitchen window and reach a drainpipe. Make himself the easiest of targets in the moonlight. Hyde looked up. *There had to be one* . . . *was*. Standing on tiptoe, he reached up, one foot on the lowest food shelf, his back pressed against the other shelves. He pushed at the small square of wood set in the ceiling of the cupboard. The hatch into the roof space. He heaved at it and heard above his own coughing the creak of the wood. The plywood slid back into darkness and he clambered apelike up the shelves as flames and rolling smoke enveloped the larder. He knelt on a joist and slid the rough plywood hatch back into place.

It was already warm in the roof space. The noise of the wind was louder. Smoke at once began seeping through the cracks in the ceiling plaster. He tried to straighten but found himself restrained, held in an awkward crouch. He experienced a moment of panic which became a grin of pleasure. It was what he had wanted, a flat roof. The restraint gave as he hunched and tensed his shoulders, his feet braced on adjacent joists. He thrust upwards, his hands linked to protect his neck. Flame was beginning to lick up into the roof space in one corner, illuminating it. He heard, very faintly, a tearing noise. Grit or pebbles bounced from his shoulders. The light of the fire grew stronger. He could see the few, thin rafters across which the felting of the roof was laid, and reached towards one of them. He heaved on it, twice, and it split, damply. Then he clawed at the roofing felt in renewed panic as a jagged ice floe of plaster collapsed beneath him and flame lurched up near his braced legs. His cheeks seemed scorched. Smoke billowed up with the flame. He tore at the felt, struggled with it—

—moonlight, watery because his eyes were streaming. It wobbled in his vision like a cork on an angry sea, but it was the moon. He levered himself out on to the gravel-scattered felt, not knowing whether the thin rafters would hold his weight. He lay there in the moonlight, stifling his coughing and his fear of the flames just beneath his body. He smelt scorched clothing.

He rose into a crouch, hearing the innocent, panicked noises of the occupants of the other flats, fleeing the fire. Cries after property, pets, family, themselves. He stood up gingerly and pointed his toe like a dancer, feeling for one of the joists. Glanced at his watch. Two minutes since the first petrol bomb had exploded. He placed his weight on the foot that had found the joist, searched for the next with his other shoe. He moved. A cracking noise. He moved again, more quickly, hearing the tears of the old felt, the creak and cracking of the joists—

—someone. At the edge of the roof, watching, as if seated casually and waiting to begin a conversation. No, not seated - kneeling on one knee, arms held out directly in front of him, a bulky shadow in the moonlight. Hyde sensed himself outlined by the fire that had broken through the roof behind him. He gripped the butt of the Heckler & Koch in the small of his back and withdrew it. He fired twice, stiff-armed. The kneeling shadow fell aside slowly, even gracefully, until his cheek was pressed against the gravel. Hyde moved and his trainer went through the old, rotten felt, making him lurch as if he had been hit. He dragged his leg free and another two steps brought him level with the body.

He peered over the roof. He had hardly heard the gunshots himself amid the hubbub from below and the noise of the fire. He could make out no threatening or purposeful movement amid the milling crowd of self-rescued people. An Indian woman was clutching a frightened cat against her large, cardigan-clad breasts. In the distance, he heard the faint noise of a fire engine's siren. There were headlights hurrying along a main road half a mile away.

He knelt curiously beside the body and searched its pockets. He did not recognise the man. He found a wallet and slipped it into his jacket pocket.

There was a drainpipe at the corner of the block of flats, and he eased himself over the edge of the roof and tested its grip on the concrete wall. It would have to do. There was no one below him at this sheltered corner. He scuttled down the pipe, an instant ahead of the tearing noises as rusting screws pulled out of the concrete. His feet touched the ground and he pressed back against the wall. No one.

He skittered like a flung stone across weedy concrete and scrubby grass, towards the Ford. He had left it parked beneath one of the few working streetlights a hundred yards or so from the shops. He passed a dilapidated tower block and heard the barking of a dog. He reached the Ford and unlocked the door, dragging it open. His breathing clouded the windscreen. He was ahead of them; there had been no immediate alarm and pursuit.

He thrust the key into the ignition. He had time – just enough – to lose them. Then something careened off the bonnet and a second bullet, almost immediately after, shattered the side window behind his head. They'd found him. He couldn't see them, it had to be a rifleman. Time to go—

—key beginning to turn, mind beginning to race ... No pursuit, but the marksman had found him at once ... Been waiting ... Key, *key* ...

He removed the key from the ignition as if it scalded him. The marksman had tried to accelerate him, make him panic and start the car. The shots were so good they could easily have killed him. They had wanted him to turn the key.

He opened the door slowly, crouching in the driver's seat against the next shot. He leaned forward and down, as if he were about to tumble helplessly from the car. He stared beneath the vehicle, hands gripping the door sill, hoping the rifleman was on the other side of the car. Sweat at the back of his neck, chilled in the breeze. His body seemed to heat up, as if orchestrated by the loudening siren ... *Yes*. His sigh was almost sexual. Against the light from the fire, he could see the device suspended from the engine block. Turn the key, and goodbye ...

When they inspected the burnt-out wreck, it might even have been blamed on vandals. The orange glow of the streetlight – stupid place to park the car – fell liverishly on his skin. He had to know where the marksman was, in which direction. If he didn't, he could be the perfect target. To find out, he had to invite at least one more shot, maybe two.

He clenched his hands in his lap. The headlights of the fire engine swept across the street, the tower block.

Now—

The lights along the river, beyond the marina which his apartment overlooked, gleamed on the sluggish water. Jessop, turning from the view, gestured with the bottle in his hand towards Cobb, seated on the cream leather sofa.

'Why not?' he murmured, holding out his glass, which Jessop generously refilled. 'Cheers.'

'To what?' Jessop smirked. 'We still haven't sent Patrick Hyde under the sod. Haven't you noticed how anxious Ralphie-boy is about that?' Jessop returned to his leather armchair. 'I'd just got out of the shower when the bastard rang me, screaming his bloody Chinky head off.' He refilled his own glass and deposited the bottle on a glass table.

Cobb snorted with laughter and lit a cigarette.

'He's a bit unpredictable, I'll give you that.'

'I sometimes wish that bastard Fraser was still alive. Then he'd be the one taking all this flak.'

'Hyde isn't even really dangerous—'

'Ralphie thinks he is. I don't know why. He acts as if he's under pressure—'

'Mind you, nice thought, eh? Pushing that Aussie prick off the edge of the cliff.'

They toasted each other, then Jessop said:

'It was easier working for Winterborne, even if he did always want finesse. And he was so obsessive about that bloody woman.'

'Hence the burglary. She's not interested in this, is she?'

'Doesn't look like it. But she's talked to Hyde now. That might change her mind. Him and that bloody Indian woman—!' He waved his hand in the air of the pale-cream lounge, as if to indicate its monklike, celibate spaces. 'We could have dumped Kumar's body in a pond or buried it in a landfill – there's enough of those places around where he lived! But no, Ralphie wanted to be *clever*. Pity we didn't know he was a pal of Hyde's—'

'You told him about Hyde. Made the bugger seem important,' Cobb offered, complacently running his hand across his neat, greying hair, then down the line of his jaw.

'Accepted. You're sure Hyde can't find anything – anything at all, aren't you?'

Cobb nodded vigorously.

'That place was gone through *expertly*. There's nothing there.'

Jessop glanced up at the clock above the fireplace, a starburst of copper and silver.

'What are they doing? They should have rung by now.'

'Wish you were there, mm?'

'Maybe. I'd like to turn the body over with the toe of my expensive shoe, yes . . .'

'Won't be much of it left!'

Jessop laughed, then snatched up the telephone from the table at its first ring.

'Jessop—'

'—running for the car now! He's in sight,' he heard. Cobb left the sofa and knelt by Jessop's armchair, craning to hear. Bromhead's voice was gaspy and excited with tension. 'He's there! Looking around . . . pulling the door open, getting in . . .' The breathing was audible to Cobb. Jessop's face was suffused with blood as if in some sexual climax. Beyond the window, late traffic slid homewards beneath the roped necklace of lights that was Battersea Bridge. Jessop's hand closed and unclosed on the leather arm of his chair. '—in the car now . . . Go on, turn the key. That's the two shots! Bound to go now – come on, *come on* . . .'

Jessop watched the clock as if it possessed a second hand, measuring the moments accurately in his head, aware of the passage of eight, nine—

'For Christ's sake, what's happening?' he bellowed, startling Cobb out of a trancelike attention.

'He's not moving—' Bromhead began.

'He's *suspicious*, you prat! He *knows*! Finish him off now – tell the marksman! Finish him *off*!'

Now—

The headlights of a second fire appliance glanced across him, enlarging his running shadow, throwing it like a gigantic target against a stained concrete wall. The car behind him shattered like matchwood under automatic fire. Then a bullet plucked dust from the wall near his head.

He winded himself against the corner of a wall, falling almost helplessly into its shadow as he heard another bullet whine away. The fire engine's siren had died down. He glanced back at the car. All its windows were empty, glass littering the pavement beneath the streetlight. He heard his own ragged breathing above the crackle of radios, the faint hubbub of those who had fled the fire. He was shuddering in reaction to the bomb beneath the car, the fifty-yard dash for cover. He had chosen correctly. The marksman had been on the far side of the car.

He glanced around him. A darkened alleyway of lock-up garages lay beyond the corner of the wall, and behind it the loom of a tower block, its lights fitful and undistressed by the blazing shops. Open space in the other direction. Beyond the garages were older, shabby terraced houses, as if the planners had become disaffected and abandoned the district to its decline.

Hyde, thrusting the pistol back into his waistband,

began jogging down the alleyway towards the cramped, twisting streets that lapped at the edge of the tower blocks and their scrubby open spaces. Pausing at the end of the alleyway, he heard a car somewhere close start up. Then, much closer, the footbeats of – one, two running men. A thrown shadow loomed then at once became cautious, the footsteps halting. He pushed away from the wall, careful of the fall of his own shadow. Slow footsteps cautiously followed, mouse-pattering noises as the two men moved in turn in quick, careful, robotic advances. People like himself, he admitted, as adrenalin exhilarated his body.

Two police cars and an ambulance whined along the narrow street towards the fire. Hyde crossed it in their wake, gaining the shadows of the terraced houses and the shelter of a parked van, before anyone emerged from the row of lock-ups. Opposite him was a narrow archway, leading presumably to the back of the terrace. A dog barked somewhere, unnervingly loud, fierce. Headlights slid over the van as a car turned on to the street. At once the two men emerged from the lock-ups and ran towards it with gesticulating arms and quick voices. A second car appeared from the opposite direction. He ducked into shadows beneath the archway and the dog, very close, barked an alarm to his pursuers. He tensed himself against the dog's assault, then heard its claws scratching at wire and a violent, slobbering growling near his hand. Moonlight showed him the pit bull's teeth, its eyes wide with glazed ferocity. It threw itself against its pen in an attempt to attack him. He heard the car accelerate and then, as it faded, the sound of running footsteps.

Light flooded over him as he was poised to swing his leg over a brick wall. He saw moonlight on what had to be water. A voice was yelling from an open window. Two figures were in the entrance to the archway. Hyde tumbled over the wall on to grass, old tyres, rubbish. A local accent cursed him and his pursuers; the dog sounded frenzied. Pigeons panicked softly with a confused rattle of wings in a wire enclosure. He rolled to stillness on an earthen path beside dark, sullenly gleaming water. A narrow strip of it, on the opposite bank of which were stunted, poor trees and the lights of a main road that curved away, leaving the district. A canal towpath. The scent of stagnant water, vegetation. As he got to his knees, he heard the noise of scrambling men, the madness of the dog. To his right, the canal curved out of sight, to his left it was swallowed, a hundred yards away, by the darkness under a bridge. A car roared along the main road, then screeched to a halt almost opposite him.

He began running along the towpath as he caught a shout behind him answered by a voice from the opposite bank of the canal. *Bridge*, he thought he heard before the car's tyres squealed as it reversed and swung its headlights towards the bridge that spanned the canal. It was racing him. There were two men behind him and one on foot on the other bank, struggling through a broken wire fence.

The car was mounting the bridge, headlights blaring at the night sky. Then it stopped and he heard a door slam. A figure was leaning over the parapet. He was twenty yards from the bridge, unlit but visible in the windblown moonlight, his shadow stumbling beside him.

'Here!' he heard excitedly from the man on the bridge.

'See him!' one of the two men behind him called back. There was cursing from the man on the opposite bank as he struggled through vegetation. He heard the noise of the car's idling engine like a withdrawn, impossible promise.

He stopped and fired twice, then ran on. His shots

evoked answering fire from behind him. Then he was in the darkness beneath the old brick bridge. Cool, dank chilliness and the scent of the water. The bridge was only yards wide and beyond it the canal curved dangerously out of sight. He could see only the end of a high wall pierced with broken windows. Above him, the car's engine continued to idle. Hyde slid his back along the arching brickwork, one step at a time. If he could get to the car, if he could only get to the—

—*second car.* He heard its approach, its gradual slowing on the road just beyond the bridge. Five of them, even six ... He shivered, as if his adrenalin had been siphoned off, leaving him empty. He must distract them—

Then he was running again along the moonlit towpath, eight, ten strides to the abrupt curve of the canal before the first shots cracked out. He felt light-headed with relief. The deserted warehouse loomed beside him, every window broken, the smell of damp and disuse filling his nostrils. Weeds as tall as himself in an open doorway. The canal sneaked away between gloomy, lightless buildings. They'd try to head him off at the next bridge—

—headlights flashing towards him as a car accelerated wildly between two warehouses across rutted concrete. The lights caught him like a rabbit, their glare hard as a blow. He ducked out of sight against the brick wall. Cold, musty air exhaled from an empty window frame. Two voices, urgently directing each other, called out to the pursuers on the towpath. Only moments now ...

He peered from the corner of the building, hearing the crackle of a car radio and someone's voice. The car's headlights flooded away to his right. Fifteen yards of concrete between himself and the vehicle. The driver was leaning against the door, the radio mike pressed like a poultice against his cheek.

'—be able to see him by now,' he heard from the mike.

'Caught a glimpse, then lost him,' the driver replied. 'He must be between me and you.'

He is. Fifteen yards, the driver alert. The car tempted like a fortune. The man's form was shadowy. He unpeeled from the car, straightening and reaching into his jacket. The mike banged against the door as he dropped it in fierce surprise. It was too far, too many strides—

—collision. Hyde wrestled the driver's arm above his head and the pistol exploded, deafening him. He headbutted the man, who was bulkier than himself, then struck his forearm. The gun rattled down the car. Might as well have shot the bastard in the first place, *his* gun had alerted them anyway. He hit the man in the stomach, then kneed him in the face as he doubled up. The radio mike was promising help. The car on the bridge accelerated. He heard footsteps. He let the unconscious man fall away from him, rounded the car and climbed into the driving seat.

He threw the car into reverse and the tyres screamed then gained traction. He swung the Vauxhall around and accelerated. The headlights flashed back from the canyon walls of the two warehouses, then the car bucked over a pavement on to an ill-lit side street. A thin cat scuttled away from his headlights. He turned on to another narrow street of terraced houses littered with parked cars. Then he stopped the Vauxhall and switched off the engine and the lights. Seconds later, a car flashed across the driving mirror and disappeared with a screech of tyres towards the canal.

Grinning, Hyde started the car, switched on the lights and accelerated. Two thirty by the dashboard clock. At once, he experienced an angry regret that he had lost perhaps half of the photographs of the murder of Kumar's home village.

But he still had the notebook . . . The Burmese, Win, that Syeeda Lal had spoken of, working in a hotel's kitchens. A friend . . . ? Should he stop the car, see if he could find an address in the notebook – or wait until the hotel opened in the morning—?

It was after three thirty before he found the address, by which time the exhilaration of danger – the luxury of escape – had dissipated. His nerves were like a collapsing electrical network, fitfully sparking, conveying minimal sensation. After he had parked the car and switched off the engine, he rubbed his face in a constant washing motion, as if to scrub away weariness.

The street was silent, dark, narrow as an alley. Grimy terraced housing fronted by patches of concrete was leprosied by the occasional onset of chequerboard stone cladding. He wound down the driver's window to the noise of a dog barking in fitful anguish and the creaking of a gate in the wind. The houses, behind low brick walls, were curtained as if to conceal expression. The moon was old, in company with the street. He wound up the window, got out of the car and locked it. Leaned against it as if for support, listening. The dog was snuffling now, the gate making the more constant complaint. Nothing else, except the hum of the traffic from the elevated section of the nearby motorway. Looking back down the street, from where it began to climb one of the few slopes of the city, he could see the aimless headlights rushing on.

He crossed the street and climbed over one low wall, almost stumbling on a garden gnome lying on its side like a drunk, still gripping its fishing rod. A cannibalised Ford Cortina stood on the concrete in front of the house's bay window. It was one of the stone-clad façades, an upturned chessboard in the moonlight. A light went on in an upstairs window across the street, but no one moved the thin curtains to look out. A stretching, weary, female figure was silhouetted. He looked away, as if he had been accused of voyeurism.

He checked the row of buttons beside the front door. *My Win.* Ground floor. There was little about him in the notebook except this address and the telephone number of the New Midland Hotel – *A Straits Royal Group* hotel, he reminded himself.

The paint flaked under his fingernails as he tested the windows of the bay. The wood seemed to shriek rather than murmur as one of the side windows moved upwards. Something fell quietly inside, perhaps a rusted catch. He paused, listening into the room, crouched by the slightly open window. Silence, the smell of stale cooking, stale sheets. The house, from its row of buttons and names, held at least three families, but only Win's name was opposite the ground-floor button.

Standing, he raised the window against its tired protests until he was able to step over the sill into the room. Through grubby, opaque net curtains that hung askew, the dull orange glow of a streetlamp showed him the outlines of the room. Its heaped furniture, the scrawls of the hideously patterned carpet, the reflecting rectangles of pictures hung on the walls and the screen of a television. He moved cautiously across the room, tiredness making him impatient and edgily angry. This man – Win – had known Kumar, Kumar had been interested in him. Kumar was dead ...

He opened the door and stepped into a narrow passageway. A staircase rose from it to the first floor, other doors led off it while a further door, half glazed, confronted him. Where would Win sleep? Would he be sleeping alone ... ? He drew the gun and pushed open the first door off the passageway. The smell of sleeping invaded the scent of damp and old plaster. A fetid atmosphere, the sound of quiet, regular snoring. Hyde listened for more breathing, studying the narrow room. A single bed against one wall, big pieces of old furniture, decrepit and out of scale with their context. The tall, narrow window letting in moonlight. The man alone in the bed.

Win had to be an illegal immigrant, or engaged in something that was illegal – drugs? – otherwise he wouldn't be hiding behind the meniality of washing dishes and mopping floors in a new hotel.

The moonlight fell on the pistol Hyde thrust against the man's temple as he knelt beside the bed. His left hand clamped on the man's mouth, his fingers immediately wet with the saliva of fear as Win struggled to open his lips.

'Win – listen to me,' Hyde whispered hoarsely, urgently. 'Feel the gun?' He pressed it harder against his temple. 'I won't fire if you agree to talk to me. Understand?'

Wide, terrified eyes in a dark face. A furious, open-eyed dreaming movement of the eyes. The moonlight shone on calculation, cunning, a feral awareness. You're no innocent washer-up, sport ... There was a wriggle of terror in the body, an impression which goaded Hyde. Win's head nodded like that of a doll as he acknowledged defeat. Slowly, Hyde released the man's mouth. Win at once tried to sit upright, as if he had no more than awoken. Hyde pressed him back on the bed.

'I'm a friend of Medhev – of Kumar, who's dead. *Murdered.* You knew he was dead?' The marionette nodded again. 'I'm looking for the people who killed him – I want them. Are you one of them?' The head shook violently on the crumpled pillow, like that of an invalid refusing death or comfort. His terror had increased at the mention of Kumar, and all sense of his safety had been snatched away. Kumar's fate foreshadowed his own. 'You're an illegal immigrant – don't bother to deny it! – and you're into drugs. Kumar knew that and I know what he knew. Understand?' The head continued to shake, as if to loosen itself from the pistol's adhesion to his temple. Hyde listened to the house around them. It remained silent. It might almost have been possible to hear Win's inward collapse. 'He came to you for *proof* that the hotel was a conduit for drugs, a laundry for the profits – right? *Right?* Like all the other hotels around the world – the one in Singapore. Is that where you met Kumar, in Singapore?'

He moved the pistol slightly, then thrust it into the taut throat. The sensation of the gun against his temple would have dulled, become less threatening. The body jerked as if surgeons were trying to shock it back to heartbeat. Then Win nodded. Hyde suppressed his sigh of relief. Felt the sweat chilly across his forehead and beneath his arms. The pistol twitched as someone stirred in the next room, beyond a thin wall.

Eventually, the coughing fit subsided into a groaned re-welcoming of sleep.

'Who sent you here from Singapore?' Hyde whispered. 'Who did you come over with?'

In Singapore, and in Macau, the casinos – which had to be the laundries for the drug profits – had been controlled by Chinese. He and Kumar had established that much. Burmese like Win, if trusted at all, were always in junior positions, like the Malays. Win must have come with at least one relatively important Chinese.

'A cousin—' Win began.

'Not *your* cousin.'

'No, a cousin of Mr Lim in Mandalay,' Win croaked. 'Sun-Chan. He is Mr *Lim*'s cousin . . .' He gobbled his throat clear of the fears that crowded it. 'He works at the hotel – he is management. It *enables* him, you understand?' Win had become confiding, calm. Shutting out present and future dangers by means of a studied explanation.

'Lim – and Sun-Chan, you say?'

'Yes, yes . . .' Hyde would go away, the voice suggested.

'And this Mr Lim – he's important, right?'

'Yes, yes—!'

'Heroin?' This time, Win merely nodded. 'Kumar knew all this?'

A flash of anger.

'Yes – I told him! He threatened me – like you – because I am here illegally!' Which was how Lim and his cousin kept control, naturally. 'Kumar was a fool!'

Hyde ground the pistol into Win's throat, making him splutter, groan.

'He's dead for it, anyway,' Hyde snarled.

'I will say nothing more!' Win announced, his wide eyes staring up at Hyde.

'Did Kumar approach Sun-Chan?'

'No.' Win had almost accommodated himself to the gun, to Hyde's presence. His imagination had left the cramped, moonlit room and encountered the Chinese, Sun-Chan and the more distant Lim, and become more profoundly afraid. Neither name had emerged from Hyde's own investigations. There would be little more to learn.

'Did this Sun-Chan have Kumar killed?'

'No—!' He did not know . . .' The man's body again began to wriggle with terror.

'Who did?'

The eyes implored. Win's ignorance of Kumar's murderer was certain and complete.

'But the hotel is used to import, distribute – the casino is the laundry?' Hyde insisted. Win nodded vigorously. 'But you know no *details*, right?' Again the furious nodding. He might, or might not know a great deal more. But he had come to regard himself as innocent of betrayal and would have to be hurt to provide anything more.

Hyde stood up slowly, keeping the pistol against Win's throat.

'Please—!' Win managed.

'They won't believe you didn't tell me everything, will they?'

He removed the gun and Win began to massage his throat, sitting upright as he did so. Eventually, he said:

'Did *they* kill Kumar?'

It would have been simpler – so *much* simpler – if they had. But they hadn't. Kumar was killed because of the photographs in Hyde's pockets.

'Maybe – maybe not. I shouldn't risk it, if I were you, Win. They might kill *you*.'

Hyde was already at the door of the room. The smell of old cooking seeped from the passageway. Then he closed the door behind him.

The taxi drew up some respectful yards from the huge portico of the Vanbrugh façade of Uffingham. Marian got out of the grubby, five-year-old car and paid the driver. As the Sierra returned down the sloping drive from the house, Marian looked out over north Warwickshire, across the lawns and paddocks towards farmland. And was strangely disconcerted. The autumn sunlight seemed to fall as if by formal arrangement on the house and its blackbird-strewn lawns. The rhododendrons appeared dusty with age, solemn and dark like the trees and the yew hedges. It was as if the house and its immediate grounds had withdrawn into a formal decrepitude, an acknowledgement of age that rejected the country around it. Uffingham had never appeared so aloof and withdrawn before, not even when she had been a child.

Then she saw her father standing beneath the portico. He had rung her early that morning, inviting her on his own and Clive Winterborne's behalf to lunch. *Have to be in London, but I've time for coffee – apologies all round . . .* The columns of the portico seemed to diminish her father's tall, spare figure. Why did she have this unwelcome impression of the house where she had known nothing but happy times? And why did it persist, making her reluctant to cross the gravel to Giles?

The morning was still autumnally cool as she moved towards her father, disguising her slight limp. *Daddy's best girl . . .* Giles pecked her warmly on both cheeks. Even as he embraced her, the mobile phone trilled in her handbag.

'Excuse me, Daddy—' It was Patrick Hyde. 'Where *are* you?' she blurted.

'Back in London.'

'Why—?' She felt angrily excluded. She'd mopped up behind his over-solicitous conversation with Syeeda, dried her tears and sent her home. And lain sleepless in the darkness of her bedroom, smoking and staring at the moonlight sliding across the ceiling – because she had felt left out. It was as if a salesman had interested her in something only to tell her his stock was sold out. 'What's *happened?*' she demanded. 'Hyde,' she whispered to her father. 'Did you find anything?'

'Yes. But don't tell the girl – OK? I've arranged to meet Aubrey and Tony Godwin, someone from the old days . . . so they can look at what I found in the flat.'

'What was it?'

'Not drugs. He had something else – which was what got him killed. Photographs. His village in Burma, I think.

CRAIG THOMAS

Wiped out by the army. A mass grave, the works. They're building a dam there—'

'Oh my God,' she breathed. 'A *massacre* . . . ?'

'There are at least seventy bodies in one picture.'

'Where?'

'I don't *know* where!' he snapped back, as if she had attempted to appropriate all outrage to herself. 'That's what I'm hoping to find out. From Aubrey and Godwin or someone they know. I need to know. It's why I'm telling you.' There was a pause, then: 'Sorry. They got close last night—'

'Are you all right?'

'Just. I went to see Win, too. He didn't know anything of any use to us. Can you get on to this? You've got contacts in Burma, and here. There can't be hundreds of dams being built there right now. If we can pinpoint the location—'

'Yes! Yes, of course! But – I mean, you're *sure?*' Giles hovered with an anxious patience near her. Curiosity lit his eyes so that they gleamed like those of a bird. 'That *many?*'

'Yes. And the army did it. One by one, then tipped the corpses into the fresh grave. You know the routine.'

'Yes . . .' she breathed, realising that she was leaning her suddenly slumped weight against her father. 'I – I'll be in London this afternoon. I'll get started on . . .'

'Sorry to hit you with it. But someone knew he knew. They may already think *I* know. We don't have a great deal of time.'

'I'll get on to it!' she heard herself shout, her voice as raw as those of the rooks that lifted out of one of the tall, dark trees, as if startled by her.

Clive Winterborne, almost as tall as her father and as old, was similarly alarmed as he stepped from the main

186

door. Sensing her weakness, Clive took her arm, relieved her of her briefcase.

'What is it, my dear?'

She attempted to speak and found her throat clogged. There was wetness on her cheeks, too. It was as if she was looking into a mirror, seeing Syeeda's features and her grief, while her own self-awareness merely aped the outburst. Except she was in tears. She sniffed loudly, wiping furiously at her cold cheeks.

'Sorry, you two...' Then she experienced a hot anger. 'It was Patrick Hyde, on the mobile. He's found evidence of an atrocity in Burma. A *whole village*, just – wiped out.' She shrugged, as if helplessly demanding an answer. 'It's absolutely bloody *appalling!*'

Her father shuffled her into the house, his arm around her shoulders. He clasped her against him, as if he had been remiss in his efforts to protect her against knowledge of the world. She squeezed his bony elbow in response.

'Can't protect me, Daddy. You used not to try.' She forced herself to smile – a rictus that became genuine at the appearance of Alder. He was standing, at first welcoming and then slightly bemused by her manner, between the two matching Daniel Quare longcase clocks at either side of the high arch.

'Hi – are you all right?' He moved quickly to her and Giles relinquished his hold. 'What's wrong?' he asked in a voice that might, in a less charged situation, have sounded theatrically over-concerned.

'Nothing... Just some bad news. About Burma.'

'They won't put the Lady under house arrest again, whatever the papers say—' He broke off, as if he had committed some blatant indiscretion.

'It's not that!' she snapped. 'Sorry... it's just the reason that boy was murdered. You know – Kumar. It wasn't drugs at all.'

'We're in the morning room,' Giles murmured. 'Come and tell us.' He ushered Marian and Alder towards the door of the south-facing room. The sunlight gilded elaborate plasterwork, roused the sullen colours of old, precious furniture.

The shock of Hyde's information rumbled more distantly through her, like a retreating storm. She began to be angry, even at her own tears, as if she had been the victim of an unthinking response to a graphic piece of newsfilm. Her fitful concern for Burma seemed expressed mockingly by her immediate reaction.

'All right now,' she announced. Alder pressed her hand as she smiled at him.

Then she saw Ralph Lau, standing at one of the tall bay windows. He turned to her, his smile lagging a moment behind his hard, certain dislike. There had always been an antagonism between them she found difficult to describe. Her reaction, when they had first met years before, had been narrow, almost housewifely. *I don't like you, Ralph Lau* . . . He was colder than David, who still had clinging to him scraps of Buddhism, bits of the Empire, Uffingham and public school. Lau, by contrast, seemed to possess no baggage whatsoever, not even something more narrowly and alienly Chinese. As he was against the light now, somehow transparent and shallow, so he had always seemed to her.

She held out her hand to him. He shook it perfunctorily, murmuring her name as if it were that of someone an aide had introduced to him for the first time. Clive was pouring coffee at the long, breakfront sideboard. Lau seemed to be studying her, then he turned away with what must have been calculated indifference to continue staring out of the windows, with that air of containment and focus that distanced him from others. Like his clothes, his manner and conversation were simply *worn* for the occasion. He dressed in a Western lifestyle, but remained wraithlike and unknowable beneath it.

Clive handed her coffee.

'Now, my dear – what on earth is the matter?' he asked, smiling.

Alder was perched protectively beside her. She luxuriated in his concerned proximity.

'It's – just the shock,' she explained. 'The death of that boy, Kumar. It seems it was nothing to do with drugs. Patrick Hyde found evidence of what amounts to an atrocity by the army.'

Lau flicked at the corner of eyesight for some moments after she began her brief account, then the window seat where he had perched seemed empty. Alder's hand patted hers, her father's features relaxed into composure and pride, Clive remained attentive. She became calm, forgetting Lau, the unknowable man she had once described to David as someone who employed real life merely for the purpose of distraction . . .

. . . Lau paused for a moment in the staircase hall as if studying some new meaning in the chequered pattern of its black and white tiles. The two clocks struck the hour, one lagging slightly after the other, as he crossed to the door of the library. He closed it and turned the key behind him. Only when he had done so did he seem to himself to exhale for the first time since leaving the morning room. His hands clenched involuntarily into fists, so that he experienced a difficulty in freeing his fingers to dial the number he required on his mobile phone.

'Jessop!' he hissed as the call was answered. 'Listen to me, and listen very carefully. You're *not* dealing with my cousin. Hyde is not only still alive but he has found something – evidence that you assured me did not exist! Don't *interrupt*–! He has passed that information to Marian, who has cried to great effect on learning it and is now regaling the morning room with details ... Your problems mount, Jessop. Not only Hyde but now the woman, too! Do you understand me? The woman *and* Hyde.' His free hand was quivering with the pressure he was applying to his fingers as he pressed them down on the leather surface of the eighteenth-century desk in the library's huge bay window. His fingers ached, but he would not release them. 'I expect speed and subtlety, Jessop. Arrange it!'

Hyde was seated on the opposite side of Godwin's desk, the phone dragged close to him.

'Listen, Evans, you Welsh windbag–' Colin Evans, in Kuala Lumpur, chuckled with an almost childlike delight. It was the pleasure of returning to their mutual past that Godwin, too, had displayed the moment Hyde had entered his office. 'I know it's not your usual beat, but this guy has to be important. Yes, L-I-M, Lim. No, no other name, but he's evidently a middleman in Mandalay. Can you find him for me, soonest? OK, thanks, Colin. Hear from you–'

The moment he put down the receiver, Godwin leaned across his desk and pulled the phone towards him, dialling immediately.

'*Economist* – Ray Cooper's extension, please.' He winked conspiratorially at Hyde. 'Ray – how's things? Yes, Tony Godwin – and yes, a favour.' He laughed. 'Burma – part of your territory. Dam projects – just those already under construction. Oh, and with an airport being built next door. Need the exact location – quick as you can.

Thanks, Ray – I owe you.' He put down the telephone and rubbed his hands together, as if anticipating a celebratory meal or a present. 'Won't take long. Ray Cooper's top-notch on South-East Asia. He'll dig into the magazine's files for us and come up with the possible sites . . .'

He was silenced by the photographs on the desk between himself and Hyde. Kenneth Aubrey, perched on the edge of his chair, was studying them sombrely. Eventually, Aubrey cleared his throat and murmured:

'I can see no obvious connection between heroin and – this . . .' He gestured at the snapshots. An autumn wind splashed rain against the wall-length window of Godwin's office overlooking the murky river. The old man sighed. 'Evidently Burmese army, so presumably with the direct instruction or at least connivance of Rangoon and the junta. But this would seem to be some infrastructure project. Important to Kumar because it was his *home*.' He tapped his walking stick impatiently, his hands gripping it tightly. 'He was summoned home, he witnessed this, and continued to pursue it—'

Hyde was vigorously shaking his head, as if to loosen thought.

'No. *Win* was the connection. From Brum to Mandalay to this. Win is nobody, he doesn't know anything, except Lim's name. But he was drug-connected. So this and the drugs could be tied in one parcel.' He sighed. 'Maybe this construction work is a laundering operation, paid for by heroin profits. Maybe one of Winterborne Holdings' companies, like AsiaConstruct, is involved. You'll go with that, won't you?'

'Very well. For the moment. Tony?'

'I don't see why not, sir. Patrick knew this Kumar. If he'd seen *this*, then it's what he would have been following up. He might have tied them together, this and the heroin, only in his mind, I suppose – but we don't have any reason to think that.' He looked beyond them at the river, stirring his swivel chair. His sticks rested against the end of the desk. The river was a sludgy grey under quick-moving rainclouds. Vauxhall Bridge seemed something ropelike and insubstantial thrown hurriedly across the Thames. 'We need to wait for Ray Cooper to supply the background, as well as the whereabouts. Coffee, sir? Sorry I didn't ask earlier—'

'Please, Tony.' Aubrey got up arthritically from his chair and wandered towards the window. Rain splashed in another gout against the cold glass, which at once misted in a targetlike circle from his breath as he leaned close to the scene below. 'Our former service,' he murmured, craning to see the green and white modernist boast of Vauxhall Cross, SIS's new headquarters on the south bank. Beyond it, beyond Lambeth Bridge, Parliament seemed small and sodden in the murk of the October noon. 'And they *really* don't mind you engaging in private commissions, Tony?' He turned to look into the room once more.

Godwin adjusted the waistcoat of his well-cut pinstripe suit and grinned, rubbing a large hand through his thinning hair.

'Privatisation – that's the buzz-word, sir. Efficiency, budgets, profit, market share ... They're some of the others. We're on a somewhat looser contract here than under the old Section Two. We do work for other government departments, business – all sorts. Sometimes for retired agents whose chickens are coming home to roost.' He grinned in response to Hyde's tired scowl. 'I suppose they rely on the fact that as I've been about for years, I don't tell a property developer which government buildings are coming up for sale or an arms manufacturer which is the lowest tender.' He shrugged. 'You won't have to twist my arm, sir, to use the office computers after hours, if that's—' There was a knock on the door. 'Come!'

A bearded, youngish face appeared round the door. He had been introduced to Hyde and Aubrey as Kevin.

'Sorry, Tone – no joy with that smart card you gave me. The codes have already been changed in the computer.' He shrugged. 'They must have been expecting us to try.' He crossed to the desk and flipped the card on to its surface, murmuring, 'Looks nasty, that,' at the splayed snapshots, then left the room. Godwin picked up the card that Hyde had supplied from the wallet of the man he had shot.

'That's that, then. John Raymond Dilkes. One of us, turned off by another one of us, and his smart card cancelled. What an epitaph.'

'So, it won't get us into the International Security Consultants' computer any longer?'

'Dilkes has been dead for ten hours. Give Jessop and his pals credit for some sense!' The access codes for the ISC computer had been stored on the card and unearthed by Kevin. Too late to matter. 'Still, what larks, eh!' Godwin added breezily. The telephone rang. He was still grinning as he picked up the receiver. 'Hello, Ray. That was quick, even for you – what news?' He shuffled a large pad towards him and fumbled a pencil into his fingers. He listened and scribbled, occasionally asking for the spelling of a Burmese name. Hyde removed a map of Burma from his pocket and began spreading it like a colourful shroud over the scenes of the atrocity. Aubrey hovered, leaning on his stick. 'That it – the lot? OK, thanks, Ray. Owe you lunch – cheers!'

He studied the list of places he had written on the pad, then turned it away from him so that his companions could read them.

'There you are, gents. Four dam projects already under construction. A couple more being discussed or tendered for, but these are the only ones being built at the time of—' He tapped the map, indicating the snapshots beneath it.

'How's Dubček?' Hyde asked as he matched Godwin's handwriting to locations on the map.

'Fat and old. I've got him a companion – President Havel, a tabby. How are your two?'

'They're at the flat.'

'You going to take them back to Oz with you?' Hyde made no attempt to reply, seeming instead to make a greater effort of concentration on the map of Burma. The pencil he had snatched from Godwin traced its way down the course of the Irrawaddy towards the Gulf of Martaban, then ascended the map again, as if he were engaged in snakes-and-ladders, until he found another location. 'Oh, the coffee—!' Godwin spoke into his intercom, ordering coffee and biscuits, then adding: 'Get a French three-course, with wine and fizzy water, set up, will you, Janice? Oh, about half an hour.' He looked up and confronted Hyde's ashen features. 'What is it?'

The pencil was poised like an arrow striking a place on the map. The north-east of the country as far as Godwin could make out.

'Patrick—?' Aubrey murmured, leaning closer.

'There,' Hyde breathed, releasing a palpable tension.

Godwin strained forward in his chair, hunching towards the map. They leaned together like men inspecting a diamond.

'There's an airport in the photographs, too. Dams don't need *airports* . . . resorts do, though. It's there. Shan state, edge of the Golden Triangle. North-east of Mandalay. That place – *there.*' The point of the pencil broke. 'Kumar's village was the site of a new resort. That dam's for an artificial lake – water sports, that stuff. The airport's for the anticipated tourist flights.' He paused, then added in a strained, hoarse whisper that sounded as menaced as Win's voice in that moonlit bedroom, 'Ros is there at the moment. Ros – she's *there*, now.'

CHAPTER SEVEN

Iphigenia at Aulis

'... try to imagine the area over which our aircraft came into land as a *lake*, and you'll begin to understand why we at Straits Royal Group think we have a real winner in this new resort complex...'

The group MD of Straits Royal gesticulated with enthusiasm towards the panoramic windows of the hotel's main lounge, then towards the elaborate, gleaming scale model that filled the centre of the huge room where the cocktail reception was taking place. A violent, quick Burmese sunset burned beyond the glass, the dust-reddened sun setting behind the curve of the new dam and glancing from the terminal of the new airport. The scale of the place stunned Ros, almost as much as her tiredness after the flight from Singapore. Bruce Pearson, Australian like herself and a salesman to the bone, continued to wax lyrical. Ros was inattentive except for her studied expression of enthusiasm.

'... our guests will have that first view of Tripitaka as they come in low over the lake – nothing less than a glimpse of Eden, as I'm sure you'll agree, ladies and gentlemen...'

Tripitaka. A Buddhist word meaning the Three Baskets of Ultimate Things. It was a clever name for the resort. It would amuse Hyde – sourly, of course. She glanced from the glare of the sunset to the large model, standing on a stilted table, then back towards the panorama. From the aircraft on final approach, the place had seemed to stretch for miles. Green liver-spots on the brown swathes of landscape were entire golf courses. New or diverted streams and rivers were little more than snail trails. There was a clump of forest that remained as a nature reserve, where the mountains climbed away to the north and east, beyond the manicured resort. There were yellow and scarlet excavators and earthmovers, toylike, everywhere. *Tripitaka*, the basket of ultimate luxury. A safari area miles in extent, complete with overnight lodges – tigers were to be imported. It would, at least, keep a dozen or so of the creatures safe.

The casinos and hotels – the money generators – were skeletal as yet. Scaffolding and giant cranes were everywhere. From one aspect Tripitaka was a vast building site; from another a jungle. To create it, a number of villages had been razed, their small populations moved elsewhere. There had been much play made by Pearson of the sensitive nature of the rehousing. There was even a picture in the thick, glossy brochure that reassured.

Pearson's voice was drowned behind the noise of an excavator trundling past the panoramic windows. *AsiaConstruct* was blazoned on its flank. Winterborne Holdings' major subsidiary, the construction company, was the principal contractor on the project. There were US and Australian, even Singaporean, logos, too.

Ros stifled a yawn as, half attending to Pearson, she covertly inspected the décor of the lounge. So far, only the hotel in which they were staying had been completed. The décor was Westernised Burmese – an obvious scheme, incapable of frightening the first tourists – but the design company had padded the final account and SRG had fired them. Pearson was known to favour Australian companies ... She glanced around the reception. Tessa and Noreen were doing as she was herself and studying the room's décor, while John was whispering into a tiny recorder. Ros felt an excitement. They'd be working most of the night in her suite, tinkering with and adjusting the fine detail of the scheme that seemed to have impressed Bruce Pearson in Singapore.

There were other design teams, from Oz, America and Europe ... landscape designers, golf tournament promoters, wildlife park experts, the heads of the big travel companies, a scattering of media people and feature writers.

Noreen passed her and whispered:

'In the bag, Ros – with a bit of work!'

Ros stifled her grin. Their designs were good enough, sufficiently Burmese to be exotic while reassuring Western perceptions.

'... want *you* to join us in this adventure,' Pearson was saying, 'which is why you've been invited at this early stage. We want your input to help make Tripitaka what it can become, that glimpse of Eden I referred to ...'

There was a small, high noise from her handbag which attracted the smirking curiosity of two sleek-suited men near her. She spilt some of her champagne as she fumbled to reach the mobile. It had to be Hyde, and *now*—! Christ,

talk about embarrassing! The two golf tournament promoters, glossy with drink and rescented with expensive
aftershave, seemed to see her as a *woman*, and dismissed
her.

'Yes,' she whispered hoarsely. 'It's not convenient,
Hyde!' she added as she heard his voice. She moved
towards the doors of the lounge, away from the crowd
that had gathered close to Pearson on his platform.
'You're like some old mother hen, Hyde! I'm looking a real
prat— What? Yes, of course I'm *there*. In the middle of the
spiel. I'm supposed to be all attention—'

'Ros, just shut up and listen to me,' she heard.

'OK – what is it now?'

She felt hot, but largely and thankfully unnoticed,
hovering just at the rear of the gathering. The tip of the
setting sun was still visible above low hills, and she
responded to it with a sense of triumph. The design theme
of the re-created hill-station atmosphere *would* work.
Hyde was instantly more tiresome than ever.

'I – look, don't ask me why, but I want you to get out of
there as quickly as possible—'

'You must be joking, Hyde! This is *business*. I'm not
budging from here. What the hell is the matter with you?'

'For Christ's sake, Ros—!'

'No. People are *looking* at me, Hyde – they're not taking
me *seriously*.'

The sun was gone, leaving the hills golden for another
moment before they purpled. The vast site stretched
away towards the mountains. Ros was painfully aware of
her posture, her *opera buffa* whisperings.

'All right,' Hyde said. She heard his reluctant sigh
clearly. 'Kumar is dead – the boy from Singapore? He was
killed over here, but died because of the place where you
are. It was his village. He saw the inhabitants murdered

and the village destroyed. The people who did it know that *I* know. They want me dead. They know about *us*, you and me. Now, for Christ's sake, get yourself on a plane, train or ox-cart *out* of there!'

She felt stunned, ossified by what she heard. The site retreated into a quick tropical darkness and she felt icily cold in the warmth of the room. Then John was standing beside her, his face puzzled, concerned.

'You all right, Ros?'

She heard Hyde ask: 'Is that John? Put him on—'

'No, Hyde! I'll – I'll talk to you later. *Later.*' Savagely she switched off the mobile and thrust it back into her handbag, her body quivering.

'You should *not*—' Aubrey began, but Hyde's baffled glare stifled the remainder of his observation.

'*Listen*—!' he snarled, then, shaking his head, he walked towards the rain-splashed window, his hands raised above his head, the fingers clawed as if he was about to explode. 'I had to *tell* her! There are people like Jessop involved, people who know who she is!' He turned to Aubrey and Godwin. 'What the hell *else* could I do? You know how bloody stubborn she is! I didn't have anything else to work with . . . And now she's turned off the bloody mobile!'

Tony Godwin experienced what, in lesser circumstances, might have been embarrassment. He had never seen Patrick Hyde so – agitated.

'Anyone could pick her out, at any moment. Someone taking care of security there, someone who worked for the service, or who's been briefed on *me*.' He glowered at Aubrey. 'What do I do – go out there and drag her away?'

'Patrick, calm down a minute,' Godwin offered tentatively. 'You're not thinking like—'

'What? Not like *what?*' Hyde snapped back. 'Not like a

field agent? I'm not a fucking field agent any longer!' he raged. 'This isn't an op, it's *Ros*!'

'Patrick!' Aubrey barked, his voice as calculated as that of an actor. 'You exaggerate.'

The silence was tense between them, with something like inflexible indifference on Aubrey's part, hatred on Hyde's. Godwin looked at the small, indecisive figure against the rainswept Thames and the vast city beyond the river.

'I used Ros once before, in India – for Shelley. In an op. I swore I wouldn't do it ever again.'

'You're not using her—'

'But she could be recognised – don't you understand that?' There was appeal and a sliver of respect in Hyde's voice. He shook his head. 'I don't give a shit about who's after me. I can't let this happen . . .'

'Jessop and his people are in London – or in Birmingham. You've no cause to suppose—'

'*One* pair of eyes, that's all it needs—'

'You should not have told Ros—'

'All *right*! I made a mistake . . . I wasn't thinking. But what do I *do*?'

'How long is she supposed to be at this resort site?' Godwin asked carefully. Hyde merely shrugged his ignorance. 'OK – look, I'll get blow-ups done of the photographs. Have a good look at them – and make sure we're talking about the same place. The computer can come up with a terrain map, if we feed enough information into it from these.' Godwin gathered the snapshots into his large hands. To Hyde, they appeared to be a collection of playing cards after losing a hand. 'She's obviously not on her own. Call her again – later – and warn her not to be alone. Try to backpedal a bit, but make her cautious . . .' Aubrey was nodding vigorously towards

Hyde, his expression parentally firm. 'If you want to go and pull her out, you need all the information and back-up you can get.' Godwin paused, awkwardly shifting his bulk in the leather chair.

'Am I going to get help or not?' Hyde challenged hotly.

'Not like *this*,' Aubrey interjected, his voice at odds with the liver-spotted, arthritic hands that clutched each other on his stick. 'Not in this unsafe way, Patrick.' There was a chill of concern at the pit of Aubrey's stomach. He had to calm Hyde, and think for him. 'There is only one safe way, for you and for Ros. We must know more about – *that*.' He sighed as if exhausted, as he looked at the photographs in Godwin's hand.

'I haven't got the time!'

'Then you must *make* time, Patrick!' Aubrey snapped, turning on him. 'You behaved unforgivably, *amateurishly*, towards Ros – as if you had forgotten everything of trade-craft . . . *No*. Don't protest. You cannot get into and out of Burma quickly enough. How long is Ros to be there? A day, two—? Now, *sit down*.'

Reluctantly, with the sulky response of a child, Hyde did so. The wind threw rain against the windows behind him, making his shoulders twitch.

'I'll get these blown up on the copier, for the moment,' Godwin announced. 'Then the computer can take them to bits later. We need faces, an exact location.'

'This way, we can ensure your safety, Ros's safety.'

'You just want to go after the big picture – I don't care about that.'

'What about Kumar and all the people dead in these photographs?' Aubrey urged eagerly. 'Seventy per cent of all the heroin in the United States originates in the Golden Triangle. Ninety-eight per cent of *that* heroin originates in Burma. Burmese heroin, so Alex Davenhill informs me, is flooding into Vietnam, India, China, Taiwan, western Europe. Laos and Thailand account for ten per cent of the world's heroin production between them, Burma for seventy-five per cent. The amount of drug money that is laundered each year is estimated at seven hundred and fifty *billion* dollars.' Aubrey sat back on his chair as if exhausted. 'The people who refine, transport and sell that heroin need projects as vast as this resort site, as the whole Mekong River project, to enable them to launder that much money. I have a dark suspicion that Ralph Lau has seen Winterborne Holdings through the disaster of David's trial and imprisonment by means of heroin.' Behind him, the rain threatened to obscure the river and Vauxhall Bridge. Parliament was invisible to Godwin, Millbank obscure. Aubrey's litany had seemed to draw the weather across the panoramic windows like heavy curtains. 'If you are going to that sorry place, Patrick,' Aubrey concluded, 'then you must go prepared.'

'So I can bring back proof – do something about the big picture?' Hyde snapped.

'Another set of snaps that match these would be a start,' Godwin offered, trying to dispel the stormy air in the room.

'Quite. It will keep *you* safe, and Ros with you. If Lau can be connected with that event, as the man responsible for the resort complex, then he will accept a compromise. Jessop and his dogs will be called off. For good.'

Hyde banged the desk with his fist, but said nothing, merely glowered at each of them.

Hyde was vengeful on behalf of Kumar, that much was obvious to Godwin. Appalled and outraged, as were he and Aubrey, by the massacre . . . But he was totally rocked and destabilised by the possibility of a threat to Ros. Godwin switched on his intercom.

'Janice, come in, will you? And how's lunch coming along?' He looked up. It was the old game; *their* game. At times, they'd even played it well, Aubrey, he and Patrick ... Olympic standard, just occasionally. 'You'll enjoy lunch, sir,' he promised. 'We'll have it in the boardroom.' He grinned, inviting a response from Hyde.

Godwin's secretary entered and he handed the tall, dark-haired woman the sheaf of snapshots.

'Sorry about the subject matter, Janice. Have them blown up as big as you can on the copier, then give them to Dennis for the proper treatment—' He paused as she studied the top photograph. The mass grave. There was a slight tic at the corner of her mouth where the first fine lines of middle age were emphasised. She absently flicked her bobbed hair behind her left ear. Then she merely nodded and left. Godwin shrugged. 'Not our usual line of work,' he murmured.

'It wasn't really *ours*, either,' Hyde commented.

'Nevertheless,' Aubrey replied, 'proof is life. We need *proof*, support for those photographs.'

'What about – Sir Clive Winterborne?' Godwin asked. 'I mean, what happens to him if all this gets out?'

'I'm sorry for Clive,' Aubrey admitted. 'After David's fall from grace to have to ...' He sighed. 'It cannot be helped. What I can keep from Clive, I will.' He turned to Hyde. 'Ingress. It will need to be diplomatic. We will have to bring Evans in. He can provide some form of diplomatic cover ... Wait!' His eyes were alight. 'Isn't there a DTI junket travelling to Burma in the next few days, in the mistaken belief that the junta are really democrats under the skin?' Hyde nodded. 'We might be able to get you out there in time to join them in some kind of official capacity. I'll have to talk to someone regarding the itinerary – Marian would know, wouldn't she? You will need to begin from Mandalay.'

'This middleman, Lim, he's in Mandalay,' Hyde offered.

'He and, doubtless, his private army. Leave Lim out of our calculation, at least for the moment. If you've got the cover to get into Mandalay, we can get you to the dead man's village. The resort site.'

Hyde's expression suggested he might at any moment double up with an abdominal pain. Then he nodded:

'All right. It's the only way. Let's get on with it. I'll call Ros again, try to play it down. You're right. She won't be there long, will she? The chances of her being recognised are slim, right? Hundred to one.'

Mozart – the slow movement of the clarinet concerto – was being piped through the lobby and out on to the hotel terrace. Huge moths seemed to drift on the music rather than on the slight, warm breeze. The sound and the moths were more calming than Hyde's second phone call with its unconvincing disclaimers and its fiction regarding the danger. Yet the beauty, the expectedness of Tripitaka at night, the big, warm stars crowding the high moon that illuminated the grey-white dam, all belied his first call and initial panic. This was not the place where something awful – *that* kind of horror – could have occurred.

Ros heard insects and nightbirds above the hum of conversation on the wide terrace. The vast swimming pool rippled gently, catching the hotel lights. She had spoken to Bruce Pearson, he had been warmly interested, seductively encouraging. Their formal meeting in the morning would probably be successful. There were noises of approval and champagne from most of the people who had flown up. The atmosphere lulled.

'Ah, here you are, Ros!' It was Pearson. He was towing a clutch of satellites in his orbit. A photographer snapped them, the flashlight dazzling, as Pearson put his arm around her and her own smile became as artificial as his. 'Excellent – great!' he enthused, moving at once to another embrace, another photograph.

She had met Pearson through her charity gala work perhaps two or three times before tendering for the Tripitaka interior design contract. He was so conventionally the business executive who had risen through sales and marketing to his present eminence that she had always divorced him from Hyde's paranoid suspicions of Straits Royal Group. She watched him promenade along the pool, gladhand or embrace, move on again. The normality of it all calmed her more than the stars, helped her to ignore Hyde. What had he said, anyway? *I jumped the gun. We can't pinpoint the site of the . . . Sorry, doll.*

Something like that. Perhaps he had meant it. She looked at her champagne flute and the approaching waiter. Another half-glass, then she ought to join the others in her suite. She let her glass be refilled. As the waiter moved away, she shook her head.

There *weren't* – couldn't be – a hundred bodies beneath the swimming pool or out near the dam. It was nonsense to think there were. This was a holiday resort, the biggest in Asia . . . People had been resettled, not shot. Tripitaka was already tamed, too much so for such a thing to have happened here . . .

The breeze blew along the platform of Coventry station as she stood opposite a hoarding proclaiming *Shakespeare's County*. Alder hovered near her, as if she might call for the support of his arm or voice at any moment. It was inhibitingly touching, his concern. He had offered to return with her to London from Uffingham and his voice had held promise, anticipation. In his company, Marian once again envisaged a mutual future.

'I'll – just call Hyde, before we catch the train,' she announced, fishing in the pocket of her violently scarlet coat as it billowed around her in the gritty breeze which promised rain. He looked at once mistrustful, as of another lover.

'Jesus, Marian – must you? The guy's paranoid – you don't *need* it!'

She shrugged and dialled Hyde's mobile, moving away a few steps and half turning from Alder, realising he was offended that a stranger's tale was more readily believed than his own. *It isn't like that, Marian,* he had emphasised again and again at Uffingham.

The garbled voice of the station announcer offered them their train, courtesy of Virgin, in a few moments. Clive Winterborne had been sympathetically neutral, her father, distressed for her, was edgily fearful of her further involvement. He would, doubtless, talk to Kenneth to persuade him not to allow her continued participation.

Ralph Lau had been as dismissive as Alder – and apparently less interested. For herself, she now felt her shock and outrage to be born partly from habit, partly from instinct, and disliked the notion. Uffingham's grand calm had soothed and distanced.

'It's me,' she announced. 'Can you talk? Are you any further—?'

'Yes,' she heard, Hyde's voice angrily sepulchral. 'We know where it happened. Exactly.' She thought she caught a murmur from Aubrey, and another voice. Then Hyde obviously moved away from them in the room. 'It's a resort site. New.' He sounded tense. 'It's a Straits Royal Group project. It all has to be tied together. They're building the biggest laundry in Asia – clever, isn't it?'

She looked in alarm at Alder. The train, entering the station, slid towards them.

'You mean – Winterborne Holdings are involved?'

'*I* think so. Your godfather wants more proof.'

'They're involved – in everything?'

'Marian?' Alder prompted. The train was level with them, almost at a stop. Grit or something else made her eyes water. 'Come on—' Alder took her arm, steering her towards the first-class carriage.

'Look, Patrick – perhaps I can help. There are people I know. Tell Kenneth, will you? I'll meet you – must go!'

Alder thrust their bags into the luggage hold and began walking her to a non-smoking seat. She glowered at his prissiness and plumped herself in a seat in the other half of the carriage, folding her coat on the seat beside her. She placed her briefcase on the table between them. The watery sun vanished without protest behind driving grey cloud, and rain streaked the dusty window.

Alder, his blue eyes angry, his hands somewhere between exasperation and dismissal, said:

'Marian – this is getting obsessional! You're dealing—' He leant confidentially across her briefcase, his fingers drumming the black leather. 'These guys are ex-*spooks*. They see conspiracies everywhere!' She recognised the urgency of a politician seeking a vote, and bridled at it. Coventry straggled into its suburbs. 'It's been their preoccupation for so long they can't think in any other way. Why get mixed up in it?'

The train passed a garage sited almost at the gates of a large municipal cemetery. There were council estates beneath the dark sky. As she lit a cigarette, Marian said:

'There are *photographs*, Robbie.' He seemed pained, as at a blow. 'The boy who took them is *dead. Is* that paranoia?'

'It's all tied up in too neat a package!' he protested, watching a herd of cows on a sloping green field. Marian saw the blur of a rabbit. 'You're making it out to be – what it needn't be. The dead guy – he was anti-junta, right? A journo, a radical. Why believe everything you hear?' She waited for him to fold his arms in housewifely triumph, so convinced was he of his own rightness.

Blowing out smoke exasperatedly, she surprised herself by bursting into laughter.

'Robbie!' she chided. 'I'm not seeking to embarrass or accuse!' Her expression became more sober. The rain shower had been left behind. Sunlight gleamed from car windscreens on a country road. 'But I can be of use here – if there is something in this.'

'Marian,' he urged, 'you say there are photographs. But *you* haven't seen them. Is there any guarantee they're not faked? Any other proof?'

After a silence, she murmured: 'No. Not as far as I know.'

'Then ask to see some proof. If it was all true, it would be dynamite. But it may not be true.'

She remained silent as his smile wooed her into compliant doubt. The sun gleamed on pastureland. It *was* difficult to believe – or too horrible to accept.

'What does this guy Hyde intend doing with these snapshots?' Alder asked.

'What—? Oh, I don't know, Robbie. I really should ask him, shouldn't I?'

Alder's expression was tantamount to alarm, discomforting her. It was as if he regarded her as a lunatic. Something dangerous, anyway—

Hyde glanced at his watch. Four thirty. The rain had stopped but the sky remained leaden. The lights in Godwin's office were brightly warm. Beyond the windows, London was thrusting itself into early evening as lights sprang out. The scene was some sort of relief after poring over the huge blow-ups of Kumar's photographs.

Aubrey dropped the boy's notebook on to Godwin's desk and stifled a yawn before pressing his hands to his eyes. The gesture lifted his spectacles to his creased, liver-spotted forehead. The poor remaining wings of white hair above his ears seemed more attentive than his expression. He shook his head.

'There is a great deal of guilt in that small volume,' he announced. 'I suspect that young Kumar *encouraged* the reluctance of the villagers to be resettled elsewhere. Some sort of stupidly brave defiance. He seems to feel that to have been the case ...' He was interrupted by Janice bringing in coffee. Her eyes carefully avoided the blow-ups that littered the carpet, an easel, the desk, a leather sofa near the windows. When she had gone, Aubrey concluded: 'There was very little description of what happened there. *Or* of what he was attempting in England. He seemed traumatised, at a loss. Perhaps he imagined connections, links? He implicates no one—'

'But he wanted to talk to Sir Clive,' Hyde retorted abstractedly. 'He must have believed in connections.'

'Giles Pyott believes in a god to whom I cannot subscribe. I can't just take his word for Him.'

'So – proof. We *know* that ...' He glanced again at his watch. 'Where's bloody Evans?' He glowered at Godwin, like a man delayed by a cancelled flight. 'And how long before we get that terrain map. I'll *need* it.'

'Tonight. Promise.' Godwin yawned. 'We already know where it is and how to get you there. Evans will come through with the papers and the technical resources. I can get the funny stuff in a Bag and out to KL the same time as you ...' His voice trailed away.

Hyde was obsessively studying one blow-up. Godwin stared out of the window. He hadn't noticed, nor had Aubrey. One of the photographs showed a line of kneeling figures, with a dozen or so bodies already in the pit. The dam wall was a blank edge to the enlargement, which was so big it was easy to see the expressions on some of the faces less bent towards the red earth. Resignation, blank trauma, terror. The face of the junior officer with the pistol – he was reloading it with a fresh magazine in the shot Hyde held upright on his knee – was fierce with nothing more than concentration. There was blue sky and distant hills behind him. Green jungle. Even the blur of a large, brightly coloured bird.

A senior officer of the Tatmadaw, the Burmese army, was supervising the massacre. Yet he was given inferior status – he seemed to be caught in a moment of deference, even apology – by the presence of a Chinese. Small, soldierly in his still authority, even though he wore an anonymous civilian suit. Middle-aged. Hyde could not decide whether he was a heroin producer – most of the drug lords were Chinese – or something else.

There was a white face; just one. Hard to tell even that much. In half-profile, light-coloured hair that might have been prematurely grey. Tall, youngish figure, turned away from the scene as if in anguish, yet without the freedom or authority to leave or protest.

Aubrey's eyesight was misty with age. Godwin didn't know the man. Both of them were interested in the *where* of it, anticipating that it was the act of strangers. All of which explained their lack of recognition—

The phone on Godwin's desk trilled abruptly. Godwin snatched it up and Aubrey became alert at once.

'Hi, Taff – how goes it? Hang on, I'll put you on the speaker and we can all chip in – there.'

Evans's lilt gushed into the room, expelling the atmosphere of strained, enclosed tension that had possessed them for hours.

'Fine, Tone – just great! Take a couple of days, though. Sorry about that, you Aussie bugger, but this sort of thing takes time!' Then he seemed to recollect Aubrey's presence, adding: 'Sorry, sir.'

'No matter, Colin. Can you put Patrick on the strength, allow him freedom of movement – at least as much as anyone in the DTI party?'

'Yes, sir. I thought he ought to be someone from the Embassy in Bangkok. Less chance of someone knowing he's not kosher. We can get him into Rangoon from Bangkok on the daily flight. I'll be there to meet him. Getting what he'll need into Burma is taking the time. Light aircraft, of course – but I can't get hold of a pilot I can trust until tomorrow. Before then, *you* decide *where*, and I'll line him up. Oh—' He seemed embarrassed. 'Sir – small matter of funds, sir. I can divert—'

'Not to worry, Colin. I think I can still remember the whereabouts of a few forgotten numbered accounts.' Aubrey chortled.

'Great! Nothing else for the moment, then, sir. I'll come back to you via Tone.' Chuckling himself, he added: 'Up all night, eh? Just like the old days. Cheers!'

Hyde looked up from the photograph of the massacre, the frozen moment of reloading, a pause in the executions. Merely a pause of machinery. He suppressed the insistent awareness that Ros was at that same place, perhaps within hundreds of yards of the buried bodies, and disbelieving his lame reassurances.

'OK,' he murmured. 'Taff's got it under control. The DTI jaunt goes all the way to Tripitaka. Where I get off the gravy train. Fine!'

Aubrey studied him with what might have been suspicion, then returned his attention to the pad that Godwin had passed to him, studying the notes he had

212

made. Godwin, like some assiduous fellow-pupil, imitated Aubrey, checking the list of equipment Hyde had demanded and Godwin knew to be essential. He flicked his intercom.

'Janice – check up and see how that map's coming along, would you?' He glanced at Hyde, who had returned to his gloomy study of the blow-up he held with both hands. Getting him in was the easy bit, with false papers, embassy accreditation and the like. Getting his equipment in was relatively simple, too.

Getting him out again would be hard, with whatever proof he managed to obtain. Exactly matching photographs, physical evidence, witnesses ...? He saw Hyde nodding behind the blow-up as if in agreement, and lowered his eyes. It was *not* going to be easy.

Hyde relaxed his attention as Godwin lowered his head. He was certain now, fiercely so. But his certainty was no proof and if the picture was blown up any further the face would dissolve into dots, losing all identity. From what he held in his hands, no one would unequivocally confirm that the white man who had witnessed the atrocity was Congressman Robert Alder. No one – not Aubrey, not Godwin, and especially not Marian Pyott—

But he *knew* it was Alder.

Peter Grainger – the rat – had rung Marian on the train to cancel their meeting that afternoon.

She luxuriated in Robbie's presence in the flat, and in the anticipation of passion. Watery blue sky filled with hurrying cloud over the river and the Physic Garden; sunlight caught the flanks of glass towers.

Around him, she felt the flat had taken on the anonymity of a departure lounge, a momentary impression that confirmed so many feelings and anticipations. Because he was there, the books, the hi-fi, the pieces of old furniture were no more than images of a solitary life. It was as if they had absorbed the autumn outside.

More than anything, she feared inhabiting the flat for the rest of her days – feared the loneliness.

'Coffee?' she enquired brightly, making for the kitchen, hurrying away from the images of containment and solitude.

'Sure,' he murmured.

She lit a cigarette and plugged in the kettle. Spooned coffee into the cafetière. Sunlight streamed into the kitchen, bright enough to catch motes of dust and her hair at the corner of eyesight.

Even before the kettle had boiled, she sensed his presence in the doorway. She shivered involuntarily, with anticipated excitement. Quietly, like a seductive compliment, he said:

'I guess I don't want the coffee after all. You ...?'

'No.'

She turned to the fierceness of his mouth on hers, his hands sliding beneath her sweater, welcome, exciting. In the bedroom, quickly naked, the sun fell warm on her body and face and seemed to arouse him further. His lovemaking was almost desperate, as if he was burying all sense of difference between them.

'Come back with me,' she heard as he approached his climax, 'come with me, please! You *want* to – we can be together ...' His eyes were wide with pleading, effort. She felt herself coming. *Yes, yes* ... It was agreement to everything; his rhythm, urgency, future. Their future ... Yes, yes, I want to ...

She stared at the early evening beyond the window as he lay on her, his face in the pillow beside hers, his body repletely still. She continued to think the no-longer unthinkable. Returning with him to Washington.

'Did you mean it?' she asked hoarsely. Then humour erupted. 'I mean, about Washington, *us*? It wasn't just something out of a lifestyle magazine, was it – how to heighten your orgasm, or something?'

He roused from torpor and rolled on to his back. His grin was boyish, unsuited to the fine lines around his eyes.

'You and me, uh? Sounds OK to me.'

'Did you *mean* it?'

He leant on his elbow, searching her face.

'Do *you* mean it?'

'I — I'm thinking about it. *More* than just thinking ... Robbie, do you *want* it? I have to know.'

'It's great – just great.' His features were alight. The bedroom seemed smaller, more cramped. 'Look, no pressure, uh? You just *keep* thinking!'

She sat up in bed and lit a cigarette.

'I won't be able to give these up.'

He kissed her breasts gently, invitingly.

'I can't give these up,' he murmured, grinning. Then he touched her hair and cheek – before he appeared startled, clicking his fingers impatiently. 'Hell, what time is it?'

'What? There ... Only five thirty.'

'I have a meeting – at six! Look, I'll make a call, cancel—'

'No you don't! Not as my partner. Duty first, as Daddy would say – though, in this case, perhaps duty second.' There was an anxiety in her smile as she added: 'Will you come back tonight?'

'Sure will, ma'am – sure will! Dinner, too. I'll just— Can I use the phone, make a couple of calls?'

Marian nodded.

'I think I'll take a shower.' She got out of bed and stretched lewdly, invitingly. Then she laughed and hurried from the bedroom.

Alder listened for the hurry of water from the shower, then he went into the lounge and picked up the telephone. He sensed his face had collapsed like that of an ageing actor at the end of a too-long performance. He hesitated, then dialled.

Ralph Lau answered immediately, at the Eaton Square house.

'Ralph – it's me. No, she's in the shower – sure, just like in *Psycho*. But listen – it doesn't have to be the way you wanted! I can handle this. Marian and me – we're an item, or about to be. She's talking Washington, the whole bit. I can keep her preoccupied, keep it all under wraps ...' In the long, ensuing silence, he felt his temperature rising, until he seemed compelled to add: 'What do you think, Ralph?'

Lau's tone was as chilly as the last sunlight falling into the lounge, reflected as a dusty gleam by the television screen. Alder was immediately aware of his nudity, that he was Lau's creature. It was as if the voice he heard was itself fully clothed, assured by its absence of nakedness and vulnerability. His eyes glanced across the book-shelves, the CDs and LPs. He stared at her handbag and briefcase, neatly beside each other near the sofa on which he sat. He said in a pained, quiet voice:

'Hey, come on, Ralph – this can be *discussed*, can't it? I mean, there's nothing in stone, right?'

He stared at his thighs, his penis. The handbag. A single earring on the coffee table. He heard the running of the shower.

'For God's sake, Ralph—!' he blurted desperately. 'This can't be happening! There's no need – not now.' His closed hand was banging at his thigh as if to bruise it. It seemed defiant, unlike his voice. 'For Christ's sake—!' he pleaded.

'Ah – you love her, then?'

'I can *control* this—'

'*I* can control this, as you call it.'

The earring, probably Victorian and a great-grandmother's, shone on the table as the sun slipped down. His forehead was wet to his hand, cold perspiration ran from beneath his arms. The room smelt of her – he did. She was everywhere as he sat crouched on the sofa as if under interrogation or torture. Appalled at her scent, at their lovemaking. Horrified that the desire he had felt for her had enabled him to blot out all thought of Lau's whispered orders before he left Uffingham. Out of sex, love, whatever – even because of the train's rhythm, *their* rhythm – he had been able to ignore until now the terrible, immediate future.

Lau, Lau, for Christ's sake . . .

Then Lau was speaking in a level, chilling tone.

'Think of our actions as identical, Robert. When you were threatened, you reacted at once. I am merely taking the same course. You were once my cousin's man, now you are mine. The woman is dangerous to me and you are too involved with her to act as guarantor of her good behaviour.' Almost sightless with tears of self-loathing, Alder stared at the earring. He envied Marian the shower's cleansing. Her scent on his skin nauseated him. He was trapped . . . 'Now,' Lau was continuing, 'I am going to pass you over to Jessop, who will tell you the arrangements and your part in them. Goodbye, Robert.'

He opened his mouth but could not speak. He simply waited for Jessop's instructions. David, his previous god, had always promised; Ralph, his new deity, merely demanded, threatened. Alder had been passed to him like a present already opened and soiled.

'Right!' Jessop announced. The earring lost the sunlight and dulled. 'You have just over an hour . . .'

***

Hyde paid off the taxi two hundred yards from Marian's mansion block and walked casually down Flood Street towards the Embankment. The parked cars he passed were empty. Traffic was thick along the river and across the Albert Bridge. A young couple getting noisily out of a new BMW startled him.

The mansion block glowed with lights, a few cars drawn up on its shallow forecourt. Hyde kept to the shadows. The sky was inkily blue, almost cloudless. Marian was probably free of surveillance ... but there was Alder to consider now. Alder, coming from Lau's house in Eaton Square, standing blurrily in the damning blow-up. Alder had *been* there, he *knew*. Mass grave ... *Ros* ... He shut out all anxiety as it threatened to creep inside him. Another day and she would be away from there. *He'd* be there instead, digging for proof.

What if he tried to break Alder? The snapshot wasn't conclusive, not against a US Congressman's vehement denial and an MP's disbelief ...

... *there was Alder*. His appearance shocked like a nightmare. His tall figure was coming out of the main doors of the mansion block. Alder ... he hesitated, then hurried, as if unnerved. He passed a man, dressed in black, on the forecourt. Light fell on Alder's face. He hesitated again and appeared about to speak, even restrain the other man. The second man was confused, uncertain, and Alder seemed on the point of assault. Then his eyes looked beyond the man, and Hyde was certain he had been seen, even recognised. It was too late to seek deeper shadow.

Then, strangely, Alder nodded at the second man before he abruptly turned away towards a car drawn up opposite the block. The second man entered the main doors.

Alder was at the rear window of the car, his arms suddenly gesticulating, his voice raised. Hyde could not discern the passenger's features.

No buzzer, no key—

The man dressed in black had walked into the block's foyer through a door left open. Alder had hesitated at the door – being careful not to close it? He had seemed about to restrain the man, speak to him. *Alder watching the execution of an entire village—*

Hyde ran for the doors. Still open—

Open—

He paused in the foyer, disorientated. The light above the lift doors was winking on and off. Stairs – how many floors? Six, eight—? He reached into his waistband for the pistol. Christ, they were going to kill her—

—kill her. The thought was immediate to Marian. The man was there, in the warmly lit lounge, snatching up the silver pieces, rummaging in her handbag. She had heard noises, they had brought her from the kitchen.

'What – what are you doing here?'

Kill her. She knew in that instant before he picked up the heavy, art-deco bronze from the table in the window bay and moved quickly towards her. Black clothes, a ski-mask hiding his face. White hands, white teeth grinning in the mask. She could not move, her mind would not react...

The man lunged at her head with the bronze statuette. The other burglary, only the previous night, now this. Her head flinched aside and the bronze grazed her arm. Nerves and torn skin shrieked. Smell of food, drops of his saliva on her face. The hand she was moving to comfort her injured arm thrust out towards the grinning, foul ski-mask. Hot, vile breathing, her hand speckled with his blood. He screeched like a wounded cat, then his hands thrust her away from him. Wet, unseeing eyes, white grin. His body followed hers across the room. She waved her arms in front of her, off balance, to stop his attack. The coffee table overturned, making him stumble moment-arily, but he came on. Her calves collided with the edge of the sofa.

'No . . .'

He sprang at her, pushing her down, thrusting himself against her. The white hands tore at her blouse, then at her skirt, plucking it up along her thighs. Her knees attempted to reach his groin, her nails tried to tear at the mask, the eyes behind it. Drops of wetness from his mouth, blood from his nose, on her face. His white hand slapped her, blinding her eyes with tears. Then he gripped her around the throat. There was no arousal pressing against her, no prelude to rape, as if the assault was being acted out rather than committed.

He was straddling her now as she was pressed to the carpet. His hands banged her head like a doll's against the floor, while they squeezed, pressed, choked . . .

Black spots before her eyes, as if the mask had duplicated itself like an amoeba. More and more, bigger black spots, coming together in an area of increasing darkness. Blocking out the mask, the square of the window's evening sky, the room, the sense of his groin rubbing the stuff of her underwear against her as the man forced himself to an erection so that he could penetrate her . . . The throttling tightness of his hands, the sense of her own hands flailing like a poor swimmer drowning . . . His weight, his rage . . .

Swallowed by the black spots that had become a smear, then a black night—

CHAPTER EIGHT

Andromeda

Eighth-floor corridor. He was gulping air, bent almost double. He heard the noise of a TV, music from beyond another door. The air he gasped in was redolent of spicy cooking. Hyde had blundered into the ordinary and for a moment it disorientated him.

One door, at the end of the brief corridor, was open, and he ran to it. Ros knew which flat it was – *Ros* – he shook her image aside.

The latch of the lock was taped back. Insulating tape. The door had never been closed behind Alder. Deliberate. He raised his hands and thrust a round into the breach of the Heckler & Koch, then dashed through the hall of the flat to reach the door of what must be the lounge—

She was already dead. First thought. It was professional, disguised as burglary and rape, then murder. Hyde's boot crushed a tiny ornament that had been knocked to the floor, alerting the black-dressed hitman who was astride her body. Her thighs were flaccid and unmoving. The man could talk, someone had *employed* him. Hyde's crouch betrayed caution. The attacker rose to meet him, confident that Hyde would not use the gun, that his life was valuable.

Then Hyde threw his body into the attack, catching the black costume across its chest, his forearm striking just above the blood that had already made a target of the ski-mask. They fell together towards the window, the hitman's body bucking Hyde's over so that he collided with the radiator beneath the window. His breath vanished. He tried to roll away, but the black costume, on its knees then quickly upright, kicked out at his head. He jerked away. A second kick made breathing impossible as it caught him in the side. The costume kicked again. Hyde parried with the pistol, gagging for breath, cracking it across the man's shin. A thin scream, distant to Hyde as he concentrated on dragging in a long, slow, ragged breath ...

As he swallowed the first air, the Heckler was pointing at the hitman. The eyes in the ski-mask were no longer certain of their living value. Hyde realised he'd have to kill—

—running for the door, the black costume vanished in a moment. Hyde's lungs shrieked for air and he did not want to get up from his half-lying position against the radiator, near her body. He heard the hitman's progress through the hall, into the corridor, down the staircase.

Reluctantly, he crawled on his knees the few feet to her body, breathing stertorously over her, on to her face, as if attempting to revive her ... Her eyes fluttered open—

Immediately, he had to grip her hands as they feebly tried to fend him away.

'It's me – *me*!' he insisted.

222

Her eyes remained wide, startled, staring at the persistent nightmare. Slowly, as if she was re-entering the world and trying to recognise her surroundings, her gaze became focused. Her mouth quivered wetly. Then the mood snapped and she sat up with his help and at once tugged down her skirt. Began shivering violently. Hyde went into the bedroom and pulled the duvet from the bed. Wrapped her hunched, feverish body in it.

'Drink?'

Marian shook her head. Her voice was a croak, causing her to gently massage her bruised throat as she managed to say:

'Damsels don't swig brandy after the white knight saves—'

She collapsed into helpless, wrenching sobs that racked her body. One hand pushed flat against the carpet as if her only support. Hyde looked for the telephone and found it knocked behind the sofa. He dialled Aubrey's number, watching Marian as he waited for the old man or Mrs Grey to pick up the phone.

'It's me,' he said, hearing Aubrey's voice. 'Can you get hold of one of our discreet doctors—? No, she's OK ...' He studied Marian's hand, the rocking movements of her body wrapped in the duvet. 'She'll be OK, bruising mostly ... Gone, sorry. Yes, I'll wait—' He put down the receiver, then, moving slowly and reassuringly, sat cross-legged opposite her. 'OK?' Marian looked at him with a watery smile. 'Good.'

Eventually she croaked: 'The bastard! He was going to—'

'Kill you? Rape you?'

She nodded furiously, her face distorted with anger, loathing.

'*Did* he rape you?' She shook her head violently. 'This

223

was professional,' he offered, judging her response. If he could distance the attack, make it part of *his* world, it might help her. Yes. It must not be personal, not an attempted violation of *her*. 'I should have guessed, anticipated—' Already, she was shaking her head, excusing him from blame.

'I could do with a drink.'

'Where?'

'In the cabinet – there.' She pointed to a small Georgian bowfront sideboard, near the bookshelves. He opened one of its cellaret drawers and poured two balloons of cognac.

Marian coughed as she swallowed. Then swallowed again, more greedily. Sniffed, then wiped her eyes.

'I wanted to black out,' she observed. 'So I wouldn't—' The sentence tailed off.

He sat opposite her on the carpet once more. 'Good stuff, this. I've been offered it once, at your father's.' The idea of her father reddened her features, and she hugged the duvet closer around her.

'Why the rape ... ?'

'They wanted you dead, Marian. A hitman with an undocumented DNA profile. One of the old tricks, burglary and sex. Who'd be looking for anything else when—?'

She was shaking her head violently. Then she said angrily: 'Don't be so bloody knowledgeable! You don't know *what* it was like!'

But she knew he was right. He ought to take the tape off the lock. But it would look as if the attacker had done it, anyway, to aid his escape. After a pause, he said: 'Who have you been upsetting?'

Alder, he thought at once. But she wouldn't believe that in a month of Sundays, nor would Aubrey.

'Ralph Lau?' she replied. 'Saw him just after you phoned

me at Uffingham.' She appeared suddenly appalled and afraid. 'I told Daddy and Clive about your call – Ralph was *there*!'

Hyde shrugged.

'There's your answer. He probably called Jessop straightaway. All they had to do was wait until you were alone.'

'Why did I have to be killed?' she asked, her voice as innocent as that of a child. He could see the snail marks of fresh tears on her blotchy cheeks.

'For the charm to stop the Thracian wind,' Hyde replied, staring into the cognac glass. When he looked up, he saw the expected gleam of her intelligence, distracting her from herself.

'Iphigenia, you mean? This isn't a Greek tragedy. Ralph doesn't have a fleet to get to Troy . . .' Her voice tailed off, as she sensed the weight of the thing, the forces ranged against them. 'I suppose he does have a lot at stake,' she added quietly, 'if you're right.'

Hyde smiled as he said: 'You can see Ros drags me about to all sorts of things – how else would this ignorant Ocker know such an arcane quotation!'

Then, shivering with the renewed immediacy of the event, she asked: 'How did he get in? Robbie had only just left!'

'Lockpick, probably. Not difficult for a professional— You OK?' She was sinking into a lethargy of self-escape, forgetfulness. But she nodded vehemently, struggling against the draining effects of her trauma.

'Is he coming back – Alder?'

'Later.'

'Good.'

'What – what next?' she asked.

'Sorry?'

'Those bloody photographs!' she snapped hysterically. 'It's why they – why ... why–' She swallowed wetly, noisily. 'You believe them, don't you?' Hyde nodded. 'What will you do now?'

'I have to obtain proof – on site.'

'Burma? Why not go to the newspapers? It's what I'd do–'

She remembered Alder's mockery of Hyde and Kenneth. One was an ex-agent, the other his former spymaster. They would simply use the photographs to protect Hyde ... and herself.

Suddenly, that was too little, and too selfish. It did not even *begin* to be enough, their being used as a bargaining counter, to stop someone else trying to ... No, it wasn't enough. The photographs were too important, they could be used to really achieve something!

As if guessing her wild thoughts, Hyde announced:

'If you rang the *Times* or the *Torygraph* – even the fearless boy reporters on the *Guardian* – they'd all be terribly excited for about five minutes ... Then they'd remember the DTI will be in Rangoon, or some bank's huge investment in Asia, or one of a hundred other reasons to stall for time while they checked around for corroboration, asked permission – and finally got told to quietly bury the story as too embarrassing.' He grinned at her contempt. 'It's what happens. It *would* happen in this case. Kumar's dead, poor sod, and so are the people from his village. Even if anyone wanted it made public, we'd all be long dead by the time the story appeared in the papers–'

She was shivering now, seeing the threat to herself as more real than anything else. She was seeing the bloke in the ski mask, feeling his hands on her throat. Her face was ashen, her eyes wide with recollected and anticipated terror.

'God, I feel *sick!*' she blurted, climbing uncertainly out of the duvet's folds. 'Sick—' She hurried from the room. A moment later, he heard the noises of her vomiting.

Getting to his feet, he walked to the window. Long gone by now ... except for Alder. Would he come back, thinking she was dead? Or was he to be the one who discovered her body? Interesting that – and dangerous. Alder had agreed to her death, prepared the ground. And was still around ...

Marian could be told *nothing*, not now. At least, not until he could take care of Alder.

Of course Alder had come back. They'd have told him the hit had failed and Jessop would have sent him scurrying to Chelsea. *Cry a lot, blame yourself for not closing the door properly, lots of cooing* ... And he was so *good* at it, Hyde thought, standing in the bedroom doorway. Around the bed with Alder were Aubrey and Giles Pyott. The two old men coddled her with a fragile, naked demonstration of their affection and concern. Alder's relief cracked out along the fine lines around his eyes, as if he was a broken egg. Yet he remained Lau's creature, and still dangerous.

Thanks – I can only say thanks, for all of us ... Alder's words. His handshake had been dry and firm, his gaze penetrating in its examination. He'd glanced involuntarily at the door lock as Hyde had let him into the flat. For a nanosecond, they had known each other utterly, then had adopted their roles of the innocent and the unsuspicious. And yet there was that moment when Alder had seen him in the dark street ...

'Daddy – I'm *fine!*' Marian protested for perhaps the dozenth time, gripping Giles's old hand on the duvet. 'No, don't go yet – it's early ...'

Hyde turned away from the scene, which excluded him.

The low, warm lighting of the bedroom gave it the appearance of a religious painting. He wanted to hurt Alder. He poured himself another cognac and inspected the balloon as if for fingerprints. Marian hadn't even taken the sedatives the doc had left; she was all right. He looked at the gilt brass carriage clock on the mantelpiece as it struck eight thirty. The clock was painted with finches against brown, autumnal vegetation.

Even out of Alder's presence, the man remained his preoccupation. The two images of him – standing above a mass grave in Burma and almost pointing out the hitman in the street. In both, Alder was present at a crime, at the same time somehow preserving the persona of an innocent bystander, rather than being partly responsible for the events.

He heard Marian say: 'Robbie, if I can fix it, I want to come to Burma on the DTI junket – OK?'

Hyde felt a cold chill in the small of his back. He moved to the bedroom door. What the hell was she up to now? He did not study her, however, but Alder—

—relief? A gleam of hope? The relief was palpable, even as he replied, in concert with Giles:

'You're not in any condition – you can't decide just like that . . .'

'Marian, be *sensible*.'

What *was* she playing at? Hyde studied her angry face, all traces of lethargy vanished. She wouldn't be refused. She was consumed with the notion that her flat, and her body, had been violated; that she had been reduced to the role of victim, impediment – object. Her hand gripped Alder's, shaking it coaxingly.

'I could do with the holiday! *Us* . . .' she breathed. She couldn't have the slightest suspicion of him. 'I can get Peter Grainger to pull strings. The junta in Rangoon will be delighted – it'll be a propaganda coup for them. The DTI will be able to blow similar trumpets.' Her enthusiasm spilt out. 'The Whips in my party will *love* it! If I don't behave, I'll end up *covered* in the deepest doo-doo!' She looked from Alder to Hyde. 'No argument – I'm coming,' she announced. Her smile dazzled.

Hyde realised her eyes were determined, unflinching. Very, very angry. It was almost as if he could see her thoughts behind them – images of the atrocity, the attempt on her life, Lau, drugs, the murder of Kumar.

For himself, there was Alder . . . Marian was demanding his approval, and when he merely shrugged, she was angrily disappointed. He turned away from her accusing gaze. He couldn't tell her – how could he? Yet ignorant, she would be Little Red Riding Hood on holiday with the Wolf. He wouldn't be able to look out for her in Burma. Would that instant of knowing recognition between himself and Alder be enough to protect her? Jessop would just love to have her on the other side of the world, defenceless. He must persuade Aubrey to stop her, somehow.

Christ, he was in danger of turning into a *suit*!

Jessop, yawning belligerently, got out of his chair and stalked with his cup and saucer towards the hotplate and its jug of coffee. Tower Bridge loomed beyond the opened slats of the window blinds. Pleasure craft on the river in the early evening. He poured his coffee, his aggressively hunched back towards the boardroom and the others around the table.

Acquisition of a US security firm staffed by ex-CIA spooks, ready for David Winterborne's invasion of America . . . Security matters surrounding the Czech telecoms deal – bribes, blackmail, subornation . . . The City security subsidiary that provided the front for ISC was being consistently underbid for new and renewable contracts, and they needed to retain the cover ...

More than the agenda of the board meeting, what enraged him was Lau. *No* ... The fact that Hyde had saved the woman and handed Lau another stick to beat him with. Fucking Hyde, turning up like some knight in shining armour and creating a monumental cock-up. The woman was still alive – only *now* she was virtually untouchable because people knew she'd been a target, and *fucking Patrick Hyde* was still alive! Lau was climbing up his arse preceded by the rough end of a pineapple, as *obsessed* by Marian Pyott as ever his cousin had been.

Chinky bastards did not even begin to describe them and their lunatic obsessions. He sipped his coffee, his back still to the room. The *business* of ISC was like a wasp attack. He didn't really need to be running the company while attempting to kill that slippery little Australian bastard. He really didn't. The real laugh was that ISC's legitimate business was enough to keep them all in quiet luxury. It was a *good* business – bodyguards for Arabs, and Jews, all the way up to big-time industrial espionage. Show us your competitors and we'll shaft them on your behalf. Much of it was either legal or acceptable.

Middle age setting in? Probably ... He still felt the attractions of the past, its dangerous glamour, like a piercing lust, but he also desired the new, sleek, safer glamour of money. He definitely was in danger, he decided, of wanting to become a suit. And snorted with contemptuous laughter at himself, mirrored in the smoked glass of the boardroom wall.

Just as Lau was about to take Winterborne Holdings – lock, stock and barrel – across the border into the badlands, Jessop was beginning to prefer *the quiet life* he had sworn would never be his. Death by pipe and slippers.

As he made to turn back into the room, he saw on the low bookshelves a sheaf of photographic enlargements bundled loosely into a file that was labelled *Tripitaka*. Paranoid Ralph Lau again! Along with all his other demands, he'd made ISC responsible for security at that bloody holiday resort they were building in Burma! To the ludicrous extent that sheaves of photographs of all visitors, company personnel, site workers and the like were faxed to London twice a week, to be checked against the computer register of every agent or ex-agent in the world, known to them or merely stumbled across – cops, Customs, SIS, CIA, any-bloody-one at all! The photos were checked against criminal files, business rivals, drug rivals – anyone who might damage Lau's operation. Lau had even boasted to him once, *Paranoia is immortality, Jessop. I would have thought you would have learned that by now – or is your own survival explained purely by luck?*

'Fuck you, Ralphie,' he murmured aloud, then laughed at his own indiscretion, sweeping the file to the floor with: 'What tosser brought these in? We don't need this rubbish just now!'

The photographs scattered across the carpet's dark blue and its discreet pattern of gold fleurs-de-lis. Jessop made deliberately to walk over the scattered, smirking, flashlit faces. Around the table, Cobb and the others had returned to discussion of a problem unresolved during the meeting: Lau's offer to the top *biznizmen*, the Russian mafiosi, of new, cheaper, guaranteed supplies of heroin out of Burma by a safer route – a spur of the Singapore-to-Beijing railway, from Mandalay to Dacca in Bangladesh. A new airport outside Dacca could fly heroin anywhere into the Russian Federation.

The Russians were holding back, jibbing at part-funding

the new airport and using their own people as couriers. The Russian mafia was so bloody penny-pinching!

Jessop stepped on the enlarged faces like a royal carpet he disdained. Ralphie-boy dreamed of being another Cecil Rhodes, building an empire on drugs instead of diamonds. Galloping megalomania ... Beneath his feet, celebrities, businessmen and women, people dealing in travel and influence, tourism and introductions. He sensed dimly that he trod on them with envy rather than malice. Then, between one footstep and the next, with Cobb already amused at his antics, *her*—

His Gucci loafer was poised above the flashlit, moon-round face of *Hyde's fat white tart*. He heard his own intaken breath. Even as he stooped to pick up the snapshot, he had the room's attention, half amused, half calculating. As he came upright again, the initial thrill of fear had become the warmth of calculation. *She* was *there*. At Tripitaka. Hyde's *inside* person. Why she was there was of no consequence. Nothing mattered except the fact that Hyde knew she was there.

'Recognise her? Cobbie? Gill?' He lunged the photograph at them, flinging it on to the table like a winning card. It fell neatly on Cobb's scribbling pad.

'It isn't, is it?'

'*Is* it?' Jessop's throat felt ticklish with excitement.

Cobb nodded, slowly at first and then more vigorously. Jessop felt seduced by the sense of an anticipated climax. Lau's kind of satisfaction, the remote and successful exercise of power. The last step through the door to who and what you wanted to be.

Marian Pyott was safe for the moment, Hyde was elusive and professional – but she, Ros, was vulnerable. And her vulnerability would bring Hyde running, without back-up, without planning.

'She's the way to pull Hyde in,' he breathed. 'The darling boy, the guy with his nose always up Aubrey's backside. We can *have* him.' He grinned, looking around the table. 'Do I have to put it to the vote? No? Good.' He looked at his watch. It was late at night in bloody Burma. All the better. His call would wake up Pearson. The expressions around the table had brightened; they'd shed their suits and executive concerns like old snakeskins.

Killing Hyde would fulfil a fantasy. The old game, the old buzz, triple-measure. It was why people went to gun clubs, bought small arsenals, killed people. For this *buzz* he felt now. He wiped his mouth with the back of his hand.

'I'll wake Pearson up, then – scare him shitless, tell him exactly what he's to do.'

'Which is what?' Cobb asked.

'Put fat Ros on ice. Hold her incommunicado until Aubrey's best boy comes looking for her.'

'And we'll be waiting, will we?'

'We certainly will. On safari, so to speak—'

'Less than another month? Full remission for good behaviour. Do I say well done, David?'

Lau's mockery was as incapable of impinging as the hardly heard croaking of rooks high in the branches of trees that seemed to float in the early-morning mist. Reg, his prison officer, was an obscure shape hardly more dense than his breathing and cigarette smoke, on the terrace of Cheveney Park. He was scarcely bothering to monitor himself and Ralph as they patrolled the gravel path between the box hedges and formal flowerbeds.

The mocking sarcasm was misplaced and habitual. He had in reality come to ingratiate, to enthuse and enlist. *David, we have to be in unison in this*, was how he had opened the conversation. Why now, though? Was he uncertain? The man Hyde was still alive, as was Marian. Both facts had been admitted by Lau, with loss of face.

'It's all coming together,' Lau insisted.

'Or coming apart?' Winterborne responded.

They paused beside a yew hedge as if to avoid Reg's desultory surveillance. The rooks seemed to be crying their location.

'What do you mean?'

'You're nervous for some reason.'

'Of what?'

'You're not entirely in control, Ralph. Why else would you be here? You're worried.'

Lau exerted a huge effort to control his expression, to render it at once confident, deferential, admissive. Let David sense he had the advantage ... He did need David, of course. It was his conglomerate as yet, even though it was really only himself who saw the future, the golden river that was *his* project entirely. It was maddening, like an attack of insects, to have to continue to admit David's necessity.

It had driven him to Cheveney Park before he left for Burma. He needed to know, before he entered a new round of negotiations with the generals of the 999 Group, that, at the very least, David would not interfere. Come between him and the light.

Winterborne watched the fierce concentration in his cousin's eyes, lighting a cigarette to hide his attentiveness. Lau's hair gleamed with the morning's dampness. Uncertainty, dislike, greed all struggled for expression on his impassive features.

'They're *my* enemies, *my* dog-mess, too – is that it?' Winterborne snapped. 'I must help you clear it up?'

They confronted each other in the mist, against the dark, berried yew hedge, their smoking breaths intermingling.

'Look—!' Lau began, hating the Eurasian face close to his own. His mother's sister's son, who had married her rich English lover, while his own mother had married a Chinese shopkeeper ... It was that ancient, he admitted, the enmity between them. 'Oh, for God's sake, David, we *have* to work together!' His hands, momentarily expressive, even violent, returned to the pockets of his stylish black raincoat. 'You *know* these people! Some of them put you here—' There was a distinct, vivid pleasure in his tone. Winterborne clenched his hands in the pockets of his cashmere overcoat. 'I - *we* - need to deal with them.'

The moment was intensely satisfying to Winterborne. His cousin, whose father had flourished with Singapore's prosperity until he was able to buy a handful of politicians and civil servants, could no longer control events.

'You have Jessop and his people.'

'Jessop doesn't seem clever enough to catch Hyde.'

'Meanwhile, dear Marian is wooing her way on to your guest list for Rangoon.'

'How did you—?' Lau smiled coldly. 'But you would, of course.'

'Of course. She is safe, for the moment. Alder can *distract* her - so long as he remains reliable?'

'He's reliable.'

'He panicked once. Watch him. Use him. Burma is a dangerous place.' Winterborne looked up towards the terrace and the house. A fraudster and a Harley Street abortionist whose patient - a Saudi princess - had died on the operating table were exchanging laughter on the terrace. A solicitor who had embezzled almost a million of some old crone's money joined them heartily. '*Now*,' he announced heavily, 'I need to know everything, my dear cousin. Everything about Burma, about the Chinese generals, your negotiations, *our* anticipated profits -

laundering, routes, covers. Join me for breakfast.'

He took Lau's elbow.

'After you've given me an entire overview of the Mekong project, together with the US expansion, *I* can decide where and how we proceed from this point.' He laughed. The rooks invisibly replied. 'Meanwhile, I'll tell you how we rid ourselves of Marian and Hyde – Jessop has an interesting plan that will work.'

Lau stared at him, his features white with shock and cold.

'I see,' he murmured.

'Of course you do, Ralph. Now, come on – I'm hungry!'

He hurried the suddenly, newly acquiescent Lau up the stone steps to the terrace.

'Well, Ros, here's to you – you did it, you beaut!' Noreen raised the paper cup filled with champagne. Some of the liquor spilt over her knuckles. John and Tessa, too, saluted her with their paper cups.

'Not without you lot!' she returned. The afternoon heat seemed to be fermenting the champagne she had drunk, heightening its alcoholic effect. Her mouth was dry, her thoughts still triumphant.

John had made the last call on the mobile five minutes earlier. They were already on the second bottle of Bollinger from the coolbox, lolling in the seats of the four-wheel drive as if they were on chairs beside a swimming pool. They had most of the necessary contractors lined up, even before they signed the contracts with Pearson immediately on their return to Singapore. *Tomorrow.* The deal was done, the handshakes exchanged. They'd landed the biggest contract of their lives. Ros giggled, her nose filling with bubbles.

'I didn't *believe*—!' she began.

'When we started—?'

'Christ, it always seemed far too big for us.'

'You were right to use the big stick on us, Ros,' Tessa concluded, her long, suntanned legs dangling over the side of the vehicle. Swallowing more champagne, she added luxuriously: 'Next time we're here, this will all be a lake – we can swim as well as drink!' She burst into laughter. Ros's own laughter seemed stillborn in her throat.

Here ... innocent water, in a few weeks' time. It was harder than ever to believe Hyde's story of an atrocity. Not *here*.

'Something the matter?' John asked.

Ros realised she had been shaking her head. The high sun pressed down on her exposed neck like a hand, as if to force her to look across the great hollow of the land's natural fold towards the white strip of the dam wall. It seemed grotesque to her now, like a bandage between red earth and fierce blue sky.

'No ...'

'Someone walk over your grave?' Noreen asked with lugubrious, half-drunk gravity. Ros shivered.

'Bit of reaction,' she muttered. 'Cheers.' They refilled their cups. The cork exploded from the third bottle. Champagne flowed over John's knuckles like water would flow over the ... 'Great!' Ros added.

What proof could Hyde possibly have? Anyway, he'd told her later to forget it. The last of the recent rain dried in the sun like old bloodstains.

Their renewed laughter roused her.

'Pearson – did you sleep with him, Ros?' Tessa asked. 'He was so keen to give us the contract!'

'I promised I *wouldn't* sleep with him if he gave us the work!' The laughter came quite easily. 'I'd have sent you in, Tess, if he hadn't come across.' She looked at her watch.

Tessa squealed with amused horror. 'Time we went, boy and girls,' she announced to a chorus of dissent. 'Time to pack, time to go—'

'It's so bloody lovely here!' Noreen sighed, dragging her frizzy auburn hair on end as she stretched luxuriously.

'Yes, it is,' Ros said quietly. 'Right-oh, John, you're the token bloke, so you can drive us girls back!' She tossed him the keys.

More champagne was guzzled as the four-wheel drive bumped and heaved its way down the slope above what would be the lake. Huge earthmovers, yellow as tropical insects, lumbered across the scene, great cranes bent slowly like flamingoes stooping to sift water for food. Butterflies seemed flung up from a bush as they passed, like scraps of coloured paper. Dust, noise, above all the sense of activity, of something vast growing towards completion. Noreen was right, it *was* beautiful; dazzlingly so.

John brought the vehicle to an abrupt halt in the hotel car park and yanked on the handbrake.

'Sorry. Bit hard to focus.' He roared with laughter.

Ros walked ahead of the others towards the foyer and into its air-conditioned chill, the shock of it becoming welcome in a moment. But it wasn't . . . The shock seemed to persist. For some moments, she was unaware of the reason, unaware of why she was staring at an enlarged snapshot of herself that had fluttered to her feet, as if expertly thrown. Herself in that same foyer, in the same frock. The snapshot was no more than hours old, she realised as its details became sharper to her. As she had entered the foyer, she had automatically looked towards the huge screen of windows on which were printed the images of the dam, the jungle, the hills distantly purple in the afternoon light . . .

... and the man had accidentally, it seemed, collided with her only a few steps from the sliding doors. A newspaper had fallen from his hand and the snapshot had emerged from the paper as if from a mouth. Herself in profile, near the reception desk.

As she fully recognised herself, the suited man bent and snatched up the photograph. Looked at her, grinned, and moved swiftly away from her. His expression was like the touch of a cold, wet finger as she slept, waking and sobering her instantly. Then he was gone, almost invisible beyond a group checking out. Ros lost sight of him near the lifts...

... and saw someone watching her as he spoke into a mobile phone. Another youngish, neat man in a business suit. He stared at her, then snapped the lip of the phone decisively shut. Continued to stare until—

—she fled, unnerved, towards the lifts.

When she glanced back to the foyer he, too, was gone. She tumbled into the lift on weakened legs, her heart thudding. Her photograph, which she was meant to see, the avid inspection of her by both men, their purposeful interest in her ... She was shivering, yet the lift compartment was hot. Shivering uncontrollably as the door opened and she tottered into the corridor. Her suite was at the end of it. She hurried towards its doors—

—a black-garbed man emerged from her suite. She raised her hand as if he was a waiter. Then he was gone, through the fire exit. She ran towards it, hand still held aloft, unable to call out.

Nothing. Ros leant against the doors of the suite, fumbling home her keycard. The doors blundered open, echoing her weak charge against them. She was giddy with fear and collapsed on to a sofa, hearing her heart and breathing amplified like terrifying accompanying music.

Her gaze took in the undisturbed exactness of the suite, her half-packed suitcase, the remains of lunch on the table, her folded clothes, the closed drawers and cupboards, the dam and the jungle and the sky beyond the room...

But someone like Hyde had been in that suite, searching it.

Hyde—

Her bag spilt its contents as she wrestled out the mobile phone. A lipstick rolled across the green carpet. Her trembling finger tapped out his number. Her left leg seemed to have gone into spasm. A breeze fingered the net curtains she had pulled back that morning, as if making a covert entry. There was cold perspiration bathing her entire body—

'Hyde!' she blurted hoarsely. Didn't listen to his response, but wailed: 'They know who I am, Hyde—!'

She was *meant* to call him, he was *meant* to know her panic, her situation. Man in her room, man in the foyer, snapshot of me, he heard, letting her talk breathlessly even as she ran down like an uncoiling spring. He needed to hear her impressions, receive the real sense of what had happened without interrupting her. Even though he felt cold and avoided looking at the other people in Aubrey's drawing room.

Eventually he snapped: 'Ros, listen to me!' It was as violent as if he had struck her. Marian Pyott flinched at the harshness of his voice. Aubrey's face was fearful, Pyott's concerned. Godwin seemed embarrassed – or perhaps afraid his eyes might betray him. 'Listen to me ...' he reiterated more soothingly as he heard her breathing subside, grow calmer.

The US satellite maps, Godwin's computer-generated

map of the resort site, lay on Aubrey's carpet like the wreckage after a fatal accident. The scheme they had been working out over the conference phone with Evans in KL was shot, blown. There was no *time* for it now! A moment earlier, he had been concerned that Marian Pyott had asked Godwin for a set of Kumar's photographs. It had seemed important, worth worrying about. Now, she and the photographs were alien, beyond his universe.

It had happened, the connection had been made. Ros had wandered into the minefield of his world and stepped on a device. The others in the room continued to telegraph Ros's danger to him in expressions of alarm and concern.

'Yes,' she responded. 'What do I do, Hyde?' she breathed wetly.

'For the moment, they're just trying to frighten you—'

'Bloody well succeeding!'

'Ros,' he warned again. Marian seemed to despise him. Hyde was aware of Evans listening intently on the still-open line to Kuala Lumpur. 'OK, don't say anything, just do as I tell you ... Check the *lampshades*. Got that?' There was a tremor in his arm that he stilled by an effort of will. Perspiration along his hairline. 'No, don't repeat *anything*.' Cold sweat beneath his arms. The image of her terribly vivid. Defenceless. 'Every one of them. You're looking for a bug ... OK, then try the power points, any adaptors.' He heard her breathing, not as stifled as his own. 'If you find nothing, look behind the pictures, the bedhead. If you find something, just cough. Cough, OK?' The room around him seemed pressurised with a great depth of water.

Ros coughed.

'OK, detach it and put it under a cushion. No, don't say anything, just keep looking!' He felt himself flinch at each breath she took. His own ceased as he recognised in hers the discovery of a second bug. Then he said: 'OK, go out on the balcony now – is there a balcony?'

'Yes.' Her voice sounded worn.

'Good—' He put his hand over the mobile's mouthpiece. 'Taff, give me a contact in Mandalay – I have to get Ros out *now*.'

'I know. OK, give me a couple of minutes. She all right?'

'Just . . . Ros?'

'I'm on the balcony – what now?' The fearful impatience of a child left in the dark. Hyde hunched further into himself, as if there was some possibility of privacy in the room. Aubrey cleared his throat and the noise startled. 'Hyde—?'

'Have you got transport?'

'A four-wheel drive on loan—'

'Where's John?'

'His room, I suppose.'

'Get him to the phone – don't argue. He can drive. There'll be an address in Mandalay—'

'That's sixty miles—!'

'On a good road,' he soothed. 'A couple of hours. Just fill a bag and go. Now, get John.'

'You'll have to wait a minute.'

'That's OK. Take it easy.'

He looked down at the maps at his feet, Godwin's and the US satellite maps. Tripitaka was scribbled in red on both of them as if a child had begun colouring the sheets. Green jungle, rivers, the winding road down from the hills, through the old hill station of Maymyo, snaking on south-west to Mandalay—

—the doorbell of her hotel suite, louder than the noises of her breathing and the distant construction work. He heard Evans on the open line.

'OK, Patrick. There's a name and a contact phrase—'

'Ros, leave the door!'

'It's room service—'

'Ros, leave the *fucking door*!'

She'd grasped at the noise of the doorbell because it was familiar, even comforting in her disorientation and slow terror.

'*Ros!*'

He heard the door open. It was so routine, so bloody *trite* ... Her gasp of shocked surprise, the muffled moment of struggle, the jar of the mobile phone being dropped, its retrieval, the emphatic breathing at the other end that did not belong to Ros. Then the phone being switched off.

CHAPTER NINE

Another Country

The dark-green jungle ridges surrounding Mae Hong Son were re-emerging from the heavy monsoon clouds like the images of a painting being restored. The small Thai Airlines Boeing spilt its passengers down the steps that had parked beside it, on to the gleaming wet concrete of the apron. Colin Evans watched Hyde coming aggressively down the steps clutching a small cabin bag. His surge of interest at once became concern, so that his wave was hesitant, disappointed. *We don't do personal.* Someone he had not liked in the old days had said that of intelligence work, and he unquietly remembered it now.

He offered his hand with an apologetic warmth, aware that Hyde was suspicious of his careful inspection of him.

'I'll do,' Hyde said sourly. 'Where's the plane?' It cut off the lagging bonhomie that Evans had suddenly felt necessary.

Hyde looked around him. The jungle climbed the now revealed hills, beyond which lay Burma. The town seemed squeezed into its narrow valley, its temples and pagodas glittering with rain in the first weak sunshine. Evans sensed Hyde's dislocation, his unpreparedness and anticipatory terrors. The apron began to steam in the midday heat. The light aircraft of the drug and gem smugglers were drawn up as neatly as guardsmen awaiting inspection. Mae Hong Son was on a major drug route from Burma. The tired *chedi* of a temple, its wedding-cake niches filled with statues of the Buddha, stared incongruously over the small airport as if disillusioned. A crop of new hotels, some half-built, others completed, seemed planted around the insignificant town, diminishing the sense of the jungle.

Evans had visited the place a handful of times. SIS hadn't the resources to be interested in the drug trade this close to the Golden Triangle. The CIA held the brief for northern Thailand and Laos, and disdained intelligence-sharing with his service. His concern was with the Malaysian post offices, the shipping companies and onward routes. Ros – the personal – was like a revenant beside them. He felt his frantic preparations, exhilarating only a few hours before, now thin and insubstantial, little more than a sketch for an extraction operation. Hyde, too, seemed inadequate.

'Parked over there.' Evans gestured vaguely. 'Bloody tight schedule you gave me, too, boy!' He shrugged off Hyde's unresponsiveness, then added: 'OK, come on then, let's get moving.'

'How do we get in?'

'The pilot's got all the right papers – don't worry. He does little jobs on the side for the generals in the junta, Thai civil servants, Malaysian ministers. And me,' he added brightly. 'Bloody lucky he was around when it all hit the – pushed the timetable forward.'

'You trust him?'

'Yes. He likes the risk, the double game. It appeals to something in his nature. And there's always the money – in dollars. Here we are.'

Parked outside a hangar was an amphibious aircraft, its two engines in tandem on top of the wings and aft of the flight cabin. The legend *Dornier* on the long engine nacelle. A small, compact Chinese was leaning out of the raised crew-escape door. He nodded to Evans and continued his impassive inspection of Hyde.

'There's two of these things stored in a hangar in Penang,' Evans explained, grinning. 'Company can't get the funds to build more. Mike Sung – say hello, Mike, this is Patrick – borrows it all the time.' Hyde and Sung acknowledged one another. 'Come in useful, this will, in a couple of hours ... Ready to board?' Hyde nodded. They climbed the steps and entered the passenger cabin. 'Ready when you are, Mike!'

As they settled into the cramped seats, Evans said carefully: 'You're not asking, so I will. You found out anything more?'

Hyde rubbed his face as if challenged or bemused. Perhaps simply worn. Evans felt doubt like a violent spasm of indigestion. Hyde looked up at him.

'I managed to get hold of one of the people with her – John. Ros ... left a message at the desk, telling them to carry on back to Singapore. She'd had an invitation to Mandalay, a possible client who knew she was at Tripitaka. I got this after landing at Bangkok. John was in Singapore by then.'

'Who's the client?'

The two Pratt & Whitney turboprops started up. Hyde

raised his voice 'A Mr Lim, who has a big house over-looking Mandalay. Complete redecoration – big order.'

'The same Lim you asked me to check on?'

Hyde nodded. 'Could be someone else - except it isn't.'

'You're sure?'

'Sure enough. It *can't* be coincidence. Lim is the middleman in Mandalay. The intermediary between Lau, the Chinese, the Burmese, and whoever else is involved!'

'Why did he use his own name?'

'To light the path for me.'

'Then Ros is in Mandalay – that's something.' There was evident relief in Evans's voice.

'Hopefully.'

'You'll do the decent thing, then, and walk into the trap?'

'Sort of, but not quite. I want to check John's story at the hotel.'

'You'll be announcing your arrival.'

'They probably know already.'

The Dornier Seastar slid away from the private hangars and the neatly parked light aircraft, towards the apron and the taxiway. The noise of the engines pressed down with the force of a tropical storm.

'You want to look through the inventory?'

'What about transport?'

'Fixed. It'll meet us when we land.'

'Back-up?'

'One of ours. Some local – if required.'

'OK, let's see the inventory.'

Hyde looked at his watch. Allowing for the time difference, it was eighteen hours since he had left London. A scheduled flight to Bangkok, then the tickets Evans had arranged, first to Chang Mai, then here – this foreign, unknown place slipping past the small cabin windows. The shock, the effort of assistance, the small communal expressions of foreboding in Aubrey's drawing room – all had haunted him during the flights, like indelible images. Aubrey's attempts at calm, the fitful sparks of contingencies, alternatives, had been stinging delays and guilts. It had finally *happened* ... what he was had enveloped Ros.

During the flight from London, he had argued himself into a shallow, fragile hope that she was still alive. If he didn't believe she was, he would never even be capable of revenge for her murder. The terror of her loss was in abeyance now, locked away – though he could still hear its screamed threats, its banging on the door for release. They would know she was an effective bait whether alive or ... They would need, in order to draw him in, to show her to him, at a window, on some terrace. In a car. She would need to be alive to answer a demand that he speak to her, hear the proof of her voice. There were a dozen frail reasons for keeping Ros alive ...

He felt himself float up again from some huge depth towards the surface of the thing. He glanced at Evans' scrawled details, finding it difficult to concentrate. As the Dornier lifted away from the single runway, climbed over the delicate white temples buried in the jungled hillside, then banked towards Burma, he felt the last terror fall away. The terrible blackness of believing she was already dead lessened. More dark hills, the sun streaking through breaking clouds, the presence of Evans, the waxwork memories of Marian, her father, Tony Godwin.

It was an evident trap, and he had to circumvent it. As if Evans understood, he began unfolding maps he drew from a briefcase.

'Lim,' he murmured. 'I'll get through to our bloke in a couple more minutes – locate this place of his.'

***

'Didn't disturb you, I hope, my dear?' Peter Grainger's avuncular, slightly mocking tones. Marian's momentary awareness of her nakedness and Alder's proximity in the bed became a reciprocal amusement. 'Some good news, Marian. The DTI and its political mistress are delightedly suspicious that you should wish to lend your considerable support. All embarrassment will, of course, entirely redound upon HM Loyal Opposition. Hence *our* masters are suspicious without delight – though realising that any scene that might occur would be the utter ruin of your political career.'

After a moment, aware again of her nudity, Marian murmured: 'I accept the generous terms.'

'Ah good!' Peter Grainger was enjoying her discomfiture. He added: 'Then George Theobald would like to give you a good going-over, as the phrase is, in the Whips' Office at, say, ten thirty? He will be issuing a severe weather warning.'

'Fine, Peter!' she rallied. Alder stirred beside her and opened his eyes. She touched her finger to her lips and then laid it on his. 'I'll attend my shriving-time with George, suitably chastened.'

'Oh good . . . 'Fraid there's been a leak or two in time for the morning editions. Bye—!'

Central Office, she thought, as she put down the receiver. Her throat still felt bruised. She had buried the attack in lovemaking; determinedly, passionately. Alder's hesitancy and gentleness had excited rather than evoked reluctance in her. She got out of bed, kissing Alder as she did so, delighted at the eager gaze with which he studied her crossing the bedroom.

The papers lay on the doormat, and she plucked them up. *Ooh, Marian!* was the headline in the *Sun*, the sub-head beneath proclaiming *MP's Myanmar U-Turn*. The *Telegraph* was more restrained, but as pointedly questioning of her unnecessary capitulation of principle. She carried the newspapers into the kitchen. What a farce, she thought, spooning coffee into the cafetière and lighting a cigarette. A stitch-up, as the criminal fraternity called it.

It *had* to be swallowed, however enraging.

Hyde had fled to Burma to rescue Ros. There had been utter panic on his part, a stunned impotence on that of Aubrey, her father, Tony Godwin. The photographs had been forgotten, lying ignored in their folder on Kenneth's sideboard. They were pictures, suddenly, of distant ancestors or events and of no further utility whatsoever. They would not save Ros.

She had believed Hyde's gloomy assessment of editorial reaction to any mention of the photographs. The newspapers would have remained silent until they unearthed their own corroboration – and even after that, perhaps the government would have become involved and demanded silence. They were valuable only to Ralph Lau in exchange for her safety and that of Hyde—

—unless . . .

When she left Aubrey's flat, she had scooped the folder into her purse. She had decided they must be used. She must deliver them herself. They must do *good* . . . Once she was accepted on the DTI trip, she had jumped the first hurdle.

Again, she swallowed her nerves. It just had to be done. She must deliver the photographs in Rangoon, where they could be used against the junta. Deliver them to Suu Kyi herself . . . *if* she could arrange a meeting with the Lady. In *The Times*, the Burmese Embassy in London was already expressing the pleasure of the junta's generals at the opportunity to demonstrate its democratic pretensions to one of its fiercest British critics. They were tying the straitjacket around her as she read.

'So, you swung it?' Alder observed from the kitchen door. The kettle boiled. She poured the water into the cafetière. 'Clever girl.'

'I did it just to be with you, my darling—'

'Really?' He gripped her upper arms. His lips smiled as his eyes interrogated. 'It's not some kind of a deep game, is it? I don't want you—'

'Screwing up?'

'I was about to say, harming your career. But that, too. Neither of us needs—'

'Damaged careers? Agreed.' She kissed him lightly, aware again of her bruised neck as he touched it. 'I'll come quietly, Officer.' She gestured at the newspapers. 'Have to, now.'

'Good.'

'I do want to be with you,' she murmured. 'That's what really matters.' He was immediately flattered, as she knew he would be, and all but convinced. She sensed her disappointment vie with her passion. Then it evaporated as he kissed her again, pressing their bodies together.

'I want to be with *you*,' he responded. 'Like *this*—' His desire was immediate, real. She let herself be pressed back gently against the wall, shivering momentarily at its chill, and parted her thighs, her heart racing, her arousal as fierce as his. 'God, Marian . . .' she heard. Felt him enter her.

Hyde's features, almost as they achieved the mutual climax. Alder leant heavily, breathlessly against her, yet at once she saw Hyde. And the snapshots splayed like a hand of giant cards. Hyde had been desperate, in a shocked, cold panic. They had Ros and he feared she would find a grave as surely as those Burmese villagers.

He had gone to find Ros, abandoning all the careful

planning that had lain suddenly like litter on Kenneth's carpet.

'You cold?' Alder whispered.

'No – no.' She *was* shivering. She had to deliver the photographs personally. Like Hyde, she was no longer a bystander. It was too late for distance.

'Down there!' Evans shouted above the engine noise as the Dornier banked steeply, poised like a raptor about to plummet towards the twisted wound of a river gorge.

Hyde watched the jungle and the hills fling themselves up towards the aircraft. The Shan plateau lay like a huge, grey, knuckled grip on the scene below, dropping away to the west towards the dry plains around Mandalay, but otherwise holding the scene vicelike in every direction. The narrow river was a pale-blue streak through the grey cliffs and dark jungle that was gouged with the scars of illegal logging.

The ex-Malaysian airforce pilot jiggled the amphibious Dornier like a dog shaking off water, aligning it with a stretch of the gorge that appeared wider, less twisted, wearing the blue river like a raised vein. Hyde absorbed the landscape as it hurtled towards him, thinking that he'd glimpsed a patch of order, away west of the plane which might have been Tripitaka. The Dornier levelled, the gorge closing around and above it like cracked grey lips.

When he'd disembarked them and the equipment, Mike Sung would fly on to Mandalay. Evans had the funds to hold him there for three days. Ros—

He squashed the thought of her. The river flashed beneath the keel of the Dornier as it bucked in the air currents of the gorge. His focus had to be someone he didn't know, had never even met. Objects of rescue or recovery in an extrication op were always just that –

entirely nameless, without degrees of value. Ros twisted in his stomach despite his effort of repression.

The water was shadowed by the plane's wing, the speed of its flow unnerving, then the keel and sponsons caught the current and overtook it. Water splashed the passenger windows. He and Evans were buffeted in their seats. The grey cliffs of the gorge were daubed with black vegetation. The amphibian slowed imperceptibly, the river current nibbling away at its onward rush, taming and unsettling the plane. The engines slowed, then Sung turned the plane towards a thin nail-paring of rubbly riverbank. It chugged like an ancient boat across the flow of the current.

There was a figure on the shore, framed by sparse trees and the broken teeth of a collapsed section of the bank. A four-wheel drive was parked above the man on the cliff edge. The engine note rose again as the Dornier faced the current and Sung held the aircraft steady.

'OK, let's go,' Evans announced, slapping Hyde's shoulder. He crouched along the cabin and pushed the main door like raising a manhole from below. The river splashed into the passenger cabin and over the sponson on to which Evans stepped. 'Come on, don't hang about, there's a love—!'

Hyde grimaced with what might have been a smile of acceptance. Evans had obviously decided to ignore his own assessment of the operation and instead re-create the past. He followed the bulky Welshman on to the rocking sponson and helped him release the rubber raft from the side of the fuselage. Then, as he held the raft, Evans transferred the bags of equipment from the cabin.

The engine noise fluctuated as the plane waltzed slowly, dreamily in the current. Sung watched their disembarkation without expression as he held the aircraft steady fifty or sixty yards from the pebbled bank. Then Evans was yelling instructions and waving to Sung, then slamming and locking the main door. He clambered into the raft after Hyde, who paddled the frail rubber craft away from the Dornier as Sung turned it once more with the current. It drifted away, then accelerated, creating a bow wave and creamy wake before lifting away from the water two thousand feet from the raft. Silver rain fell from its keel in the sunlight. At first, the tiny plane was almost lost in the glitter of the water, then lost altogether as it climbed out of the gorge and banked out of sight before the raft's bottom grazed on the pebbles.

Nothing but the noise of the river and the grinding of the raft on the bank. Evans' boots splashing in shallow water. The hard, bright arguments of invisible parrots. Hyde paused in the raft for another moment; one last deep breath for his mind, his whole body. Then he helped Evans and the other man drag the raft up on to the bank, hardly glancing in the second man's direction; uninterested in anything other than the new, invigorating tension that shivered through him. He was no more than thirty miles from Tripitaka, and only hours away from Lim's estate in Mandalay.

Evans' contact had supplied the location of Lim's guarded, gated hillside estate. Evans had ringed it precisely on the map. He would check the hotel first, to confirm that he was meant to follow the trail to Lim. It was two o'clock. Mandalay by tonight, then. Evans' play of urgency had become real. His reputation as a field director, back in the good old dark ages, had been high.

Hyde straightened after pulling one of the heavy bags from the raft. What was this local contact like? SIS, with a World Health Organisation cover. He looked across the raft—

—to find Phil Cass grinning at his surprise.

'Hi, Patrick.' A momentarily sombre expression on Cass' more lined features, then they were shaking hands. Cass' hair had greyed and thinned in the few years since Hyde had saved his life by hauling him wounded out of Pakistani Kashmir.

'Learned the local language yet?'

'Burmese? Karin, Shan, Kochin? English ...?' He appeared for a moment to consider voicing the object of their meeting, then merely offered: 'I've got him under at least a sketchy sort of surveillance. No evidence as yet. Sorry—'

'D'you think Ros might be there?' Evans asked, as if he knew that Hyde could not.

Carefully, and watching Hyde, Cass shrugged.

'She – could be.'

'Has to be,' Hyde announced with finality. 'Fucking waste of time, all this, if she isn't.'

He knew his cynical flippancy was the only way he could make it work. Cass grinned with relief and Evans was suddenly more relaxed.

'It's good to see you again, you Aussie bugger,' Cass said.

'Let's get this stuff into the four-wheel drive,' was Hyde's response as he smiled.

'Good to see you, Phil ... OK, how long to the resort?'

'Not much more than a hour. Then less than another two to Mandalay. OK?'

'It'll do. I'd like to see Lim's layout as soon as I can.'

'Can do.'

It *was* becoming easier, he admitted, but as if confessing to a crime or a betrayal.

It was hot, struggling up the broken cliff with the heavy bags of equipment, the sun burning his neck. If they killed him no one else would come after them. There *was* no one. Aubrey and Pyott didn't have any troops. He flung the bags into the open rear door of the vehicle and clambered in after them. The interior was stifling. His impatience mounted like his temperature.

I'm coming, Mr Lim, just as you expect.

'Get on to your local help, Phil. I want to know Lim's routine. Every day, every detail—'

The woman, seated on the rickety chair in the yard of the Soho restaurant, was younger than twenty-five but appeared middle-aged, even prematurely old. Insein prison, a forty-minute drive from Rangoon in a windowless truck, produced that accelerated ageing in most of its political prisoners. Those who survived, and were eventually released, called it *the regime's rubber stamp*. Clubs and fists, boots, darkness and vile food, infectious water, stamped them with their government's image. Myint San had been so remodelled. She limped, too, and many of her teeth were missing. She wore her crooked, gaping smile – if she smiled – as a badge of honour.

Marian had ensured, four years earlier, that her application for political asylum in Britain had been successful. Since then, the young woman had been her London conduit to the democratic opposition in Burma. Supplying Marian with the appalling facts, the vile details, enabling her to speak and write on behalf of Suu Kyi's National League. Now, of course, Myint San was outraged, betrayed. The jaw they had broken in Insein worked furiously but loosely, as if grinding a meal of stones.

'It has to be done,' Marian offered once more. 'I had to do things this way.'

'You are compromised,' the woman responded, staring

at her hands that seemed to have been moulded in plasticine by an impatient, unobservant child; and the splayed, sticklike fingers. They barely enabled her to write now. She could, of course, wash dishes, which she did in the kitchens of the Thai restaurant in whose untidy yard they now sat. '*Why?*'

It was as if Marian had inflicted some private nightmare on her. She could do no more than shrug in response. The old chair on which she sat, too worn to be used any longer in the restaurant, croaked apologetically as she moved her weight. Then she murmured:

'Will you do it? Tell them I wish to see Suu Kyi, or someone very close to her?'

'Can we trust you now?' Myint San's habitual manner was as ugly and uningratiating as her tortured body. Her tone had threatened the success of her appeal for asylum on many occasions. The interrogators had deformed her nature and her body equally.

Exasperatedly, Marian snapped: 'What I have can be used! I could use it here, I could sabotage this whole trade mission—'

'Then why not do so?'

'Because the National League alone has the right to decide how and when. Not me.'

'And Daw Suu Kyi would be a purer source than any British politician?'

'Perhaps.'

The President of the Board of Trade had crowed and warned in equal measure in her abrupt, ruffling, domineering tones. Chanting the same psalm as Central Office over the sinner that repenteth. Her local chairman had been informed. She was utterly compromised – and now regarded by this young Burmese woman with undisguised contempt. The mid-morning sun fell into the narrow yard like a disappointed optimism. Two Thai waiters smoked and laughed in the kitchen doorway.

'Will you *tell* them?' Marian pleaded. On the paper in her hand were scribbled her hotel, time of arrival, the number of her mobile. She looked at Myint San. '*Please...*'

'Even the trashy newspapers are critical of you,' the young woman replied, her eyes like shrivelled black fruit. Anger stared out of them, the suspicion of someone previously disastrously betrayed; the contempt of the tortured for someone banned from driving for a speeding offence. 'Why should we go on trusting you?'

A small, autumnal breeze plucked at Marian's fawn jacket and silk scarf. It stirred the dust of the yard. She thought she glimpsed a furtive rat sidling through a bower of black rubbish bags. The waiters' laughter seemed mocking.

Myint San refused the cigarette she offered. Marian lit hers and exhaled loudly.

'You'll miss a great opportunity, *Tekkabho* Myint San,' Marian eventually replied. The honorific recognised the young woman as a university graduate. The form of address was politely Burmese, deliberately respectful.

After a long silence, the woman said: 'Very well, *Ma ma* Marian Pyott.' Elder sister. It was as if Myint San had laid her brown hand on Marian's.

'Thank you. Give them these details.' The broken brown fingers clawed the piece of paper into the pocket of the thin coat drawn over her narrow shoulders. 'I'm sorry I felt I had to do this myself. That there was no other way. My help will be compromised – from now on.'

The black eyes were suddenly greedy.

'What you have is worth that much?'

Marian nodded.

'In my judgement, yes. It will – *may* – halt *all* foreign

investment in Burma, for years. Mobilise international opinion. There are all sorts of possibilities . . .' She knew she sounded like a seducer with a bribe as her sole accreditation.

'Good. Now, I must go.' She stood up, her head on one side, regarding Marian with the suspicion of a perched bird. It was as if she was struggling to acknowledge a sacrifice less damaging than her own, but still genuine. 'I will tell them – tonight.' She nodded. '*Daw* Marian Pyott . . .' *Aunt*, respectfully so. The woman almost smiled. Then she was gone, past the loitering waiters into the kitchen already heady with scents.

Marian blew smoke, watching her hands quiver. She had committed herself as completely as Hyde now. As dangerously, too . . . ?'

From the window of Godwin's office, Aubrey watched the autumn sun on the Thames and the green glass of the SIS building, as he listened to Colin Evans on the conference phone.

'—Pearson's already left, we know that. Phil's pretty sure Lim has Ros stashed at his place outside Mandalay. Patrick's just going into the hotel to check on the tale he was meant to be told.'

'Was it necessary?' Aubrey murmured.

'Sir – with respect – he's not listening to us. He can't think straight—'

'Very well, Colin. Neither you nor Cass must endanger your official status or your covers. Understand me? *Help* him, but do not become involved.'

'Yes, sir.'

Aubrey had turned from the window and gestured helplessly as he spoke. Reluctantly, Godwin nodded his agreement. Aubrey rubbed his temple with uncertain fingers. Godwin cleared his throat.

'Colin – Tony here. The stuff he wanted has followed him out in the Bag, to Rangoon. The money, too. Can you get it sent up to Mandalay without problems?'

'Yes.'

'What d'you think he'll do, if Ros is there?'

'God knows, boy! Something bloody daft, I expect!' Then he added: 'Like I would.'

'Best not to ask, then. OK, Col – talk to me when he gets back.' He switched off the phone, but sat contemplating it as a means of not meeting Aubrey's enquiring stare. Then he did look up. 'I'm right, sir – best not to ask. You can't really order them *not* to get involved.'

'No, no,' Aubrey snapped, patrolling the screen of the window. 'Damnable, this loyalty business.'

'There'll be no trail back to us.'

'I'm not worrying about my own skin, Tony!'

'Then stop worrying about theirs – sir.' Godwin's plump features were pink with anger. 'They're old enough and ugly enough to look out for themselves, after all,' he added by way of apology, together with: 'I'll order us some lunch, sir. Anything you'd especially—?'

'By your tone, perhaps a lollipop or ice-cream would suffice, Tony?' Godwin glanced down and Aubrey at once added: 'Sorry. It must be this infernal lack of support and resources. The object is sufficiently important, but the operation is *feeble*.' He clenched his hand on air for an instant, then returned it to its soothing task on his temple.

It wasn't really Hyde, of course, it was Marian. Neither he nor her father had been able to dissuade her from what was utter recklessness. To take those photographs to Rangoon, to attempt to hand them secretly to the democracy movement was – totally insane. Romantic and utterly dangerous.

Patrick's danger, however immediate, was no more than a prelude to hers.

He turned the four-wheel drive into a parking space in front of the hotel and switched off the engine. He was comfortable, even in the suit that Cass had brought from Mandalay to help fulfil the transitory shadow-life Evans had created for him. Aussie businessman tied in with Ros, one of her suppliers, supposed to meet her in Mandalay – no show. Appropriate frustrated rage, tie askew, time's money, where is the stupid Sheila ...? Comfortable with the tricks and moments of identity.

Hyde picked up the black briefcase and the mobile phone, slammed the vehicle door behind him, stormed across the dusty tarmac. The sun was low, perched on purple hills to the west. Tripitaka, which he had studied for hours through binoculars, as carefully as a major investor, shrank to the tinted glass doors that opened on the foyer of the hotel where she had been until—

Stop it.

John, Ros's friend, had said the man's name was Chris. This was his shift on reception. His was the story about Ros, Lim and Mandalay. He was the signpost on the road Hyde was supposed to follow. *He* was the one who had to be convinced that Hyde was alone and desperate, that he was hurrying towards a collision with Lim.

Blond hair, slim, neat, freckled, Australian – John's description of the reception clerk. *Chris.* There it was, worn on his lapel as unwaveringly as the professional smile he was using to dispatch a middle-aged couple as he turned to Hyde.

'How may I help you? Are you booking in, Mr ...?' Slight tightening of the face, as if it had been coated with a sudden astringent. He'd have seen photographs of Hyde.

'Never mind. I want to know where bloody *Mizz* Woode is, one of your guests.'

'Ms Woode?' There was an unpractised, almost endearing moment of excitement, a single bead of perspiration at his left temple, the slightest tic of an eyelid. Hyde savoured the instant. 'I—' Chris tapped at his reservations keyboard, studied the screen with pretended concentration. Then: 'Ah, yes. Ms Woode booked out, I'm afraid. With her party ... No, I remember. *They* returned to Singapore on Mr Pearson's flight, while Ms Woode took a business trip to Mandalay. A Mr Lim, I'm certain that was the name—'

His affected, confident campness flickered like a failing bulb as Hyde banged on the desk with the flat of his hand. Short, tie askew, red-faced, sweating ... Chris, he saw, was absorbing the image he presented and was finding it surprisingly ordinary, unthreatening. He'd tell them it was going to be easy, and there was the faintest chance they'd believe his assessment. The cover had to appear no more than the lid on a pressure cooker, *anything* to suggest that there was no plan, no patience, only panic. *No* back-up. Evans had understood that – the cover was hurried and flimsy. Was this bloke smart enough to read the evident signals?

'Listen, you—!' Hyde blurted. 'I have to get hold of her – she *owes* me money! She owes me business! Understand, *Brenda*?'

Chris's cheeks flushed at the coarse insult. His nostrils narrowed like his eyes. *I'm pretty sure he's gay.* John's assessment. He was one of the thinner-skinned variety, and was antagonistically alert, and contemptuous. Good.

'Ms Woode has checked *out*,' he replied, his anger making him spiteful, incautious for a moment. He wanted to mock with knowingness, grant Hyde a glimpse behind the curtain.

'How do I know that? I've just come from Mandalay – you expect me to drive all the bloody way back there on your bloody say-so?'

'Look at this – *sir*.' Chris turned the screen towards him on its thin stalk. '*There*...' he purred.

Hyde flinched at her name, the dates of arrival and departure. His hand fiddled nervously and was watched as if it was a crab waving dangerous claws. Dribble out the cover story now, he told himself, show him it's a bucketful of holes, that you're desperate, can hardly get the fiction right. It was not difficult to continue to stare at Ros' name on the screen, and breathe raggedly.

'I have to see her – I was supposed to be here with them, couldn't get away. She owes me, I have to have the money. I got here as soon as I could... I have to find her!' He looked up for the first time, pleading. 'Can you give me an address, a telephone number for her – anything?' His eyes expressed weakness, uncertainty. 'I have to be paid, it's a fucking *mess* back home—' A small, sidelong shame at having to confess as much. It evoked pleasure, encouraged certainty, knowledge of him. 'Christ, mate, have you got this Chinese bugger's address somewhere – *please*?'

Don't believe anything you've heard about me, just believe the pathetic jerk in front of you now ...

... he did. He *did*. Chris was arrogant with contempt, with the ease with which he envisaged Hyde's entire situation. He saw how Hyde was hanging on to his cover story, saw the effort of disguise for what it was. His thin lips smiled condescendingly.

'I'll ask, sir.'

He left the screen facing Hyde, who leaned towards it across the reception desk's dark wood. He rubbed his wet face with one damp hand while the other beat a muffled, senseless measure of the passing seconds. Chris appeared to consult a telephone directory, then returned, having scribbled a number.

'That's it, I'm sure.'

'Thanks—!' Hyde snatched the slip of paper with eager desperation. 'Look, sorry about – I'm knackered, haven't slept. Had to get hold of her – she can bail me out. Sorry.' Chris remained silently aloof. 'Can I use your phone? I have to talk to her tonight – it'll take me hours to get back to Mandalay—'

'I'll try the number for you. A pleasure.' He took back the paper with his fingertips, turned away and dialled on a phone at the rear of reception. He paused, then spoke inaudibly, quickly. The hotel foyer was noisy with guests, business, the explosive bonhomie of strangers engaged in deals. Through the window, the sun was no more than a gilding along the rounded peaks of the hills. 'I think it's one of Mr Lim's staff . . .' Chris startled him by announcing, handing him the receiver.

Hyde slapped the telephone against his cheek and said: 'My name's Stewart.' If Ros heard the name mentioned, she'd know it as an old cover. 'I'm sorry to bother you – you have a Ms Woode with you, a guest of Mr Lim. I need to speak to her urgently.'

He knew it was Lim at the other end of the line. Had to be. He'd want to make his own assessment.

'Is there a Ms Ros Woode there?' he asked, more desperately. 'My name's Stewart – I was supposed to meet her at Tripitaka on business. I'm told she had a meeting with Mr Lim. Is that right?'

'Mr Lim is not here. He is with Ms Woode, who is his guest. They will not be returning for some hours.' Hyde sighed loudly with studied, grateful relief. 'My apologies on behalf of Mr Lim. You say that your business with Ms Woode is urgent?'

'Very. Life and death, near enough.'

'But – business?'

'Urgent business. Can I arrange to see Ms Woode? Not to intrude or bother Mr Lim . . .'

At the corner of his vision, Chris' mouth tasted small emotions of satisfaction, confirmation. Someone would be searching the four-wheel drive by now, and finding nothing except a small pistol, fake hire documents, his suitcase as supplied by Cass. An airline ticket from Oz to Thailand, then Mandalay.

'You are staying in Mandalay, Mr Stewart?'

'Innwa Hotel, yes.'

'I know it. A business hotel. You will be there tonight, tomorrow?'

'Yes, but—'

'I will convey your request for a meeting to Ms Woode, and Mr Lim. If it is convenient, a message will be left at your hotel.'

'Listen—'

The connection had been broken. Lim was satisfied – of what? That he was coming to Mandalay, alone? Hyde put down the receiver, and shrugged with exasperation.

'That's it . . . uh, thanks. Back to fucking Mandalay. Christ, I just hope tomorrow's not too late!' A moment of disorientation and uncertainty. Then he picked up his briefcase. 'Thanks again. G'day—'

Hyde trudged towards the doors as if the weight of what confronted him weighed on his shoulders – which it did, indeed.

Alder believes it is the irresistible attraction of his penis that keeps the woman distracted from us. What do you think, Jessop?

I'm not interested, sir, so piss off. He hadn't, of course, replied in anything like that manner to Ralph Lau's enquiry. But it could be true. Marian Pyott was thirty-eight and lived alone. Getting it on a regular basis from Alder could be right up her street. Why not? She was allowed a passion awayday every once in a while. She'd never exactly been a nun.

He had soothed and half agreed, therefore, in order to get Lau off the line. The Chink had rung only minutes after the young Australian poofter from the Tripitaka hotel. He was a good observer, and the tape recording of his conversation with Hyde, played down the line, was helpful. He agreed with the young shirtlifter – Hyde had swallowed the bait and gone careering off to Burma without back-up and with a sketchy cover, helpless to do anything but follow the trail to Lim. And a certain body bag.

It was, of course, intensely irritating to have to wait to fly out there himself. Lau had some bloody banquet in the City to attend the next day and wouldn't be flying out to Rangoon in Winterborne's Dassault Falcon private jet until after it was over. Hyde could well be dead before he, Jessop, took off from Heathrow. Pisspoor anticlimax that would be.

Hyde was using one of his covers and old or hurried documentation. His nerves were shredded. Aubrey might have slipped him the necessary, via Godwin, but the old bastard had been able to do nothing else, except wave Hyde off at the airport.

Jessop sat back in his chair and watched afternoon cloud shadow Tower Bridge and make the river pewter-grey. He recognised the trick Hyde had been using, it was in every syllable he spoke. Using his genuine panic as part of the cover. But he was coming apart at the seams, that was obvious ... He'd always been sure of Hyde and his fat lover, that one was the key to the other. His hands grasped the edge of his desk as if he intended lifting it, even throwing its rosewood bulk across the room. Hyde was on his own, couldn't think straight, wouldn't live another twenty-four hours.

But he wanted to *be* there when it happened. Not afterwards, unzipping the body bag for a quick gloat before it was dumped in the Irrawaddy. Because of Lau, he and Cobb wouldn't reach Mandalay before Hyde's corpse developed rigor mortis and was stored in a freezer to stop the maggots breeding . . .

CHAPTER TEN

Flow My Tears

The quick tropical dawn caught him climbing the shallow hill towards them. Lim's white, imitation-colonial house sprang out of the darkness, its walls gleaming, the huge swimming pool suddenly dyed blue. Trees massed in the quick light like servants peremptorily summoned. Beyond the house and its guest bungalow and outbuildings, the Irrawaddy's wide, python-brown shape slid past Mandalay as the first golden pagodas climbed out of the dawn. The sun rose above the Shan plateau and the rice country to the north like a spread carpet. Hills as small as boulders jutted from the plain.

'She's not there, is she?' Colin Evans murmured. Cass shook his head in reply. 'Well,' Evans continued in a whisper, watching Hyde moving more cautiously up the hill, 'not unless she's in a cellar where the bugs and the thermal imager can't pick her up.' Evans shivered. Cass' cheek was gilded by the new sun. 'How's he going to take it, her not being there? You don't think—?'

'No, Taff. She isn't a dangerous prisoner. Easy to keep her harmlessly alive, in case they want to show her to him.'

'Fair enough.' He yawned. 'I'm knackered – out of practice for all-night surveillance. Bit easier being security liaison for the Commonwealth Games in KL ... All right?' he concluded as Hyde dropped into the shallow gouge in the hillside which, together with straggling, thorny scrub, hid their presence from the windows and the occasional security patrol.

Hyde rubbed his face with a hard washing motion, then nodded.

'All right. What are you picking up?' He nodded again as Evans handed him the brandy flask and a thermos of tea. He swallowed the brandy greedily, coughing and then silencing the noise as if he had betrayed his emotions. Then he sipped the tea.

Cass gestured towards the receiver and its aerial.

'Usual early-morning sounds – lots of lavs flushing, noisy breakfast cereal ...' He grinned, the expression tasting the air as carefully as a snake's tongue. He wore the headphones askew, listening with one can to the noises and voices transmitted by the bugs Hyde had placed. 'Nothing – significant.'

'You wouldn't,' Hyde responded flatly. 'She's not there.' He raised his eyes and his hands as if to employ both to fend them off.

'Lim's giving orders,' Cass interrupted. 'Wants the car ready in a half-hour.' He released the knob on the set that tuned him to whichever of the bugs he chose to hear.

Hyde unslung his nightglasses and the portable thermal scanner from his shoulder. Unhooked the earpiece and mike and then released the webbing of the radio harness. Evans packed each item into the bag as carefully as a valet.

'Everything you know about him, Phil,' Hyde announced.

His features remained unwarmed by the rising sun and without colour, even as the tints of the city, the plain and the plateau deepened and became richer. Pagoda pinnacles and roofs, statues of the Buddha, goldened. Rafts ferrying bamboo, looking like wrecked buildings in the river current, moved slowly on the Irrawaddy. The Kathadaw pagoda at the foot of Mandalay Hill was a blinding tower surrounded by its seven hundred *pitakas* – the white beehive miniatures of the pagoda that housed the marble tablets recording the entire Buddhist canon, the *Tripitaka.*

'OK,' Cass responded, 'the man's probably all you say he is – the crucial middleman between the Golden Triangle and the Straits Royal Group. What he does *legitimately* in Mandalay, from a suite of offices in one of the new highrises near Zegyo Market ... That one, appropriately golden-glassed. See?' Hyde nodded. 'He imports and exports, mainly to China. Gems, hardwood and textiles, sugar, dried fruit. He's been in the same business for years – which,' he added apologetically, 'may be why I haven't given him the attention he merits. He's a man of old habits, routine. He still *appears* to spend all his time doing what he's always been doing.'

'Perfect cover,' Hyde observed sourly. '*How* routine is his day?'

'From what my guys have managed in the lack of time, he's almost like a robot. Office every day, all day – except for Thursdays, which is when he visits his mistress in the house he bought for her in Maymyo. Then he's home every evening, unless he has business dinners or the like.

Mr Clockwork. Hello—' He was still wearing the one ear-phone. 'That accent's Russian, unless I'm mistaken—'

Hyde took the headphones and listened. When he returned them, he said: 'He's not buying textiles or dried fruit, Phil. There's a German or Dutchman there, too. He didn't want any toast, just coffee. Lim's office – underground garage?'

'I'll check.'

'Let's hope his routine is the same today as every other day.'

'Want anything to eat – pancake, Shan sausage?' Evans asked, opening a coolbox. Hyde nodded.

'What's in the pancake?'

'Shrimp – not bad.'

As Hyde ate, he said: 'Lim isn't worried about me. He won't even be expecting a call today. Just some half-arsed rescue attempt, some time. We need to take him before he begins to wonder what I'm up to. Agreed?'

'Wouldn't that endanger—?' Cass began.

'It could lead to a trade,' Hyde countered. 'If Lim is as important as we think he is.'

'He's coming out,' Evans murmured, adjusting the focus of the binoculars. 'Shaking hands with two men – good suits. One could be Russian. Big black Merc, would you believe? His guests are leaving.'

They watched the car move away from the house towards the high iron gates, which swung automatically open. The car dipped down the hillside towards the city, trailing red dust. Lim returned indoors.

'Is he going to the office?' Hyde asked.

'What's today – Thursday? Office in the morning, mistress in the afternoon.'

'There's another Merc outside the front door. Chauffeur, two others. Armed – folding-stock Skorpion machine

271

pistols, or similar. One rides in front, one in the back. Price of dried fruit must be going up all the time ... Here's Lim.'

Lim's slight, rotund figure ducked into the rear of the Mercedes. Then the limousine moved smoothly away from the white façade of the house, through the gates and down the hillside. The sun made its black paint as iridescent as the shards of a beetle.

Cass switched off the receiver.

'Grabbing him could get very messy – every which way,' Evans cautioned. 'Set off all kinds of alarms.'

'Then we've got to take all of them – survivors and others. Does he spend the night in Maymyo?'

'I'll check. We may not know.'

'Let's hope he rogers himself to a standstill every Thursday. In which case, we'll have all night. Is someone watching his office?' Cass nodded. 'Tell them he's on his way – and so are we.' He smiled wearily, his lips trembling slightly. 'She's alive – somewhere. He knows. He'll just have to tell me, won't he?'

Evans was appalled by the savage bleakness of Hyde's stare as he glared balefully down at Mandalay.

Marian swallowed coffee as she read her own words in the early edition of the *Telegraph*. Pathetic bluster, she judged. *Transparent* bluster. Her political enemies were hugely enjoying her discomfiture. One of them, in her own party, was offering odds she would become a Euro-federalist by Christmas. The remark made her smile.

Why on earth had she done it? What was it Dickens called it – *telescopic philanthropy*? The easy concern at far-off indignities and injustices ... Politicians bored with old ladies' complaints about vandalism in their constituencies? The hint of *hybris*, the illusion that mere mortals like herself could make a difference?

Or was it because she knew, on a suitably romantic balcony in Rangoon, probably by moonlight, that Alder would make her an offer she could not refuse? Was all this just one last hurrah before she deliberately chose a private world of enthusiasm and passion? A last duty to a life she had already determined to leave behind?

She was committed to Alder now, and the rearrangements she must make in her life seemed no more important than formalities; resigning her seat, moving to Washington, living with him rather than in her habitual solitariness.

She had known and liked him longer than any other man. She was ignited by him sexually as by no other. Because of him, she could no longer devalue the merits of company. Her fear of loneliness had become real during the past days. Unlike most of the men she had known, Robbie neither feared nor resented any disparity of intellect or taste between them. With him, she could continue her inner life.

He makes me laugh and I desire his company, she had admitted in one bout of reflection. Not bad, on the whole. Enough for her to commit herself. But only for the long haul – not for anything less permanent than marriage or fashionable *partnership*. Anything less would have an insufficient meaning.

So, Rangoon was the grand finale in some way, the best of exit lines. It wasn't even because of the attempt on her life; not really. Rather, it was a kind of vanity that drove her to it, one last big gesture.

So, knickers to everyone and to all reflection on the matter, she announced to herself, finishing her coffee. Pushing the newspaper aside, she looked around the small kitchen. It was already strange that she was alone in the flat. Robbie was at the DTI, then going on to the

Burmese Embassy, oiling the final wheels. *Lady of the Lost Cause* caught her eyes above her photograph in a tabloid. Most of the article, dutifully supportive of the government, was positive about moves towards democracy in Burma and hoped she would notice. Government and Opposition alike saw the success of the trade mission as a consummation devoutly to be wished. The junta were even promising to crack down much harder on the heroin trade from Burma. Token destructions of poppy fields in Shan state had begun . . . Oh dear, the black Mercs would have to go back to the showrooms, she thought, then sobered at once as she recollected the photographs of a hundred and more people massacred and buried in a pit.

She must not reveal the source of the explosives when the bomb went off, she instructed herself. Robbie would never, *never* forgive her for sabotaging billions in investment and trade, and neither would anyone else.

The phone rang in the lounge and she left the kitchen and picked it up. It was Myint San. Her self-satisfaction evaporated.

'I'm alone,' she answered to the young woman's anxious caution. 'Have you heard from—?'

'Yes.'

It was as if suspicion of her had returned to the young woman overnight, like a malarial chill. She sensed Myint San's hostility. Perhaps that morning's newspapers had renewed her mistrust. She had been demoted in the order of Burmese spirits.

Marian smiled bitterly. She was about to prompt the almost truculent Burmese woman when she heard the entryphone ring. Ignore it—? It rang again, urgently.

'Hang on a mo - someone at the door,' she breathed, and went into the hall. A distorted, round-faced, big-nosed male on the tiny CCTV screen. Familiar, though. 'Yes?'

'Tony Godwin, Ms Pyott—'

'I'm just on the phone—'

'Um, could you let me in and stall the caller till I get there?'

She pressed the door release. Looked at the telephone receiver in her hand, puzzled, and opened the front door.

'Sorry,' she murmured, 'can you hang on another minute?'

'Yes.' The sullen tone was now convinced that her disdainful suspicion was justified.

Godwin and a younger man came out of the lift, Godwin moving crablike on his sticks. It was, for a moment, as if they were about to barge past her. Looking up, Godwin saw the undisguised but embarrassed pity in her expression and his features clouded. Impulsively, she apologised by laying a hand on his arm, gesturing him into the flat with apparent eagerness. At once his expression became affable, but he nevertheless shook his head.

'Can we remain out here for a moment, Ms Pyott?'

'Marian.'

'Marian.' He grinned. 'Kevin knows what to do.' He looked down at the receiver in her hand as his lightly bearded, spectacled companion continued into the flat, carrying a heavy, black briefcase. 'How important is that call?'

'My contact – why?'

'Have you said anything significant – names, dates, that kind of thing?' Marian shook her head. 'Good. Have you spoken before, over the telephone?'

'Yes – but not names. That's always been at her insistence.'

'Good. Oh, you can carry on with the call out here. I'll just see what Kevin's up to.' Godwin stumped away down the hall.

'Hello,' she offered into the receiver. 'Sorry about that.

You've made contact, you said? What arrangements?'

Myint San was exasperated, in an ugly mood. Marian hated the judgement she made. The woman's damaged body rebutted her irritation. Myint San and Tony Godwin – both the victims of undeclared wars.

'Someone will contact you at the Inya Lake Hotel, where you are staying. I have given them the details and dates. You will be given instructions. Do you understand?' It was deliberately belittling, patronising.

'Yes—'

'That is all I was told to tell you.' The angry, bristling suspicion of Marian seemed to run down like exhausted clockwork. 'I must go. Good luck.' She was gone immediately, as if hurrying away from her own warmth.

Slowly, Marian wandered into the flat. Godwin and Kevin appeared mutually smug. Two metal buttons lay on the coffee table, no bigger than a pair of earrings. 'Good job your contact's the cautious kind. Probably has cause to be—?' Marian nodded. 'These two little friends would have picked up everything ... One in the standard lamp, one in the power point – they don't put them in the phones these days. Too many mobiles in use—'

'Someone's bugged my flat? *When?* How—?'

'Probably when you were out. We should have swept it before. Our mistake. Sorry.'

'It's like bloody Euston station, this flat! How many people have been in here in the past few days?' Her anger was not directed at Godwin. She sat down suddenly, opposite the two men, shivering. The day was fine beyond the window, with briskly hurrying white cloud.

'It's normal – like a burglary,' Godwin soothed. 'Violation of privacy.' She merely nodded. 'Get us some coffee, Kev, there's a good lad. Kitchen there, is it?' She nodded again. 'Good.'

She blurted out: 'God – if I can't cope with a couple of bloody bugs, how am I going to cope over *there*?' Angrily, her hand swept the bugs from the table on to the carpet.

'OK,' Cass whispered urgently, 'he's left the office and he's on his way down now.' One of Cass' Burmese locals was dressed in overalls posing as elevator maintenance. Cass shivered with excitement. 'Three of them – Lim and the bodyguards.'

He waved the R/T aloft as a signal. On the far side of the high-rise's underground garage, another Burmese on the payroll waved back, then climbed into the delivery van that had brought them all into the garage.

'OK,' Cass muttered, watching the doors of the lift, then the black Mercedes, its chauffeur invisible behind the tinted windscreen. Finally, he glanced at Evans crouched beside him and Hyde on his haunches behind the flank of an American limousine.

The garage was like a huge, concealed safe in which the new wealth of the shabby, sprawling town was stored. Ranks of gleaming limousines, sports cars, four-wheel drives. Some of the prosperity had already sprouted into the streets, like the building that housed Lim's offices.

'All right?' Cass asked Evans.

'Hope so, boy – we'd better be able to take a couple of Chinks, hadn't we? Not much bloody good if we— *Doors!*' he ended in a harsh whisper. He saw Hyde tense as the lift doors slid open.

Hyde focused on the first bodyguard as he scanned the garage, his eyes narrowing against the midday light spilling moltenly down the ramp from 26th Road. He remained unsuspicious of the delivery van as he crossed to the Mercedes, which had drawn up near the lift doors. Hyde rose into a crouch behind the Lincoln. Lim, followed by the second armed man, moved casually into the garage, hardly glancing around him – he paid the body-guards to do that.

The delivery van, as if just arrived, rolled slowly across the dusty concrete towards the Mercedes. The long striplights in the low ceiling reflected hypnotically from its windscreen. Lim ducked his head to climb into the rear of his car. One bodyguard was on the far side, the second at his elbow. Routine ... The van came doggedly, unsuspiciously on, then turned slowly as if towards the unloading bay. Its proximity alerted the bodyguards. The crash and tinkle of perspex, and the scraping of metal. The van had grazed the headlight and wing of the Mercedes. Lim backed out of the rear and the bodyguards began to remonstrate—

—*now*.

He dodged the Lincoln like a matador, running at the bodyguard closest to him, glimpsing Cass and Evans hurry into the cover of the van. Caught the raising of Cass' arm, the blow coming down on the other guard as he moved to threaten the van driver—

—collided with Lim and the bodyguard, hearing their breaths explode, the machine pistol bang against the roof of the car. Struck across the surprised, winded face, which immediately bloodied. The car's engine roared, the Mercedes held on the concrete until the driver was certain Lim was inside. The collision had half knocked him into the rear seat, sprawled him across the cream leather.

Hyde thrust the barrel of the Heckler against the crease of fat above the chauffeur's collar.

'Off!' he yelled, kneeling on Lim's chest, ignoring his clawing hands. 'Switch off – *off*!' Reluctantly, the engine died. Hyde slapped the pistol at Lim's waving knuckles. He

heard bone crack, the man gobble with pain. 'OK—?' he
shouted. 'Phil, Taff?'

The chauffeur's hands closed around his and the pistol.
He had twisted in his seat, was tipped half over it between
the two head restraints. Teeth bared in a snarl. His grip
strong, twisting at the gun. Lim, too, was pulling at him
with his uninjured hand, kicking upwards with his knees.

'Christ!' Hyde bellowed with pain, his groin on fire. Then
he was deafened by the explosion of the gun, blinded by
sticky redness. He wiped savagely at his eyes. The
chauffeur was bleeding over his hand and arm from a
stomach wound.

The other rear door opened.

'All right?' Cass.

'He isn't – get them in the van, all of them. This one too –
keep fucking still, Mr Lim, or I'll blow your balls off!' he
bellowed, thrusting the pistol into the crotch of the silk
suit. The chauffeur was groaning ominously. Then he
screamed and fainted as Evans pulled him back into the
driving seat. 'Come on, let's sod off!' Hyde snapped.

Evans and the van driver dragged the chauffeur across
the concrete like rubbish and hoisted him into the rear of
the van. Then the unconscious bodyguards; finally Lim.

Who knew who he was. His sleek, sallow features retained surprise at the attack, at their numbers, organisation. But he wasn't really afraid. Not yet. Short, paunched,
accustomed to authority, Lim's dark eyes were contemptuous rather than terrified.

'In the van, Mr Lim.' Hyde prodded him with the gun,
wildly, carelessly. Convincing Lim of his own danger had
to begin at once. 'I'll drive the Merc. OK, let's go, go, *go*!' he
shouted at Lim, ignoring the doubt in Cass' expression.

Her suitcase lay on the bed, closed, her black briefcase

beside it, together with a cabin bag. She glanced at her watch. It was darkening outside, early evening in the sky upriver, the lamps glowing on the Embankment. Milk and newspapers cancelled, central heating switched off.

'Yes, Daddy, I will,' she assured into the receiver. 'I'm your *grown-up* girl now.' She laughed, touched by his concern, as always. 'Listen—' She held the receiver out towards the lounge. 'Hear it? *Messiah*. Which goes to prove I was already well aware of your parental concern.' She listened, then, masking her impatience, murmured: 'I'll keep in touch ... No, no silly or unnecessary risks ... I promise – yes, I'll call you as soon as we get to the hotel. Bye, Daddy – love you, too.' She put down the receiver on the palpable disquiet, the tangible effort to disguise anxiety. Oh, *Daddy* ... She wandered into the lounge, sipping the gin and tonic. The taxi would arrive in another ten minutes.

Knowing Giles would call, and perhaps as some kind of touchstone, *Messiah* was playing on the hi-fi. Or was she mocking herself ... ? It was one of the very few pieces of serious music Giles enjoyed or even recognised. He had sung in the chorus at umpteen amateur performances, dragging Mummy and herself as a child to most of them. Unknowingly opening the door to music for her, creating a passion in her that only now seemed somewhat dry and academic ... Was she playing it as a way of saying goodbye to all that?

If we can go to Burma together, then maybe we could try Washington ... ? Think about that, Marian.

Robbie had said that on the phone an hour ago. I am, I am ... She studied the tumbler in her hand. After all, she already used American measures of ice in her drinks – it was a start. She smiled at herself in the mirror. *Rejoice greatly*, the soprano sang out in the familiar room that suddenly, in the subdued lighting, appeared to need redecoration. Giles only ever needed music when memory was to be indulged. Then he usually played his scratchy dance-band 78s and held Mummy again in his arms as they fox-trotted or quickstepped. *Rejoice greatly, O daughter of Zion.* Robbie probably indulged his musical appetites in elevators – ah, well. She laughed delightedly.

The music made the room smaller, cramped almost.

Nevertheless, despite the warmth evoked by the recollection of his voice and the promise it had held, she could not treat her future impulsively. She was not her mother, swept off her feet on the dance floor at eighteen by a dashing young captain in his full regimentals. She was thirty-eight and the veteran of a number of minor skirmishes and actions of the sex war, *two* of them her previous brief liaisons with Robbie. She realised that an important, ingrained part of herself still clung to her books, music, career ... *He shall feed his flocks* began as she drifted into her study. Genius, passion, the familiar shiver at the manner in which the music pierced.

The photographs lay on the desk, as if she had forgotten to pack them; or was reluctant to do so. She quailed once more at the sight of them.

... *and gently lead those that are with young.* Without faith, she shared Giles' eye-prickling response to the mezzo's promise. She recalled a late-night television debate with a prominent bio-atheist, one of the new stormtroopers of the godless, where she had ended up arguing against rather than with him; because of passages of music like this rather than for any shred of belief. Ridiculous, the potency of great music.

She picked up her reading glasses and looked at the snapshots once more. Perhaps a hundred of God's images had been executed and thrown into a pit. She couldn't just

walk away, or simply forget. The future frightened her.
She felt endangered. She steeled herself by studying the
photographs again. As far as she knew, Kenneth had not
even noticed that they had been purloined. At that
moment, she hated the small theft and its consequences
for herself.

You have to go on with it, she told herself. However
frightened you are ...

Come unto him, all ye ... that are heavy laden ... The
soprano now, the music climbing towards its certain
heaven. She wondered, for a moment, whether the
atrocity mocked faith or its absence.

... ye shall find rest ... She picked up the magnifying
glass, using it without removing her glasses. The music
always caused her eyes to prick. But she was crying now,
her tears falling on the photographs, on the glass she held
quiveringly over one picture. Her tears streamed helplessly, her chest ached with tearing, cardiac sobbing.

Ludicrously, she blamed herself for using the magnifying glass. If she hadn't, she would not have recognised
him, not even have taken any special notice of a white
man's presence there. She could have forever been
ignorant of the fact that he had been there. Robbie *had
watched it happen*. Her hands beat helplessly at the air,
fending off the terrible evidence of the snapshot. Alder
had *been there—*

The dilapidated warehouse overlooked the Irrawaddy
and the wharves along its eastern bank. The building was
scheduled for demolition like the slums, warehouses,
shops and shanties that sprawled around it. The place, in
the afternoon light, had looked like nothing more than a
landfill bulldozed to the water's edge and then forgotten.
Except by the whores, their pimps, dealers and addicts,

and the ships and huge rafts that unloaded at the wharves.

In the late afternoon, Hyde had seen buffalo pulling great logs from the water; a ferry had left for Bagan as women had done their washing. The boat had been ramshackle and overloaded, like a small, crowded corner of the town that had broken off and was drifting away. As he returned again and again to the dirty, broken windows on the warehouse's upper floor, the river had appeared the only urgent thing in the scene, sluggish as it was. It seemed to suggest the futility of his own distracted nervous energy.

Across the river, pagodas and stupas had risen white and gold out of the red earth and green vegetation, timelessly. The sunset had ignited the dusty sky, as if the air had become molten. The temples had looked as black as ash-heaps, the river like smelted ore. Weak lights had flickered out of the night that had followed, signs of an uncertain encampment.

It was almost one in the morning now. The chauffeur was certainly dying, slowly and in great pain. *And he hadn't cracked*... He still feared Lim too much, more than death at his elbow. Lim was smug and certain, his power not falling away from him. They seemed unable to frighten him, and the theatre they had created seemed no more convincing than a hasty travelling puppet-show. Tied in a chair, sweating in the night heat, his broken finger causing him pain, Lim remained somehow aloof and unthreatened. It wasn't working—

The smoke Cass exhaled splayed like a grey hand against the window and the night outside. His presence made Hyde newly aware of the chauffeur's groans from the farthest corner, where he was lying on a sleeping bag. Lim was in another corner, as far away as possible from the dying man.

'I've untied his hands,' Cass murmured. Hyde began what might have been a growl of dissent. 'He seemed to need them free to clutch at his stomach, the bandaging...' Cass hesitated, then added: 'Patrick, don't bollock me, but the guy hasn't got long. He might not even *know* where Ros is—'

'I think he does.'

'Then he's more scared of Lim than he is of dying.'

'I know that,' Hyde hissed through clenched teeth.

They had played good cop, bad cop with the chauffeur for almost two hours. Cass had promised him hospital, Hyde indifference to his death. It hadn't worked. The two bodyguards – unwounded and therefore even more under Lim's authority – were locked in a tiny storeroom. Evans spoke sufficient Mandarin to eavesdrop by means of a bug. They'd been threatened, kicked a bit, not given food or water, but they'd given nothing away even when left alone. Maybe they didn't know.

It required days, perhaps as much as a week. They didn't have enough time, because Lim would be missed by morning and Jessop, who must have organised the trap, couldn't be more than a step or two behind.

'I know that,' he repeated. Cass exhaled more cigarette smoke against the smeared window. The waterfront's sparse lights reflected in the river. Hyde, his hands clenched, turned to Cass and added: 'Once more. Tell him I won't let him go but you think you're beginning to persuade me. I'll leave the room – take Lim outside ...?'

Cass nodded.

'I'll try it.' He ground the cigarette beneath his shoe and retreated across the dusty warehouse towards the groaning chauffeur. Hyde approached Lim.

The man's sallow complexion was made muddy by the few poor lights suspended from the ceiling that still worked. Muddy, but defiant and contemptuous. Hyde raised his fist, but Lim seemed little more than amused by the gesture. His eyes watched Cass in the opposite corner, bending solicitously over the chauffeur. The eyes were suspicious, guarded.

'We're going outside for a bit,' Hyde snapped, jerking Lim to his feet so that the Chinese had to bend forward, the chair protruding behind him, lashed to his arms and legs like a donkey's burden. 'Come on, you can bring your chair with you,' Hyde mocked, pulling at Lim. The man waddled humiliatingly beside him.

Then he began shouting in Mandarin, for the chauffeur's benefit. His tone abounded with threat. Hyde shut the door behind them, pushing Lim backwards so that he settled awkwardly on the chair, almost upsetting it. Lim turned his head, realising that his back was to the steep, rickety flight of stairs. Another yard and he would have tumbled down them to the ground floor.

'Want a push?' Hyde sneered. Lim spat. 'Filthy habit, that,' he observed, lighting a cigarette as much for theatre as tension. 'I thought *we* were the barbarians . . . ?'

'You are all dead men,' Lim growled. 'You are all *dead*!' The shout was one of insulted superiority.

'Fuck you, Chink,' Hyde murmured, his back to Lim. 'We've got that tart of yours from Maymyo. Nice place you've put her in.'

Softly, and following a silence: 'You are lying.'

'You think there's only *three* of us? Don't be stupid. We wouldn't try muscling in on Ralphie's drug business, just *three* of us – would we? No, we've got the woman – just as you've got mine. In the case of yours – you could well end up being found by the cops, lying beside her dead body. Knife in your hand, I shouldn't wonder.'

'I do not believe you.'

'You'd better. Want an ear of hers for proof, do you? When you're out of the game, Ralphie might even *give* us a piece of the action. We could be your successors. Think about it, sport.'

The story was simple. It was also desperate – which was why he hadn't discussed it with Cass or Evans. It might, just might, be believed by Lim that the three of them were the vanguard of a group of ex-spooks muscling in on the heroin profits. It had happened before, in other parts of the world . . . It was the only story he had. So they had to appear to know everything about Lim, not just be interested in Ros' rescue. They wanted a slice of the cake, either by arrangement or force. It even explained Hyde's own long, close interest in Lau and Straits Royal . . .

'You are all dead men,' Lim repeated, but with less certainty. The suggestion of numbers, a danger much greater than Lim had imagined, and directed at his *business*, unnerved him.

'Change the record, sport. We've got you. Do what we like with you. Talk to Ralphie ourselves, maybe. I mean—' He turned for the first time to face Lim, then moved towards him with violent, animal speed. Lim flinched in the chair, aware of the stairs and the gap of dark air behind him. Hyde gripped the chair and tilted it back-wards. 'If you won't give my woman back, or even tell me where she is, what fucking use are you to man or beast?' he shouted into Lim's face. His arm quivered with the effort of holding the chair with its front legs off the floor. Lim's feet kicked feebly at him. Hyde tilted the chair more off-balance and Lim at once became still and deeply afraid. 'I mean,' Hyde snarled, his breathing louder than Lim's on the narrow landing, 'what bloody use are you alive? Eh – what bloody *use*?' he shouted into Lim's muddy, strained features. Spittle flecked the man's face. Then

Hyde added at once: 'Christ, I'm getting a bit tired of holding this. Why should I bother with you? You're not going to tell me anyway! I'll have to try to beat it out of one of the others!' The chair groaned, its back legs slipping on the creaking floor.

He *wanted* to let Lim fall . . .

The door behind him opened.

Cass exclaimed: 'She's alive, Patrick! In *China*—'

He wanted more than ever to let Lim fall backwards, break his neck tumbling helplessly down the stairs . . .

Even at the altitude at which the Dassault Falcon was flying over Athens, the floodlit city shone out starkly in the night below him. The Acropolis jutted up from the city hazed with pollution, the Parthenon – Athene's temple – was bone-white in the hard lights. It was little more than a fleeting image before it was behind the aircraft and hidden by its port wing.

As Ralph Lau turned his gaze away from the electrical circuitboard of lights that Athens had become, he saw Jessop coming towards his armchair from the flight deck. The man and his even more uncouth companion, Cobb, were seated towards the front of the cabin, forward of the grouped armchairs and bar and dining area he occupied with his team. Lau resented Jessop's approach like a trespass, even as he was alerted by what struck him as the shifty hesitation in Jessop's expression.

The man hovered and Lau, with condescending reluctance, indicated that he might occupy the armchair opposite him. The Aegean was suddenly black after the city, its islands like stars, so that the sea might have been nothing more than a mirror of the night sky.

'What's wrong?' he asked quietly, picking up his champagne glass without offering Jessop a drink.

'A – message, sir.' Something had gone wrong.

'Yes?'

'From Mandalay – Lim's number two boy. He was on the phone—'

'Yes?'

'Lim was seen. Thursday's his day for a shag – he goes to Maymyo, his mistress—'

'Yes?'

'He was seen at the airport' – Jessop looked at his watch – 'an hour ago. Not with his own pilot. With someone who could have been . . . could have been Hyde, sir!'

After a long silence, in which the islands of the Cyclades slipped like water lilies on an illuminated pond beneath the Falcon, Lau breathed:

'Where were they heading?'

'A flight plan was filed for Ruili.'

Jessop's gaze avoided him, then the man's head came belligerently up. 'He has to have recruited help to get hold of Lim – Lim underestimated Hyde! I warned him not to—'

'Be quiet, Jessop – unless you have a suggestion? An hour ago – how far are they from Ruili now?' He answered his own question. 'As little as ten minutes away. This man Hyde will walk into *my* house and make Lim hand over the woman, just like that!' Lau snapped his long fingers.

Then he seemed to react like an actor to the sudden, tense silence that possessed the cabin. His arm, quick as the movement of a snake striking, reached across the low table. His open palm slapped Jessop's face, fingerprinting it like a sheet of paper. Jessop's mouth hardened and his eyes burned.

Eventually, he muttered: 'Lim is the one who screwed up. Letting himself be taken. I warned him—'

Lau's hand moved and Jessop flinched. The hand waggled dismissively.

'What *now*?' he asked.

'Lim's become expendable. He *loused* up, he's been compromised. He might even have told Hyde something. Give the order to eliminate him. Sir.'

'Too inconvenient.'

'Lim can be replaced by a dozen others. You can look decisive if you give the order. A warning that you'll tolerate no sloppiness.' His voice faded in self-consciousness, and Lau smiled at the man's embarrassment.

'In Lim's case, not yours? I'll consider it.'

'There's not much time—'

'Shut up, Jessop!' Lau hissed. 'I'll let you know what I decide.'

'Have them eliminated, sir – the woman, too.'

'I'll *consider* it. Go back to your seat. Now.'

Jessop stood up. The silence clung like a hair shirt to his body. Islands dotted with the lights of towns and villages far below the aircraft. David Winterborne's aircraft ... Fuck Lau ... he *had* to agree. Hyde was within ten minutes of Ruili, taking Lim as a hostage and a means of releasing his fat tart of a girlfriend. Come on, Lau, you bastard – *decide*!

He did not dare look back at Lau in order to assess the effect of his argument.

From the window of the Bell 407 Hyde could see, even in the faint pre-dawn greyness, the border town of Ruili spread like a skin disease on the low hill-slopes. Beside him, he felt Lim twitch with sudden tension. In the pilot's seat in front of them, Mike Sung – Evans' pilot – nudged the helicopter's nose down. The three of them seemed to drop helplessly towards the town. The border fence was visible, straggled across the hills like some enormous fuse in preparation for dynamiting Ruili.

Hyde scanned the hillsides beyond the town's lurid glow. Bulldozers' lights already moved like fireflies, levelling shanties, creating factory space and the bare earth where new hotels would be planted. Large, discreet white houses and bungalows rested coyly within dark, new plantations. Hyde wondered which of the low factory buildings near the reservoir was the one that contained three hundred bears, caged in one-cubic-metre spaces, and hideously milked for the bile in their gall bladders.

From the reservoir, the town flowed down into a pool of hard light. Beyond the outskirts of bamboo and corrugated-iron slums were tree-covered hills, paddy fields, tea plantations.

The helicopter dropped lower, searching among the bungalows and houses like a sniffer dog. Lim stirred beside him like a more dangerous animal. Cass and Evans – the latter by now at Mandalay airport for the morning flight to Rangoon – had tried to persuade him against this course of action. Then given in and planned it in a couple of hours. *Five minutes in and out – no more than seven. After that, Lim will think of taking risks to stop you ...* Their voices came to him like snippets of a pilot's dialogue with a control tower. Crucial, but disembodied, unreal.

Cass had fought with him to save Lim from being tipped down the stairs of the warehouse. The brief struggle had calmed him – more importantly, with the chauffeur's collapse, Lim himself, already terrified, had subsided like a bank of eroded earth. Told them where Lau had his estate, confirmed that Ros was there, alive. Hyde's relief had been immense, and he'd turned away to mask it from Lim.

Lim flew to Ruili two or three times a week, ostensibly as a gem trader, in reality as the heroin middleman. Cass knew that much already, but not about Lau's estate—

'There!' Hyde shouted to Sung, his arm pointing. 'The big white house with the pool to the side! Got it?' Sung nodded. 'Is that a helipad?'

'Yes. I will put her down there!'

Hang on, doll – I'm coming.

Lim would, with a gun in his back, give the order to release Ros. It would purportedly come from Ralph Lau. Sung would fly them back to Mandalay, ninety minutes to the south-west. *Hang on, Ros . . .* His excitement was fierce, even exultant.

A hundred feet up now, no more. The white, circled cross marking the centre of the concrete landing pad floated up towards them. The swimming pool caught the first daylight. She'd hear the rotor noise by now – it had probably woken her up. Fifty feet. The Bell wobbled in the slight dawn breeze. Dark trees stirred, the grass rippled like water in the downdraught. Beside him, Lim was tense, angry, calculating. Hyde drew the pistol and nudged the Chinese in the ribs. The house remained solidly unconcerned at their unexpected arrival.

Hyde scanned the façade, the pool area, the lawns, the trees through the night pocketscope. There were still deep night-shadows filling the estate like a black fog. Twenty feet, fifteen . . . Nothing, nothing . . . Ten feet—

It could have been a Russian RPG-7. It was the same kind of jutting tube. The man's figure was at the corner of the house farthest from the swimming pool. His head was cocked to one side like that of an inquisitive animal as he squinted through the sight mounted on top of the portable rocket launcher.

He felt the helicopter's undercarriage bounce softly as it touched down. He shouted at Sung:

'Take her up – *up!*'

His right hand was on the door lever, the straps of the backpack in his left before he finished shouting. He saw terror spread like ink over Lim's features, and was certain he saw the spit of flame as the rocket was launched. He thrust the door open as the helicopter tried to struggle into the air. He fell sideways, towards the lawn, the pack dragged after him.

The helicopter lurched, he felt a hot breeze on his face, then he was blinded by flame, deafened—

CHAPTER ELEVEN

Unexpected Guests

Lim was haloed in orange fire, his arms waving as he drowned in flame. Then the breath was knocked from Hyde's body as he hit the ground and the big backpack fell on to him. The lawn sloped. He rolled a few yards.

All he could see was something like the retinal image after staring at a lightbulb, a corona around a dark mass. Nothing else. The mass moved and lurched, enlarging, and the corona shone more fiercely. The noise of the rotors was engulfing. Something had flown out of the corona like a small comet. It might have been Lim. The burning helicopter leapt down at him like a spider dropping on its prey. Then a second rocket hit what remained of it, showering him with hot fragments. The Bell rushed at him, its crazed rotors leaning drunkenly in his direction. The noise screamed in his head and its heat enveloped him as it hung for a moment in the air. He could feel the scything wind of the rotors. He stared up, terrified, as the burning wreckage pursued him like a boulder. He was still running, though his legs seemed to surrender to the inevitable—

—tripped on something smouldering on the lawn and fell. The burning shadow passed over him, a few feet above the grass, before a rotor blade buried itself in the ground like a ploughshare and vaulted the wreckage into thick trees and shrubs which immediately began to burn.

The fuel exploded. Whiteout. He was blinded—

—*they'd be blinded, too* ... Their nightscopes and telescopic sights would be flooded with white-grey fire. They wouldn't even have seen him drop out of the helicopter. He'd tripped over Lim's body, and could hear the man's last breaths gurgling in his scorched throat. Only yards away, the trees and huge rhododendrons were alight.

Hyde dragged the pack after him into bushes the fire had not yet reached, hearing voices raised in alarm and confusion. He remained blinded by the flames of the explosion, and shook his head angrily, trying to see and orientate himself.

It would take minutes for them to bring the fire under control and find two bodies rather than three. He could feel the heat, smell the burnt fuel and vegetation, and began to make out the shape of a bush, the black trunks of trees—

—good enough. The pocketscope was still clutched in his hand. He scanned the façade of the house. Running men, dragging a hose, others watching, arms waving. One still clutching the launch tube of the RPG-7.

Face at a window. White, moonlike. Then it vanished, dragged away by someone he didn't see. Third from the right, first floor. Ros.

Hang on, doll—

He shivered with cold as the shock loosened its grip.

Kneeling, he opened the big backpack. *Just in case*, Evans had told him. *Just in case*, he had repeated ... Rations, comms equipment, weapons, maps – full kit. He pushed the first round into the chamber of the Sig Sauer pistol. Thirteen-shot magazine. Spare clip. Pistol in belt, clip in pocket. Then he fitted the thirty-round curved magazine to the silenced Heckler & Koch sub-machine gun, before standing up and hefting the pack on to his shoulders, settling the harness to comfort.

He could hear voices clearly, but they were still concerned with the hose, the burning rhododendrons and pines. Hyde breathed deeply.

Then he pushed his way through the dusty bushes, away from the lawn and the men. The Bell, tilted against a tree, was little more than garden rubbish that had been set alight. He emerged from the ornamental thicket on to another sloping lawn and a gravel path leading towards the house and the swimming pool. One minute—

He sprinted towards the angle of two white walls and the broad patio beside the pool, the map of the house clear in his head. The Welsh windbag had reconstructed it from the chauffeur's pained ramblings in the car that had taken him to hospital ... A map that possessed the clarity of gratitude, relief, hope. He heard his boots on the grass as he ran beside the gravel path. Trelliswork, an arbour, then the patio. The pool caught the dawn and the fire like petrol catching torchlight. First floor, third window. He skittered along the wall of the house as if dancing quickly between shadows thrown by the flames. The short, stubby silenced barrel of the sub-machine gun was pressed against his jaw.

The pool rippled with the morning's first breeze. There were mountains beyond the town, walking away like an endless herd of huge grey animals. It was quickly becoming lighter. His breathing was audible—

The kitchen door was open and someone had come through it. He struck the sallow face with the bulk of the gun, then hit the back of the head. The shirtsleeved man staggered, toppling into the pool with a lazy reluctance.

Kitchen. Beside the door, in the dim light from another room, he saw a pegboard from which dangled sets of keys. He snatched at one set after recognising the logo on the keyfob. Hall and stairs beyond a corridor. He moved quickly, cautiously, the voices from outside retaining their ability to startle and alarm.

He paused at the foot of the staircase in a teak-floored hall. Dying firelight through the glass of the main double doors. The place smelt rawly new with wood, paint, plaster. Chinese vases, carved ornaments. The pack was already heavy. Now—

He bolted up the stairs. Wrought-iron balusters, polished teak handrail. Third window at the rear of the house. He turned at the head of the stairs. Another forty-five seconds gone. Now—

He kicked open the door, ducking out of sight and then reappearing briefly. Three-shot burst. The silenced gun bucked, puffing like someone recovering breath after running. Ros' expression was one of stunned terror. The body of the guard flew backwards to sprawl across the single narrow bed near the window. His arm had flown up, and the gun it held cracked the window. Shit. Ros's terrified eyes were looking beyond him. He fired through the open door. The body on the other side held it open, its legs sliding into view. Ros's gaze transferred to himself. Voices outside.

'OK?' he asked as she shrank away in the armchair beside which the first man had been standing. '*Ros?*' Sharply, like a slap. Her features immediately crumpled into the muddiness of confusion, disbelief, reawakened fear.

'Hyde ...?' She remembered him with the effort of senility.

'Come on, doll, let's get out of here — *come on, Ros!*' Another verbal slap. She was newly conditioned to orders. His lips quivered like his hand, with frightened relief, as she got to her feet. She was dressed in loose black silk trousers and a bright, gold-dragoned padded jacket. He was at the bedroom door as someone called up to the window from the gravel walk outside. A note of enquiry. Repeated. He turned and she immediately flinched at his glowering expression. He turned back, instructing in a hoarse whisper: 'Keep close to me. Do everything I say.'

'Hyde, how did—?'

'Not *now*.' Then, more gently: 'Legs OK?' She murmured in response. 'OK, let's go!'

Top of the stairs. He faced the armed man at the foot of the stairs for what seemed like minutes. Ros' soft collision with him seemed to jerk his trigger-finger. The shots knocked the man aside, into a crumpled heap against the wall, creased like the silk rug his fall had distressed.

'Now.'

He ran down the stairs, hearing her follow. Noises of alarm from the kitchen. Ros' breath on his cheek, the noise of clockwork quickly running down. He snatched something from one pocket of his jacket, tugged at it as at a beer can, then rolled it towards the kitchen.

'Turn away!' he snapped. He was sweating now.

Red light flared over them. He smelt the smoke immediately, and flung open the main doors as Ros dawdled in renewed shock near the crumpled body against the wall. Voices were shouting, there was coughing beyond the roiling smoke from the grenade. He dragged Ros into the cool of the dawn, their feet suddenly noisy on gravel.

'Garage block — there!' He pointed with the Heckler.

Ros' concentration vanished into alarm once more. He half pulled, half bullied her into a stumbling run. The sky lightened as if a black cloth had been swept aside. 'Come on, doll!' he urged.

He fished out the keys he had taken from the pegboard. Japanese four-wheel drive. He pressed an electronic pad and the garage doors slid upwards. Hyde ducked beneath them, dragging Ros with him. Dawn light glinted from windscreens and chrome.

'That one!' he urged, pulling her with him.

He unlocked the driver's door of the Toyota, then whirled round. One-handed, the barrel resting on the wing mirror, he fired a three-shot burst, then another as the gun jumped unstably. The man fell aside, wounded, dropping his own gun. Hyde clambered into the driving seat, thrusting the backpack into the vehicle's rear.

'*Ros—!*' he bellowed, startling her slow attention into obedience. She climbed shakily into the passenger seat as he started the engine. He let off the handbrake, revved the engine.

Pulled at another grenade's pin and threw it from the window. Four other vehicles, a Merc, two four-wheel drives, a Porsche. Incendiary grenade, two thousand degrees centigrade, burn time thirty seconds. Lovely mess. He let out the clutch and the Toyota careered out of the garage. Then he saw, again at the angle of the house, the man with the RPG on his shoulder. He braked violently and threw the Toyota into reverse, waiting for the missile's launch and the incendiary grenade to explode. Christ ... Two seconds, three ... Saw the spit of flame as the projectile's motor ignited. It flipped like a swift under the door of the garage. Four seconds. One second to... The Toyota screeched out into daylight as the projectile hit the rear wall of the garage and the grenade exploded. The mirrors were blinded. He believed he could feel the heat of the explosions.

He glimpsed the man with the launch tube, screaming like some demented child for another projectile. Raging helplessly, half blinded, pulling out a pistol. Sweat soaked Hyde's body. Ros was oblivious, drowning in shock. The rear window crazed in the driving mirror from a gunshot as he swung the vehicle out of the main gates, which had opened automatically.

The Toyota lurched on to a steep tarmac road that descended the hillside towards Ruili. The reservoir caught the sun, becoming another blind mirror. The shanty town huddled sullenly against the border fence.

Hyde glanced at Ros. Tears were streaming down her cheeks from dark-stained eyes. She was shivering malarially, utterly knackered. He'd just opened a termite mound to get her out, stirring up a degree and ferocity of activity he could barely imagine – and Ros was already done in. Her silence contrasted with the exhilaration he experienced.

'Bad, was it?'

'What? Yes.' It was as if he had enquired whether she had slept well.

They were inside China, two or three days from Mandalay by road. Mandalay? They weren't safe anywhere inside Burma. And the pilot was dead. The garage fire whisked out of sight of the mirrors as the Toyota rounded a bend in the steep road. He'd got her out alive, thank Christ ...

Now for the difficult bit: keeping her alive.

He felt shock nibble at his attention, the destruction of the helicopter coming back to him now. He glanced surreptitiously at Ros. She didn't appear to have been physically ill-treated, but she'd been in their hands for days, totally isolated. She now stared through the windscreen, idly watching the trees flowing past, somehow oblivious of her rescue. Her hands did not even leave her lap to reassure herself that it was really him.

He gripped the steering wheel more fiercely, to prevent the tremor in his hands that was the consequence of the past minutes, and the hours and days that lay ahead.

The Dassault Falcon lowered itself, suddenly clumsy in the air, towards the runway. The raw, half-finished international airport, south of Bago and forty miles north of Rangoon, emerged from the early-afternoon heat. Incomplete terminals and hangars lay like old crab shells on a beach. The new highway snaked away through the darkness of jungle and paddy fields. The undercarriage touched the still-gleaming concrete as the last rainclouds of the morning slid towards the Andaman Sea.

The new airport had been how he, and AsiaConstruct, had got into Burma. And how he had encountered the generals of the 999 Group – their temptations and their power. *And now General Feng had discovered the escape of Hyde and the woman from Ruili* ... The vast delta flattened into an horizon as the Falcon slowed on the runway.

'Yes, General,' Lau murmured. He felt the cold perspiration along his hairline. 'It is being organised—'

'Lau Yen-Chih' – the voice was like a threatening hiss – 'do you know where these people are? What resources do you have at your immediate disposal?'

The plane turned on to the taxiway. The limousine to meet him was already and expectedly pulling away from the main terminal building. In concert with another car, a fawn Mercedes.

Lau glanced away from the window towards Jessop

and Cobb. They seemed to relish his discomfiture.

'My people know this man. They will have the best—'

'Insufficient. A military flight is waiting for them. I know who they are. A Shaanxi transport of the Myanmar airforce is on the runway now. Tell them to transfer to it. There will be other troops on board, more at Ruili. There is *openness* and co-operation, Lau Yen-Chih. You understand?'

'Yes.' He had tried to keep the lid on, silencing his people in Ruili until Jessop could fly up. One of them obviously worked for the Chinese generals.

'Good. This is tiresome.' The plane had come to a halt, as had the two limousines. His own car, cleaner and newer, gave the illusion of choice. 'My car will bring you to Yangon.' Feng always scrupulously employed the junta's terms of reinvention for Burma – Yangon for Rangoon, Myanmar for the country. The codewords of oppression. 'We will talk while others act.' Then the phone was put down on him. He stared at his own receiver, then quickly replaced it in the armrest of his seat.

'Something wrong?' Jessop asked with the shock of a hot needle.

'No!' he snapped back. Jessop soothed a satisfied smile from his lips. 'No. General Feng is aware of the situation. Probably for our benefit. He has a troop carrier standing by. For you and Cobb. Military units are also—'

'Who's in control?'

'I think that's obvious, don't you? *We* are *responsible*. Make sure you succeed. You do *know* this Hyde well enough to be able to anticipate him?'

'I know him. I don't know who's been helping him. Not that it matters any more. He and his fat tart are in hostile country, aren't they?' Jessop grinned.

Lau thought the expression exaggerated. 'Make

certain.' He looked out, enraged, at the two limousines that were not alternatives.

'OK, let's collect our gear,' Jessop announced to Cobb.

'Make certain,' Lau murmured, almost to himself. His long fingers tapped uncertainly on the armrest. His fate – *his!*– was now linked to this man Hyde. Unless he died, and the woman, and their knowledge along with them, he would be demeaned and further subordinated. Lose face ... lose *power*, with Feng and the other 999 generals. Maddeningly, because David had fallen for Jessop's over-elaborate trap for Hyde, *he* was now uncertainly placed. 'Make certain this time!' he snapped.

Jessop's shoulders flinched; not as if he had been struck but as if he contemplated turning and striking out himself.

Late afternoon. The sun beginning to burn like a furnace as it seemed to rest on the jungle to the west of the military airfield ten miles from Ruili. A collection of barrack huts and a control tower. The parked aircraft were mostly drab-painted transports. Cobb, standing at the top of the lowered rear cargo ramp of the Shaanxi, squinted into the low sun. There were a couple of Qiangjiji fighters parked on one of the taxiways.

'You always know you're in one of the nicer places in the world when the goons in uniform are all wearing Ray-Bans,' he observed. 'What a dump.' He nodded towards Burmese army officers standing beside two trucks. Two of them were smoking. There was a deal of braid and the ubiquitous sunglasses. 'They're just going to do whatever we tell them, are they?'

'If Ralphie's generals say so, I suppose they will,' Jessop replied. 'They'll be good enough, anyway. They've fought almost every bugger who isn't in their army to a standstill.' He watched the troops beginning to file past them down the ramp towards the parked trucks. There were other trucks near the single low terminal building.

'They haven't had so much as a sniff of Hyde yet.'

'He can't be far away.'

'It's ten or more hours since he—'

'Shut it, Cobbie,' Jessop snapped. He experienced an alienation he realised must be similar to that of Hyde. This place, and Shan state just across the wire, was a huge, unmapped minefield. He had been dumped, blindfold, into the middle of it, just like Hyde. *Because of Hyde* ... 'OK, let's talk to these little brown chappies about what they're doing and what they need to do.'

'Sure.' Cobb suppressed a slight shiver. A cool breeze from the mountains had nudged aside the afternoon heat. 'Sure.'

'We've got this lot,' Jessop reassured, waving his hand. 'Hundreds more across the border if we need them – *all* of Shan-bloody-state if required. Helicopters for the asking, courtesy of the Chinks.' He pointed towards the airfield's perimeter fence. 'See, Z-9s. Gunships the Frogs helped them to build under licence. Isn't international trade a wonderful thing?' He laughed more easily, with returned confidence. 'Come on, let's find out where they've already searched, and where they haven't. See if they've got all the roads and airports fully covered.' He studied Cobb. 'Come on, you miserable sod. It's our *job*, after all – and we've got Patrick-bloody-Hyde as the target, just for added frisson.'

He waved his bundle of maps in the direction of the waiting officers like banknotes. A Chinese colonel climbed out of the cab of one of the trucks. The Burmese officers at once became attentive, distracted from Jessop's approach.

Thanks for the reminder of who's in charge ... The

mountain breeze was cold. Ralph Lau was a fucking humanitarian, an amateur do-gooder alongside the Chinky generals—

'I'm Jessop, Colonel,' he announced, at once offering his hand. 'We need to talk—'

He was wearing Kunming Military Region flashes at the collar, and military intelligence insignia on his shoulderboards. He inspected Jessop and Cobb in turn, and eventually seemed reassured, as if he had perceived beneath race a family likeness. He held out his hand.

'Yao Fan,' he announced in a studied, prim English. 'Certainly, Mr Jessop, there is a great deal to discuss. Come.'

Jessop winked at Cobb as he turned away. *Hyde is stuffed*, he mouthed. The gaggle of Tatmadaw officers, a couple of colonels and three captains, fell in behind them. A slim Chinese finger tapped Jessop's bundle of maps and Yao Fan announced:

'You will recall from the maps that there is only one good road to the west. He took that. A peasant saw him at eight, in a Toyota four-wheel drive, red in colour. It is confirmed as the vehicle he stole.' They reached the nearest of the barrack blocks. 'He will have taken the Bhamo road north or the Burma Road south towards Lashio. The mountains offer few alternatives.' He looked up as a Z-9 gunship drove in low from the west like a raincloud. 'Ah – let us hope, new information.' The helicopter settled noisily, dustily on to concrete, its downdraught chilly as it buffeted Jessop. 'Since we were informed' – he paused, as if anticipating an apology – 'two helicopters have been flying the roads all day. A third and fourth crisscrossing the mountains north, west and south of the peak of Lol Song— Please enter. We may continue where it is warmer, since you appear cold.' A narrow smile, then he went through the door, at once lighting a cigarette.

Hyde is stuffed, Jessop again mouthed at Cobb as they followed the Chinese inside.

It was the bats, flung suddenly up into the dark all around the limousine, that disconcerted her. Or so she chose to believe. They had replaced the crows and other birds so quickly, as if an omen. A projection of her fears, or the product of her worn and wearied nerves. Both, Marian decided, as Alder, seated beside her, directed her attention towards the last of the sun shocking Inya Lake into a sullenly burning mirror. There were heavy, darkened trees, the expanse of water, as the car moved along a wide boulevard lined with white-painted colonial houses. He seemed to be inviting her to see only the façade.

She wanted to scream, because Alder was selling her an image of a place marooned, innocently, on a colonial sandbank, and able to make some kind of painless transition to the modern. If only she ignored the disease of the junta's red and white posters everywhere, then she would see Rangoon through his eyes. She wanted to scream – because he remained oblivious to her stretched, drained mood. But most of all because he had *been there*, this stranger seated beside her in the rear of a limousine that smelt of leather and the heat of the Rangoon day. Because he had known, all along. He had stood beside a Chinese in civilian clothes, watching people being executed.

She wanted to scream because she could not even accuse him of it, because she must continue to play this exhausting role, go on pretending . . . when all she wanted to do was to ask him *why, in God's name why?* On the plane, at the hotel, over their gin and tonic, now in the car – *why, why?*

'The Lady's house,' he murmured almost in her ear, pointing across her breasts. His proximity revolted her now, made her feel the need of another shower – as rape victims must feel. Shower after shower. 'I respect her, God knows, but she's wrong—'

'Is she?' she challenged. '*Why*, Robbie?'

He seemed surprised at the vehemence of the question. The limousine was past the house on University Avenue in a moment. Marian glanced back at the signs warning vehicles not to slow down or turn, and at the uniformed guards at the closed gates and stationed at intervals beneath the high wall. A trishaw seemed to hurry past the gates in the gloom under the trees. Would *she* have to be smuggled in there to meet Suu Kyi?

'Cold?' he asked, touching her arm.

'No—' It was betrayingly abrupt. 'Jet-lag, I expect,' she added.

'Sure.'

The limousine passed a Buddha seated near a brick washing trough. The figure's posture was that signifying the moment of enlightenment. Soon afterwards, they passed the Shwedagon pagoda's small forest of stupas and terraces. She glimpsed groups of unmarried girls seated on grass, weaving new robes for the monks. The full moon, in the last of the daylight, hung swollenly above the stupas, catching the setting sun in red-gold. The streets were suddenly more crowded.

Marian focused her attention on what she saw, as if attempting to make some complex mathematical equation soluble. The buses, bicycles, trishaws, the pedestrians, street markets – soldiers, even – were unreal, but if she concentrated sufficiently she was less aware of Alder's body close to hers, less conscious of their mutual, intimate past.

And less aware of her own danger and of the photographs, hidden in her suite at the Inya Lake Hotel . . . Even so, the city remained alien and aloof. The posters and the uniforms oppressed. There was the sense of people being made afraid, ground down, corrupted, even when she saw them laughing or caught the noises of the streets. Men and women smoking cheroots, white shirts in the dusk, *longyi* skirts worn by both sexes, a dead dog. A building eaten by damp or fire, near the Sule pagoda, was glimpsed as they plunged into the mildewed colonial relic of downtown Rangoon. The air-conditioning seemed to bring the scent of neglect and decay into the car.

Cinemas, theatres, crowds. Fruit stalls. A Buddha, standing in the *mudra* that promised tranquillity. Grey brick and red, the High Court, the new banks. The broken-teeth gaps where new hotels were being constructed like dental fillings.

Then, quickly, the Yangon River and the waterfront along Strand Road, the harbour indistinct in an ochre sunset haze. Steamers moved ladenly while small boats rowed by figures standing upright seemed to worry them like insects. Pavement cafés, mobile phones, Western sports cars, a high-rise hotel. Modernity lurching against the colonial past as if to shoulder it aside. Money was more visible. Long white or black limousines, many of them queueing, like theirs, to deposit their passengers beneath the portico of the British Embassy.

She felt immediate relief at their arrival. Familiar Victorian architecture, echoing both Georgian mansion and Greek temple. The sky darkened swiftly and ships' navigation lights sprang out. Alder took her hand and she shivered as at an electrical charge. Her thoughts seemed wild, incoherent, segmented like an orange. Alder's presence, what she now knew of him, what she must do, the unnerving city, the imminent reception—

A saffron robe and a dark business suit passed each other on the wide pavement.

'I'm all right,' she reassured. 'Fine! Just tired.'

'Go easy on the champagne,' he chuckled.

She wanted to scream ... The limousine reached the red carpet lying like a dog's tongue across the pavement to the doors of the Embassy. The chauffeur opened her door. Scream ... The evening air was like a warm flannel against her cheeks and an assault on her nostrils. The river, the spices, the heat and dust. She got out, careful of the long, sarong-like skirt.

At once, she recognised a government backbencher, and was forcefully grateful as the familiar enveloped her like oxygen, allowing her to breathe.

'Hi, Greg!' she called. 'Trust you not to be late for the buck's fizz!' His smile, thank God, was genuine.

'Hi, Marian – ah, Congressman.'

The men shook hands, then all three of them climbed the short flight of steps beneath the portico. Marian felt herself hurrying into the known, the safe. By the third step, watching how she placed her slippers and holding the sarong skirt that glistened like petrol in the lights, she was calmer. Greg was the familiar, solidly so. A young and ambitious member of the new intake, he was – others said – a suit trying to become empty. Occasionally and awkwardly, even apologetically, he opposed his party. He had found, like a barrier to ambition and office, a genuine concern for the inner-city constituents he represented. Marian liked him. Not all ex-PR men were to be condemned out of hand.

Remembering jokes against Greg, seeing the other familiar faces in the big reception hall and on the curving staircase, she felt like an actress, not walking on to her favourite Westminster stage, but at least appearing in one of her most famous roles in a provincial theatre. Portraits of HMQ, some antique furniture dulled by years and humidity, photographs of former ambassadors and Prime Ministers, including the callow child who was the present incumbent of No. 10. The rotund ambassador and his taller, angular wife. Wear on the stair carpet and the scent of dust in the long, heavy curtains.

She shook hands with His Excellency and wife. Both seemed amusingly on their guard, as if she was a gate-crasher. She *was* ... Her smile was consciously dazzling, disarming them, then she passed on to the staircase. Even the number of Burmese military uniforms could not, in these surroundings, unnerve her. Alder, a step behind her with Greg, had already attracted Burmese officials and some of the DTI civil servants, like satellites of a larger planet. Marian was struck, for the first time, by the significance attached to his presence. He was conferring an American imprimatur and legitimacy on the occasion.

She passed, champagne flute in hand, into the double reception room on the first floor, to be at once buffeted by the noise, and to be further reassured by the crowd. A slight Burmese bore down on her, almost like an attacker, dissipating her fragile complacency. He bowed and smiled, announcing:

'Miss Pyott – I am Mung Thant, Minister of Hotels and Tourism. May I welcome you on behalf of my government to Yangon.' She touched his cool hand with her fingertips.

'U Mung Thant, I thank you,' she replied. The minister was delighted at the Burmese honorific. He glanced at her costume, the *longyi*-style skirt and black silk jacket, and evidently concluded that her respect was intentional, lacking deceit or mockery.

'This is, I believe, your first visit to Yangon – to Myanmar?' Marian sipped her already warm champagne. Alder, nearby, seemed pleased at the minister's attentiveness. 'I express the hope that much of what you see will please you.' The light of the huge chandelier above them dazzled on the minister's spectacles, increasing her sense of his polite, self-effacing harmlessness. The sudden images of the atrocity that had sprung into her thoughts faded.

'I – I hope so, too . . .' she faltered.

The President of the Board of Trade passed, gathering an apologetic Mung Thant into her orbit. Peter Grainger, hugely enjoying himself, his face sleek with pleasure and self-importance, winked at her as the group passed. Marian thought she caught mistrust and suspicion from a junior minister and a brace of senior business figures. Then they were gone, into the room's undergrowth of influence, money, power. She was again aware of the preponderance of military uniforms. Evidently, the junta was unabashed and easy in its confidence.

The power groupings were already moving in small, purposeful shoals around the room, like those fish that emit constantly changing electrical signals varying in colour and vivacity. It made her realise her own smallness and impotence. She watched Alder as a stranger, grasping hands, pumping shoulders, as he authorised so much of what was occurring. Knots of uniformed or dinner-jacketed men approached him, spent moments, appeared to depart satisfied. Flashbulbs seemed to fire only at him. He held healing and banknotes in the hand they all gratefully shook. At that slight distance, and for a moment, he was innocent again.

But he was not innocent . . . The realisation affected her like a nerve gas, maddening and tormenting her. Fumblingly, she lit a cigarette. Coughed. Then wandered towards the room's windows. The Embassy was perched on Strand Road to overlook a trading port, as it always had done. It would go on doing so. *Everyone* was keen on that idea. Teak, oil, gas, minerals, rubber, gems, rice, fish to sell, and the whole of the modern to buy and import. Sounds fine ... Turning back into the room, she at once saw Alder's tall figure, head and shoulders above a group of Chinese and Burmese. Heroin to export ... She felt her breath catch and her heart thud quickly but leadenly. It was appalling to have lost him, as much as the realisation that he was involved in—

To distract herself, she picked out the CEOs of a dozen UK and European conglomerates, some Japanese with British subsidiaries – oilmen, the gas companies, construction firms, the electronic giants, the defence industry. Civil servants from Rangoon and London moved between the groups like sparks bridging contacts. A deal of silent toasting as the future was pledged and redeemed, bought and paid for.

Alder again—

A Chinese approached him, conspicuous in the severe, old-fashioned Mao jacket he was wearing. The spirit of socialism at the feast? The cigarette and the joke calmed her. Someone at the PRC Embassy, doubtless. China was Burma's biggest trading partner, strongest political ally.

He was a slight, almost insignificant figure, less than ten yards away. Alder appeared startled and uncomfortable. For her, it was at once difficult to breathe. Her chest ached with recognition. He had worn a Western-style suit the last time he had stood next to Alder; on red earth above the pit and the bodies which had fallen into it. She couldn't *breathe*...

'You all right?' Someone had grabbed her elbow to steady her. She had, involuntarily, tried to shake off the man's hold. His eyes were concerned, his mouth smiled. Colin Evans? 'OK?' he asked earnestly, still smiling. Then his eyes followed her intent gaze. He seemed puzzled, though he evidently recognised Alder. Then he forcefully turned her away, waving his arm as if to indicate night on the river, framed by the windows.

'What is it?'

Her hand rested on his.

'I'm all right – Colin?' He nodded. 'All right.' She smiled, then her expression became startled, unnerved, as Alder loomed.

'OK, Marian?' he asked. 'Something wrong?' She shook her head.

'Just a bit hot in here.' The slight Chinese was beside Alder, more like his jailer than a fellow criminal. The man's gaze inspected her minutely in an act of forced intimacy.

'I'm Colin Evans – embassy staff. I recognise you, of course, Congressman ... How d'you do?' he offered towards the Chinese.

'Feng,' he replied. He waved his cigarette airily. 'An acquaintance of the Congressman – and you are Miss Marian Pyott, of course. I recognise you. Your photographs do not do you justice.' He smiled, his eyes withdrawing from her.

'You want to sit down?'

'No – don't fuss, Robbie. I'm all right now, honestly.'

'I'll look after Miss Pyott,' Evans assured. 'My job, really ...'

'Congressman Alder, perhaps you might introduce me to the British minister. I wish to ask her ...' Feng seemed to lead Alder tamely away.

'What *was* all that?' Evans demanded. 'Do you know Feng? I don't – except I think he's Chinese military. Recognise the manner.'

'He is.' She was nodding furiously. 'He – he was *there*.'

'He's in those photographs? Shit – oh, sorry. I don't like his interest in you, in that case.' He studied her, then added: 'I'd say he's sure you know him from somewhere. He could work out exactly where, if he knows there are photographs—'

'Even Robbie doesn't know – know I have them, that is. He hasn't seen them, anyway.'

'But you've made Feng suspicious of you, that's more than obvious. I'd better check him out with our blokes here. Someone must know him.' He added, in a sharper tone: 'You're still looking at him. Try to show no interest at all – please! Look, I'll be back in a minute. Just circulate.'

Evans moved off towards one of the waiters behind the long trestle tables masked by dazzling white linen on which the buffet was drawn up like an army for inspection. He took the waiter aside and began talking urgently.

About Feng, obviously – Feng, who had stood beside Alder, and who was now interested in her. She shivered, even though her whole body was hot with tension. She felt her eyes unwillingly drawn back to Alder and—

—yes. Feng was watching her. Then he looked towards Evans. Then back to her. His gaze was a renewed assault against which she felt helpless. It was as if he already knew about the photographs and what she intended to do with them.

And was confident he could prevent her.

The quick dawn caught the gold of a stupa which sat like some fierce, giant helmet amid the ruins of other pagodas and an overgrown, jungled city wall. Closer, the market town of Bhamo was already dusty with traders and animals moving into it from the surrounding countryside. The muddy-coloured Irrawaddy lay like a snake's discarded skin, broad enough to be regarded as a lake rather than a river. Closer still, almost beneath the rocky outcrop which concealed them, was the tiny airport with its single runway, scattering of hangars, and one-storey terminal building. And the army trucks, unconcealed, and the lounging, unalert soldiers; two of the officers were smoking. The rising sun caught the windows of the terminal.

As Hyde lowered the binoculars, Ros stirred behind him. She shivered, then groaned at her stiffness – or the realisation of where she was. There was a helicopter down there, too. It had brought more troops and was being refuelled before continuing the search for them. The Toyota was hidden in a thickly wooded defile half a mile behind them, well off the track he'd driven in the dark the last twenty miles or so to Bhamo—

—and the airport they couldn't use. Stupid to have ever thought they might. They were less than fifty miles by air from Ruili. A helicopter, even fully loaded, could fly that in fifteen minutes. He rubbed the stubble on his cheek, as if erasing Ros' warm breath as she crouched beside him.

'No go?' she asked quietly.

'No bloody go.'

The Myanmar Airways Fokker sat on the apron in front of the terminal, a fuel bowser nuzzled against it, its two turboprops still. The only flight of the week from Bhamo to Mandalay. Goodbye to Phil Cass' great idea; their way out was blocked. Cass had had two of his locals fly up on the plane with return tickets. They'd be waiting in the terminal now, ready to pass on the tickets to Hyde and Ros – in vain.

'You'd better talk to him again.' Ros was still weirdly detached, a passenger on a train whose timetable she did not know, having no real reaction other than a sleepy vacancy. Hyde understood it. He'd got her out, she was with him, *he* decided things.

'I'll have a think, first,' he murmured, scanning the airport and then the town and the riverbank with the binoculars. The wide marketplace at the hub of the town was already crowded with stalls, bright awnings, people, animals; above it hung a gauzy dust that the sun reddened into a peppery spice. 'Have a think,' he repeated, keeping all anxiety and doubt from his voice.

The river lay like poured silver across a fertile plain, sliding south and then west towards purple hills. A rice crop was growing. Even the jungle seemed clipped and cultivated where it pressed down from the Shan plateau and the mountains to the north. A double-decker ferry like a floating bus was unloading petrol drums at a wharf.

Hyde felt himself relaxed rather than poised. The ease of their escape and the immediate border crossing – one sleepy soldier at a barrier already raised for early-morning workers and peasant traders to cross into Ruili – had been followed by hiding up in the hills before finding the narrow, climbing, twisting track to Bhamo. The full moon had given him light enough not to wreck the Toyota. The journey had been slow and uneventful; soporific, he admitted now. Cass had come up with the escape route to Bhamo, and even when it hadn't worked he felt himself slow to realise that he had collided with a brick wall. As if it was all happening to someone else. Rescuing Ros had been the object, and he'd done that.

He had to shake himself out of it. He saw the rotors of the helicopter begin to turn down on the runway apron. Ros' hands gripped his arm, her languid body pressed against his. He touched her forehead with his temple.

'All right?'

'Bit woolly – sort of asleep from the neck up. You?'

'Sounds about right.'

No one had hurt or threatened her; it was only the wear and tear that had been impossible to avoid, the devouring of her own reserves. 'OK, let's get back to the Toyota. I'll have a good look at the maps—' He hefted the pack on to his shoulders and climbed over the lip of the outcrop.

A narrow track led down the steep hillside into the wooded ravine. He looked around at Ros, nodded and then continued. Nerves began to open, slow as flowers. Cass would have to come up with another idea – a pick-up or something. Helicopter . . . ? The pilot would have to be good; they'd be expecting it. But it couldn't be by road; they were too exposed, and Mandalay was two days and nearly two hundred miles away.

He flinched as the Chinese-built helicopter flashed over them, its rotor noise masked from them until it lifted over the outcrop. He and Ros flattened themselves instinctively against the rock face as the Z-8 climbed away from them, making for the road from Bhamo towards the Chinese border. He watched it become a glinting dot, then a star, then sun-sized. It had turned and was coming back—

'Ros, get down! Behind the rocks!'

It grew in size, coming directly at them. *They can't have seen us.* It went into a hover only hundreds of yards from them. A flare curled up lazily in the morning air, then exploded at the end of its unwound length of smoke. An answering flare rose out of the ravine less than a half-mile away.

It was the Toyota. The helicopter was hovering directly above where he had hidden it. There were obviously troops no more than a few hundred yards from it. They'd found their only means of escape.

The Z-8 continued to hang above the hidden vehicle like a huge spider on an invisible thread. He heard, clearly above the rotor noise, the first shots. They'd riddle the vehicle before they approached it, just to be on the safe side.

There was no way out, not now—

PART THREE

A Burma Road

But the lust for power never dies—
men cannot have enough.
No one will lift a hand to send it
from his door . . .

Aeschylus, *Agamemnon*, 11.1355–8

It is not power that corrupts, but fear.
Fear of losing power corrupts those who wield
it, and fear of the scourge of power corrupts
those who are subject to it.

Aung San Suu Kyi (1989)

CHAPTER TWELVE

The River and the City

Her mood of detachment survived the first dousing of the shower for long enough for her to be grateful that the Soviet plumbing had been removed along with much else during the refurbishment of the Inya Lake Hotel. Plentiful hot water, adjustable shower head. All mod cons ... The water took her out of the nervous self-absorption she had inhabited during the reception. She was washing herself *clean* of Alder.

She had been able to simulate passion and even determine that the photograph in which he appeared would not be given to Suu Kyi. Been able, albeit fitfully, to sleep beside him. The message that had been left for her at the hotel desk – *Noon, the terrace of the Shwedagon pagoda, near the Bodhi Trees* – had increased her fears and brought Feng into a prominence in her imagination that was omnipresent. He was her real danger – and he had somehow made Alder less criminal, less guilty. She had engaged in casual sex with this new stranger, and kept Feng at bay ... until now. She shivered beneath the hot downpour and soaped herself violently, as if enraged that the shower gel would not cling to her skin.

The waiter to whom Evans had spoken was SIS. He had checked with the military attaché, and others. Feng was indeed a Chinese general, into heroin by rumour and linked to the former Communists who had gained control of most of the Burmese production of the drug. Alder had described him, in the limousine on their return, as a businessman he had met *when I was last here*. Alder had wanted sex as some kind of rich dessert to the entrée of power, influence and money he had enjoyed at the Embassy.

She continued washing her breasts, her thighs, again and again. He had been almost childishly vulnerable after his climax, tender and requiring proximity, comfort. Was that Feng's influence on him? She soaped her shoulders and arms. Secretive, too. Feng again? She let the water drum on her head and face. She would have to skip a seminar and a visit to an electronics factory to meet the contact at noon. Evans had ordered her to do *nothing* until he had consulted Kenneth and dug up more background on Feng. She wanted to obey.

She switched off the shower and stepped out of the cubicle into the steam-filled bathroom, towelling herself vigorously. She dried her hair, perfumed herself and entered the bedroom. Alder was to have ordered room service. She dressed quickly, putting on a long-skirted, brightly flowered frock and a pair of strappy, low-heeled shoes. Dressing would somehow cancel the night, she believed, brushing her hair. She was reluctant to renew their presence in the same room.

Eight o'clock. She walked into the sitting room, her attention at once caught by the view of the lake, dotted with islands and early-morning yachts. The smooth water mirrored pagodas and dark trees, and white colonial bungalows on the far shore. An illusion of tranquillity which the toy-sized traffic near the university did not dispel. The cloudless sky dyed the water an identical blue. She turned, her mouth opening as if to protest. Alder, in his dressing gown, was kneeling at the side of the room, the photographs of the atrocity spread out around him like the pieces of a giant puzzle. He looked up, startled out of abstraction. They stared at each other in what seemed a hot silence, as if the air-conditioning had failed. His baffled, angry sense of exposure, his understanding of her deception, made Marian quail; even though her genuine distress seemed to cow him.

'You know, then? The one thing I never thought of – you know everything.' His hand gestured feebly across the spread photographs. It did not hesitate, even at the one near his left knee – of himself, Feng and the dead. 'How long?' He did not wait for her to answer. 'These belonged to Kumar, right?' he growled, his eyes focused on something not in the room. His hands closed into fists as he returned his clouded, fierce gaze to the photographs.

'Kumar . . . ?' she asked, as if never having heard the name. She remained standing stolidly, a few paces from the bedroom door. Birds flickered at the windows like a prurient audience. 'Yes,' she recollected.

'The guy Hyde, right?' He did not look up. 'He found them.'

Suddenly, she wanted to scream at him. 'You were there!' she wailed. 'Kumar *saw* you *there*!'

'Of course I was there!' he yelled back at her. He got to his feet and walked to the windows, arms flailing. 'I was *made* to be there! *It made me his creature!*' He turned, glowering at her, the sofa between them. 'Feng planned it this way. That's Tripitaka, my last visit. I was David's man, not Ralph's. They wanted me locked in—' He paused, watching her take a cigarette from her purse. It was a means of silencing herself, suspending thought. She lit the cigarette and put the purse down on a low table. He continued: 'It locked me in real good. I had no idea, *no idea*. I knew all about Ralph, about Straits Royal and the laundering operation, the distribution through Winterborne businesses, the whole heroin thing—'

There seemed something other than shame or even self-preservation in his mood, something still hidden which puzzled her. As if the photograph that incriminated him was somehow secondary.

'How did you guess I had the photographs?'

'What?' He seemed surprised at her interjection. 'Oh, Feng. He knew you recognised him, so he believed you must have seen something—' Then, enraged: 'Otherwise, why the hell were you and Hyde coming after us? What was driving you? Not just curiosity; it had to be *knowledge*. I hid from that, but you couldn't deceive Feng. Christ, Marian, you gave the whole game away, the way you looked at him last night!'

The fear in his voice chilled her. He was terrified at her knowledge of him, and for his future, but also afraid on her behalf. Then he said, almost with contempt:

'What were you planning to do, uh? *Confront* me?' The small yachts glided as remotely and inaccessibly as paper boats on the smooth lake. 'What did you think you could *do*, Marian? Stop the train by standing on the railroad track? This isn't just *me*, Marian. This is in the hands of grown-ups who play for keeps – people like Feng. For Christ's sake—!' He was infuriated with her, an emotion that seemed entirely inappropriate. 'What did you think you could do about *that*?' He waved dismissively at the photographs.

'Something – nothing . . . I don't *know*!' She felt bereft of motive, then blurted: 'Something – I didn't know about *you*!' She was now the one signalling helplessly with her arms, as if to be rescued.

'And now you do know?' His look was scornful. 'You don't know *anything*.'

She ground out the cigarette in the big glass ashtray beside her purse, then retreated from the coffee table.

Alder seemed to come to some momentous decision. He rubbed his chin, staring at her as at a hostile stranger. His lips moving silently as if he were making some huge, complex calculation. Then, exasperated, he announced:

'OK – so you want to *know*? Truth time? Then this is how it is . . .' He paused, then asked: 'Answer me just one question first. What involvement do the Brits have in this? Uh? Why is Aubrey fired up, what's Hyde's interest – are they trying to take a hand in this?'

'In *what*, for heaven's sake?'

'The entire ballgame. Us, China, Burma – the whole Pacific Rim. Development; spheres of influence. What is it with you people? Your empire's long gone, you're down to trade missions now – or are you?' He moved towards her and she flinched back. 'OK, OK,' he reassured. 'You're just getting in the way.'

'What in God's name are you talking about?' she flared. 'It's *you* in the photograph, not me or Patrick Hyde! You make it sound as if it was no more than an *embarrassment*!'

'It was – necessary. You think I *wanted* to be there?'

'Why were you?'

'To get closer to Feng, of course!' he snapped

contemptuously. 'I was getting closer all the time. That gave him the hold over me he wanted—'

'You *planned* it? Why? Why were you there?' She was quivering with rage. He was accusing her, as if she was to blame for something much greater than the evidence in the photographs. Almost helplessly, she offered: 'I didn't even suspect until I saw you in the snapshot.'

'And right away you felt dirty,' he sneered.

'And all at once I felt cheated, Robbie.'

'OK, here it is,' he announced after an interminable, dragging silence. His words fell as slowly as stones through amber, and at a great distance from her. 'You shouldn't hear any of this, but I guess I owe you this much – and maybe a lot more.' He sighed, as if still restrained by complex bonds and loyalties. 'China controls Burma. Simple fact. People like Feng control the heroin trade, which means the Chinese army controls it. And controls the Burmese junta—'

'A lecture in geopolitics – *now*? For heaven's sake—!'

'Listen to me, Marian,' he growled, 'If you've ever listened in your life. You've blundered into something like Alice in Wonderland. Except that Burma isn't wonderland. You have no idea how big this is. Now listen.'

After another hot, tense silence into which she wanted to scream, Marian nodded and lit another cigarette.

'I'm listening, Robbie. But I can't really believe I am. How can there be a *reason* for it?'

'OK. It would have been a damn sight easier if you'd gone ahead and disbelieved the photograph – or believed a little more in me . . . But, OK.' He breathed deeply. 'My government – the White House, the State Department, Congress – the Company, too . . . We have two policies in China. Engagement and interdiction. One's public, the other's covert.'

'And you—?'

'Just listen.' He stood at the window, his hands in the pockets of his dressing gown, almost relaxed. Marian felt herself held in coils, a rabbit confronted by a snake. Or by his secret self, the person who was now acting as an informant on the man she thought she knew. Strangest of all, she knew that what she was about to hear would be the truth...

'Engagement and interdiction. I'm part of both. Helping open up Cambodia, Laos, Burma to our influence and investment ... and getting close to Feng and the other generals at the same time. Because they think I'm a crook from way back, long bought and paid for. First, I became David Winterborne's man. When I ran for Congress, David funded my campaign. That's illegal in the US. Then David went in the slammer and Ralphie-boy bought me all over again – and I let him do it.' He turned to face her, his features dark with anger. 'Then I began to get real close. Feng wanted a piece of me. He didn't trust me, and he was right, so he tricked me up to Tripitaka and – made me watch *that*. He has a whole album of photographs of me. He thinks he has me by the balls.'

'Has he?' She found it hard to catch her breath.

Alder shook his head.

'Only because it was meant to look that way.'

'Did you *have* to be there?'

'I didn't know what to expect – some kind of compromise of me, that's all. It turned out to be that. But I'm real close now.'

'To what?'

'The whole ballgame. The big picture. I have almost enough to go public ... for the White House to go public. Expose the Chinese generals and bring these countries into our sphere of influence. China will have to renounce the Nine-Nine-Nine Group. It will help free up Burma. The junta will have to let us in. It's that big, Marian.'

'It's foreign policy, then?' she mocked.

'You're so damned myopic, Marian!' he flared, arms waving. 'And so smug. You don't get it, do you? Deng's the bogeyman here, even if he's long dead. Because he *understood* how to make China work without democracy, human rights, freedom. Not like the Soviets – they never saw it. He did. How to run a capitalist dictatorship. And the guy who taught *him* was Adolf Hitler. Don't laugh, Marian, I'm deadly serious. No middle class, no intellectuals. And instead of Krupps and the rest, let the army run industry. It's working, too. People are getting richer but no freer. The Chinese model. Every damn country in Asia will want to copy it if it's a real success. And if they don't like it, maybe the Chinese will foist it on them anyway. Most of them are trying to replicate it already – especially right here in Burma, for Christ's sake! Half the damn *world* could rush into China's arms if we just let it happen.'

He had turned back to the window and returned his hands to his pockets. He seemed to be waiting like a pedagogue for some assurance that his pupil had understood the lesson. As if he doubted it, he added:

'Get rich and shit on everyone else. The West got it wrong; this is the way things work. Killing, repression, the boot in the face – that's the *real way forward!*'

'I see,' she murmured eventually. 'You're really working for the CIA—'

'For the White House and State. The Company provides back-up, it doesn't make *this* policy.'

She felt weak and hot. It was plausible, even convincing. Horrible, too. Horrible that he accepted the atrocity as a device, a guarantee of his pretended villainy. He remained the stranger on whom she had stumbled, looking at the photographs. Not so criminal, perhaps, but more secret and distant than ever.

'What – *now*?' was all she could ask.

'Now?' His gaze focused on her, as if he recognised her for the first time. Marian felt numb, but as if she had broken something as precious as the Worcester urn he had bought for her when they had first met. Valuable in money, invaluable in associations, emotional investment. She wished, at that moment, she had never seen the damning photograph of him, or that she could disbelieve it; could mend the broken porcelain. 'Now, I have to think this thing through. How to convince Feng there's nothing. Trade on my value to them—' He looked up at her and shrugged away her disdain. 'Maybe they'll listen. Not like the boy. He wouldn't ...' The dialogue was with himself and the past. 'That ought to have stopped it ... It didn't.'

She was kneeling on the carpet, collecting the photographs together, placing them on the low table. It was an automatic thing, a means of staving off thought. She allowed him to move closer, listening to nothing but the soothing, quietening tone of his voice, as if she were a pet animal.

'Why he was at Uffingham, God only knows – but he was. He wouldn't listen ... I never wanted it to happen. But he was crazy about it, about *me*.'

She looked up at him. 'No,' she breathed. 'Not *him*, not Kumar?'

'I had to – he wouldn't listen!'

'No—!' she wailed. He'd killed Kumar or had him killed. The boy who had taken the photographs, Syeeda's fiancé. Alder believed in what he was doing; he was even brave. But he had killed Medhev Kumar. His confession was too much for her.

She got to her feet, thrusting him away. Alder grabbed for the snapshots and they struggled for them.

The doorbell startled them both.

'Room service,' they heard.

He glared her to silence and went to the door.

A uniformed waiter smiled, pushing the breakfast trolley forward into the room. Marian remained rooted to the carpet, the photographs in her hand. The purse now, too—

The waiter had pushed the trolley to the table at the window and locked its wheels. He bent, oblivious, to open the heated box beneath the cloth, and removed a plate covered with a tin dish. Marian watched him as if he were performing some sacrament. He began laying the table—

—she moved jerkily, like someone learning to walk on prosthetic limbs.

'I'll see you later, then—' she announced loudly.

He moved to block her path, his hand raised towards her, or perhaps the photographs she clutched.

'You can't!' he whispered urgently, glancing at the waiter as he hovered for a signature and a tip. Marian smiled at the man. Then she said hoarsely:

'Goodbye, Robbie. If you try to stop me, I'll scream the place down.'

'For God's sake, you can't leave – *please!*'

'I have to. Tell them, tell them I disappeared – anything!'

He grabbed her arm, squeezing it painfully.

'You and your fucking sense of what's right! I can't let you do this—'

'Let me go, Robbie – *let me go!*'

'Get out!' he shouted at the waiter, dragging her further into the room. 'Beat it!'

The moment was being snatched from her. She had to get away from him, couldn't let him persuade her.

Kumar's murderer. She thrust at him with the sheaf of enlargements. The sharp edges of the prints caught the corner of his eye.

'Christ—!'

His grip slackened and Marian lurched through the door into the corridor. There were two maids with a trolley, a guest waiting at the lift door. She stumbled towards them as if she had forgotten how to run.

'*Marian!*' he screamed after her. '*Marian—!*'

She was running now. The lift door sighed open. Alder continued to yell after her like an animal in pain. She blundered into the lift behind the surprised guest, oblivious of the other passengers and their embarrassment. The door closed on his figure in the corridor, yelling impotently at her. She wanted to be sick.

Ros watched him as he crouched in the angle of a crumbling wall like a beggar, talking to Aubrey in London. The box of the radio system he had tugged out of the pack was in his lap, and the receiver was concealed by the hand he held against his face. His head was bent over the microphone. She was reassured by his tense, hunched posture, his clipped questions and responses. She turned away from him to watch late-arriving peasant farmers driving bullock carts or bearing huge bundles on their heads as they converged on Bhamo's central market-place. Enormous butterflies drifted through the dense foliage that overhung the road, and parrots quarrelled invisibly.

Hyde glanced at her, then continued his murmured conversation via the satellite link. The tactical radio was frequency-hopping – *just in case, even though it's heavy.* Evans' words and grin came back to him.

'No, there isn't another way ... Yes, the Toyota was

spotted, so they know we're in the area. But they're concentrating on the airport ... Get Cass to organise something. By tonight we'll be in Katha—' He traced the course of the Irrawaddy west, then south towards Mandalay. Two days, perhaps four, depending on how many loading and unloading calls the boat made. 'If we can get as far as Katha, then there's the train,' he insisted. 'Got that? Get Cass to send up a couple more locals on the train – no, I'm not going near the airport! *New* people – to Katha, with train tickets, new papers. OK? Or we stay on the boat, doing the tourist thing. What? Yes, Evans provided a cover of sorts – don't laugh, Godwin. American missionaries. Lot of Christians in Kachin state, apparently ... Yes, I know—' He glanced up once more at Ros' back. 'No, I can handle that. No other way out or means of transport. Yes, I will. I'll make contact again at Katha. Thanks.'

Ros turned as she heard him closing the straps of the pack. He held two books in his hand as he got to his feet and shrugged off his immediate surroundings like a shawl. They were hidden in the ruins of a burnt-out house on the outskirts of the town. Must have been the army or Kachin rebels – the place still smelt scorched.

Ros watched Hyde study her, saw his pleasure at her returned confidence. He had expertise, wore his skills like a skin. She was, in his company, able to put the days of isolation and insidious collapse behind her; beneath her immediate awareness anyway. And strangely, he was more attentive, even loving, because of her new dependence on him. He touched her face, announcing:

'Right, it's the boat as far as Katha. The old bugger will make the arrangements for what comes after that. All right?' His dirty fingernails pushed her hair away from her eyes. Ros nodded. 'OK, here we are. Carry one of these—'

Two small Bibles, bound in leatherette. 'This is the elaborate disguise.' He grinned. 'I've had less.'

'What?'

'American missionaries – probably the Welsh wind-bag's idea of a joke. Evans always tries to cover all the eventualities. Lot of Christians in Kachin state. Usually – he says – missionaries aren't targets for the army or the rebels. Aussie accents – they won't be able to tell the difference round here.'

He was, she realised, already looking beyond her shoulder, towards the hill they'd descended to Bhamo. Looking for their pursuers. Neither of them had heard the helicopter or seen any soldiers in the hour it had taken them to retrace their steps to find and descend a narrow, jungled track down the hillside to the road. Peasant farmers and traders, heading for the market, had seemed lethargically curious rather than suspicious of them.

He put his arm around her as they reached the road. Huts of thatch and bamboo matting straggled away as if seeking the shelter of the great trees that crowded them. Two wooden houses with corrugated roofs, belonging to the more affluent. The outskirts seemed preserved, as if they represented the village that Bhamo had once been. The town declared itself in rows of houses raised on posts, concrete-based, wooden-walled. Cultivated vegetable patches, scratching chickens. Shops, the stupas of a monastery, a woman weaving a blanket on a narrow porch.

A green world, though the trees and undergrowth wore a hurried, raw look like new skin after plastic surgery. And failed to conceal pitted stone and shattered wood, eroded bomb craters and the signs of scorching. Hyde talked to her incessantly, as if to distract her from any awareness of this former battlefield or no-man's-land through which the road led them. Ros sensed him coiled like a spring, though his tone remained casual. Luminous butterflies drifted like great scraps of coloured tissue-paper through streaming sunlight.

Hyde was satisfied with her. She could have been in much worse shape. She'd talked about it, briefly and with the interrupted transmission of a weak radio signal. They had told her nothing, for which he was grateful. She hadn't been aware of herself as the bait in a trap, hadn't anticipated his death. She had dissolved into fitful sleep once she had ended her narrative.

There were signs of the brief, undeclared war between the Tatmadaw and the Kachin Independence Army everywhere. A war zone bandaged by the quick, lush tropical undergrowth. Bhamo itself was already decaying and peeling; mounded with rubbish while still raw and new, as if the climate had surreally accelerated its ageing. As the road became more crowded and narrower, lined with shops and stalls, piled high and leaning drunkenly, they reached the marketplace. Amid the smells of animals, human sweat and dirt, morning heat and dust, there was that of the river.

Startling them for a moment, the flight to Mandalay climbed away from the airport, its engines drowning the noises of the market. Hyde gripped Ros' arm reassuringly. She breathed deeply, even smiled.

'We need something to eat,' she remarked almost casually.

'Clothes, too. Buy a shawl or something you can wear to cover your face and shoulders.' He studied the Chinese clothes. 'Your trousers are better than a *longyi*. You'll do.'

'Won't they be looking for an outfit like this? Someone my size?' The smell of spices and earth-clodded vege-tables. The scent of oxen pulling a cart.

'OK, try to get some peasant's clothes.' He looked around him at the press of costumes, at the Kachin, Shan, Lisu traders and farmers. His look was returned with polite curiosity. The hubbub and frenetic activity of the crowded market seemed, however, to explain or excuse their presence. 'I'll go down to the jetty and get the tickets.' He thrust a bundle of high-denomination *kyat* notes into her hand, and a narrow fold of dollar bills. 'Use the local stuff if you can.'

He hesitated for only a moment, then began working his way through the alleyways between the rows of stalls, the animals and children, the now-importunate traders who looked on his light skin as grinning currency.

The double-decker ferry was already crowded with passengers, bundles of goods, saffron-robed monks, basketed and tethered animals. A goat looked down imperiously from the railing of the upper deck as the ferry sat like a betrayed promise at the end of the decayed jetty. There was a short queue for tickets at a drunken booth, and he joined it. He watched the few hundred yards of dust between himself and the marketplace, then studied the jungled hills beyond the town. A bird or helicopter circled in morning thermals. It was already hot, humidly so – but that did not explain his sweat. The queue inched forward. This was already beginning to be a bad idea—

An army truck, towing a dust cloud, emerged from the marketplace towards the jetty. It passed a shawled woman taller than native ... It was past her before he realised it was Ros, in dark cotton trousers and the black shawl. He turned away, unnerved, hearing the truck stop, its brake rasp on. Soldiers debouched from it, and he heard snapped orders. The man in the booth, wearing a battered trilby hat and offering a gap-toothed grin and betel-nut halitosis, held out his hand.

Hyde bought the tickets to Katha. He turned slowly, aware of the pistol in the waistband of his denims and of its futility. Ros passed him, her hand emerging from the shawl to take her ticket. She reached the jetty, hardly hesitating before she walked down its length, showed the ticket, mounted the gangway. Then she disappeared into the crowd of passengers.

He studied the soldiers. They seemed purposeless now they had left the truck. There was no officer, just one NCO. Two of them were smoking. He was caught between the noise aboard the ferry and the market's hubbub. He heard the sound of an ancient truck, piled with Chinese goods, trying to start. And the noise of a helicopter. He squinted into the sun. It was enlarging like a sunspot. He began strolling in a casual, sauntering way – his sweating increasing – towards the truck whose engine wouldn't catch. He reached the jetty. The driver was enraged, the soldiers amused, the helicopter louder ... The downdraught plucked at his hair, his damp shirt. Another ten yards to the gangway, which was about to be hauled aboard. He tensed against a shout. The draining clatter of the truck's ignition, grating like a dentist's drill, seemed enlarged into the menace of the rotor's noise. People were watching the descending helicopter as if reliving an old, bad dream.

His feet on the gangway – which was hauled up after him. Mild curiosity at his skin colour, recognition of the Bible he held in his damp hand. His legs felt weak and he all but lost his balance as the ferry jerked itself away from the jetty, out into the river's current.

'—contact again at Katha.'
'Good luck and take care.'
'Thanks.'

Then Hyde was gone. Godwin stretched the tension from his upper body. His raised arms, against the windows of his office and the lights strung along the river, seemed to Aubrey a gesture of ineffectuality. The digital display in a lump of onyx told the old man that it was after two in the morning.

'Is it sufficient, Tony?' he asked heavily. 'Just to ask Cass to ensure that there are rail tickets at this place?' His forefinger found it on the map spread between them. 'Katha? There is no alternative in view,' he added heavily, 'and that I dislike.'

'Me, too, sir. More coffee?'

'Please.' Aubrey stifled a yawn. His hand wavered, like someone blind seeking to locate an object on the desk. 'No, I don't like it. The search for them will be highly organised, thorough. Any escape by *public* means is unsafe.'

Godwin refilled Aubrey's cup from the percolator on the windowsill behind him. He swivelled in his chair to replace it on its hotplate, then said:

'Phil Cass is accountable, sir – and not to us. There's only so much he can do.'

'Which gives me further cause for concern. Evans is a somewhat freer agent, but his primary concern is with Marian – especially now that Feng has become suspicious of her.'

'Can't you stop her trying to get those photographs to Suu Kyi?'

Aubrey wearily shook his head.

'Giles himself couldn't. I have no hope. Evans will protect her, *if* she does nothing too foolish. However, Patrick and Ros ... Any ideas, Tony?' His hand waved over the map once more, like that of a conjuror no longer at ease with his former repertoire. 'South lies the only road and the sensible direction. From Mandalay, they can be got out, diplomatically if necessary. At that point, we can enlist Peter Shelley.'

'Have you thought of asking our next-door neighbours *now*? Shelley would set up an extrication op for you, wouldn't he?'

'From Myanmar – during a DTI trade mission, all flags waving, smiles to the fore? Perhaps not even for Patrick. Peter has to be our last resort. Do I tell him Patrick was on holiday in Burma?' He sipped his coffee and lit a cigarette, adjusting his spectacles as he returned to the map. 'Patrick has no proof now; we have only the photographs, the provenance of which would be disputed. There is something at the back of my mind about Burma, the Irrawaddy. Yet I'm damned if it will come to me! It isn't Giles, myself, even Clive. None of us ever served in Burma ...' He plucked at his lower lip. 'Katha – it was the name. I stared at it as if it evoked a memory. A long, long time ago ... Damnit, I can't remember!'

Godwin hoisted himself out of his chair with his sticks and stumped across the office, calling out:

'I'll get a signal off to Phil Cass, sir – leave you to think.'

Aubrey finished his coffee as the door closed behind Godwin. He stared out at the neon night, the city stretching away northwards under cloud that reflected its glow like a huge conflagration. His irritation at the failure of memory masked a profounder impatience. Hyde, not to mention Ros, was more vulnerable than when he had returned from Penang. He trailed his enemies after him as a comet trails its cloud of debris and gas. A cloud which, in Hyde's case, constantly enlarged. He removed his glasses and rubbed his eyes. Then replaced them, and stared once more at the map, which remained as unevocative as the night beyond the windows.

How could Hyde survive Burma ... or Lau, or Winterborne Holdings, the junta, the heroin trade, China ...? His enemies enlarged and spread like a storm across smooth water. There was no means of forcing a trade-off with any of those opposed forces. Aubrey ground his teeth in frustration. What was it, for heaven's sake, in the depths of memory? Like an echo of the present – Katha? drugs even? the Chinese? ... There was someone who had known the area, who had related all this to him like a drunk slumped against a bar ...

... or lounging in a cane chair! 'Ha!' he barked triumphantly. He could *hear* the man now, even before his image came to mind, could recapture his own boredom as he listened to—

Scudamore. He remembered now. Scudamore knew Katha; there had been a heroin problem of Chinese origin – yes ... Scudamore.

The Chinese involvement with Burmese heroin pro-duction and smuggling was as old as the remnants of Chiang Kai-shek's KMT army that had retreated into Burma in the late forties and early fifties. They had financed border raids into Yunnan province against the government of the new People's Republic by means of heroin production ... Good God, Scudamore's narrative had seemed to take hours to complete! The heroin was smuggled south to Mandalay and, and *west*, into the newly independent India and East Pakistan, to Imphal and Chittagong, into Assam and Manipur. He saw, almost with surprise, his hand scribbling the place names on Godwin's notepad.

He lit another cigarette, his hand moving over the map as if on an instrument he had that moment recalled how to play. The Burmese government had asked the old colonial power for expertise and manpower to combat the trade. MI5 and Special Branch officers in the main. Scudamore had been drafted in from Malaya because he had served in northern Burma as a very young military intelligence NCO.

Scudamore – the Errol Flynn of post-war Burma, as someone else present at the interminable narrative had labelled him . . . Aubrey realised he was smiling.

Nothing new under the sun. At least not in the case of the Burmese heroin trade. And fat, boastful Scudamore knew more about its origins than most. *And* about the old and secret routes the smugglers had used to get the heroin *out of Burma.*

He was all impatience now, and preternaturally wakeful. Where was Tony? He needed to talk to Colin Evans at once. He knew which hospital they'd removed Scudamore to in Kuala Lumpur. He rose from his chair and scuttled to the door. It was a chance, and perhaps a real one. A fallback plan at the least, a slender means of getting Patrick and Ros out, if all else failed. The outer office was empty – where *was* Godwin?

'I think you should come here. Shall we say at noon?' The instruction given, Feng was gone and the connection broken.

Alder stared at the receiver for a moment, then replaced it. He rose from the sofa and walked to the window, hands thrust into the pockets of his slacks. The smell of the breakfast that had long gone cold caused his stomach to churn. He had managed only coffee since she had disappeared into the elevator. With the photographs . . .

No, there's nothing here – yes, I've searched her luggage, the suite, everything . . . No, she left nothing with the desk or in a deposit box – yes, even her handbag. I think you're barking up the wrong tree—

Was Feng convinced? Before he had called, he had

practised his assurances over and over, like a raw student for a high-school play. Written down the key phrases, too, to prompt himself. It had taken him an hour to calm down, to coach himself in what he must say, how he must sound ... And to forget her, because she and the thought of her enraged him, and would cause him to falter as he lied to Feng.

If he had convinced the Chinese, then Marian was safe for the moment. What would she do? Hand the pictures over to Suu Kyi or her people? Alder poured himself a small bourbon from the bottle on the table and sipped meditatively at it. Should he let her run?

He had to, he decided, watching the boats on the lake as if their sails were small semaphore messages. Had to. Unless he had her stopped by the people who looked out for him.

Who would kill her to keep her quiet, just as Feng would. The game was that big.

You can lie to Feng, he assured himself once more. You have to. Then the question pressed on him: why had he told her? Love—? The need to be candid with someone other than his handlers and minders, with someone who believed you only got good things done by being upfront? Marian was a hopeless romantic, but he could not despise her for it. Perhaps he had just needed her to know the importance of his deceit, the pivotal nature of his covert life. Anyway, her interpretation of the photograph had stung him into it. He couldn't have remained impassive in the face of the storm of her accusations and contempt.

He'd intended the revelation to stop her, and recover her respect. Now he could not harm her, or cause her to be hurt. Even if he had never fully loved her, he'd glimpsed a future he desired, seen something warmer and better through a crack in the door. Besides, her outrage was as great as his own ... So, if she ran with the ball, would she fumble it? Would it be enough, if Suu Kyi's people exploited the photographs properly and the West came on heavy enough with the moral outrage and trade sanctions – would it achieve what the White House wanted? The Chinese generals would have to be disowned, their grip on Burma and other Asian countries would be prised loose ... Wouldn't it?

He had to leave it there, at hope. The White House and State wanted *everything*; for him to go on and on to an always unspecified goal, one that kept diminishing in a desert perspective. Marian could stop that, even by exposing him. He'd become inoperable, unusable. The Company already had the alibi of a clumsy frame-up standing by. He could get out ... And he *was* tired of it. All excitement, all sense of the work's importance had long vanished. He lied and pretended out of a dogged determination now, even out of habit, with petty successes and deceptions as his comforts. Perhaps that had been why he had dived into a new affair with Marian with such hunger ... ?

Kumar's death was an operational necessity. She didn't understand that and she would not forgive it ... But the villagers in the photographs, Marian was right there. The experience had settled on him as the flies had settled on their bodies. You couldn't just go on and on with things like that. He wasn't a machine.

Maybe nothing between himself and Marian could be recovered. He couldn't even try until he had gotten himself out of all this. She might not even survive the day, he admitted, then snapped his mind shut on the thought. He went into the bedroom, and opened his suitcase on the bed. He removed the pistol. *You can lie to Feng* ... He moved the first round into the chamber. Just in case.

'The American was lying,' Feng announced, putting down the telephone. General Wang Wei, smoking another of his innumerable daily cigarettes, was framed by the study window. Across Inya Lake, the hotel from which Alder had spoken to him squatted in the sun like a white toad. Rather like the wizened features of the senior general. 'The woman was seen by one of our people, hurrying from the hotel. She appeared panicked and perhaps afraid—'

Wang Wei affected indifference, his gaze straying beyond Feng, who stood at the desk, towards the main reception room of the luxurious bungalow.

'You give too much credence to these minor matters, Feng Zedong,' he observed. Feng's features remained impassive. 'We have much still to discuss. I am here only for today.' He barked out a cough that was expressive of his impatience.

A warlord, Feng thought, a political commissar, an authoritarian provincial governor. A cunning, ruthless peasant too, and a viciously brutal capitalist entrepreneur. The very spirit of the 999 Group, he reflected sourly.

'Wang Wei-chin,' Feng announced with careful formality, 'I wish only to be certain—'

'The certainties are in the next room,' the old man replied, gesturing towards the group around a large, ornate table of carved and inlaid teak. Their voices could be heard through the half-open door.

'They are interdependent certainties.'

Wang Wei sighed angrily.

'An American, a woman, a renegade British agent in the jungle, are equivalent to the matters we are discussing?'

'They threaten them.'

'How?' Wang Wei continued to watch the people in the

adjoining room as avidly as a starving peasant might have watched rich men dining. The university- and academy-educated Feng retained an impassivity of expression. 'I do not see it. You were always suspicious of the American. You were permitted to go to the foolish extreme of testing and entrapping him once again at Tripitaka. Yet even now you are not satisfied, having made him your ox. Waste no more time on these fantasies.'

Like Deng, the dead paramount leader he physically resembled, Wang Wei belonged to the culture of the Long March and the pre-eminence of the Party. When Deng and the Party declared that capitalism was the necessary road for China, Wang Wei had embraced the new ideology with fanaticism. But fanaticism was always blinkered. Wang Wei was still an automaton, following orders and the Party's dogma.

Feng moved to sit in the window bay opposite the old man like a favoured grandchild. Leaning forward, he quietly urged:

'Why has this man Hyde, a well-known British agent, been pursuing Lau Yen-chih for so long – and unofficially? For sport? It cannot be that. Why is the woman, a British politician, so concerned with proof of a minor incident in northern Myanmar? Moral outrage alone?' he concluded with deliberate scorn.

Exhaling acrid smoke, the old man asked bluntly, his words jabbing like a pointing finger:

'Then *why* are they interested? *What* proof?'

'The woman has something, I am convinced. From the young man Kumar. The man Hyde must have found a diary, photographs, something . . . ?'

'This is *petty*, Feng Zedong. In there, they are discussing billions of dollars, vast power, the future of three countries! And yet you persist in this tale of proof and threat. Explain – or become silent.'

Feng was vividly aware that Wang Wei spoke with the authority of someone who had ordered the deaths of a great many people, over decades.

'Very well.' The old man's eyes hardened. Feng continued in a mollifying tone. 'The man was at Tripitaka, looking for proof, for a trail he could follow. The woman must intend to hand whatever she had to NLD people, even to the Suu Kyi bitch.' He glanced out of the window. Sunlight was calm on the lake. Mung Thant, the Minister for Tourism, possessed a very charming house.

'Why?'

'Because it is a *plot*!' Feng burst out. 'It must be a plot by the British, at the behest of the Americans. By factions who wish to exclude China from influence in the region, who wish Myanmar to fall into their sphere, their form of capitalism. Suu Kyi is Western-minded. If ever she were in power, she would attempt to limit our influence.'

Wang Wei's features were a caricature of concentration. Yet Feng realised he had touched a nerve of habitual paranoia. Eventually, after lighting another cigarette, the old man said hoarsely:

'Are we sensible to see plots everywhere?' But he was uncertain. His contemptuous assurance had vanished. 'The Americans? Or the British?'

'Both of them desire a market – *this* market. That is why the British are here now. The Americans appear unopposed to the regime in Yangon – why? Trade. They wish to invade our sphere of trade.'

'Does *your* American know any of this – if any of this is true?'

'I suspect not. He is merely corrupt.'

'And you believe we must be certain?'

'We may be exaggerating the danger, but we cannot afford to believe so.'

Wang Wei listened more intently to the talk that floated like incense from the adjoining room. Dollars, dam projects, the Mekong project, the investment of heroin profits, via Hong Kong banks, in Myanmar, Laos, Cambodia ... each dollar a unit of influence rather than currency. Then he said:

'Find out what your American knows. Then kill him.'

'But he may continue to be valuable—'

'Kill him.'

'As you wish. We need to know what it is the man Hyde knows, who employs him and for what—'

'Then ensure that your people and Lau's people catch him.'

'I will. And the woman, too. She must be stopped.'

'Of course.'

Wang Wei rose with difficulty from his chair. Coughing, almost bent double, he rasped out:

'I, meanwhile, will attend to the meeting. Among other things, I look forward to informing Lau Yen-chih that all future success for his companies depends entirely on his expanding his capacity to deal with the heroin. And perhaps I shall demonstrate to him his recent catalogue of blunders, which borders on the recklessly criminal ...' His smile was savage.

'Another reason for taking no more risks. If Lau was exposed we would be damaged.'

'I know that. I do not believe in your grand conspiracy theory for a moment, but I *do* understand that our progress could be temporarily halted if Lau Yen-chih's companies are lost to scandal over dead peasants or heroin.' He ceased coughing and straightened, looking up at Feng. 'I understand how much damage *might* be done.

Your education and success have made you fanciful, Feng Zedong. But your sense of danger is that of a good guard dog' – the insult was deliberate, unanswerable – 'and like a good guard dog, you will catch these people and tear them.' He patted Feng's arm. He was a slighted but still favoured grandchild. 'Now, I wish to hear the music that money makes.' His laughter was crowlike, even angry, and Feng felt the power of this dwarf of a man whom he could have knocked to the carpet with the vaguest gesture of his arm. 'I will leave you to make your arrangements.'

Wang Wei gathered up his files and pushed wide the door to the main room. Feng heard sighs of satisfaction and an immediate, new animation among those present. The Emperor had consented to hold audience.

Feng picked up the telephone and dialled.

'Get me Tin Hla, Minister of Security. General Feng ...' He savoured the respect at once offered his name and rank. Savoured, too, the coming humiliation of Lau by that cunning old man. After the fiasco at Ruili, and the escape of the man Hyde, projects on which he was counting would be withheld from his companies and awarded elsewhere. 'Quickly,' he said into the receiver, 'the matter is urgent.'

Lim had died needlessly in the helicopter crash, partly for the sake of spectacle. Hyde had walked in and out as if staying at an hotel. Alder, Lau's creature, had lied about the woman. Lau had been prodigal, over-ambitious, foolish. He would be offered not a single scrap from the table until these matters were settled. No gas pipeline, no dam projects – not so much as a cowshed to be built until Hyde and the woman politician were dead.

Marian watched a long, curving line of women, in short

blouses and *longyi*, sweeping the marble terrace and gaining merit. Their slow, methodical progress across the hot noon space between the Large Pavilion and the Wish Fulfilling Place's small shrine and gold-leafed Buddha angered her. It was as if they were nothing more than mocking automatons marking off the slowness of the passage of time. They denied urgency even more vividly than the heat. She was surrounded by stupas, pagodas, temples, shrines, images and pavilions. The place, crowded and busy, was nevertheless serene and timeless and it seemed to have hypnotised her.

She held her shoes in her hand as custom dictated, and the marble burned her feet even though she was standing in the brief shadow of the pavilion. It was ten minutes past noon. The Shwedagon Paya had sucked her in like slow, inexorable quicksand. The place was a *nibbana* that enervated, destroyed perspective and priorities. Sacrilegiously, she almost loathed the place because it rendered her distress, appalled disillusion, and even her danger, unreal.

Joss-stick incense was heavy in the unmoving air. The two Bodhi trees, one from a cutting of the tree beneath which the Gautama Buddha received enlightenment, seemed crowded into the north-west corner of the terrace, and were childishly decorated with flowers and small flags. The hot sunlight hurt the eyes as it beat on the bright gold of the main stupa rearing into the cloudless sky. The contact was not coming ... Incense, the wonder-working Buddha surrounded by the faithful, monks walking clockwise round the terrace, red-robed, shaven-headed, the stupas, hundreds of them, narrow as spearpoints ... Alder had had Kumar killed ...

Feng must know about the photographs by now because he seemed to know everything ... Marian pressed her hot fingertips to her throbbing temple. It was an increasing, almost impossible effort to prevent herself from panic, from fleeing that enervating, maddening place. They would be looking in earnest for her now – the police, the army, Feng.

She started at the noise of a siren floating up from the city which lay below Singuttara Hill, surrounding it like a dirty tide.

She had believed every word Alder had spoken. She could even imagine an idealism like her own pressganged into a secret life. But he had had Kumar killed in cold blood to protect an intelligence operation, and that was anathema to her. He was excommunicate, cast out. She had loved a murderer ... It was an idea that continued to bully and shake her until she was revolted, despairing. And it urged her to rid herself of the photographs as soon as possible and then let Evans take her somewhere safe.

She had rung Evans from the rear of the shop in which she had bought the sunglasses she wore and the straw hat that hid her blonde hair. He had ordered, then pleaded, she come to the Embassy. She had refused because, otherwise, it would *all* have been nothing but deceit, illusion, betrayal. She had said nothing of Alder, only that she had surprised a waiter who had discovered the photographs in her suite. He had fled empty-handed. Evans had sounded almost frantic on her behalf.

A second siren, then a third, rising like the scent of petrol and crowded humanity from the streets below the Shwedagon.

The small Burmese in white shirt and *longyi* seemed embarrassed at intruding upon her tears, unnoticed by herself until that moment. He held his rubber slippers in his hand as he bowed formally. It was twelve thirty.

'You must forgive us, Miss Pyott. We had to make certain

that you had not been followed.' He bowed again.

'What—?' Marian sniffed loudly, wiping her hand savagely at her eyes.

'We have kept you waiting. I apologise. Also, I am sorry that your meeting must be postponed until this evening. You can return here at sunset—?' He was disconcerted at the distraction on her countenance.

The policemen, barefooted, three of them, all armed, had emerged from the crocodile-guarded western staircase. They were inspecting the faithful, the sweepers, the monks and tourists. Marian shrank back into the shadows. The sirens—

'They are looking for me,' she managed. 'I'm sorry – I can't come back later . . .'

'Then please give me what you have brought with you.' The young man's voice was suddenly peremptory. Marian automatically reached into her purse, then exclaimed:

'No! You must help me – *please!*'

'Why are the police looking for you?' Another young Burmese had moved closer to them. He, too, was watching the policemen as they stopped two blond tourists in shorts and check shirts. The woman appeared concerned at having to produce her passport. *Passport* . . . Hers was in the hotel suite. The realisation slapped her into alertness.

'Someone knows I have the photographs—'

'Then give them to us.' For a moment, he appeared about to snatch her purse, and only habitual politeness restrained him.

'Please, I have to have help. They're looking for *me!*' Even as she pleaded, she realised that their danger was more persistent and real than her own. And accepted their anger at her.

The police had stopped another white woman. Too old. The two Burmese spoke rapidly to each other. The woman the police had stopped was American. Her surprised protests brought her small party and their tour guide to distract the police.

'Please!'

One of them nodded.

'Very well, Miss Pyott.' She was distanced by the formality of the address, the Western honorific. Politeness alone seemed to motivate them. 'Please walk towards the staircase.' Again, quick, bright exchanges in Burmese, then: 'Try to appear unconcerned.' They moved swiftly apart from her. If she was stopped, they would not be involved. 'The *eastern* stairway, over there,' the one who had first approached her whispered fiercely.

Walking clockwise round the terrace from the Bodhi trees, as observance and anonymity required, she would have to pass the three policemen – and there must be others, at each of the staircases . . . With an effort of will, she made herself leave the shadow of the pavilion, then pass the image of the Buddha that worked wonders. Then the Chinese pavilion, and the lifesized Indian guards who, with a dragon, protected a footprint of the buddha. The crowd of Americans surrounded the policemen, berating them and being berated. Her legs felt weak, the sun pressed like a monstrous hand as if to bully her uncertain steps in the direction of the police.

The two Burmese had gone—! She couldn't see them. Panic was a sweet nausea in her throat, cold perspiration on her forehead and beneath her arms. She reached the shade of the Two Elders pagoda, a miniature of the Shwedagon. The shadow was inky. Looking back, she saw that the police were contemptuously dismissing the American tourists—

—and one of them called out, waving an arm, pointing. At her. Marian remained immobile with fear, her hand resting on the hot wall of a pavilion. The policeman began moving towards her along the marble terrace, the automatic rifle he carried incongruously at odds with his respectfully bare feet. There seemed a gleam of satisfaction on his face—

She never knew if the Burmese had grabbed for her arm or her purse. Perhaps he did not know himself. But she was dragged off-balance, then pulled away, around the curve of the terrace. She began running in panic, clutching her shoes and purse, his hand still holding her arm. Someone was lighting candles at a planetary post, a monk was jostled aside, she heard the shouts of the policeman behind her, the gasped surprise of tourists and locals, then the noise of a whistle shrilling—

—the Buddha, with palm upward, watched stoically, compassionately unmoved. She tripped and almost fell over the loosened rifle and scrabbling hand of another policeman guarding the head of the eastern stairway. She was hardly aware that he must have been knocked down by one of her protectors. Then she was plunging with them down the stairway, through its bazaar of stalls and shops. Whistles, perhaps as many as three or four, their noise bullying after them. An old man was sent tumbling, his *longyi* flying aside to reveal thin, brown sticks of legs.

She was dragged into a small, dark, close shop that smelt overpoweringly of flowers and incense. Candlelight gleamed from glass jars, copper bells. A tiny woman was shocked into recognition and surprise at her protectors, then at Marian's taller, paler form. Then they were in the rear of the shop, through a narrow door, and she was confronted by a sunless high stone wall. She panicked afresh at its blind-alley solidity, before she was dragged to her right, following the wall, above which now was a narrow slit of sky. There was hard-baked earth beneath her feet, sloping downwards. Tiny *kyaungs* - monasteries - before the riot of colour, noise and people of the Bahan bazaar and Arzami Road.

Marian tried to catch her breath, catch at the place and her senses as they were whirled like dust-devils. She glimpsed police vans, a line of police herding people suddenly fearful. Hawkers and child prostitutes scuttled into shadow.

'This way,' one of the two young men ordered, his features distorted by breathlessness and anger equally. 'Quickly!' Already, as he glanced again at her purse, he seemed to regret the impulse to rescue her rather than rob her of what alone was valuable to them.

The police were selecting each white face, each pale arm, from the crowd. As the two young men hurried her away, Marian felt alone in their company.

Katha was a fitful, lamplit glow a mile or more downriver, before it was drowned in the sunset. The sky and the great swath of water that was the Irrawaddy were dyed holy saffron, then an unearthly orange, as if the sun had changed colour. Ros's face and hands, his own, were dyed the same impossible hue. The river's banks were dark strips like charcoal scribbles on the single orange element of sky and water.

Then, in what seemed only a few more moments, the scene drained of colour and the scattered small lights of Katha emerged from the quick darkness and the dim oil lights of the ferry's upper deck reflected from the black water. Near them was the platform set aside for monks. Their robes were smudges in the evening, the glow of their cheroots like fireflies. The first stars appeared like pale candle flames. In the darkness, the distant, jungled mountains behind which the sun had fallen had disappeared. The paddy fields, too, were invisible. The ferry, no more than a loose alliance of lamps and noise, moved on a flat, unpolished surface through an absent landscape.

'Only another ten, fifteen minutes,' Hyde murmured. Ros nodded. 'Be all right then.'

Behind them, as they stood at the rail of the upper deck, there were noises of anticipation and preparation. Petrol canisters, for unloading at Katha, were being moved, bicycles were resurrected from the mêlée of goods and people. Hyde heard chickens, other fowl, smelt beer and betel nuts, the smoke of cheroots. Fish was being fried. Sacks of peanuts were dragged across the deck's planking.

The ferry had made three stops during the day. At one of them, early in the afternoon, boys had unloaded heavy sacks and crates while a soldier lounged against a jetty rail, idly scanning the crowded decks and the few passengers who had disembarked. Helicopters – or the same helicopter again and again – had swept over the ferry at intervals, following the river's course. There seemed little urgency or concentration of troops, vehicles or aircraft, as if the stealth and heat of the river discouraged all strenuous activity, even in those pursuing them.

At Katha, the beginning of the railway line to Mandalay, it might be different ... The town's few lights grew stronger, but remained as small as glowing spiders isolated on the night's huge web and as individual as the stars. People pressed around them, searching for the town in the darkness. And, as if to satisfy their curiosity, more lights sprang out. The wharf and its jetties became illuminated like a stage. The town's evening electricity had been switched on. Hyde saw low warehouses and stores, wooden jetties on piles rising from the lamp-freckled water.

A parked army truck and a platoon of Tatmadaw soldiers spread out along the wharf. The town was suddenly distanced beyond the high sandy embankment. Accident, or design?

Design...

Even at the distance they were from the riverbank, Hyde sensed their purpose, expectation. They were alert, focused, their rifles held positively across their chests.

As if to confirm Hyde's impression, a white man appeared from the shadow of a warehouse, dressed in a safari jacket and light slacks. He stood for a moment and a cigar glowed. Then he walked casually, confidently towards the jetty. The loose-limbed gait, the posture, the size were all familiar. There was no mistake; it was Jessop.

Design indeed—

CHAPTER THIRTEEN

The Lady

Behind Jessop, coming into the light theatrically, was Cobb, Jessop's dog. And a Chinese in military uniform. His hand tightened on Ros' arm, alarming her.

'It's all right—' he began.

'Doesn't look much like it,' she replied, shivering, turning to him as he drew back into the shadows beneath the wooden roof over the upper deck. An escaped chicken scuttled and flapped out of their path. 'What now?' The chicken's owner scrabbled after it, the fowl's claws clicking on the planking.

There were shouts, then the slight lurch as the ferry bumped against the tyres suspended along the jetty. Ropes flew in the hard light as they docked. The chicken, clutched in an embrace, passed them, shocked by its recapture.

Hyde looked over the upper deck, down towards the

water that was shadowed by the bulk of the ferry. Passengers crowding towards the stairs to the lower deck moved away from them, as if aware of their condemned status. The drag of heavy bundles across the deck, the protests of children and cooped animals and birds.

'Have to swim for it,' he remarked.

'What?'

'We're Aussies – misspent our childhoods on the beach, didn't we? Piece of cake. Come on, doll, let's get down to the lower deck.'

They pressed into the polite, excited throng of passengers. A bird's gleaming, enamelled eye glared from the shadow of a woven cage. He held Ros' waist in the crook of his arm. The crowd jostled the backpack. Jessop would only have to ask – *two white faces, man and a woman?* – to know he'd found them. Hyde's heightened senses smelt petrol, cigar and cheroot smoke, the river, betel nuts, scorched fish; he saw Jessop and Cobb, the line of soldiers. The monks from the upper deck hemmed them as they reached the narrow stairs. A group of squatting men continued their game of carromme, the clicks of the discs like the noise of rounds being thrust into the chambers of guns. He held Ros' shoulders as they descended, his lips against her hair.

At the bottom of the stairs, they forced their way through the eager press and noise of the passengers. Most of them, even if their passage was for Mandalay, would disembark for the hour or so that the ferry was docked. More papers and tickets to inspect would give him and Ros additional time ... His hands gripped the rail. The engine was silent, but the babble of sound from the wharf and the ferry was a fog of noise.

'OK?'

Ros nodded. Her face was jaundiced by the oil lamp's sullen glow.

'Where?'

'Swim away ahead of the boat. The bank's lower beyond the lights. Railway station and the town are that way, too—'

'Hyde, does this make sense?' she demanded.

'Ros, for Christ's sake—!' Then, more calmly: 'The white men on the dock know me – they'd recognise you, too. We can't *choose*.'

'OK – you'll have to help me over.'

She straddled the rail, then lowered herself over the side, her feet scrabbling against the hull. He heard shouted orders as he held her forearms. The lower deck was already sparsely populated. He nodded at her fearful expression, and then let her slip into the water.

She disappeared, frightening him, then her head bobbed to the surface, her hair plastering her face like dark seaweed. She began swimming slowly, laboriously away from the ferry. Quickly, he scrambled over the rail, clung then dropped, the pack splashing into the river beside him. He surfaced, at once seeing her head bobbing in the river ahead of him. The waterproof pack was beside him like a corpse, kept heavily afloat by its buoyancy bag.

Hyde struck out, almost at once drawing level with Ros. The water, after the evening's heat, seemed icily cold. There were more shouted orders from the ferry and the jetty, the stamp of boots on deck planking.

'OK?' he spluttered.

'Bloody cold!'

'Just a bit further—'

He looked back, believing he could distinguish Jessop on the wharf. A white man waving his arms, anyway. He could see the big stars above the halo of light around the wharf and the ferry.

A searchlight mounted on the back of an army truck

flicked its beam across the water. Its pointing finger probing at the river's creased surface. It wavered upstream, then swung back towards them like a baleful glare.

'Hyde, I'm getting cramp—!' Ros all but snarled at him, her tone incongruously suggesting irritation as much as fear.

He grabbed her arm, drawing her close to him. Her weight was leaden. The pack dragged at him, and he felt her panic as if it was his own. The weights on either side of him forced him to tread water as the searchlight beam crawled like a white finger across the dark river. They were thirty or so yards from the bank. The sluggish current of the Irrawaddy now seemed possessed by a huge, swallowing undertow that was irresistible. The beam of the light slid closer.

He kicked out, pulling at Ros, who flapped at the water with her free arm like a child splashing. The pack resisted him like a dog as the light skimmed the water. His legs, too, felt the onset of cramp, his body the numbing chill of the water . . . The light, Ros' weight, the pack's resistance, the current of the river . . . The bank seemed to retreat, the wharf and ferry become no more than a fuzzy, light-glowing smudge. The searchlight caught them, blinding Hyde, then passed on. He struggled frantically, kicking his legs, wriggling his body . . . The beam of light swung back towards them, a white pendulum. Kick, *kick* – his feet were leaden . . . in sand. He was able to stand on the bottom. As his feet touched, the current of the river seemed to strengthen. The searchlight scythed the water only yards away as it reeled itself back in towards the wharf.

He held Ros upright against him as she tried to stamp ashore against the sand and her cramp. Hauled out the pack after them like a third escapee. Ros stumbled and fell, covering her sodden clothing with sand. Hyde exhaled noisily before crawling to the lip of the shallow bank and raising his head above its parapet. Already, in the evening heat, his clothes had begun to steam.

The unloading of the ferry had been halted. Soldiers scurried over the almost empty boat like ants. He listened to Ros' quiet cursing, her rubbing of cramped muscles. Jessop, Cobb, other individuals were no larger than miniatures. The searchlight flicked back and forth across the black river like the tail of a fly-maddened animal. Someone must have seen them climb overboard. He turned his head towards Katha. An avenue of cloudy raintrees stretched away from the riverbank towards the railway station. Beyond the station, Katha seemed more like jungle than town, lights dotted like campfires amid the omnipresent, century-old trees. A few nearby houses offered only the slightest hint that there was a town of perhaps thirty thousand hidden beneath the trees.

He scrambled back to Ros.

'How's the cramp? Can you walk?' *Run ... ?* He helped her to her feet. She stamped her feet awkwardly, then began to walk more easily. She nodded cautiously. 'OK, time to move, doll. Just follow my lead – don't worry. I'll get us out.'

He worked his arms into the sodden harness of the pack. Taking her hand, he led her up the bank and across a sandy track to the dirt road that paralleled the river. There was no traffic, and only the ghosts of white shirts and pale blouses in the gloom. The virtual absence of streetlamps and headlights made the handfuls of people spectral. The lamp of a trishaw wobbled towards and past them. As they reached the avenue of raintrees, there seemed to be more people in the gloom, but their lack of substance perpetuated the unnerving sense of the town's unreality. Quiet voices murmured from beneath trees and half-glimpsed verandas and garden plots; oil lamps swung, catching small faces in their glow, a gleam of eyes, the colour of cloth.

Hyde felt like an intruder into some mysterious, contemplative ceremony. There was the occasional streetlamp, archaically elaborate and dim. Moonlight filtered like dust through the leaves. He saw an ox-pulled wagon, bicycles. A single parked car, ancient and polished. Laughter and the scents of cooking. Ros hurried beside him towards the brightening glow of the railway station, her drying clothes and skin wrapped in the shawl he had taken out of the pack.

He heard the noise of a vehicle, then saw the lurid splash of its headlights as it blundered around a corner into the avenue of trees. He pulled Ros into the shadow of a huge trunk as the truck roared past them towards the station, soldiers revealed inside by the flapping of its canvas.

'Shit.'

Jessop had guessed. He watched the truck come to a halt and the soldiers debouch. A white man, smaller than Jessop, was among them. Cobb. The armed troops hurried into the low, toylike station building.

'What do we do now?' he heard Ros ask, almost in his head. Her tone was fervid, but unafraid; almost peremptory. 'Hyde – what do we do?' Then her eyes widened in the glare of the new headlights turning into the avenue.

'Let's find somewhere quiet to think. I'd better talk to Cass – or the old man.' He forced optimism into his voice.

'How do we get out of here, Hyde?' Ros demanded.

A jeep passed them at speed. Hyde glimpsed Jessop and the Chinese officer. When they found the station empty, they'd start searching Katha. They might even have enough troops to cordon off the entire town. Beyond Katha were endless paddy fields, the river, and the Mangin Taung ridge. It reached down from the north, jungled and trackless; almost impenetrable. On the river or in the fields, or on the one good road, they would be like flies on a white wall.

He tugged absently at her hand to reassure her as his forebodings grew. Then he heard the distant but approaching sound of helicopter rotors. Jessop was certain they were in the town – in the bag, really.

Ros' moonlit face was a mirror of his own fears.

Marian watched the tiny frame and childlike figure of the woman as she bent forward on the low stool on which she sat. She was leaning towards the photographs spread out before her on the small, round table. There was an electricity failure in that district of Rangoon, and the warm light and shadows cast by the candles and the paraffin lamp in the cramped room added to the air of conspiracy. And gleamed on the high-cheekboned face and huge eyes of Aung San Suu Kyi.

She was almost anorexic in appearance, as if she had lived too long on her inner convictions. Marian saw the pain of discovery on her face as she studied the massacre. It seemed, too, a reaction of recurrent distress, as to a disease long borne and which she had schooled herself to confront.

She was dressed in a silk blouse of orange flowers on a cream ground, and a dark-brown *longyi*, her hair tied back with a large bow. Marian felt hot and crumpled, even ungainly by comparison.

The room in which she sat with Suu Kyi and three other members of the National League for Democracy was on the first floor of a narrow wooden building squashed into a row of shops in a street north of the Sule pagoda. Below the tiny, barely furnished room was a woodcarver's workshop. The scents of fragrant wood seemed to seep upwards through the floorboards. The noises of the evening open-air market outside assailed them through the window shutters.

Suu Kyi had arrived only ten minutes earlier. How she moved undetected around the city while under virtual house arrest in her home on University Avenue, three miles from the shop, Marian had no idea. Perhaps the junta and the police wanted her to move about, revealing her contacts, the NLD network in Rangoon; hoped, at least, that that might be the outcome. She did sometimes receive covert Western visitors, usually television and other journalists, at her home. Perhaps Marian – or the photographs – seemed too threatening to be entertained there.

The two men who had rescued her from the Shwedagon were downstairs, with other bodyguards. They had brought her to the woodcarver's shop, given her water and a little food, then left her alone in the upstairs room. The quick evening had come and turned to darkness outside as she waited. She had heard the occasional police siren, the gradual increase of market noises from the street, a lathe turning or careful hammer taps from the workroom. She had thought little of her own danger. There seemed only a growing impatience for the moment when she could dispose of the photographs and call Evans. She had thought, almost exclusively, of Alder. The now-stranger with his secret life, his hidden purposes and ideals, his ruthless pursuit of his object, his murder of Medhev Kumar. She felt a desperation at losing him and a swelling outrage that he had felt Kumar's death to be so casually, unthinkingly necessary. She had said nothing of him, merely used the story of the waiter searching her room as the reason for her flight.

She looked up from Suu Kyi's concentration at the balding, rotund Burmese who stood behind her stool, looking over her shoulder. Observing *her*, Marian realised, with a gaze that seemed as intent as some telepathic inquisition of her thoughts. She sensed mistrust and suspicion, a fierce and calculating protectiveness towards the tiny woman over whom he stood. He seemed on the point of speaking when Suu Kyi looked up, sighed with a shiver of her whole frame, and murmured, her eyes preternaturally bright:

'Daw Marian' - the politesse was studied, but compli-mentary - 'why did you not give these to the English newspapers, *The Times*? What did you expect *us* to do with them?' Behind the politeness, there was suspicion, even challenge. A lack of trust? They'd never met, of course, but Suu Kyi knew of her and had sent messages of thanks for her support in the past.

Why hadn't she? Marian asked herself. Suu Kyi's effect on her was compelling, subordinating.

All four of them seemed to study her with the same quizzical, intent gaze; the expression was magnified by distrust on the face of the Burmese who stood over Suu Kyi. Khin Myo. The other two were an Indian and a Chinese, younger men. Was Suu Kyi deliberately display-ing the ethnic diversity of the NLD? The Indian, tall and thin, was a mirror of her intensity. His thumbs stuck out at unnatural angles. A torturer had broken them at some time in the past. The small, bespectacled Chinese had said little but had made notes of everything Marian had said. He had offered her a silent respect for her intermittent moral outrage on Burma's behalf.

Khin Myo continued to smile at her uncomfortable silence, as if he considered her unmasked. Then the young Indian with the ugly hands asked:

'Daw Marian Pyott – you explained that Medhev died in England. Did he give you the photographs to bring to us?'

'No . . . They were – found.'

At once, Suu Kyi said softly: 'After his murder?' Marian nodded. 'Were they found by someone who understood their value?'

'Yes.'

Triumphantly, Khin Myo exclaimed: 'It is some kind of operation by British Intelligence, then!' Suu Kyi raised one narrow, long hand but did not gesture him to silence. 'Isn't it? You were asked to bring the photographs—'

'No!' Silence, then she added: 'I thought it right to bring them. Others disapproved.'

'We apologise, Daw Marian.' Suu Kyi's smile dazzled unrevealingly. 'We sometimes cannot dismiss the habit of suspicion. There is, nevertheless, much to gain from an explosion such as this, set off by others and at a distance.'

'I can see how you might think that. I didn't realise.'

'Your newspapers believe you are now sympathetic to the regime,' Khin Myo pursued, undeterred. 'You have changed sides. If we were to reveal who brought the photographs, you would be in considerable difficulties . . . ?'

'Then,' Marian began, pausing to clear her throat and combat the sudden thought of Feng, 'then you must reveal who brought them.'

Now Suu Kyi patted the man's arm and he fell silent, though his eyes, gleaming in the candlelight, continued to study her.

'Who murdered Medhev?' the young Indian asked. 'The same people who did that?'

'Yes.'

'Thank you, Daw Marian.' He had evidently known Kumar, and lost a comrade. 'And it was because he had the photographs? And it was someone working on the orders of—?'

'Ralph Lau and the Straits Royal Group. As I explained, the hotel chain is a vast laundry for drug money. Those poor people were murdered to hasten the building of a resort in order to quickly increase the capacity of the laundry. It's rotten from top to bottom.'

'Of course,' the Chinese murmured.

She sensed their weary knowledge, their angry impotence, their reluctance. And, as if divining her disappointment, Suu Kyi said with a bitter smile:

'I am sorry that we cannot act as your agents in this matter, Daw Marian. I understand that you must see us, not unkindly, as your representatives here, who have let you down.' She raised her hand to silence protest. 'Yours is the comfort of liberalism in a liberal society. It is apparent in most of the Westerners who interview me or write to me. After they have expressed their admiration and taken their photographs – always my best side' – the smile dazzled – 'they begin to wonder why I appear to be *doing* very little. Their sympathy, like yours, is sometimes used as a prod. If only I – we – did more, to justify their faith and support.'

Marian flushed in acknowledgement of the accusation. She felt humiliated, stupid. She had taken up Burma once more, like an old acquaintance she had felt obliged to ask to lunch, and now she was shocked by their lack of excitement and gratitude.

People she had known, journalists in the main, who had met Suu Kyi possessed a kind of consensus view of her with hindsight. As one of them had put it, *an indomitable spirit is very like a hedgehog – prickly.* It was not intended to insult or demean, and withheld no jot of admiration; but, as she now realised, it captured the sense of distance, even superiority of a soldier observing a comfortable civilian world, one that waved flags and knitted comforters and wanted the war to be won whatever the sacrifice. The constancy of danger, the acute and profound knowledge of oneself under the greatest pressure, Suu Kyi shared with that soldier. People well away from the battle were objects of quizzical amusement, even mild derision, with easy values, comfortable ideals. They didn't *see* as Suu Kyi did.

Her slow-moving, expressive hands made recurrent movements. It was as if the reminder of Kumar's death had prompted the gestures and she was attempting to add the tragedy to some arrangement already made. Marian understood how many times Suu Kyi must have heard news of the death of people close to her, who had worked for her, for the cause.

'The Burmese officers could, perhaps, be identified. Exposed?' Marian suggested quietly in the aftermath of her alarm at a passing siren. 'The Chinese is General Feng. I recognised him yesterday.' She had not shown them the photograph of Alder; could not.

'We know about Feng,' the Chinese announced without inflection. 'This evidence is not surprising, given Chinese involvement. We understand only too well China's support for the junta, Daw Marian.'

She remembered Alder's confession, and almost as if she had adopted the role of his mouthpiece, she said:

'But that support weakens *you* in the NLD.' It was easier and less real, when she was not addressing Suu Kyi directly. 'You might use this evidence to expose the Chinese involvement. It could prevent the growth of China's influence in Burma, for a time at least.'

Khin Myo snorted, growling out: 'This evidence would be denied as a fake. We cannot excavate the site for further proof. We would simply have to wait until Western outrage and sanctions brought sufficient pressure to bear. And in the meantime, hundreds and perhaps thousands of us would be arrested, even disappear! Perhaps we would have a week in the spotlight before *this* had to contend with all the other horrors in the world for space in British and American newspapers and on the television ...' He broke off to listen to another siren in the street. He was still standing behind Suu Kyi, his hands poised almost reverently over her shoulders.

Marian realised that the Lady was a priceless religious relic, too invaluable to be risked by exposure, by the proximity even of worshippers. They had made her the vessel of all their hopes, all their dreams. She was their hair or footprint of the Guatama Buddha in its tiny, frail pagoda of flesh. So much so that they dared take no risk whatever with her. They were blind to dramatic gesture, deaf to the temptations of a quick cry of triumph. Theirs was a siege against the regime, not an assault. It had to be, she admitted.

'It seems to me, Daw Suu Kyi,' she urged quietly, 'that a blow struck against the companies owning and building Tripitaka' - there was distaste at the word, the use of the Buddhist canon for the name of a holiday resort - 'would achieve a great deal.' She cleared her throat, hearing whistles blown in the distance. 'The hotel group, the construction company, the umbrella conglomerate that owns them both - could be removed from Burma. As would be the present focus of Chinese influence, the conduit for the heroin and the means of laundering the profits. If the photographs could be used to full effect, it would cause disarray. Delay.'

She was leaning forward, her shadow enlarged on the wall, urging her arguments as if they were physical blows. Suu Kyi was thoughtful, even persuaded. They had known about the heroin, the Chinese, but not much of Lau and Winterborne Holdings. Yet she sensed they still acted like scholars of their oppression, merely recording, filing, interpreting the information. Another siren, more whistles...

'Investment and tourism would be frightened away,' Marian continued quickly, as if pressed by some vague threat. Suu Kyi smiled, her eyes sparkling as she nodded in agreement. 'SRG and Winterborne Holdings – Asia-Construct, too – would withdraw from Burma. They'd have to.'

Khin Myo seemed to writhe for a moment as if in the clutches of an octopus, and then, even though he glanced down at Suu Kyi with apologetic misgiving, he burst out, enraged:

'How do you expect us to achieve so much without your help? You, and people like you!' Suu Kyi raised her hand to restrain the outburst, then returned it to her lap. 'You in the West have a responsibility, Daw Marian – we *cannot* do this alone! The media who could use this effectively lie in Europe and America, not here. Yet you bring it to *us* ...?' He wound down like a piece of propagandist clockwork. But his eyes were pained as he added: 'You know the people, you can persuade the media—' Then finally, as if ashamed of the pleading note in his voice, he snapped: 'We are always here. The room remains even when the light is put out and the door closed.'

In Suu Kyi's eyes there was agreement. And understanding. Marian opened her lips, but remained silent. All four of them were looking at her. *To* her. She knew, now, what she had concealed from herself. From the moment she had seen the photographs, she had treated them like stolen money, desiring their quick return. At best, she had behaved like a distant, detached benefactress, anticipating gratitude rather than involvement.

She lit a cigarette, the first since her arrival. Exhaling, she said: 'Yes . . .' Then she sighed. 'It was rather up to me, wasn't it – from the beginning?'

Government and her own party alike would never forgive. They would hound her. She kept the pain of that certainty from her expression.

'Thank you, Daw Marian.' Suu Kyi's fingertips briefly touched her arm.

The politeness of their gratitude stung and then sedated. Removed self-consciousness as if by anaesthetic. The warm room was dreamlike, as were their faces in the candlelight. She, like a butterfly in chaos theory, must flap her wings and cause an earthquake on the other side of the world—

—if she lived. A whistle, closer, pierced her reverie. Alarmed the others.

'I – I'd better call Colin Evans,' she mumbled. 'Ask him to bring me in.'

The door of the room opened. One of the men who had rescued her appeared, his features filled with urgency. His politeness, even awe, towards Suu Kyi remained intact. He spoke rapidly in Burmese, and his words stirred them as a wind the dust.

'There is a house-to-house search of this street and those nearby,' Suu Kyi translated unhurriedly. 'We must leave.'

'I'll need help, until I can—'

'Of course.'

The photographs were gathered from the low table. Marian crushed out her cigarette. The noises from the street had become sullen; there were shouted orders. Suu Kyi handed Marian the photographs she had scooped up as if it was now they who wished to be quickly rid of them. In a tight group near the door, they seemed diminished, even helpless.

'Quickly!' the Burmese who had brought the warning urged. Then he seemed to pounce forward, reaching for the cheap tin ashtray on the table. He held up the smoked cigarette. 'English!' he snapped. 'This could have killed the woodcarver!'

'I'm sorry—' she half protested.

They weren't helpless, merely hunted, stamped on. Suu Kyi had been no more than truthful. Marian understood that now. Her respect, even as she hurried from the room, was enlarged. She realised how much courage it required merely to stand still, speak out.

The second young man was waiting at the foot of the stairs. There was a peremptory, not-to-be-denied banging at the door of the shop. She saw an old woman shuffling in darkness to open it. She was hurried out into the cramped, noisome yard behind the shop. The air struck fetid and dank. She was just like them now, a hunted animal, a *nuisance* – something to be washed from a wall, a slogan in chalk. Wiped out, washed away—

It was over in a few minutes, the transformation of the town into a war zone. Hyde pushed Ros back beneath the thick shadow of the raintree's canopy as the searchlight on the helicopter wiped and flicked like a long white whip up and down the avenue leading to the station. Near the river end of the avenue, more soldiers dismounted from two trucks. A second helicopter droned over the town, farther off. The station was ringed with troops. Ros' breathing was as quick and feverish as if they were making love against the trunk of the tree. Her lips were wet against his neck as she whispered: 'Let's get off the street!'

The light flicked across them. They had to be visible to the people drawn from their houses by the noise and activity. Jessop had all the men he could want, and more. Burmese army, the Tatmadaw, but run by Jessop and the Chinese officer. Everyone was at the party—

Deeper shadow? An empty house? Why bother - they'd closed the gate, the town was sealed, infested with them.

'Hyde!' he heard her saying. 'Don't go crook on me now! Snap out of it - let's get off the street!'

A voice speaking Burmese, amplified and distorted, stunned them both. The tone obviated the need for translation. It would be the usual crap, *criminals or dissidents, report any strangers, you will not be harmed*, and so on. The garbage of uniformed governments.

Someone was pointing at them, talking to a neighbour in a high, batlike, clicking voice. Their white faces were visible in the shadows beneath the branches. A truck roared past, screeched to a crawl, a soldier laid like an armed egg fifty yards farther along the avenue - Christ, this was *good*. Jessop and the Chinese—

A voice called to the nearest soldier and an arm waved, pointing. They didn't want trouble, their homes invaded or wrecked; who could blame them? The soldier stuttered forward, alarmed, calling to his comrades. There were dozens of people on the street or on the verandas of tiny houses now. The soldier was being encouraged to follow the pointing arms, and his nearest companions were attracted by the birdlike, urgent calling taken up by more and more of the bystanders. The PA system boomed out again. It, too, was closer. The searchlight caught the

370

approaching soldier and froze on him as if he had stepped on to a stage. The light increased as the helicopter dropped lower—

Hyde shot the soldier and then dragged Ros away from the tree. She instinctively struggled against him as the soldier collapsed balletically in the searchlight beam. But he pulled at her, and then they were both blundering through rhododrendron bushes, other vegetation. Dusty, prickling. Someone was already crying fearfully.

Hyde parted branches for her as if leading her into a bower. There was nothing but darkness and starlight and the sense of other running, fleeing bodies. They blundered into another street, narrow and twisted, almost lightless. People were already staying indoors, terrified. Earth hard as concrete underfoot, then more undergrowth.

As he looked back, the helicopter lifted over the raintrees and the scattered houses raised on posts like an enraged, winged beetle. It was black against the stars, its searchlight lashing to and fro like a wounded tentacle. Then the firing began, insane, untargeted, from a heavy machine gun mounted in the helicopter's open door. Hyde watched the tracer rounds spit groundwards like molten droplets, rip through the wooden walls of a house whose main pillar was a tree trunk and rattle off its corrugated roof. The machine gun continued to spray the ground, flicking aside the bamboo walling of another tiny house raised on stilts. Everything was black and green as the searchlight flickered over the trees, until one of the stilted houses caught fire.

Hyde glimpsed bushes in flower, washing on lines or frames. They stumbled through one vegetable plot, then another. Fat ripe things were squashed underfoot. The rotor noise maddened as it passed over them. He kept Ros as close to him as if he was wearing her like the backpack.

A narrow earth track, tiny house lights hiding in the trees, a truck roaring and bucking over the uneven ground moments after they reached cover. He thrust bushes aside and then he and Ros were swallowed by them. Then they were colliding with the wall of a house, and someone inside it cried out in helpless fear. Another narrow earth track—

—searchlight, catching them in its glare, like an eye opening on them. The truck on which it was mounted roared towards them. Ros was as still as a rabbit, even as he fitted the curved box magazine to the Heckler submachine gun and fired. Thirty rounds on automatic. He emptied it in an instant. Darkness, the truck careering into a house and demolishing it, its windscreen without glass or driver. He pushed Ros across the lane and into a tiny avenue of raintrees, while the PA system bellowed distantly after them. The searchlight still dazzled on his retinae. His vision slowly cleared as they thrust on towards the town's outskirts.

It was no more than another ten minutes before they came across the empty, dilapidated house that was more like a chicken hut. Ros's progress was no more than a stumble, drunken and exhausted. He could hear her teeth chattering. Her face was ashen in the moonlight as he leant her like a sack against the rotting wood of the low, overgrown hut, and scanned the sky. Big, warm stars, but none of them the moving navigation lights of the two helicopters. They must be away north and east of Katha. They had, by accident and speed, apparently staggered outside the mesh of the search. The town was a painted glow to the north-west. Hyde could hear the sluggish, slurred voice of the Irrawaddy and smell the river on the still air. Beyond the town, lit by the full moon, he could see the Gangaw Taung range of hills.

Carefully, he pushed open the hut's sagging door and stepped inside, flicking on the narrow beam of a torch. A rat scuttled away from the light. There were no snakes. A broken table, a single hard bench. The place had been empty for years. There was little left of the thatched roof and there were gaps in the flimsy wooden walls. A Buddha in a niche, a couple of photographs of ancient, wizened Burmese, a calendar askew.

Ros subsided into a doll-like posture, her back against one wall of the hut, her senses remembering gunfire and the crashed truck, the proximity of death. He handed her the water flask.

'Hungry?' She shook her head. She watched the sub-machine gun slung across his chest as if it possessed a malevolent intent towards her. 'I have to talk to Aubrey,' he added, hefting the pack to the earth floor and lifting the tac radio out of it. The batteries were the best but wouldn't last forever. He extended the antenna, remembering his basic training, twenty years ago. *Always* assume that your comms are about to pack up. OK, Aubrey, you old bugger, you'd better have a bloody good plan.

It was Godwin, almost at once. The set was switched to whisper function, but Godwin might have been less than a mile away as Hyde held the receiver against his face. Ros remained hunched against the opposite wall, her breathing becoming steady. The dim moonlight filtering through the broken thatch showed his free hand shaking with reaction.

'Me.'

'OK?' Godwin's concern was vivid, breathless. 'Phil's been on – thinks the two passengers who had your tickets have gone into the bag.'

'Jessop's here, with half the Tatmadaw. We're safe for the moment.'

'Great. There is a back-up. I'll put Sir Kenneth on.'

Hyde's free hand would not become still.

'Patrick? How much time do you have?'

'Not much.'

'Ros?'

'OK.' He looked at her. She *was* OK. She'd even shaken him from a moment of desperation, under the raintree.

'Good. You'll need the map. I have Scudamore patched in. There's an old smuggling route over the mountains. It ought to be secure and usable – by vehicle, if you can obtain transport.'

'Maybe. Scudamore *knows* this part of Burma?'

'Some time ago, but well. Shall I have Tony patch him in? He's still in hospital in KL. Evans' people have moved in secure communications. Ready?'

'As I'll ever be ...' He unfolded the map. Its crackling startled Ros.

Katha was a dim black spot on the wriggle of the Irrawaddy. The river scribbled itself southwards through Burma. *Over the mountains?* The thin beam of the torch wavered. He heard the distant drone of the two helicopters. 'Where's the destination?' he asked.

'The border with India – as close to Thaungdut as possible. At the northern end of the Kabaw Valley, the course of the Chindwin. Once you're over the mountains, it's one huge lowland area all the way to the border ... Yes?' The description ended in apology.

'What then?'

'There will be a snatch operation. Helicopter, probably. Yes, almost certainly. You will need a vehicle. Tony asks that you keep in touch, report your progress—' Then, as if Aubrey himself stared into vacancy, he added: 'We will get you out, Patrick!'

'Yes,' Hyde returned as he directed the torch over the

map. A civilian helicopter would dare penetrate only a handful of miles into Burma – if one came at all. He began estimating distances, time.

'Can you obtain a vehicle?'

His free hand continued to quiver in an independent fever. 'Have to, won't I? Patch Scudamore in.' The immediacy with which Scudamore was bellowing in his ear, as if confronted with alien technology, symbolised Aubrey's eagerness to end his own contact with Hyde.

'You're in the shit, then?' the fat old drunk was shouting.

'Looks like it.'

'Aubrey wants me to get you out of it.'

'Can you?'

The noise of a helicopter approaching and then fading again, a wavelet of threat.

'I'd better, you saved my life. Got your map in front of you?' He could hear Scudamore's stertorous breathing. The night outside the hut was silent again, and Scudamore seemed at a much greater distance than Aubrey had been. It was a distance of trust.

'Right – get us out.'

'They used mules, even bullocks, in the old days. Later, it was trucks—'

'This route? It's a long time ago – is it still usable?'

'With the amount of heroin they shift these days? Don't be daft, lad!'

'Is it usable?'

'Could be overgrown in places – at the beginning. You'll need a machete. They poisoned the earth to keep the track clear. It shouldn't be too bad. Elsewhere, it's ravines, defiles, ledges. I bloody walked it enough times to know.'

'OK.'

'It starts just north-west of Katha, off the road to the Gangaw Taung. There's a Buddha in a niche of rock, two miles from Katha. To its right, the track begins. There's a ruined hut. It winds through the foothills, crosses the railway half a mile from Naba – got that?'

'Yes.' He scribbled the description on a pad and marked the map.

'The trail's marked with *nats*—' Scudamore chuckled, a noise which became a gravelly coughing. 'You know what they are? They're every half-mile or so, on hollow trees, rocks. Painted or carved. Some are just scratched or daubed. All of them are the *nat* pictured *standing* with a sword over his *left* shoulder. Got that? I can't remember the bugger's name—'

'Doesn't matter. Standing, sword on left shoulder. OK. And I do know what they are!'

Nats – the figures of demons and spirits of primitive beliefs that Buddhism had never really managed to chuck out. The Burmese still feared, even worshipped, the *nats*. Christ – what a bloody pig's ear of a bloody plan!

'Go on.'

Ros stood upright against the ruined wall of the hut, stared at him for a moment, then went out into the night before he could speak to prevent her.

Angrily, he snapped: 'OK, the trail's marked with *nats*. What next – after Naba?'

The moonlight fell on Ros like something that cleansed her. She paused a few steps from the hut, inspecting her crumpled, now-dry clothes. Then she returned her gaze to the moon, clustered about with big stars. The drone of one of the searching helicopters was distant enough not to concern her.

He wouldn't have smelt the burning, intent as he was on keeping them alive. To her, it had sprung up on the still air in instant horror. That helicopter, firing wildly into the trees and houses. The cries of panic of birds and people.

She continued to stare at the pale, blotched full moon, its disc no more than nibbled by its waning quarter. The minutes passed without thought. She heard him murmur occasionally from the hut. He would do his best, his utmost, to keep them alive, but he would have to kill again to do it – just like that enraged helicopter . . .

She shivered as she sensed him beside her. He snorted with exasperation, then lit a cigarette. She sensed his alert nerves, the tightening of the spring within him. Then he was standing challengingly in front of her.

'OK, doll,' he said quietly. 'I can get us out. That old soak Scudamore knows the track through the bush. I can do it – but it's going to be worse than you ever imagined, Ros, you do understand?'

After a short silence, she nodded. He shook her arm gently as she asked: 'Can we make it?'

He grinned. 'Christ, my reputation's at stake! I've saved some good, some bad in my time. I have to be able to save *us*, don't I?'

'They said a vehicle. Where do we get one?'

'The wharf. They won't expect us back there – not yet. You ready? Want some chocolate?'

'No.'

He re-entered the hut and emerged carrying the backpack, settling it to comfort on his shoulders. The sub-machine gun was slung across his chest. Briskly, he announced:

'Let's go.' He held out his hand to her. She took it eagerly.

Beyond the noisome yard at the back of the woodcarver's shop was a narrow, ragged lane, twisted as a broken limb. It smelt of rot and filth, and was slippery underfoot. Marian stumbled again and again in the first lightless hundred yards, and one or other of the young men, pressed as close as assailants, reached out a hand to steady her. Beyond another twist of the lane, there were lights and whistles. Marian was stunned into immobility, her feet in the open sewer that was gouged out of the lane's packed earth. She choked on stench and shock.

Torches and lamps, dancing off the drunken wooden backs of shops and huts, illuminated terrified faces in the deep shadows of narrow verandas or balconies. The lights threw up startled pigeons as if from angry hands. She was dragged off-balance as one of them pulled her back the way they had come. The market noises from nearby streets mocked.

One of the young men thrust her after his companion back into the yard of the woodcarver's shop. The torchlight danced up the lane towards them. The whistles were hideously real. There were running footsteps. Marian stumbled—

—the old woodcarver, a hole that still leaked in his neck, lay inside the door. She had added the final indignity of stepping on his body. Lurid light flowed over her, coming from the front of the shop, and there was heat. Marian choked back acid vomit as she was surreally dragged upstairs and through the room in which the meeting had occurred, before being pushed into a narrow passageway.

Smoke had been seeping through the floorboards of the room. Her sandals had left soiled footprints on the smoking floor. Then her heated cheeks encountered cooler, outside air as one of the Burmese flung back a hatch and they clambered on to the flat roof of the shop. She could hear her own blood and breath, their noisy exhalations. Flame emerged from a hole in the roof like a curious observer, innocent by comparison with the noise of whistles and the bullet hole in the old man. In no more than a minute, they had questioned him, decided his

A BURMA ROAD

ignorant worthlessness, and dispatched him.

She was sick, then, in great retching heaves, oblivious of everything else. Her face streamed with tears and mucus. Her hands waved the two men away – everything, *everything* away ...

Eventually, her stomach was empty. Her whole torso seemed hollowed, shivering and shrunken. As she raised her head, she realised that she had fallen to her knees. Was aware that flame had become an audience, licking out of the roof in a dozen places. The two Burmese were already on another, adjacent roof, watching her with apparent dispassion. She was wiping furiously at her eyes, mouth, nose. They were probably debating whether to leave her, vanish across the rooftops of the market district. Tugging her hair away from her face, she stood up and confronted them.

It was as if she willed them to rescue her. One of them waved her towards the next roof. Clutching her purse and the photographs inside it, she joined them. She knew she was endangering them. To erase the sudden guilt, she urged them forward. One of them nodded, then all three of them moved to the parapet at the edge of the roof, their flame-thrown shadows crouching ahead of them. Marian peered down into a side street.

A police van was nudging its way along the fissure between the buildings, the police in its headlights checking doorways, windows. Marian was gestured towards a plank thrown across the narrow ravine of the street below. The taller of the two young men danced across it and beckoned her after him.

She paused on the brink. *Don't look down*, she remembered in Giles's gruffest voice. She stepped out on to the plank almost carelessly, as if the involuntary memory had strengthened her sense of herself, and made

379

the entire nightmare something that would not swallow
her. She teetered at the noise of a siren, then grabbed the
young man's outstretched hand. The second Burmese
was, she realised, only a step behind her.

'Quickly!' one of them hissed in response to a new
outbreak of whistles and the noise of shots. Marian
hurried after them . . .

. . . to slump against the angle of a roof, her feet
stretched out towards a flat area where, in huddled cages,
disturbed pigeons cooed and grumbled softly. She was
breathless, exhausted. It had to be a half-hour since they
had climbed out of the woodcarver's, half an hour with
hardly a pause. They were near the railway station. Like
birds, they had descended to the ground only a handful of
times, at the impassability of wider streets. The two
Burmese, Thu and Zeya – she knew their names now –
comprehended the geography of the roofs as well as they
did the streets of Rangoon.

Recovering her breath, Marian stared at the full moon,
crossed by a single cigar of cloud, then at the lights of the
station and the Dagon Hotel. Thu and Zeya whispered
together more light-heartedly, in a self-congratulation
that did not exclude her.

'I'll talk to the people who must come for me,' she
informed them. Then added: 'Shall I—?'

They glanced at one another before Zeya, the taller of
the two, said: 'Yes. It is OK for us to rest here. You have
time.' His relief was politely masked.

Marian wiped the perspiration from her forehead and
beneath her eyes, then fished the mobile phone from her
purse, touching the snapshots with an electric shiver. The
dead old man in the shop. She dialled Evans' number with
an uncertain finger. The noise of a departing train was
louder than the distant sounds of the search for them. The

shops that had caught fire from the blaze at the wood-carver's were half a mile away, their immolation as innocent as a candle flame. The city rumbled and gabbled beneath her perch. A steam engine began hauling its coaches laboriously out of the station. She saw the sparks and glow of its open firebox.

'Colin?'

'Is that you? Thank God!'

Colin Evans realised he had not even paused for confirmation of her identity, merely snatched at her voice and the relief it offered. His hand, clenched on his desk, punched the air. He mouthed at the ceiling of the cramped, borrowed office, *Thank God*, once more.

'Colin, I need rescuing,' he heard her say, almost as good-humouredly as if she was trapped by a bore at a cocktail party. He admired her effort at calm.

'You all right?' Aubrey and her father would not have sounded more relieved. 'Where are you?'

Her laughter was all but hysterical. She choked on it.

'On a rooftop, near the station – on a *rooftop!*' The laughter was almost manic, purgative.

'What happened?' he asked abruptly, as if slapping her face.

'What—? Oh, no sale. I still have them. *My* job, apparently.' She wound down like an automaton whose range of gestures was exhausted.

He looked down, for the first time since he had heard her voice, at what had preoccupied him for the last few hours. It lay on the scratched utility desk, a photograph, monochrome. The man's face was turned to the flashbulb. Sodden clothes, the water of the Royal Lakes reflecting the flash, as did the staring dead eyes in the drowned white face.

Alder ... murdered, then dumped. The back of his head

stoved in. A mugging – just that, and something to be regretted and then ignored. US Embassy business – a stink in the papers back home, uproar in Congress, condemnation from the White House, and the ruling junta in Rangoon whitewashing itself in the local press. Tears from Marian Pyott . . .

An hour after he had almost accidentally received the photograph, a chap he knew from KL and now at the US Embassy in Rangoon was denying all knowledge and wanting to know why he wanted to know. There was a news blackout, no uproar, no diplomatic panic. It had all gone very quiet . . .

Alder was some kind of spook, evidently. Or working with the Company. The silence confirmed it.

And now there was madam on the phone. *Look after her, Colin – yes, Sir Kenneth.* He and her father had been screaming for her safe return all day. She was Alder's lover. Was she working with him? Couldn't be. She saved the world for democracy with impeccable moral outrage! No wonder she was sleeping with Alder; they had political naivety in common!

'Are you still there?' he heard her ask, and sensed her fear like an electric shock. 'Colin—?'

'OK, I'm here,' he soothed, disregarding the shapshot of Alder's body. He surrendered his speculations. By morning, the US Embassy would have got the story straight. The news blackout would be lifted and the mugging theory, in all probability, confirmed. Someone would have to be arrested, of course . . . 'I'll get you in – but I need a bit of time. Two or three hours.' He heard her breathing quiver. 'No longer than that. Can you stay safe that long?'

The buggers in the Ray-Bans and the chests full of medals were after her, he reminded himself. Just bring her in, before they kill her too.

A BURMA ROAD

'Yes...'

'Leave your phone on. I'll pick a meeting place, set up cover, give you a time. All you have to do is stay safe for a couple of hours—?'

'Yes...'

'If you're in – other company, or someone's close, switch off the phone. Otherwise, leave it on.'

'OK.'

Marian glanced up at the two Burmese, and was aware once more of the evening traffic, sirens, the glare of light from the railway station. The city, alien again, seemed to thrust itself up towards her in successive, drowning waves. Beyond the lights there was a vast darkness which the moon left unilluminated. She was no longer a visitor or stranger, but a fugitive. From people with power and guns. Even Colin Evans was distant from her, a lifeline become a thread.

'Please hurry, Colin,' she heard herself say. A siren, very close, unnerved her. 'Please—'

'Quick as I can,' he replied. 'Just keep out of sight for a couple of hours.'

A Burmese soldier, watched by a lounging officer, was pouring fuel from a jerry-can into the tank of an army jeep parked near one of the warehouses that lined the wharf. The ferry had left, heading downriver. The wharf was almost deserted, most of the unloaded cargo already transported into Katha or into the warehouses. There were fewer lights, so that the place looked like an ill-lit backstreet. He could smell the river, the diesel, heard the fuel slop.

There was too much open ground. The planking of the wharf creaked betrayingly as the soldier shuffled his feet. The officer was too many yards from the jeep. Even if he shot both men with a silencer, he had too much loud distance between himself and the vehicle not to alert other troops. There were a half-dozen or more in the vicinity, dozing or playing cards. Cheroot smoke puffed up intermittently into the overhead lighting—

—darkness. Surprising the soldier. Hyde heard fuel slop on to the planking. The officer laughed and arched his cigar butt towards the water. Hyde saw it fall as a spark. Ros grabbed his arm, breathing hard.

'What's happened?' Yet her grip seemed more to restrain him than anything else, as if she anticipated his being harmed.

'It's all right – I forgot. The electricity supply. They only have it on for a few hours a day in places as remote as this. We saw it come on – show's over for tonight, by the look of it.'

Jessop would be disconcerted. An oil lamp was lit at an open warehouse door, and its light spilt like a small, warm pool on to the planking. The soldier abandoned filling the jeep's tank, returning the jerry-can to its stacked companions. The card game continued by oil-light. The stars glowed. Jessop would be making contact with this lot soon, warning them to be alert. The officer lit another cigar. The searchlight beam of one of the helicopters walked like a white leg across a floor of dark treetops in the distance.

Ros' arm still held him as they crowded together behind stacked crates that smelt of salted fish, peanuts, molasses. He turned to her and touched her face, shaking her grip gently away. Then he moved upwards into a crouch. The light from the lamp and the moon was sufficient. Distance?

Twenty yards to the jeep. He'd need spare fuel, at least three jerry-cans. Cover?

He would be seen from the open door of the warehouse

by the officer and the card players. The key needed to be in the ignition. He prayed that the officer had not removed it when he had parked the jeep, twenty minutes earlier. Hyde adjusted the Heckler across his chest, then inspected the pistol before thrusting it into his waistband in the small of his back. He kept the knife hidden, slung beneath his left arm. Then he removed the bulky grenade from his pocket.

The Multiflash grenade lay in his hand like a tin of baked beans. Gently, he eased out the pin and placed it silently on the nearest crate. When he moved, he knew he would be spotted before he could roll the grenade towards the card players. The submunitions it contained would go off after two seconds. They'd be too surprised at his sudden appearance to shoot in that time, but the moonlight was worryingly bright.

Likelihood?

Borderline.

'Just be ready to jump in when I pull up beside the crates. Head down. OK?'

'OK.'

He shook her shoulder and stood upright. He hesitated for a moment, but it was no use giving her any alternatives in case he went down. There weren't any. If he was killed or injured, Ros was lost, too. She'd never get out alone.

Distance . . .

Gradually, the scene became as still as a painting. The shadow of the jeep in the moonlight, the lakelike expanse of the Irrawaddy beyond it, the little profane activity of the card players in one corner of the canvas, oil-lit. Someone laughed, someone else spat in the moonlight.

He was two steps forward now, at the edge of the shadow caused by the stacked crates. He cleared his head of Scudamore's belligerent instructions, the times and distances to the border with India ... Distance, fifteen yards. His moonshadow fell briefly behind him as he skittered across the wharf towards the jeep. Then he turned on his heels like a machine, weighed the grenade, rolled it—

—the first cry, a craning head as the soldier tried to see clearly beyond the lamplight, out into the vast, moonlit darkness. The right hand, holding a playing card, pointed. The officer's hand reached for a holster at his hip. A leaning rifle tumbled away from a snatching hand. The innocent-looking tin of the grenade continued to roll towards the four players and the officer, each of them assuming what seemed exaggerated poses in a tableau.

Two seconds, one shot from the officer's pistol which buzzed near Hyde's head. He hunched away, hands over his ears. He'd warned Ros to do the same, and *don't look*—

Four deafening blasts, the jeep lit by the first flash. White light. White-hot sparks. Firing, terror, panic. He jumped into the driving seat of the jeep. More detonations, more sparks, and blinding, disorientating light. The ignition, the *key*—! He switched on the engine. Jessop would see the light and hear the explosions, even from the railway station, and know exactly what kind of grenade it was.

The soldiers looked charred in the light that was already dying down, and severely disorientated. The officer was firing blindly into a night he could not see.

'In!' he yelled at Ros, revving the engine, holding the jeep on the handbrake. '*Get in—!*' She, too, was disorientated. Hyde grabbed her arm, hauling her into the vehicle. She retained the presence of mind to drag the backpack in after her like another rescued person. He let out the clutch and the jeep jerked forward. The light was almost gone. He flung three jerry-cans into the rear of the jeep, stretching from his seat to gather them—

—shots. He roared away. The diesel cans exploded on the wharf. More blinding light, gouts of burning fuel, sparks. Ros was rubbing his hair and clothing. He smelt his singed hair, then only the petrol as the jeep bucked up a slope towards the road, hurrying them into the shadow of the raintrees.

The scent of the sawmill was heady in the humid night. Now that the noises from the crowded, riverfront shanties were no more than punctuation, Evans could hear the river slithering like a huge snake a hundred yards away. Hear, too, one of the locals he'd been loaned shift position. Moonlight caught the man for an instant as it poured through broken windows and the distressed roof. SIS at the Rangoon Embassy owed him favours, and, besides, he was in control of British Intelligence's haphazard, indolent drug-smuggling investigations.

The DTI party was missing Marian, of course, but with a tone of relief and amused disrespect rather than suspicion or concern. Alder's death was not yet public and, for the moment, the dead American provided her with a prurient alibi. He and Marian were an *item* ... Causing much ribaldry and some envy.

I promise you, Marian, you're not going to become an item with him now, in the morgue.

'Anything yet?' he whispered hoarsely into the R/T against his cheek.

'No.'

'A couple of beggars.'

'A Mercedes, uniform inside with a woman.' Evans heard the engine purr along Monkey Point Road.

'A police patrol, cruising. Nothing for them to see.'

The cover was operating efficiently. They were posted

along Monkey Point Road, at the Syriam Jetty, the Botatung pagoda, and on the corner of the bazaar. The bazaar's night-time noise and crowds had dissipated and the police activity had seemed to evaporate with it. There had been plenty of black vans and olive-drab Tatmadaw jeeps and trucks throughout the evening. Now, just before two, Rangoon had fallen asleep and so, hopefully, had the frenzied search for Marian.

Evans listened again to the city. It grumbled in its sleep - the sirens of the search, a ship hooting from the Yangon River, the bark of a dog, even someone spitting. The lights were fitful, too, like the flickering eyelids of a shallow sleeper. The electricity supply in Rangoon was notorious. Locals claimed you could tell where the junta, the army and the corrupt businessmen lived, just by looking out of a window after midnight. Their homes and streets were the only ones with lights.

'Report,' he instructed.

'Police van, not curious' ... 'Nothing' ... 'Couple of drunks' ... 'Two beggars - same as before.'

He'd selected the sawmill on the waterfront because it offered the river and the mazed grid of downtown Rangoon to foil any trap or pursuit. It was also quiet and dark, and populated with derelicts, shanty-dwellers, black marketeers and muggers. Just the opposite of the sort of place you'd expect a rescue operation for a white female politician. Smiling, he stood up and stretched away cramp. The piled planks of teak ranged away from him into the darkness. Through open doors, he could see stacked timber and the river gleaming in the moonlight. He could smell the wood shavings that stirred under his feet.

He'd instructed Marian only to contact him in emergency or when she had the sawmill in sight. She seemed to trust the two Burmese who had got her away and were keeping her out of sight. To Evans, they sounded competent, if reluctant. Someone flung rubbish into the river from the deck of a freighter at one of the jetties.

'Three here,' he heard. 'Another police van ... going away. Those two beggars, sir - I think one of them might be a woman—'

Evans studied his watch. Five minutes past two. He'd said two, but expected caution to make her late.

'OK, keep tabs on them, Three.' He lifted the night pocketscope to his eye, picking out the three men he had dispersed through the teak mill. Moonlight gleamed light grey on toothed circular saws. 'Stay alert. Other scouts report.'

He heard the infection of Three's suspicions in their voices.

'One, sir - no activity' ... 'Two here - army jeep going north, one taxi. Nothing suspicious' ... 'Four, sir - same here. Should we close in?'

'No. Leave Three to tail them. If it is them, they're on their way here. Just watch for traffic—' He felt the perspiration beneath his arms and across his forehead, no longer the consequence of humidity. 'Three—?' he whispered.

'It is a woman - tall. Burmese costume, though—'

'Doesn't matter; she's taller, you say?'

'I think so. She's hunched up.'

'Keep close to them. Any traffic?'

'No.'

'Good. Where are they now?'

'At the corner of Botatung Pagoda Road, inspecting some rubbish behind a bazaar food shop.' There was doubt of her identity and a fastidious distaste in the voice of the middle-aged Burmese. Evans grinned. 'They're moving again. Crossing Monkey Point Road. Two hundred yards from you.'

'Good. All of you, close up. Inside crew, full alert.'

He ignored their responses. The teak sawdust smelt more powerfully and the noise of a distant and retreating car seemed important. He heard the river's slither clearly, and the tinny noise of a radio on one of the moored freighters or small boats. A baby was crying with hunger in one of the nearest shanties of petrol cans and cardboard.

'A hundred metres . . .' Then, almost at once: 'Fifty now. Must be them, they're not hesitating now.'

'One, Two, Four, close up. Let's get ready to move.'

He raised the pocketscope and focused on the doors. Seconds now. Thank God.

'One, Two, Four?' he whispered. 'Have you got them in visual?' He listened to the silence. 'Come in, One, Two, Four – *Four*, come in!'

He saw them framed in the doorway, the Burmese man and a taller woman. A frozen tableau.

'One! Two! *Four*, for Christ's sake!'

The light changed in the nightscope, as if the two figures were outlined against an explosion. The sawmill was bathed in hard white light that flooded in through the doors. The R/T offered him nothing but chilling silence and static. A voice boomed through a PA system. He heard vehicles braking. Evans felt panic, felt himself mocked by the two figures caught in the searchlight, ridiculed by the easily accomplished silence from the R/T.

The voice from the PA system was repeating its orders in Burmese – to *remain still, do not move*. Move, he thought, drawing his pistol and thrusting a round into the chamber. Move, don't *stand* there, *move*—! Then he realised he was shouting the words: 'Marian – *move! Marian*—!'

Marian . . . Her name startled her out of immobility. But the light, even her disguise, restrained her. She was caught like a butterfly, with Zeya, pinned in the hard light.

Even the amplified voice was like a restraining grip on her shoulder. *Don't move, stay where you are, we know who you are*... There was no disguise, no escape. How—?

How, for Christ's sake, *how?* Even as he thought it, Evans was running towards the doors and the lights that seemed anchored to Marian. She was still standing there, hesitant, the Burmese beside her, also immobile. *Come on, girl, for Christ's sake—*

He ran heedlessly. The imperative was to get her out safely. He squinted through the pocketscope as he ran in an attempt to locate running figures, guns, the positions of vehicles. *She was still standing there!* One soldier, a policeman – Evans fired. The man fell away. He knew his cover troops would already be fading away into the scenery. That was their priority; they were only on loan. Alder was dead and now the woman was about to go the same way—!

'Marian!' he all but screamed. '*Move!*'

He fired again, at a second moving figure. Fuck diplomatic immunity; this was Pyott's daughter and Aubrey's godchild.

'Marian!' he screamed again.

Marian ... It penetrated the fog, like a cattle prod rousing her. The pudgy, selfless figure of Evans was running towards her, firing wildly – one soldier about to lay hands on her was down, rolling in agony on the floor ... She lurched forward, as if to run into Evans' open arms. The teak mill was full of shadows. One of them was hers, and there was another running beside her, fleeing from the lights. Zeya.

Then her shadow was alone. She looked wildly round and saw the body of the young Burmese stretched on the sawdust. She flung herself away from it in horror and collided with Evans. His pistol fired again, deafening her.

There was other shooting, more lights, the noise of sirens and now rotors.

'Come on—!' Evans yelled wildly. Then his features were no longer elated but instead surprised by pain. He slipped on the sawdust, down on to his knees, as if to pray. He looked up at her, puzzled, then yelled: 'Run for it, woman! I'll be all right!' She still hesitated. 'Fucking get— Oh, Christ—! It's *you* they want dead – run! Do as I say!'

He was leaning back against a stack of fresh-cut planks, dragging himself upright. He waved her away, pointing with the gun towards an opening in one wall of the mill, no more than yards from them.

'Get down to the river – go on, *go* ...' He thrust something into her hand. 'You'll need this – go!'

She nodded, gathered up the filthy *longyi* in which they had dressed her, and was running immediately she turned away from Evans. She had no idea where her other protector, Thu, was. Perhaps they had killed him too.

Fetid, humid air, less light. She stumbled away from the teak mill, finding herself at once immersed in lines and clumps of shanties. She splashed through a crude drainage channel that stank unbearably, and almost flattened a cardboard shack. Someone inside cried out in fear, someone old. There were other figures moving, alarmed by the lights, fearing a police operation to cleanse or arrest them.

An oil lamp overturned, cooking pots spilt, a baby lay in the dirt. Terror on each face that the moonlight or the roving, maddened searchlights betrayed to her. There were whistles and shouting behind her, as if she and the shanty-people were animals being roughly herded. Evans – Thu? They had slipped away from her like figures in a dream.

She realised that what Evans had thrust into her hand

was a pocketscope. She held it to her eye and adjusted the
focus, smelling her own unwashed fear and dirt amid the
noisome stench of the shanties. Petrol cans hammered
flat for walls, cardboard, mud, straw, bamboo – and
people running, possessed by fear. The helicopter swung
over the teak mill towards her. Soldiers were firing indis-
criminately, yelling orders to *halt, stay still.* Uniformed
police, dozens of them with the soldiers, all running
through the shanty-town like a wind. A truck was bulldoz-
ing shanties flat. Screams, fear – terror everywhere . . .

People were wading into the river to escape, as if from a
fire. Small, terrified, half-naked creatures, a different
species from those in uniform who were in pursuit of them.
She was unnoticed. The *longyi* clung around her legs as she
at first waded, then swam towards the shadow of a rotting
jetty. The helicopter hung like a toad over the shanties, a
searchlight in its nose stabbing at running figures as a
finger might have squashed ants. The heavy machine gun
mounted in its open doorway fired sporadically.

The uniforms now marched in a tight formation towards the river, driving the shanty-dwellers in front of
them. Three trucks were blundering towards and flatten-
ing huts and shacks like maddened elephants. Gunfire,
screams, orders, rotor noise, quieter splashing near her in
the water, even the chatter of teeth from the shadows as
someone cowered in terror, like herself . . . On her heated
body, the water seemed icy. She began shivering. Terror
was infectious, a plague that had spread in minutes.

Zeya was dead, Evans might be dead by now – dozens of
these people were dead or dying, because she had fled
through their shacks . . . She was alone, terrified, clinging
to the rotting wood of the jetty in the vile river. She began
to flinch uncontrollably at each shot, each yelled order,
each stab of the searchlight at the ants . . .

CHAPTER FOURTEEN

Jungle Warfare

The tiny figure of the *nat* with a sword over his left shoulder was just distinguishable on the rock without being caught in the headlights of the jeep. The dawn lay like a silk robe, pearl grey, along the horizon of the jungle and the hills of the Gangaw Taung. East of them. Behind them. Katha, the road and railway, the Irrawaddy – all were invisible beyond the spine of hills they had already crossed. Ahead and around them were the foothills of the Mangin Taung, defiantly jungled like the beard of a ferocious enemy.

Hyde stopped the jeep in the lee of the rock on which the *nat* had been painted decades earlier, and switched off the engine. The sudden silence was as palpable as an attack. Ros yawned, complacently. Hyde suppressed a sigh of satisfaction. Ros had been temporarily lulled out of their real situation. She had narrowed it all to the two of them in a jeep driving a narrow track by the light of a full tropical moon. He was grateful for that, if for nothing else, as he watched the horizon's silk change colour, becoming palely orange. A dazzle above the hills where the sun would soon be—

—emerging from that glare, like a black flea, was a helicopter. His hand twitched on his thigh, but Ros failed to notice. A second black flea followed the first. The search had been widening like ripples on a pond all night. He'd detected the pattern early, the helicopters flung out from Katha in ever-expanding circles. They hadn't concentrated in any one particular direction – yet. The jeep's progress had kept him and Ros *just* beyond the search, but only because he hadn't rested—

—and he was tired now, very tired.

He stifled a yawn, and his nerves. The two helicopters were skimming the jungled horizon, heading north for the moment.

'Hungry?' he asked, climbing out of the jeep, stretching innocently. The horizon drew him again. It had come to resemble one of those car windscreens with a tinted upper edge. The helicopters moved like insects inside the screen, troubling him, threatening a fatal accident. 'Anything you fancy?' he added with forced lightness.

During the night, as they were crossing the paddy fields of the valley between the Gangaw and Mangin ranges, and as Ros dozed heavily, the helicopters had swept a circle they had been no more than a mile outside. At the next cast of the net . . . ?

The jeep was beneath old, gnarled bushes and stunted trees that leaned drunkenly out from the rock on which the *nat* had been painted. The track, just wide enough for the jeep, wound between bouldered scree and looming jungle, upwards into the hills. Safe enough.

'What is there?' Ros asked.

'The usual.' She wouldn't know the usual for survival. 'Porridge, chocolate, various spreads – usually chicken – on biscuits. Soup sachets—' Evans always packed well. 'Rice,' he added. There was a tiny butane stove in the backpack.

'Biscuits – anything.' She was coming out of the trance-like state. 'Toilet paper,' she added. He handed it to her from the opened pack.

'Don't wander off – round there will do.' He pointed. By her expression, Ros seemed to find the intimacy of the exchange unnerving. She hurried away from him.

He unpacked biscuits, the chicken spread, some raisins, chocolate. There was two days' supply in the pack, four thousand five hundred calories a day. *Enough to sustain a high level of physical activity – like saving your skin, killing people, being shit-scared, all that*, the instructors always added, smiling. He chewed a handful of raisins and apple flakes. Then, still watching the helicopters, which had not yet enlarged, he filled the tank from one of the jerry-cans. Diesel corrupted the freshness of the morning air. His eyes measured the progress of the two machines along the stubbled chin of the distant hill range. The circle was a wide one. Soon, they would turn west—

After he'd hacked at the undergrowth near the Buddha in a rock niche, just as Scudamore had remembered, the poisoned earth of the track remained driveable. They'd crossed the railway, climbed the foothills, passed through a narrow defile in the Gangaw, and descended to the sleeping, moon-bathed valley.

Then the helicopters, walking on their searchlights, had flashed through the valley as he halted the jeep in a paddy field. He'd heard frogs and crickets and the plop of something into an irrigation channel before the rotor noise drowned everything. Ros had woken as the noise retreated, not revealing whether she had identified its source. He hadn't asked or explained.

He now flung the empty can over the edge of the track. It crashed through the trees below. Ros was walking back up the trail, clutching the roll of toilet paper like a baby against her breast.

'I've seen the helicopters, by the way,' she offered belligerently. 'Heard them last night, too—' Then, before he could reply, she thrust her hair away from her face and added disconcertingly: 'How many did they kill, in that village? Where Tripitaka is ... ?'

'It was just a small Auschwitz, a little Tiananmen Square. It was people getting in the way.' She spilt water on her hands and lathered them. 'A hundred ... ?' She shuddered. 'They must have thought I'd sent you for a look-see ... They *all* knew about it, including your mate Bruce Pearson!' He was suddenly enraged. The helicopters were larger black dots against the climbing disc of the sun. He shrugged. The anger was pointless, like shaking a fist at the coming day. 'Your pal Marian's trying to interest the Lady in the souvenir photographs right now.'

'Is she in danger, too?'

'Probably. That's her choice.'

'A hundred ...' she breathed after a long silence. Then she burst out in fury: 'No wonder they want to add us to the bloody list!'

Larger black dots against the pale sky. Ros dried her face and hands on a scrap of towel. There was a hum, not of insects, on the air.

'They bloody kill people so *easily*,' Ros was saying. 'We've got to get out of this alive, Hyde. I'm not going to be – *erased*.'

The dots were resolving into objects. The helicopters appeared to be driving at them like falcons in the stoop, their rotor noise loudening, filling the air.

'Ros, get in the jeep now – *do it!*'

The rotor noise was already banging back off the rock like surf as the two helicopters closed with frightening speed.

Marian washed at the side of the brick trough as if she wished to cleanse herself of her surroundings rather than her dirt, repeatedly tipping water from the leaking tin bucket over her head, lathering her face and arms with the coarse soap. Moss and algae clung to the sides of the trough, which was opposite a decayed colonial building on the other side of the pitted road. Nearby, on trestle tables at a market stall, Burmese men in chefs' hats were skinning and preparing snakes for foreign, expense-account lunches and dinners. Lustrous banded skin was peeling back to reveal pale-pink flesh, wet-looking. The calm, indifferent skill unnerved her. The newspaper seller next to them was raucously unconcerned.

The Burmese at the wash trough looked at her and wondered. Seeing herself as they must do, she realised they saw a tall white woman in soiled native costume, weary and barefoot, with broken painted fingernails. That unkempt, unclean appearance was the best of her disguise. She could hide in plain sight, like some pauper tourist abandoned, sloughed off like the snakeskins by lack of money, or a taste for drugs. She simply *could not* be a woman of any importance.

A hat pedlar with filed gold teeth amid gaps in his broad grin passed her. With a small stick, he politely raised the topmost of the half-dozen hats piled on his head.

She moved unobtrusively away from the trough, her

facial skin tight with soap and rubbing. Beneath the river-stained *longyi*, the photographs of the atrocity remained taped to her stomach in their polythene cover. In the belted purse Zeya had given her was her mobile phone, credit cards she could not use and some Burmese currency.

She shivered, sensing herself as something as decrepit and rotting as the building across the street. She flinched as an ancient van backfired. Whitewashed, crumbling buildings stretched away. A line of monks carrying polished bowls paused at a roadside eating stall to receive the gift of breakfast which bestowed merit on the giver. A thin dog watched them suspiciously, as if its own meal was endangered. The poverty, the weary dilapidation, the dirt and rubbish, the smells – all blundered against her like bullies rather than sensations. They clung to her skin and seemed to enter her pores like nerve gas, numbing and deadening. She staggered, leaning against a drunken wall. Whitewash on her fingers in flakes—

Evans was dead, killed trying to save her, dead like the bodies that had floated past her as she had cowered under the jetty, numbly treading water. The army had taken the opportunity of her having been there to flatten the entire shanty-town, kill dozens of people. Screams, firing, the noise of bulldozers, the lurid light of fires . . .

Her stomach heaved and she vomited on her dirty, bare feet, sickened through her whole frame by what she had witnessed, what she had occasioned. Bile followed food . . . The shivering would not leave her. She couldn't move – unlike her eventual escape from beneath the jetty. She had swum with the current of the river after the gunfire had ceased; weary, semi-conscious from her terror and aching cold, moving loglike as if waiting for an elephant's trunk to drag her from the water. She had floated in the terrible shelter of a man's dead body. As they had drifted together with the current, a dead dog, bloated with gases, had joined them in a ghastly parody of company. Searchlights had flickered over the water and along the shore. Filth in the river, other bodies. Once she had ducked beneath the surface for what seemed like minutes while a soldier casually sprayed bullets towards the dead man and the body of the dog. Then they had gone on together, the current taking them towards the ill-lit, early-morning shore. The wake of a freighter had washed them further in. The sky had become grey.

Eventually, she had sensed mud beneath her feet and seen the blurred image of a steamer at a jetty. Small, thin boats were being rowed across the harbour by men standing at oars. Fishing nets were cast.

She had crawled into the shelter of a rotting, upturned boat and fallen into an exhausted sleep. Thu, the other Burmese, who had been shadowing them in a taxi, near the timber mill, had disappeared, probably believing her dead. The thought loomed over her like an armed man discovering her hiding place, but it still could not prevent sleep. The thought was there, however, the moment she woke, chilled and hungry in the morning light. Isolation bullied her into panic more than the distant signs of a search for her – or her body – along the waterfront. Alder—

The mobile wouldn't work after being in the river. She had thrown it into an alley somewhere near the river, screaming at it, attracting the curiosity reserved for the mad or abnormal. She had tried the Royal Lakes hotel from a public callbox. Alder was not in his room. And Colin Evans was dead; she'd seen him shot and wounded, and they would have finished him off in a moment. Otherwise, someone would be looking for her. Instead, she was alone ... The river had been a baptism of sorts, into the life of a scrap of a thing crouching on a broken pavement and afraid for its next few minutes of life.

She stood up and wiped the slime from her lips. Sniffed loudly. She could not make an international call to Kenneth or her father except from the Central Telephone and Telegraph Office. She had passed it on Pansodan Road. Even to her untrained eye, it was under heavy surveillance. They hadn't found her body and would know she was alive somewhere in Rangoon.

Where was Alder? She *needed* him.

As if to deny the present, and in a parody of normality, she bought a newspaper and retreated with it to a narrow, filthy alley. The smell of the river still clung to her. A thin mongrel sniffed at her then moved away to urinate. Marian slid into a defeated crouch against the wall, staring at the front page of *The New Light of Myanmar*, the junta's English-language rag. A thin, striped cat watched from its perch on a rotting windowsill, with evident disdain. A one-legged man on crutches passed her, oblivious. She smelt cooking ...

The picture on the front page was difficult to make out. Her tears blurred it. Traffic hurried past the entrance to the alleyway.

Alder's features stared at her from the corner of the front page, beneath the small headline, *US Congressman Dies in Robbery Attack*. His dead eyes stared at her. His body had been hauled out of the Royal Lakes. There was a wet, uniformed sleeve at the edge of the picture. They'd killed him. Found him out in his double game and just – disposed of him.

She wanted to be sick again, but her stomach – all of her – seemed too empty for even that response to his murder. Her eyes wandered over the page, as if she expected to read of her own death, even that of Evans . . .

. . . near the bottom, a brief report of the shanty-town's destruction. *A Raid on Drug Smugglers*, an event of the tiniest significance. *Regrettably, a few innocent people were caught in a fierce crossfire and were killed or injured . . . among the wounded was a British government official . . . cannot be named . . . assisting the police Drug Intelligence Unit . . . comfortable in the Diplomatic Hospital . . .*

It had to be a lie. Colin was dead. This was just something to smoke her out . . . Colin Evans was dead.

A thin shaft of sunlight glared down into the aquatic green murk of the jungle. Hyde stood as if transfixed by the climbing palms and wait-a-bit rattan, whose fish-hook thorns glistened like washed, miniature knives. All around him the sunlight danced on the points of the thorns as he turned very, very slowly. Ros and the jeep were ten yards away, invisible. The curved blade of the parang remained raised beside his cheek, ready to chop down again at the jungle undergrowth that had obliterated the old smugglers' track.

Sweat streaked his face and chilled his body. The sweating seemed to increase, malarially, as he attempted to remember in which direction Ros and the jeep lay. There, *there* . . . ? Claustrophobia was sudden and unnerving. The green light, the shaft of the sun, the thicket of thorns surrounding him like a fence . . . And all the hours behind him that had stolen his reserves of energy and confidence, so that he could be stunned into a paralysis by thorns.

More sweating. The track had simply vanished beneath the jungle's reinvestment. *Scudamore, the bastard, claimed they'd poisoned the track; it should still be here.*

402

The thorns gleamed, thousands of them, and plucked at his bush jacket, his trousers, his hair. *Wait-a-bit*, that was what they called the rattan on which the thorns sprouted. Wait-a-bit – if you didn't, if you moved quickly, they tore you to ribbons. Slowly, he stilled the quivering in his body, though his sweating continued unabated. Then he moved his left arm carefully, turning his body and head gently and slowly, as if courting the thorns in a dance. His sleeve came clear. There was no opponent, no enemy except the rattan thorns. Slowly, he moved his right hand. Ants moved violently beneath his shadow, over his boots, on some urgent operation of their own. Huge, garish butterflies wafted above his head, where he could see a spot of sky.

He could hear the noise of falling water, close but invisible. He studied his raised right arm and the gleaming blade of the parang. The curve of the blade protected his knuckles as he struck downwards and across at the rattan and bamboo. The knotted, ropelike stuff parted. He moved his left foot, striking again with more confidence. Another foot or so of vestigial trail appeared beneath the struggling undergrowth.

He heard the water more distinctly. Then Ros' voice. His panic had been no more than seconds long.

'Hyde – all right?'

'All – right,' he answered, his throat tight. Christ, frightened of thorns now ... 'OK.' He looked back and could now make out the way he had come, where the jeep must be, less than twenty yards away.

Reinvigorated with an inordinate relief, he slashed carefully at the thorns, watching the rattan part now like rotting curtains exposed to a wind.

The parang embedded itself in a fallen trunk and he wrenched it free. The carved, mossed figure of a *nat* studied him disdainfully. He struck more and more vigorously. Now the undergrowth seemed thin, a mere disguise. Grinning, he struck again, tasting his lunch as he belched. Cold fish curry that tasted slightly of the plastic container in which Ros had kept it. The *ngapi* dried shrimp paste mingled queasily with the chocolate from the rations.

The jungle seemed to open ahead of him, the rattan and bamboo now like a door he had forced—

—immediate noise of rotors. His smile froze. The track was exposed, curving around rocks over which a waterfall coolly spilt itself, glittering in the midday light. He glanced wildly around the enlarged sky above him, already mottled with cloud, blinded for an instant by the overhead sun. He heard the helicopter's noise louden. *Ros*—

He looked back. The jungle seemed impenetrable once more, Ros and the jeep lost on the other side of its dense wall. Insects swirled around his face and eyes. The waterfall fell away into what might have been a bottomless green well, after arching out over a rockface.

One helicopter, not two. Coming back to make sure? They hadn't been spotted earlier, he was certain. The sun's heat had brought on the sweating again. They couldn't *see*, anyway! Not through the leaf canopy of the palms, or the rattan and bamboo. He was exhilarated by that realisation, as his temperature mounted.

Heat. The noise of the rotors changed as the invisible machine went into the hover, somewhere away to his right. Only hundreds of yards away, it seemed. If they even suspected their presence, they'd be using a thermal imager. And he was *hot*, a bright orange shimmer on a thermal imager's screen.

'Ros!' he shouted. 'Ros, can you make it through?' He couldn't see her—

'Hyde, I'm coming. What about the jeep?'

'Just come!' The jeep's engine had been off for an hour. It would be no hotter than the air around it. 'Ros, hurry up!'

He forced himself to move back among the thorns, wielding the parang like a swordsman, widening the narrow track.

'Hyde!' He knew she was trapped.

'Stay still – don't *move*!' he yelled.

'Hyde—!'

He slashed to either side of a point just ahead of him, cutting away the rattan, slicing the thorns aside, hearing the helicopter maintaining its fixed, intent, bird-of-prey stillness in the air. He slashed again and again—

—terrified white face, the parang quivering above it. He teetered with the effort of keeping his arm harmlessly aloft. Gradually, the shudder deserted his arm. The thorns were in her hair, her sleeves. He brushed them gently aside with the blade, as careful as a valet or maid.

'Come on, quick!' he whispered hoarsely.

Water, he thought. If they hadn't spotted them yet, there was still time. He moved forward, hurrying, her hand in his . . .

. . . something moving?

'What's that, there?' Jessop asked, his finger jabbing towards the display screen while he held the thermal imager to his eyes. A video recorder stored the shifting, ghostly patterns he saw. 'Moving – it's fucking moving! What is it?'

The Chinese colonel, standing beside him in the downdraught at the main door of the helicopter cabin, glanced from display to jungle, jungle to display . . . A cooler wash on the screen appeared suddenly as Jessop tracked the imager binocularlike across the scene.

'Moving quickly,' he murmured. 'An animal? A deer startled by the noise? It's not there now.' He looked down at the jungle as it tilted slightly in the proscenium of the open door like a world on its axis. 'Ah, the waterfall.' It filled almost the whole screen now, coolly blue. The hotter spots and streaks around it belonged to trees, other vegetation. 'I wonder—?'

Colonel Yao Fan's unfinished remark was intended to irritate Jessop, one of the most typical of barbarians. On a folding table bolted to the bulkhead were taped the enlargements of the grainy photographs from the dawn surveillance of the other helicopters. A jeep was bolting like a squat wild pig into the cover of jungle. The blobs of two white faces were clearly visible. Jessop's delight had been savage. Hyde was evidently attempting to cross the Mangin range, then the Kabaw's fertile lowlands towards the Indian border. A rescue might possibly have been arranged. India was the nearest border; the plan was obvious. Yao's eyes left the photographs and the thermal imager's display, and looked towards the densely jungled hills and the hazy green plain beyond them, then at the border where higher peaks rose up like a barrier. A long grey spine of the Himalayan foothills marked the entire horizon, from north to south.

If Hyde and his woman crossed the hills to the plain beyond, they would be as exposed as flies on green paper. Let them, for the moment, have the cover of the jungle – there would be more than enough time and miles after that in which to find and eliminate them. Yao was satisfied. He had read the man's file. He was not a boar, or a deer; they were hunting a tiger.

'The terrain here is difficult – for us and for our quarry,' he announced, leaning his head towards Jessop's ear and raising his voice. The other man, Cobb, was crowded to the other side of Jessop. 'If he is indeed crossing the Mangin, then we need only wait.'

Jessop glared at him.

'I can't—!' he began, but seemed at once quelled by Yao's uniform, his impassive certainty. As if swindled in some obscure way, Jessop shouted: 'He's down there – he's close! I can feel it.'

'But you cannot see him.' Yao pointed. 'He must cross – *there.*' He gestured towards the strip of green between the Mangin and the more distant mountains. 'Patience, Mr Jessop – a little patience. And more organisation—'

'OK, OK! What can we put into that area – how many choppers, troops, vehicles?' Jessop challenged. His belligerent, almost fearful contempt was tiring. His hatred of the man Hyde was blind, but useful. Yao was, anyway, ordered to work with him.

'Sufficient. If we begin now. *If* we return to Katha at once.'

Jessop snarled, 'OK, let's get out of here!' He glanced with longing at the snapshots of the jeep. 'Tell the pilot. Let's go, Colonel!'

Yao gestured at one of his junior officers, who opened the door to the flight cabin. Jessop continued to stare down at the snapshots, at the small white spot that was Hyde's face in profile.

You won't make fucking India, son, not in a million years . . .

The rotor noise loudened as the helicopter flipped out of the hover like a flung coin. The landscape tilted, exposing the strip of green, the distant mountains, and the sky stretching away over India. Then the scene was gone as the helicopter turned towards Katha, its rotor noise banging back from the crowded hills . . .

. . . noise slowly diminishing, its echoes fading quickly into the sound of the waterfall, behind which he crouched beside Ros. Hyde listened, drenched and chilled, as intently as an animal as the racket became a distant drone, then was lost.

Ten more minutes, to be on the safe side. He pulled Ros, who seemed little more than a sodden heap of clothing, against him, hearing the uncontrollable chatter of her teeth, feeling the frantic shivering of her frame. It was so bloody *cold* in the shallow cave behind the curtain of water, which dazzled with the midday sunlight only feet away. He kissed her wet, straggling hair, suppressing his own tremor of relief.

The noisy water was penetrated occasionally by the cries of parrots. Gradually, her breathing steadied. They must have been spotted at dawn, but not now ... But Scudamore's trail was much more exposed once they left the Mangin for the valley beyond. Unprotected almost all the way to the border. And they must know he was heading for India. The trail crept beside a river, sneaked through rocky outcrops, patches of jungle, but it was more dangerous at every point after the mountains. Cultivated, populated land, flat and open for the most part. He'd have to talk to the fat old bugger again.

He looked at his watch, pulling in the line his thoughts had cast ahead of him.

'OK?' he asked. 'Ready to go?' Ros nodded quickly.

The letter, propped against the jug of water on the bedside cabinet, was difficult to bring into any kind of focus. Eventually, the envelope addressed him as *Taff*, before slipping back into the room's general, post-anaesthetic muzziness. The noon sun filled the room from a window that hurt his eyes. His mouth was so dry that he could barely move his tongue against his palate. The water jug came out of the haze once more, and then vanished again. But he had located it and struggled upright in the metal-framed bed.

His head lurched as if some huge cargo had shifted in a dark, empty hold. Sickness rose into his throat and he swallowed, then coughed drily. *Christ*... He held his head in his hands as if cradling an egg. Hangover—? His side erupted in pain as he reached for the jug, and water and the envelope spilled into his lap. His left hand clutched the bandage across his side. Very slowly, the padding and strapping came into focus... He could smell the teak mill in the hospital room. Saw *her* running away from him, heard the Burmese voices and felt hands turning him and searching his pockets. Remembered their quick debate over his ID... then passing out as they lifted him.

Colin Evans wiped the film of perspiration from his forehead, then reached with a groan for the glass. He drank greedily, refilled the glass, swilling the water in his barren mouth. The pain in his side lessened.

He'd come to a few times, he remembered; in the back of an ambulance, a hospital corridor, in the operating room just before the injection... And now. He turned his lurching head towards the window. It was midday, or thereabouts. The sweating subsided. He had almost emptied the jug of water. It was making him nauseous – better lie down...

Taff, on the envelope in his lap. With a small asterisk in the top right-hand corner, too ... He struggled to remember something. Had he woken earlier? Who had left the envelope? In the ambulance, barely conscious, he had been able to gabble out some wild tale of following up a tip-off about heroin to a plainclothes copper who spoke good English. The detective hadn't asked about *her*. Perhaps he'd hoped Evans would give something away, semi-delirious as he must have been from his wound. He hadn't, and they evidently didn't want his body on their hands – too political. So they'd taken him to hospital.

Taff, and an asterisk . . . He remembered and tore open the envelope.

Taff – call me when you wake up. Glad you're not dead, by the way. I need to know the current whereabouts of a certain item, particularly in light of the loss of another important package. No connection – I hope! The spin doctors are asking for the urgent return of the item. Grapes on next visit, I promise! Bill.

Bill Braxton, the military attaché at the Embassy. The use of his nickname, but more especially the old signal of the asterisk, had told him the letter had come from someone like Bill. Intelligence. They must be panicked or furious or both at Marian's disappearance. Bill had guessed that Alder must have been some kind of spook and wondered whether Marian was involved.

She's on her own crusade, Bill . . . if she's still alive.

Was she? Unlikely, he concluded almost immediately. He could still hear the gunfire in his head. Indiscriminate killing, by dozens of troops and police. They had been determined to kill her, and probably had done. How they'd picked her up and known the rendezvous, he didn't know. He'd been as careful as hell. It might even have been luck. They had enormous manpower . . .

He shivered and let his body fall gently back against the pillows. The odds had been against him; time and lack of support had been his enemies. The ache in his side made it difficult to apportion blame to himself, or even to blame Marian . . .

He dozed. A doctor came, inspected the bandage, asked a few questions, purely medical though not without displaying a suspicion of him, and left. He refused food and the nurse, too, departed. The Diplomatic Hospital, he had elicited. But the starch and expertise would have told him as much, even if the nurse had not. There was a phone in the room. He would ring Braxton . . .

. . . the ringing of the phone woke him slowly, like a gently shaking hand on his shoulder. He opened his eyes luxuriously. The phone continued to ring. He remembered, as he gingerly reached for it, that he must call Braxton. He sat up very slowly.

'*Christ*—!' He paused to regain his breath and wipe his forehead, then he picked up the receiver.

'Colin—?' he heard, from a voice more clogged and dry than his own. 'Colin . . . ?' The enquiry was whirling almost at once into disbelief and fear. The tone made it certain it was her.

The line was probably tapped. They knew he'd been there because of her. He might even have been kept alive in order to lead them to her. They could have put his survival in the bloody paper—

'Hello, love,' he enunciated emphatically, 'thanks for ringing—' The tone had to knock her into suspiciousness until he could find the right words to spell it out while saying nothing.

'Colin—! I read it in the paper, that you weren't—' The relief was like the recovery of hearing or sight. Blissful, ecstatic. She'd tell them everything in another minute—

'Not me, love. I was there following a lead and suddenly all hell broke loose. *Drugs* again. I just got caught in the crossfire, it was an *accident*.' Christ, working with civilians – they took bloody ages to catch on!

'What do I do?' she asked oblivious, confused and frightened by his manner.

'I can't have visitors just yet,' he said slowly, deliberately. *Come on, girl, wake up!* He was sweating profusely in the hot, glaring room. 'Maybe a little later . . . ?'

She was silent for some moments, as if speech was impossible while slow thoughts coalesced.

'Yes,' she murmured. 'Is the phone—?'

'*Possibly.*' He had to assume it was, and get something else organised. 'Call box, is it?' She'd have to call him on that phone at least once more.

'Yes.'

'I suppose you nipped out in your lunch hour? From the Embassy? Too nice a day to go back inside, I'd say.'

'You think—?'

'*No.* Just go for a walk. Enjoy yourself – enjoy the crowds. You always liked crowds, didn't you . . . You should buy a map!' he concluded, forcing laughter. 'Listen, call me in a hour and I'll have had time – to ask the doc when you can visit me. OK?'

'Colin—!' she all but wailed, sensing the imminence with which she would again be alone.

'It's all right,' he soothed. 'Just a matter of *time*, that's all. Now, go for that walk.'

Eventually: 'Yes.'

'Good. Crowds – and Tin Pan Alley and Penny Lane,' he added, praying that she caught the slight emphasis on *alley* and *lane*. That she must stay in the back streets.

Shakily, he replaced the receiver. The sweat made him blink, and his side protested at his breathing, his anxieties, all effort. He'd been pretty amateur himself, hardly able to frame the coded hints with any skill.

'Oh, shit!' he exclaimed, lying back against the pillows, struggling with his pyjama buttons. Hospital issue. He was so bloody hot—

He snatched at the phone, as if she might still be there at the other end of the line, then hesitated. Aubrey had to solve this one – and Aubrey could play the game. But he'd need secure comms to keep in touch with London, via Godwin probably, and a mobile that Marian could ring without going through the hospital switchboard. He'd have to check the room for bugs, too. They wouldn't risk planting them now he was awake, but it might already have been done ... He was sweating again, more than ever. First off, do the difficult thing and *remember Aubrey's number*!

Bill Braxton could supply and bring in a mini-Sat radio telephone. That ought to be powerful enough ... And he could supply the mobile, no questions asked. Bill couldn't be involved officially. If he was, then someone would make sure the photographs would be lost, and Patrick Hyde be flushed down the bog. Bill was a mate and Bill enjoyed secret games. And owed him. Ring Bill, then, not Aubrey—?

He dialled Aubrey's number. The phone rang out distantly like a child's voice at the bottom of a deep well. His last call to Aubrey had been a fudge, because he'd been confident then he could bring her in without much of a fuss. Aubrey and Pyott didn't even know she was in danger.

'Sir Kenneth—'

'Colin! What's happening? For God's sake, where have you—?'

'Stop yelling at me!' The disrespect was the code.

'Yes?' Then he heard Aubrey, his hand muffling the receiver, snap at someone else in the room. Probably her father.

'You have to talk to someone soon as you can. Clive's little nephew. You'll have to draw lots of pictures for him. There's a whole pack that needs putting back in the kennels right away. No time for delicacy. *Someone needs a warm bed.*' That *was* jargon. Someone needed bringing in. He'd know who. *Food* would have meant there was just enough time; *bed* meant it was an emergency. 'I'm getting myself kitted out – I'll call again. Draw Boyo a colour picture!'

He replaced the receiver and stared at the window. The light hurt almost as much as when he had woken. His head remained filled with its loose, dangerous cargo. *Could* Aubrey use the photographs of the atrocity in some way, to save her?

If he couldn't, she was dead for sure.

He swallowed a renewed sensation of sickness, and held his wet forehead with one hand. Secure comms and a mobile phone. In less than an hour. Evans groaned aloud. His side hurt like hell.

Silently cursing, he dialled Braxton's number at the British Embassy.

The sun was already impaled on the peak of the six-thousand-foot Taungthonlon. It threw a long, ugly shadow across the broken, mutilated flanks of the mountain, and was already nibbling at the plain towards which they were descending. The mountains in India were gilded like temples. The steering wheel bucked in Hyde's hands as the rear wheel on the driver's side climbed a boulder then dropped back on to the ledge of rock. It overlooked a slit of a gorge through which a river fled whitely, a hundred feet below them.

He wanted to close his eyes. The dusk shadows were too difficult for his tiredness to overcome.

Ros wasn't well, it could be dysentery. Despite her anger at her condition, she was dull, listless, constantly drinking water. No fever, no violent abdominal pains. He'd given her Flagyl tablets from the first-aid kit. It had tired her, concentrating on the trivial and talking constantly in order to keep him awake. She wanted him to stop before he wrecked the jeep, or tipped it into the gorge. The helicopters had been back a couple of times during the afternoon, but at a distance, scouting the wet patchwork of paddy fields dotted with clumps of jungle. They hadn't been spotted again. He believed . . .

He couldn't stop. He had to reach the plain and cross it in darkness. Their only chance of avoiding the search was to make that crossing at night. The rain had stopped around four. By then he'd found another *nat* scratched on a rock as if clinging to it in the last of the downpour.

The jeep lurched again, threatening to tip him out and down into the river, then righted itself.

'You've got to bloody *stop*, Hyde!'

'Don't nag, Ros. This isn't the bloody M25! We have to be down there before dark—'

'You won't listen, will you?'

'I can't stop. I'd have to use the lights to get down there safely if we don't do it now.'

She exhaled noisily, clutching her stomach. Drank more water. The blander, quieter country lay ahead like a promise. He resisted an urge to accelerate. India was less than eighty miles away. He'd spoken again to Aubrey. Phil Cass was having problems. *He has to send in a chopper to lift us out!* he had yelled. Aubrey had tried to reassure him. Cass hadn't enough big favours he could call in. He'd spoken to Scudamore. The smugglers' trail wound from outcrop to outcrop of forest across the plain, *nats* carved on the trees. They had used the irrigation ditches and raised banks that marshalled and fortressed the paddy fields. *At night*, as he was aiming to do.

The steering wheel wrenched itself from his grip. He wrestled the jeep back into a kind of submission. Ros's face was deathly white in the gloom of the narrow gorge. Another thousand feet of descent before they reached—

The near offside screeched, the engine raced. The jeep bucked like a savage dog restrained by a rope.

'What is it?'

'It's jammed in a rock cleft,' Ros replied wearily. Her hands clutched her stomach as if a baby kicked there. There was a dew of perspiration on her forehead. 'I'm all *right*!' she managed.

Hyde got out of the jeep and moved to the nearside rear wheel. Jammed was right. Between the cliff wall and a boulder too big to move. The jeep leaned drunkenly towards the drop to the river, which was ghostly in the dusk, its rushing noise unnerving in the silence. Rock it back and forth, jiggle it out . . . ? It seemed a momentously difficult task, something complex and remote; higher mathematics. The air was cool, as if it rose out of the river like a mist. Pointlessly, he kicked the wheel and swore, then scuffed at loose stones.

The shadows increased as he collected the loose rubble from the track. He told Ros to stay seated on a rock. Her body sagged with the enervation of the dysentery, her face white in the gloom that was belied by the sunlight still streaked across the distant paddy fields. He jammed the rubble into the cleft beneath the trapped tyre. Eventually, he was satisfied. Gesturing Ros to remain still, he unloaded the pack and the other equipment. Then he got back into the jeep and started the engine.

Gently, he let out the clutch. The tyre, whining against the cleft, vomited the rubble. The shadow of the mountain stretched over the plain like a huge, dark finger. Sweat ran into his eyes as Ros watched, her anxiety plain. He rocked the jeep back and forth. Again . . . again . . . again . . . *come on, come on* . . . once more, in reverse . . . Rubble machine-gunned against the subframe, the vehicle lurched, was free, careering backwards and sliding before he could regain control. A wheel whined over emptiness, his body tilting slowly. He was curious as to the reason, even as the Chinese helicopter passed down the gorge at speed towards the plain, its belly-light flashing off cliffs. Hyde was stunned into inaction as the helicopter swung in a tight arc like a skidding motorcycle and began coming back towards them. His body was at an angle, the white river gleaming in the evening shadow—

Hyde jumped clear as the jeep toppled slowly over the edge of the track, towards the river. It bounced, then exploded. Lurid flame lit the shark's belly of the helicopter as it loomed above him.

'Alex – thank God! Marian's still alive! Evans has her call him every two hours. And Phil Cass is doing what he can for Hyde.' His old, breathless enthusiasm ended suddenly.

Aubrey was alone in the drawing room. Davenhill smiled with soothing reassurance as Mrs Grey closed the door behind him. The gilded French clock on the marble mantelpiece struck one with a shivering, silvery sound. Aubrey looked very tired. His eyes, however, burned with the fever of his prime, as he blurted:

'Can we do it, Alex? Can we bring if off?'

'Where's Giles?'

'Oh – feverishly impatient. *De profundis* – despair to something like ecstasy. I sent him on an errand to occupy him. Evans is bedbound and without a back-up team. Giles has gone to unearth some old Burma hands of his acquaintance – someone who might provide local contacts. We need people, a place to bring her to . . . If you have a feasible plan for her rescue!'

'A large Scotch would be welcome. Mrs Grey has taken my sandwich order . . .' He yawned. 'Sleepless night, thanks to you.'

Aubrey poured the drink and handed it to him. He sipped at it gratefully. Mrs Grey entered with the sandwiches.

'Smoked salmon – delightful!' When she had again closed the door, Davenhill said purposefully: 'Sit down, Kenneth, while I explain what we must do. The *only* course of action open to us.'

Aubrey perched on a leather chair at the Carlton House desk near one of the windows, as if to exaggeratedly mime a rediscovered professionalism. Davenhill plumped on to the sofa and opened a wedge of files and a large scribbling pad. He studied the worn, impatient old man, and felt an immediate and unreasoning anger towards Aubrey, and Giles Pyott, and especially towards Marian.

Holy fools, all of them. Angels fearing to tread and all that. Were Colin Evans dead, as well he might have been, nothing could be done to save Marian. Even now, it was a damned close-run thing ... He was tired and a migraine threatened. Kenneth's panic and Giles's desperation had leaked down the telephone line to him, dispelling the pleasures of supper and the young man he had encountered. He'd since been checking and double-checking, finally dismissing everything and everyone but Lau from the equation. Damn all crusades, he thought, and all self-indulgent old men and politicians!

'The sole object is Marian's safety,' he announced. Then, sharply: 'You agree, Kenneth!'

Eventually, after a play of emotions like swift clouds across his face, Aubrey murmured:

'Yes. Very well, yes. Not the Chinese, not Alder, not the heroin. Marian ...' Then, more brightly: 'How?'

CHAPTER FIFTEEN

Impatient Diplomacy

'We bring pressure to bear on Ralph. And the DTI – one by means of the other, in fact, so symbiotically are they related at the present time.' Davenhill sighed and finished his Scotch, refusing Aubrey's offer of a refill with a slight wave of his hand. 'Background first – a little, anyway . . . Hong Kong returns to the Motherland, bands play, ships sail away. End of empire. At least, the end of our last crown colony as a base of influence for HMG, and especially the DTI, in South-East Asia. Interest at once transfers to Singapore. Not our colony, but friendly. What banks, individuals, conglomerates should we cultivate there to further the interest of UK plc? So asks the Office, the Treasury, the Department of Trade and Industry. *Who* might be best placed to carry our modest banner in his briefcase—?'

'Ralph?'

'Winterborne Holdings, anyway. Winterborne Straits, AsiaConstruct, all the other tentacular interests under the holding company's umbrella.'

'Even after David's—?'

'—criminality? Fraud was what was on the charge sheet. Dear David is paying his debt to society. And Clive as chairman, poppet and patriot as he is, and Ralph the coming man, were both pathetically eager to make amends. Clive, at least, was genuine. Ralph Lau became, in the event, a kind of businessman-at-large for Her Britannic Majesty's government. It must have amused him mightily, to see himself so trusted while rebuilding a shattered empire on heroin profits.' Davenhill laughed acidly. 'The DTI and the Office have sung Ralph's praises so long and so loud that they can't disown him entirely in a moment. Not, at least, without jeopardising this current junket to Burma and covering themselves in the proverbial should the photographs ever come to light. They *mustn't*, by the way. Not afterwards, not ever. All copies to be handed in at Lost Property – mm?' Aubrey merely nodded. 'That will have to be our threat, that they will somehow emerge – and our guarantee will be that they will not.'

'You're certain about this closeness between Ralph and government?'

'Yes. That was what took the time, gathering the impressions, *weighing* Lau's importance.'

'Can we bend him?' Aubrey rubbed his hands together with a dry, sandpapery noise.

'Yes – if he is approached via the Office. Ralph has played pandar and introducer, been a conveyor of whispers. He's acted as a conduit for approaches for a great many exporting companies and potential Asian investors. Under the old government and the new.'

'Ah.'

Unrequested, he refilled Davenhill's tumbler, then reseated himself near the window.

'Before you ask, I can't do the same for Patrick – except personally with Lau. Just as we cannot approach Lau directly about the photographs.'

'How do we make our approach?'

'Via the unspeakable Salter would be my choice of direction. He is on the passenger manifest for the present jollities in Rangoon. Salter would be terribly disturbed by these revelations.' His smile was one of feline, predatory gloating. 'They have to allow me to talk to Lau, semi-officially, perhaps under the pretext of checking out the substance of some rather ugly rumours. Once the *Office* had persuaded Lau that he must talk to me, Ralph may just see that the game might possibly be up. What we must do is circumvent the politicos, for the moment – and the spin doctors who throng the rafters of government.'

'What is the pretext for your call – for the urgency?'

'The Foreign Secretary's in Washington with the PM. I will have been approached – for *confirmation* – by some obscure news agency. Someone who was up with me at Oxford, perhaps. They, in turn, will have been sounded out. The details are sketchy – photographs, hints of something quite appalling ... As to time? It is evening in Rangoon. There is a grand reception, I discover, tonight. Just before it is scheduled to start, I would think, would catch Salter and Ralph on the hop. Perhaps a couple of hours' time? I—'

The telephone trilled and Aubrey snatched it up.

'Colin—!' he exclaimed.

Keep her alive, Davenhill silently mouthed. All night, if necessary, he added to himself, glancing away from Aubrey's expression.

***

A wild pig, nothing larger or more dangerous, moved in the undergrowth, rooting and snuffling. Roosting chickens in a dilapidated shed muttered and clucked, then settled to silence. Hyde could see the river now, not merely hear it. Silver in the light of the full moon, it flowed south-west across the plain towards the Chindwin, forty miles away. A line of narrow, canoelike boats were drawn up on the smudge of sandy bank for the night. Someone in one of the huts behind them cleared a half-asleep throat, then spat loudly. Ros, beside him, twitched in alarm.

He listened, above the background interference of insects, to the tropical night. Eventually, he was certain that the only other sound was their breathing. Ros' was harsh and ill-sounding. The dysentery was dehydrating and exhausting her – even more than the loss of the jeep or the five-mile trek to the river and the sense of night falling over the jungle.

The helicopter had ricocheted along the river gorge like some maddened insect in the dusk. In the moment when the crew might have seen them and been certain they were not in the jeep, the vehicle had exploded, blinding them. The helicopter had used a searchlight, then lowered a man on a winch to check the wreckage. But the jeep had tumbled into the river and their bodies might have been swept away by the fierce current.

There had been enough doubt to make a door through which he and Ros had slipped into the deepening darkness.

He'd unloaded the pack and some of the spare diesel to lighten the jeep as he tried to free its wheel. He'd carried the two cans the five miles to the river. They needed another vehicle and that would require fuel.

Ros, already physically weak, was drawing on dwindling reserves of determination and outrage to keep going. She seemed more enraged by the atrocity at Tripitaka – talking of it constantly – than by the hunt for them.

They had stumbled across this tiny village and the river and boats by accident. Now, squatting on his haunches, his hands resting on the fuel cans either side of him, he studied the outlines of the boats. Their small outboard motors were silhouetted against the gleaming river. Fuel ... Diesel *ought* to work. Had to. He leaned his head against hers.

'I'll check the boats. That hut, too.'

She seemed to wish to restrain him, yet the touch of her hand on his arm might as well have been a gesture to hurry him. He slid from the bushes almost on all fours, across the strip of sand to the boats. Looked inside the first. A pole for steering or punting, a paddle, the smell of fish – scales gleaming in the moonlight like broken glass – and the scent of diesel. His relief was palpable. He crawled away from the boats towards the one hut squatting close to them, rigged with nets and lines, and rose snake-like against the single window and peered in.

An overwhelming smell of fish and old firesmoke. The curing hut. He flicked on the pencil beam of a torch and inspected the walls. The light picked out straw hats like small, bossed shields hanging from pegs, and a ragged cloth jacket that had been used to wipe bloodstained knives. The hut door was unlocked. He removed two hats and the filthy cotton jacket before crawling back to Ros, who said:

'What the hell is that stink, Hyde?'

'Our new wardrobe,' he whispered back, grinning. 'OK, help me get one of the boats into the river?' He waited and she nodded bravely. 'Good. I'll paddle it a way downstream before we start the engine ... OK, let's go. This river flows into the Chindwin. The Chindwin flows south *along the border*. We should be able to reach the river's closest point to the border by midnight.'

'You have been a busy little bugger, haven't you?' Her voice was stronger.

'I love you, doll – and I'm getting us out of this. Now, let's get started.'

Ros moved awkwardly ahead of him. A dog snuffled in its sleep, somewhere close, momentarily disturbing the chickens. They pushed the punt on its flat bottom down to the water, and Hyde loaded the fuel, the pack, then Ros, before pushing the boat out into the current. As it began straining to pull away from him, he clambered aboard and began paddling.

Ros' face was white in the moonlight. The punt slipped away from the straggle of tiny huts. In midstream, the current was tangible beneath them, and the background ether of insect noise was lost in the sound of water hurrying around the hull. The last of the jungle, and all sense of a landscape, retreated from the river's banks, to be replaced by the vastness of the night sky, jewelled with warm stars and dyed with moonlight.

Last stage, he thought. *Endgame.*

He began listening for the noise of helicopter rotors.

Ralph Lau realised that he was already drunk. Not because of the Krug copiously served by the waitresses, more because of the noise created by the others in the huge sitting room of his hotel suite. He was drunk on their mutual congratulation, their exalted success, the gratitude they heaped on him with touches, grins, whispers and jokes. The scattered pages of faxes and contracts littered the furniture and the carpet like fallen, solid expressions of the room's heady talk. Cigar smoke rose, signalling success. The reddened, confident faces of the men he had assisted were all effusively eager to laud him. The heads of investors, the gas companies, the construction executives, the mining companies, the engineering, electronics, communications conglomerates, the UK arms of Japanese giants, all seemed turned to himself like flowers towards the sun.

The triumph of the moment swept away all sense of what remained unresolved. This snapshot of complete success was his to have gilt-framed. Poor, imprisoned David Winterborne was not here to witness the redemption of Winterborne Holdings. A shame that he could not enjoy the acknowledgement in David's eyes of *his* success, David's eclipse.

Another word of thanks from a soft-drinks manufacturer, a pat on the forearm from someone global in communications . . . The minutes passed with a sensation of mounting arousal. In another half-hour they must all descend to the hotel ballroom for the formal dinner with the politicians and for further, if condescending, congratulation. *A job well done.*

In his own briefcase in the bedroom were enormous contracts for AsiaConstruct in Burma, Laos, Cambodia, his promised share of the Mekong project. His success was awe-inspiring, dazzling even himself—

—then Feng was like a patch of shadow at the corner of his eye, as the Chinese general entered the suite. His appearance forcibly reminded Lau that his own contracts remained as yet unsigned, conditional on the deaths of Marian and Hyde. Their two lives still stood between success and himself. That was probably why Feng had appeared now, as a visible reminder of his subordination. The Chinese haunted him like a vengeful spirit.

'She is still alive,' Feng murmured in his ear. Lau realised that he had moved halfway across the suite to meet Feng.

'Yes!' he snapped. 'Yes, but not for much longer.' Angrily, feeling his triumph draining away, he added: 'Why are you so *insistent*, so impatient?'

'Because she should no longer exist.' Feng gestured at the room, its coteries of power and wealth. 'It is impermissible that anything concerning myself or my associates – our grouping – should become public. If the matter concerned no one but yourself, it would be of little importance. A brief setback. There would be other legitimate faces to replace yours.' Lau felt cold in the heated, excited room. 'Those photographs include myself. In compromising Alder, I am potentially compromised. I am linked to a *strategy*. That was what interested the American and brought about his death. If the hand of Nine-Nine-Nine Group should—'

'It will be done!' Lau felt himself perspire with nervous humiliation. 'My people are—'

'As yet unsuccessful. This woman is dangerous – kill her.' There was a vehemence on Feng's habitually inexpressive face and in his black eyes. Lau sensed increasing pressure on the man, from Wang Wei, his senior, and the other entrepreneurial generals who stretched away like a chain of forbidding mountains. Feng's long fingers gripped his arm. 'You understand the utter necessity of this?'

A smirking CEO from a fast-food franchiser approached them, but then seemed rebuffed by the invisible field of Feng's injunction. The hot night beyond the windows was a scatter of reflected lights on Inya Lake.

'Yes, yes!' Lau protested. 'I will speak to the Police Minister at once.'

'Good.' He released Lau's forearm, which prickled with cramp. 'She is your only obstacle. Remove it.'

'Avoiding the mission-control people will be the problem, Kenneth.' Davenhill held the telephone receiver loosely in his hand. Afternoon sunlight beyond the windows filled Regent's Park. 'The monstrous regiment of spin doctors.' He smiled. Aubrey's nerves placed him beyond any light response. Davenhill was grateful that Giles Pyott had not returned. He had called, weary as a supplicant, desperate as a condemned prisoner. 'Shall I begin?'

Aubrey wiped at his lined features with a nerveless hand, studying Alex. He had to let him play his hand. Yet it was so wrenchingly hard to surrender his responsibility for Marian's life and to accept a passive role. He nodded.

Davenhill stifled his sigh of relief, then his own nervousness.

'Salter, then,' he muttered. 'Our respected head of the Far Eastern and Pacific Department. A shiny new KCMG to his moniker, to signify the importance of China in the eyes of the Office.' His smile was humorously malicious. 'Motto of the Order of St Mike and St George – *Token of a Better Age.*' He laughed comfortably, and glanced at the gilded clock. 'The formal dinner's about to get under way. Division of the spoils and a great deal of congratulatory backslapping. Let's ruin *Sir* Maurice's appetite! He should be tying his black tie just about now—'

'Be careful, Alex,' Aubrey could not but warn as Davenhill began dialling.

'Don't worry, Kenneth, I know my man. We're not dealing with the people you and I once knew at the Office. People like Salter are just figures on celluloid. Unfortunately, the projector does not possess sufficient candlepower to make them seem real ... Ah, good evening. Sir Maurice Salter, please. Foreign Office matters—' He winked at Aubrey. 'Good evening, Gerald – Alex

Davenhill here. Maurice around the place, is he? Important? Well, possibly – you know. Maurice's advice would be helpful– How are things? Excellent! Yes, I'll wait.' He placed his hand over the receiver. 'One of Maurice's turnspits ... a young man more poisonously ambitious than ninety-nine per cent of the new Commons intake ... Ah, Maurice – Alex. Sorry to disturb–'

'Yes – Alex?' The slight hesitation in acknowledging professional intimacy with Davenhill was habitual with Salter. 'I'm running a little late – could Gerald or someone else handle this?'

'No. I wanted to avoid mission control altogether, if possible, Maurice.'

'Yes? Why would that be, Alex?' Salter's ingrained asperity was tinged with his homophobia, and with his customary straining after a *gravitas* which lay forever just out of reach of his vocal range.

'At the moment, Maurice, because it's just a small cloud on the horizon, no bigger than a man's hand, et cetera ... But with the possibility of becoming something of a typhoon. Embarrassing.' Almost as if it was audible, Davenhill sensed the cabalistic interest that clicked in like a defensive armament.

'You say so?' Then, to the young man: 'Gerald, tell the minister I may be a few minutes. Hold her hand until I get there.' Silence, then: 'Very well, Alex, what seems to have ruffled your feathers?'

'Maurice, you know that I have disreputable, certainly unattributable, connections in all parts–' The tone was apologetically ingratiating. 'One of them rang me at home in the early hours of this morning. Someone from one of those small-circulation digests that feed other, larger–'

'I see,' Salter murmured dismissively. There was a

theatrical sigh. 'Is there a point to this background, Alex?'

'Yes. 'Fraid so. At least, there might be. A matter of your overview, Maurice, your judgement . . .'

Aubrey watched and listened as to a home movie of some younger self. Alex's nerve-endings guiding his mind, his antennae, like the sonar of a swift negotiating the complexities of a cathedral's spires. It was – *delightful* to watch, and all but enough to allow him to ignore Marian for whole moments together.

'Yes,' Alex was insinuating, 'very possibly very murky. Though there may be nothing at all in it . . . Reports from Rangoon are good, I gather from Gerald. Much as hoped and foreseen? Well done. Our masters must be euphoric. Much of the praise being hurled in the direction of Ralph Lau and Winterborne Holdings, I imagine . . . ?' Again, he winked at Aubrey. The old man appeared fidgety and restless. *Sit down, Kenneth.* 'Ah, ahead of me there, Maurice. It *is* to do with Lau and Winterborne Holdings, the Light Brigade of your offensive . . . Yes, I use the analogy deliberately.'

'Time is pressing,' Salter replied querulously, but defensively. 'I really must—'

'I'll hurry on, Maurice. It seems to be a matter of photographs, a whole sheaf of them, that have come into my disreputable friend's hands. They impinge. How important does Lau *remain*, now that his good offices have been employed with such success? Any thrown mud likely to stick to people *other* than Ralph were he to – fall from grace?'

'What?' The crucial moment was upon Davenhill almost before he recognised it.

'Not best loved by either of us—' he began, sensing Salter's outrage and disbelief.

'Alex, you've always treated the Office as some kind of

personal games arcade. What *is* this nonsense? Ralph Lau is not my favourite individual, but he remains important. Why do I receive the impression that this is some kind of malicious game and nothing more?'

Bluff...

'You make him sound essential to our entire foreign policy, Maurice,' Davenhill mocked.

'You won't bait me that way, Alex. What *is* this? Do you have anything, anything at all, to convey?' There was a wrong note in the line of music. Salter had to doubt – not to do so might lead to egg on face. Davenhill winked his own huge relief at Aubrey.

'Very well, Maurice. Difficult for *me* to believe, so I understand your reluctance.'

'What?'

'That holiday resort of Ralph's up-country – aren't you and the other chaps booked in for a spot of R and R after the trade mission concludes—?' That had been a delightful nugget thrown up by the computer which he had kept from Aubrey, whose old eyes glinted with malicious admiration. 'Not virtual reality, I'm afraid, Maurice.' He must press now, before Salter's black-tie image of himself was caught in a mirror in his suite and reawakened his confidence and dismissiveness. 'Photographs. Of some form of extreme persuasion employed against the former residents of the site. The extinction of a place, people – in the cause of business. As with Troy, fire and ruin. Then, above the ruins, a new citadel rises. Hotels, to be precise. Tripitaka, a resort complex. That's a Buddhist term, isn't it, Maurice?'

A long silence, into which Salter dropped inadequate pebbles of resistance.

'What do you mean – precisely – by fire and ruin?'

'Huts ablaze – gunfire. I gather there were a great many

bodies, if the pictures do not lie. A deep trench, like Katyn or Babi Yar – there's a long pedigree.' He hurried on: 'My disreputable associate wouldn't handle them – he says. Though he's thinking of one of the nationals that might – or a French rag . . .' Salter's breathing was hard and quick. He had woken beside a plague carrier. Then he burst out with:

'Who are you suggesting might be involved in this? Lau, directly? That must be preposterous—'

'No, no – surely not. If these photographs were to prove genuine, then it would be the work of some local bigwig or a Tatmadaw commander . . . life and death being a more casual affair in somewhere like Myanmar. We shouldn't be too hard on Lau—'

'Alex, for God's sake!'

'Sorry, Maurice. But it is Ralph's resort, unfortunately. He built it. What would have seemed a sensible "site-clearance" business decision by someone local would all rebound on Ralph. On HMG—' He paused briefly, then pressed on. 'But I think were we to move quickly . . . Better still, if Ralph could *reassure* . . . give the whole thing the lie, I could then, perhaps, clear things up at this end.'

Another interminable silence. Salter had to seize the opportunity of containment. Aubrey seemed caught like a ghost by the afternoon sun coming through the tall windows.

'You think I – I must speak with Lau. Evidently, he must clear this matter up, squash these ugly rumours. I will call you, Alex. Where are you?'

Davenhill gave him the number of his mobile. Then he added: 'I have arranged to call my contact within the hour, Maurice.'

'Yes, yes! I will see to it, Alex.'

'Bye, Maurice. Good hunting.' Davenhill put down the

receiver, suddenly exhausted. Aubrey advanced violently on him, and in irritation Davenhill raised his hands to ward him off. 'Patience is a virtue!' he snapped. 'Practise it, Kenneth!'

He looked at the mantel clock. The official banquet, the comforting blankets of power and success, enfolded Lau and Salter alike. Would his story begin to seem incredible to Salter, once Lau began soothing denials, feigned outrage?

If it became unreal, Marian died . . .

Evans wiped his forehead with a towel. The telephone was clammy in his hand. She'd rung in half an hour late; it was dark outside the window, and he'd begun to believe he'd lost her. He stared at the receiver, still uncertain she had been at the other end of the line, afraid for her once more now that she had cut the connection.

She was slipping away, going into hibernation. She was vague, hesitant with her words, possessed no concentration. She was drained – so much so that she might even forget to ring back again in another two hours.

His wound ached as he got off the bed and slumped near the satcomms unit the military attaché had loaned him, *no questions asked* . . . A wry smile, a percipient expression in his eyes, but no questions from Bill. Evans couldn't ask for men, for back-up – just the satellite telephone and the mobile she could ring to avoid the hospital switchboard.

'Tony—!' he blurted. 'Colin again. Get the old man moving, and bloody Alex Davenhill! There's not much time left. I've told her over and over to hang on a bit longer, but she's slipping away from me. If they don't hurry, there'll be no point in doing anything at all!'

***

Giles had returned, desperately eager, with the names of three men from his old regiment, ex-soldiers now employed by an international gas-exploration company in Burma. They were currently enjoying R & R in Rangoon from their unnamed security duties and would, on agreed financial terms, put themselves at Evans' disposal. A senior officer in MoD had already made the arrangements, strictly on the qui vive.

Now, within a half-hour, Giles was as stricken and enraged by circumstances as Aubrey was himself. They were like two bears unspeakably imprisoned in cages for the purpose of draining off their bile; unable to move, unreally and nightmarishly alive. In their case, forced to sit on upright old chairs watching Alex, who alone held the spidery thread that connected them to Marian's survival. Aubrey was appalled at his own impotence. For so long, he had possessed *so much power*... Now he could do nothing; all his effectiveness lay in the past.

Lau, so Salter relayed, had not even been ruffled by Alex's story. Alex's face was creased with suppressed fury as his listened to Salter pour oil on waters he did not even admit were troubled.

'Assured you ...' Alex repeated dully, his gaze unfocused. 'Enemies, business rivals. This sort of thing has come up before, you say ...' All as if learning Ralph Lau's dialogue by rote. 'No, I'm equally certain there are.' He was slightly more animated.

Alex seemed so utterly defeated. Aubrey realised how exhausted he must be from the hours of patient delving and research. Now he was like someone who had just witnessed his matchstick model of St Paul's Cathedral crushed by the playful family pet. Risible – and dangerous. He was losing Salter.

'Yes, I realise the formal dinner is about to commence,

Maurice—' Alex looked towards Aubrey, an actor desperately catching the eye of the prompter.

How could he help—?

Obvious. So obvious that Alex couldn't see it. His baffled weariness invigorated Aubrey. Giles seemed to have caught Alex's defeat like a cold. Aubrey scribbled on the large pad at his elbow and held up the message. Sunlight caught the big letters on the white paper.

You've got the photographs.

Alex continued to stare with the myopia of disappointment, then slowly his expression changed. His smile was beatifically grateful. Then he said into the mobile:

'Did I not mention, Maurice?' His grin bloomed. 'I was sent *one* example of the photographs in question by my friend. Usual in matters of this kind . . . sample of what is on offer – yes, Maurice, a *print*, not the negative. Yes, it's very clear . . .' Salter was evidently on the ropes. 'Of course – it may be a fake, it may be somewhere entirely different, it may even be old news. Only Ralph is likely to be able to tell us which.'

Davenhill listened greedily to the winded silence, feeling his own sluggishness entirely fall away. Salter had nearly had him in a fall! God . . .

Eventually, a thin, almost piping voice said: 'I – I'll get him to the phone, Alex. This must be sorted out, cleared up. It would seem to be best if he—'

'Yes, Maurice.'

'I'll call you back. Immediately.'

A rat crossed her lap in the darkness and Marian shivered. She had slumped into a dozing, fitful sleep – again. She turned her watch in the moonlight that fell weakly through the high, ruined roof of the locomotive shed. Its cathedral-like size became more distinct around her. How long had she

been there? Since dusk? It had to have been still light ...
Her thoughts collided clumsily, as if blindfolded.

During the day she had moved north-west from the
business quarter and the wider residential boulevards
into crowded suburbs of factories, leaning tenements,
narrow streets and alleys; always following Evans'
instructions. Reporting to him every two hours or so from
call boxes. To end up here, in the shunting yards behind
Kyemgindaing railway station.

In the darkness around her other derelicts slept; the
homeless, beggars, thieves. Evans thought her safer here
– and perhaps she was. Away from the sirens and whistles
of the police and Tatmadaw. Cheroot ends glowed fitfully
in the darkness. Occasionally there were the noises of
urination, spitting, eating, snoring. The quarrel of a drug
sale nearby. The whimpers of dogs and children before
she had dozed.

She had bought food from a family huddled around a
smouldering fire of cardboard and scraps of wood, little
brighter than a match. The food had made her stomach
churn, but she had kept it down. It had served only to
increase her hunger and thirst.

'I can't get someone to you,' Evans had explained when
she had last rung him. 'These blokes your father rounded
up – they're OK, but they've got white faces ... And
they're a bit iffy about any direct contact with the police
or the Tatmadaw. Worried about their bloody company
pensions, I expect ... Anyway, I don't seem to be able to
lay my hands on any locals who can be trusted. You'll
have to stay put for a bit – OK?'

Marian was very weary. Metal struck against metal
somewhere in the night. Steam hissed. Neither sound roused
her to alarmed wakefulness. Someone coughed and spat.
Rats scurried and an owl swooped from the invisible rafters

near the high roof. A train passed. Marian did not bother to look at her watch again. She just wanted to sleep . . .

General Feng listened to the faint sounds of Lau moving from the bedroom back into the lounge of his suite, where so recently he had entertained the powerful and the greedy. Then one of the bugs in the lounge picked up Lau's voice and that of the senior civil servant, Salter. Feng hovered behind the junior army intelligence officer operating the recording equipment. Lau and the Englishman were as clearly audible as if he had joined them in the suite, instead of being in a room on the floor above theirs.

'You really must answer these disturbing rumours, Ralph.'

'Maurice, I can and I will. Give me the number.'

'Here it is . . . Look, I really do have to be at the President of the Board of Trade's elbow when she is welcomed by the Burmese government – this is most unsettling!'

'I'll handle it, Maurice, you run along. I'll report what happens. This can be put quietly to bed, there is absolutely nothing in it.'

Feng listened to the long silence as if hearing the two men's thoughts. Then:

'Very well. Tell Davenhill I wish to talk to him later.'

A door closed. Lau sighed. Then the silence returned. The operator increased the amplification. Feng leaned forward, as if to snatch at the voice at the other end of Lau's call. He bit at his thumb, infected by the nerves Lau must be experiencing. He'd seen Lau summoned away. Salter's face had been darkened with suspicion and anger. He'd followed them on an impulse.

He heard Lau's room phone bleeping as the man dialled. Feng loosened his uniform collar. The operator increased the amplification once more.

'This is Ralph Lau – I take it I am speaking to Alex Davenhill? And who else?'

'Ah, Ralph – thank you for returning my call.' The Englishman's voice was assured, mocking. 'A matter of some urgency, I'm afraid. Maurice agrees—'

'What is it, Davenhill?'

'Your Tripitaka thing – Maurice has briefed you, of course?'

The distance at which Davenhill's voice was placed, even by the tiny bug in the telephone, and the boom of Lau's voice did not represent the relative strengths of the two men, Feng realised.

'He has. You can tell your friend the theory is nonsense. There can be no photographic evidence, since the incident you claim never happened.'

'They'll be under sixty feet of water by now, will they?' Davenhill asked lightly. 'I hear the dam is about to come into operation and that the new boating lake will look an absolute *picture . . .*'

'I am not a travel agent, Davenhill.' The irony was too naked.

'My apologies, Ralph. Shall we come directly to the point, then? There *is* proof, Ralph . . . But let me explain. It could not be a picture of *anywhere.* Computer analysis places it precisely' – Feng heard his own indrawn breath as if it had been Lau's – 'at Tripitaka. Should I describe the scene?'

'Go on.'

'A deep trench. Bodies. Soldiers of the Tatmadaw doing the killing. There are more than forty dead in one of the shots, I'm told. In the example I possess, there are two Burmese and one Chinese officer.' The shoulders of the operator flinched as Feng gripped one of them. The silence went on and on until it hummed in his ears. Then Lau said:

'You could not use those photographs against me. It would embarrass your political masters.'

'Yes. In foreign newspapers, however, with the source protected ... ? But Ralph, it needn't be like that. Silence can still be – bought.'

'How?'

'By the exercise of your undoubted influence. You draw back, simply that. Marian. Our silence for her safety. The photographs – all copies, all negatives – to you. *When* Marian calls us from the Embassy?'

Abruptly, Lau stormed: 'Is Aubrey there?' The hatred was venomous.

'Yes, Ralph. And Marian's father. Both privy. Both agree with my proposition. You have our solemn word – to speak or to remain silent. Call off the dogs, Ralph. From Hyde, too. We can guarantee his silence—'

'I can do nothing about Hyde. I am not in contact ...'

'Very well. Reluctantly. For Marian alone, then. You accept?'

'Can I trust you?'

'You can.'

'Then I must.' There was a twisting, sullen rage in Lau's tone, but little defiance. Nothing but defeat, the reply of a whipped dog.

Feng crossed the room and picked up the telephone, stabbing out the number he wanted. The Minister of Police.

'Feng. Lau will call you soon. You will pay no attention to his request, even though you will appear to agree to it. Your people will continue the search for the woman and kill her. The body must be secured until *I* identify it. Good.'

'... and her copies, yours, the negatives,' Lau was saying. 'Delivered to me.'

Lau would consider himself safe. Would doubtless

438

attempt to explain that he had bribed or blackmailed the photographs out of the woman and Aubrey. Expect matters to be as simple and pleasant as walking through a door into an ornamental garden. But he, Feng, must see the photographs, discover exactly what they knew. He, of course, was the Chinese officer – though perhaps unidentified. He must have the photographs from the woman's body. Eventually, have *all* the photographs.

He dialled the Minister of Police again.

'The woman,' he announced, 'will be brought to safety by the man Evans – yes, the one wounded by your people. He is at the Diplomatic Hospital. Increase the surveillance there. That is where she will go.'

Aubrey picked up the receiver. Davenhill and Giles were seated together on the sofa, sunlight spilling over their hands.

'Tony?'

'Yes, sir. I've got Phil Cass for you, hanging on the line. Wants money, I think. A lot of it,' Godwin added gloomily.

'Put him on.' Was it coming together? 'Philip, what's happening?'

Cass sounded as if he had been running. 'Got hold of some smugglers, sir – tip-off from the local police, who are probably on the take themselves. Never mind that. They use an old Cheetah helicopter for bringing out jade and rubies. Two crew, *three* passengers. I can hitch a ride ... Trouble is, they know I'm on the rack and the price is sky-high. In dollars. I haven't got enough—'

'How much?'

'Thirty thousand – fifteen each.'

'I see.' The unofficial operation had emptied the little, disparate clutch of old and forgotten SIS accounts on which he had relied. The cupboard was bare. 'My account.

I'll have the money transferred at once. The sort code is . . .'

'Yes. Got that, sir.'

'I'll instruct the bank to take an enquiry from you that the necessary funds are available. These smugglers of yours can listen, if they require confirmation. The money will be telegraphically transferred to any account number they supply the moment you inform me Patrick and Ros are safe . . . Or not. So long as you are certain either way.'

'Yes, sir. I'll get on with it—'

'Hurry, Philip. I'll make the necessary arrangements.'

He put down the receiver. Davenhill, exhausted, was still on a cloud of success, and Giles's soothed anxieties were oblivious. Just as well. The mantel clock tinkled four, prodding him. As he picked up the phone again, he experienced a guilt towards Patrick for having ignored their plight in the effort to save Marian.

He hurriedly dialled the number of his bank.

The gunship, its searchlight probing at the trees and undergrowth like a finger, went into the hover at the confluence of the Chindwin and the tributary Hyde had taken. It seemed to sniff like a dog at the water. Hyde, less than a mile into the foothills from which the tributary flowed down to the main river, held the boat against the bank, his arm crooked around the narrow bole of a leaning tree as he watched the helicopter.

Ros was fitfully asleep in the bow, curled on her side like a child under a thin blanket. Her face was hidden by her lank hair, then further concealed as another sliver of cloud slipped across the declining moon. It was almost eleven o'clock. He shook himself awake once more and stared afresh at the nosing gunship. A more distant glow came from the searchlights of the troop carrier.

Too obvious... He'd known it the moment he chose the tributary that flowed almost straight from the Indian border. But there had been no alternative.

The cloud still wrapped the moon. The gunship was moving slowly, sniffing at either bank of the river. The current, flowing against them, would make their progress slow. He tugged at the starter and the engine fired like a detonation, half waking Ros. He steered the boat a little away from the bank but kept it beneath the shadows of figs and other twisted trees that leaned out over the water. The jungle pressed down on the water like a herd of thirsty animals, and the river ahead of him was squeezed between high, damlike banks, weaving like an intestine into the higher country. Against the current, the boat would never take them as close to the border as he wished.

Ros struggled back into exhausted, dehydrated unconsciousness. She'd never walk into India over the mountains ahead. All her reserves had been drained by the dysentery.

The troop carrier was nosing behind the gunship, just as fervently interested in the river banks. Its two searchlights flicked out from either side of its squat body like an insect's legs. They were less than half a mile away. Shadows of trees fell across the tributary like mercy as the moon emerged from behind the cloud. The boat's narrow wake shone like a slug's trail in the moonlight. Shit—

Hyde steered the boat closer to the bank, nudging underwater roots, bucking away again, opening the throttle as he righted the boat. The rotor noise was becoming audible above the racket of the outboard. He glanced fearfully back. The gunship seemed huge in the night air, its rotors like a veil across the face of the moon. Only hundreds of yards away—

The river was narrowing and the current pushed

against the boat. Moonlight, spilling through overhanging branches, leprosied his hands and arms, and blotched Ros' face as she sat upright in response to his urgency. He watched her face and the landscape ahead, reading the narrowing distance between the gunship and the boat in her expression.

If he could only make another half-mile, before the gorge rose sheer on either side, squeezing the gunship's manoeuvring space. A bloody half-mile—

—no. He heard the change of engine note as more power was fed to the big twin turbines of the Mi-25. Export version of the Hind gunships he'd dodged in Afghanistan.

Then it was over them, the huge spider descending on its thread. The water around them was ripped into frenzy as if by a shoal of piranha. The water's violence stunned more immediately than the machine gun's noise. Leaves fell into the boat amid a shower of wood chips; a small branch fell across Ros's lap, stifling the scream she was about to begin. Hyde grabbed and held on to a jutting branch as the trees crowded over them like a damaged roof.

The gunship snouted for them, the pilot careful of the encroaching trees. The weapons operator would be eager for a glimpse of them in his electronic sights. He saw for an instant the tandem multiple eyes that were the two cockpits, then the water a little ahead of them was lashed into a savage froth by the machine gun. The wake of the stream of twelve-millimetre bullets moved towards them.

'*Get down!*' he yelled at her, barely able to hear his own voice.

Pulling at her, almost falling on top of her, he pressed Ros into the bottom of the boat. Branches severed like limbs; the outboard sprayed diesel over them, then caught fire as the stream of bullets moved on, tearing at the earth of the bank. Flame ran towards the spare fuel can, and licked up from the motor into the lowest branches.

He dragged Ros into the water, mud churning under his boots. The stream was icy from the mountains. He dragged the pack, too. Ros fell helplessly against the bank, her breath not coming in the panic that assailed her. Hyde tugged the backpack over the exposed roots of a tree, wedging it. Then he put his shoulder under Ros and pushed upwards.

'Catch hold, *for God's sake—!*' he bellowed above the rotor noise. '*Grab something!*' His terror enabled him to push her into the tree's roots and scrabble after her, the seconds still precise in his head – *eight, nine* – the fire brighter, the helicopter becoming a still weapons platform. He pulled at her arms, dragging her across the ground further into the trees, away from the bank. Then he staggered back – *fourteen, fifteen* – and pulled at the pack, hauling it towards her. Branches lashed in the downdraught, the flames from the boat dancing in it—

—eruption. He buried his head in his hands, lying across Ros. Trees groaned, the earth shuddered under them. Stones and mud fell on their bodies.

Seven, eight, nine, ten ... The silence after the detonations struck against his eardrums like a continuing explosion. Something crawled on the back of his hand and fell away as he moved. He could not hear his own voice as he urged Ros to her feet and then began dragging her and the backpack further into the crowding undergrowth. The silence continued, whining and then humming. Each pod on the gunship contained twenty rockets, there were *twenty pods*, this was just a slap on the wrist—

The detonations threw him off his feet in a half-somersault. Ros fell behind him. The backpack jerked his left arm painfully. The jungle glared with reflected light as small trees were uprooted, heavier branches flung down. The concussive shockwaves made him struggle for breath. Rocks, mud and wood rattled through the undergrowth.

Hyde crawled back to Ros. The trees behind them were aflame. He saw the fire reflected in the river and on the flanks of the gunship. Ros stared at him as if blinded—

—*blinded*. They were safe from the infra-red and the nightsights. He held her against him, crushing her frame to his, as fire dazzled them. He gabbled in her ear, not hearing or understanding his own words, not sure that she could hear them. He pulled at her – and she struggled to her feet, stumbling uncertainly through packed, hampering undergrowth.

Then she tripped and fell, dragging him down with her. The backpack was like a third person as it tumbled on them, heavy as a rock. The trees and undergrowth around them were lit by the fire now raging along the riverbank, still no more than hundreds of yards away from them. Above it, as if gloating, the black gunship. He remained seated in the leaf mould their fall had ploughed up, still holding Ros in his arms.

Then he saw them, descending on wires from the troop carrier, a little distance from the burning trees, like sparks falling from the helicopter. He released Ros and fiddled in the backpack. He pulled out the sub-machine gun, extended its retractable stock and fitted the magazine and the nightsight.

The soldiers continued to fall down the wires from the troop carrier. Nine, ten, a dozen—

'Oh, Christ, Hyde!' she wailed.

'It's all right, all right,' he soothed, as he resumed his count, anticipating another rocket or cannon attack.

Endgame—

CHAPTER SIXTEEN

Chaos Theory

Jessop watched the Chinese troops, slipping like toys down their wires to the burning skeleton of Hyde's narrow twig of a boat as it drifted away from the bank. *A pisspoor Viking funeral for Hyde* ... except that the bastard wasn't in the boat, but was probably still alive behind the blazing screen of jungled riverbank. The boat, still smouldering, accelerated with the current.

The pocketscope was useless against the burning jungle. Should have thought of that, but it had been such *fun* bombarding Hyde with rocket and cannon. Great fun ... He grinned, despite his disbelief that Hyde was dead. Which Ralphie-boy no longer wanted, apparently, but the men behind Colonel Slit-Eyes standing beside him did – so Hyde was finished. As he glanced at Yao-Fan, Cobb asked almost gleefully:

'Think we incinerated the Aussie bastard?'

The colonel moved towards the radio equipment and the troops on board the gunship poised to descend, and only then did Jessop reply.

'Knowing his luck, I doubt it. He's still in there somewhere with his fat tart. Maybe with a leg blown off, if we're lucky. But he won't be alive much longer, Cobbie, I promise you that.'

He watched the winchman take his position and the first of the troops slip his body harness to the cable that had been dangled above the jungle. Ten troops aboard the Mi-25, another two dozen already offloaded from the troop carrier. The gunship nudged over the trees, towards darkness. Gabbling Chinese voices as comms equipment was checked and the colonel instructed a lieutenant and two NCOs. Jessop watched, gloating. He wasn't going down there, not on your life. A boot into the ribs of Hyde's dead body would be pleasure enough. The first man, folding-butt automatic weapon slung across his chest, disappeared through the cabin, followed immediately by a second.

'You think Lau will blame us?' Cobb asked.

Jessop snorted in derision. 'Ralphie-boy knows which side his bread's buttered. It's the Chinks who call the shots. And he's in with them for the long haul.' He waved his arms expansively. The sixth, then the seventh soldier disappeared through the doorway, like conjuror's props.

Anticipating the first gunfire from the jungle below, they raced each other to the open cabin door, laughing aloud.

Her leg was dragging and her back ached with a wearying pain. She shuffled through the night like someone broken by beatings. The noises from the zoo startled her; the strollers in the park and beside the lake alarmed her. The park and the Royal Lakes floated like a dream of pleasure on the surface of Rangoon.

The hospital towards which Evans had told her to come was on the north-western shore of the long-fingered lake, less than half a mile away now. She could hear the muffled music from the Karaweik, the huge restaurant that was a replica of a royal barge. It was almost midnight.

Just offshore was a floating shrine to Upagot, the *bodhisattva* whose power protected people in mortal danger. Marian hoped it was protecting her. There had been a few recurrent faces in the strolling crowds, one of them white, but she was too weary of fear to be unduly alarmed. She was just as incapable of believing in rescue. Someone brushed against her lightly. She was close to Natmauk Road. The man was white, and he nodded to her, as if confirming her identity. Then he vanished like a memory.

She looked up. The Diplomatic Hospital rose palely in the night on the opposite side of the thinly trafficked boulevard. It was set in tidy grounds, behind neat trees. Could Evans see her yet? Suddenly, the man's brushing against her was very terrifying. Could he see her?

There she was – thank God. Evans heard his breath sigh out. It momentarily clouded on the glass of his fourth-floor window. He studied the grey, photographic negative that she was in the binoculars, hesitating at the park entrance. She looked as feeble and distracted as an addict, and he was shocked by her posture and air of vacancy. Behind him, his room was in darkness.

He swung the glasses across the hospital grounds. Even such minimal movement caused the wound in his side to throb. Marian's ghostly image reminded him too forcibly of the ambush at the teak mill, her narrow escape, his own wounding. He pressed his hand gently against the thick bandaging. *Come on, girl, just a couple more minutes...*

There were still cars passing along the tree-lined boulevard. Innocently. The pedestrians seemed uninterested in her as she hesitated at the kerb like an uncertain diver at the end of a high board. She was staring dreamily and unrecognising at the hospital. No one had followed her out of the park except Cormack, one of her father's ex-regimental recruits. Over the R/T, Cormack had reported her dazed condition. He'd been right not to identify himself and alarm her into panic.

She remained stranded at the kerb.

'Marian – Marian, cross the road,' he murmured intently, willing her to move. She looked up towards the hospital as if she had heard his voice, her attentiveness as grey and blanched as her features in the night-glasses.

She began to move slowly from the kerb towards the hospital. Evans realised he was sweating uncontrollably. The few parked cars beneath the trees of Natmauk Road and in the hospital car park had been checked. Clean. Marian was halfway across the boulevard, walking more purposefully. Less than a hundred yards now. Cormack was ten yards behind her, beginning to cross the road . . . His sweating increased. The other two gas-company security men that Giles Pyott had brought in were watching the car park and the main entrance. Once she got to Evans' room, she was protected diplomatically. And he would ring the Embassy the moment she—

She reached the near kerb. The tarmac drive up to the main entrance was foreshortened in the glasses. Evans scanned the boulevard again. Nothing untoward. She had reached the drive and was walking firmly, head bent, shoulders hunched, like an athlete on the last few yards of an exhausting race. Nothing moved except innocent traffic and Cormack, dodging the swerve of an ancient taxi as he gained the near pavement. Fifty yards. He picked out the other two, Neill and Omer, who had spotted her. Cormack was increasing his pace to close up behind her. Traffic flowed, there was no one else near her except a male nurse in a white coat. Nothing – sweating. His side was agony. Nerves—

It began to go wrong. Behind the double-glazed windows in the hot, darkened room, it was like a silent film of a minor disaster. He saw the brief exhaust plumes from two cars. The local help was moving in with Neill and Omer. Marian was striding out. Both cars careered into the hospital drive, tyres skidding, windows blank. Marian half turned. Neill and Omer, yards from her, were woken to alarm. Cormack had turned to face the cars, was drawing a pistol.

First, Neill, then Omer, fell . . . Evans watched, appalled. White faces, grey blood spurting. Their bodies were at once sprawled on the tarmac, while Cormack fired at the blank windscreens, shattering one of them. Marian began running, as if across a muddy field—

Evans lurched across the room, screaming, into the empty corridor, towards the lift. A shocked nurse was framed by its opening door. He flung her aside like a curtain between himself and the scene he had witnessed. His body was bathed in sweat. The bandage over his side was damp, his fingers reddened. He wrapped the dressing gown tighter around him. *Third . . . Second* – lights above the doors. Oh, Christ, his side was agony.

The doors opened and he tumbled out of the lift into the neat, aseptic foyer. People were moving with submarine slowness towards automatic doors that had already opened in response to a passing shape. Neill and Omer down – must have been a sniper; there hadn't been firing from either car at that point.

Nurses stood at the reception desk with a cowed

security man. He saw the two cars swing like the panels of an animal pen in front of her. She was still running, with Cormack yelling behind her, urging her on—

—as he reached the doors, shouting to the hospital staff to *Get down, lie down*, as he drew the Browning from the pocket of his dressing gown. He thrust the first round into the chamber as his wound screamed at him not to move—

Cormack was on his knees, shirt dyed with blood. Still firing. A light suit emerged from one of the cars and grabbed for Marian. He fired, saw pieces fly from the man's head and Marian's face receive some of the gouting blood. He fired again and again. Marian barged aside the injured second man, who was unable to restrain her. Evans heard screams as from a great distance. Cormack, back on his feet, limped like a wounded chimpanzee. Evans fired again, then twice more, bracing his body against the door frame. Return fire crazed the reinforced glass near his head.

She lurched into him like a reunion of drunks. As she fell against his side, he almost passed out. Instead, he clutched her and dragged her inside the doors, firing over her shoulder. Cormack was still firing. A third body lay across the bonnet of one of the black Mercs. He stumbled and she fell on top of him. Pain, then he blacked out—

She was lying on Evans, she realised, his face grey and damp. Everything hurt. The man from the park sat listlessly bleeding on the steps. The doors closed and people at once fussed over her, as if reality had suddenly been re-established. She fought off ministering hands to sit upright, roll away from Evans—

And saw the two cars slide away towards the boulevard. Bodies remained in the drive. The man on the steps was trying to light a cigarette. Nurses in white uniforms hurried out into the night towards him. Evans groaned and opened his eyes. Thank God . . . She was safe. There were too many witnesses. They'd had to leave, once Evans had dragged her through the doors . . .

The photographs of the atrocity at Tripitaka must have been torn away from her when Evans saved her life. They lay scattered on the tiles of the foyer like huge flakes of confetti. She gathered up those closest to her. A nurse collected others, more shocked by what she had just witnessed than by their contents.

She placed the sheaf of photographs on Colin Evans' chest. He groaned, and was then able to wink at her. She held his hand. Safe now—

No more troops were being spilt like droplets of thick oil down the cables from the two helicopters. He had counted more than thirty, seen their weapons. Folding-stock sub-machine guns, AK-47 assault rifles, a couple of light machine guns, a flamethrower, the tube of an RPG anti-tank weapon . . . He'd taken the inventory through the pocketscope. They were *invading* the fucking place . . . He continued to fumble in one of the pockets of the backpack. Pills—

He picked out the Flagyl tablets. Didn't really matter now which kind of dysentery Ros had – she swallowed the tablets with water. He held the other pill, the Spring Lamb. Two hours or more as Action Woman guaranteed, then total exhaustion, just like turning out all the lights.

He couldn't take one because all that adrenalin made you selfish as hell. Spring Lambs were for endgames, but only when you had just yourself to consider . . . Hyde hesitated, wondering at the effect of the pill on her debilitated system. Then gave it to her.

'Take this, too – do you good,' he called in her ear above the rotor noise. She swallowed it automatically.

There was little more than pinched moonlight beneath the trees. The gunship moved off, resuming its station above the river. The fire was burning out. They needed relative silence now. They'd hear nothing if the MiL was too close. Through a new rent in the trees he could see the foothills. He stood up and heaved the backpack on to reluctant shoulders.

The Indo-Burmese border was the heaviest-manned in the country. The Tatmadaw and the Indian army pressed against either side of it, nervously. The Burmese had Chinese intelligence, some Chinese officers. It was an unofficial Chinese border, one of the places where the two most powerful countries in Asia warily faced each other.

Sometimes nervous frontiers could be less hostile . . . If they wanted to avoid starting a border incident, then they'd avoid using the Tatmadaw. Military manoeuvres would appear hostile to Indian satellites and watch-towers, could look as if an invasion was about to begin.

The border with the Indian state of Manipur was beyond those mountains, five miles away. On an outcrop, the moon revealed the distant shape of a pagoda, a small white building jutting out of the jungle. A mile and a half away. The pagoda, Cass said, was a landmark for heroin smugglers - now a signpost for Hyde and Ros.

He reached a hand down to her and she rose to her feet with pleasing speed. Her eyes were brighter and the skin of her face shivered with adrenalin.

'All right?'

What was in that—?' she began, her voice cut off by the rasp of ether from an opened radio channel.

'Let's go.'

He held her against him for the first few steps, then she moved slightly away. Hyde nodded, pushing back undergrowth, then urging her past him, leaning thin bamboo aside for her. Moonlight filtered down like dust. The undergrowth closed in behind them, around them. Hyde pushed against it as if shouldering open a door, fearful of using the parang until it was necessary—

—then he swung at the dense undergrowth, the noise betrayingly amplified to his heightened senses. Sweat bathed him. He swung again and again, causing randomly spaced sounds, hugely relieved when he sensed the leaf-mould beneath his boots begin to slope gently upwards...

In a pause, to regain his breath, he listened intently. Muffled rotor noise, the rustling of an animal or reptile, Ros's small, agitated movements as if she was limbering up for an imminent race... *There.* The whisper of ether – something moving through the jungle. Off to their left and ahead of them, more than fifty yards away ... definitely moving off.

Her heard his own exhalation over the faint noises, that were more laboured now as the unseen soldier climbed the slope. Beyond his noises were those of another man, like an echo. Ros' face was eager in the moonlight, her eyes moving in a wideawake dream. He waited for silence then hacked at thin, whipping branches and creeper, cutting low as if to make a tunnel rather than a corridor. The bamboo fell away sideways, more easily, so that he began to hurry forward...

... pausing to listen more infrequently. Ros pressed behind him, filled with artificial, redundant energy. The gradient of the slope increased and he could see the moon-stained sky and dimmed stars more often. His breathing became laboured. In the few brief silences he allowed himself, he heard nothing. Even the rotor noise from the helicopters was like the background noise of crickets...

He stumbled on to a path, his last swing of the parang biting air and almost overbalancing him. A tiny, beaten track, too narrow for smuggling, made by small deer or wild boars. It wound through bamboo and tall trees in a narrow, uncertain tunnel. But it climbed the hill in the direction of the pagoda.

'OK?' he whispered, flicking the pencil beam of the torch on to the US army satellite map for an instant before looking up.

He studied the pagoda through the pocketscope. It became ash-grey instead of bone-white in the lens, its concentric terraces railed with waves of stone that passed protective carved monsters as they climbed to the central stupa.

'OK . . .' he murmured to himself. The place was lifeless.

'Can't we get a move on?' Ros asked impatiently. She was all but shuffling from foot to foot.

'You having trouble again?' he asked, grinning.

'No, it's that damned pill you gave me, Hyde. Let's get moving before I bloody well explode!' Then she added: When this wears off, I'll be paralysed, right?' He nodded. 'Right, come on, then—!'

'Hear anything?'

'Not for twenty minutes. Where are they?'

'Behind us, I hope. IR's no good in jungle. They need to pick up our trail. They're not up there – yet.'

'Is Cass up to it?' she asked after a moment.

'I hope so.'

'You want me to have a gun?'

'Not in your mood and walking behind me!' He stood up. 'OK, quick as we can manage.'

They moved off, jogging slowly, the slope increasing as the narrow track twisted upwards through the massed trees. Soon, they slowed to a plodding walk.

'All right?' He turned to her, settling the Heckler across his chest, holding an arm out towards her.

'It's like a bloody *dream*, Hyde! I keep feeling I can fly, but I'm stuck in *this*—!' She rubbed her hands down her breasts and stomach, her eyes unnaturally alive.

He was about to reply, but saw her eyes widen further, as revealing as a mirror. He bullied her to one side and off the track. She fell into the undergrowth, the noise broken by the tiny sound of his safety catch and the laugh of a macaque high in the branches of a tree ... Then their safety catches and the kisses of their weapons against other equipment, all apparent to him as he turned to face them.

Two of them, squeezed together and blocking the track. They were more like the silhouettes of targets than men. Hyde fired even as he dropped to one knee. The silenced MP5 coughed with whispered politeness in three-round bursts. Then again, six more shots. Bark was gouged from a tree beside his face, and the chips stung his cheek. Leaves ripped, earth was torn. The two targets fell, their noises in the bushes emerging from the din of their assault rifles.

'Ros!' he yelled. 'Come on!'

The pagoda was still lifeless in the lens, the hum of rotors still distant and constant. No nearby radio noise, no calls. Ros blundered into him.

'Keep behind me – right behind me!'

The pack weighed heavily as he bent and snatched at one of the bodies, hardly pausing. Chinese face, very young. Assault rifle, ammunition. They used seven-six-two, not nine mill ... He tore a spare magazine free of the dead boy's uniform, then started running, straightening up with a huge effort.

'You there?'

'Yes!' Her voice was close.

He could hear little after that except his own breathing. The slope was defeatingly steep now. He could no longer hear the hum of rotors above his exertions. Where was it, the fucking gunship, *where*—?

The pagoda was white in the moonlight. Stone elephants around a steepled wedding cake. Firing—

—returned fire into dense trees at nothing he could see. He ran on, after ensuring Ros hadn't been hit. Tried to grab her but she waved him on up the slope. Two hundred yards to go.

They reached the wall around the pagoda, and clambered over it on to a weed-strewn stone terrace, into the shadow of a gnarled, stooping tree.

The jungle was swallowing the pagoda like the slow, green jaws of a huge python. Hyde shed the pack and rolled on to his back and saw the MiL gunship sitting in the hover above the trees only hundreds of yards from the pagoda.

He crawled to the low wall and raised the pocketscope to his eye, scanning the jungle below the outcrop for moving forms. He heard Ros crawling to him, then felt her flank against his.

'OK?' he whispered.

'Don't keep asking! A gun - now?'

He held up the Sig Sauer and clicked off the safety catch. The Sig was good for small hands like hers.

'Thirteen shots - here's the spare clip.' He demonstrated the removal and replacement of the magazine. 'Got it?'

'Yes.'

Why isn't the gunship moving?

'Aim, arms steady, squeeze.' Ros nodded. The stimulant made her eyes and face feverishly eager for the gun; as if her whole personality had been changed.

'Good.'

Hyde fitted the laser lock sight to the barrel of the Heckler, then inspected the Chinese AK-47. Folded the nightsight up into position – not great but good enough in the bright moonlight. Checked it on the hovering MiL – *why isn't it coming in?* Tested the laser lock system after switching it on. A red dot on a figure that immediately removed itself from the frame of the helicopter's cabin door. He lowered the sub-machine gun. The AK-47 had the greater range. The Heckler would be better once they closed in . . . He swallowed away the taste of the thought.

The gunship remained in the hover. The white pagoda with its gold-tipped stupa looked fragile and vulnerable in the moonlight. The MiL could demolish it – and them – in one attack. *Why not, then—?*

From the backpack, startling him into a shivery reaction, he heard the peremptory bleeping of the radio. Someone wanted to talk. He dared not think it was Cass, even as he scrabbled the set from the pack and opened the channel.

'Patrick—?'

'Phil – Christ!'

'I've got the bloody thing at last! Take-off now, if you want it – a HAL Cheetah, enough room for the two of you . . . Ros?'

'She's OK—'

'Great! The old man's money came through – fucking greedy sods!'

'How *long*?' Hyde blurted. 'We're at the pagoda—'

'Fifty miles,' Cass announced after a moment. 'Uh – twenty-five minutes max—'

'Then get a bloody move on, Phil – half the fucking PLA is trying to crawl all over us! Don't tell the pilot—'

'No way,' Cass replied soberly. 'OK – good luck!'

Cass was gone; as if the call had been imagined, Hyde shook his head furiously. Not in disbelief, but in realisation as he looked up at the gunship. The Cheetah would be unarmed and a hundred m.p.h. slower than the MiL; it was more like a dragonfly than a warplane. He'd invited Cass to come and be killed along with himself and Ros. The gunship would take no more than seconds to down the Cheetah, and only a little longer to destroy the pagoda ... *Then why the hell didn't it?* his thoughts screamed.

He scanned the jungle slope through the AK-47's nightsight, depressing the change lever with his thumb to single shot. One ghostly figure, then a second, slipping up towards them through the mass of darkness that was the trees. He lowered the rifle.

It would be impossible to protect the entire circumference of the terrace. He couldn't send Ros to cover a second position on her own – didn't dare ... He studied the terrace. The jungle creepers and undergrowth invested almost two-thirds of it and had begun to close over the pagoda itself like a huge, dark hand. Anyone coming through would make a lot of noise, but remain invisible until they reached the terrace and had a clear field of fire. The rotor noise might even keep their approach undetected ... Why don't you *move*? Ros was quivering against his side. It was working, the terror inspired by that hanging weapons platform. The troop carrier was an unarmed dot further down the hillside, floating on the treetops.

Two minutes since Cass' call – airborne now. He raised the nightsight to the MiL. Someone descending the wire into the trees, the downdraught plucking at combat jacket and hair, making the leaf canopy angry. The figure disappeared – it was Cobb. He waited, tensing. Any moment now. Yes ... Jessop, like a monkey on a stick,

suspended in the air. His finger began to tighten inside the
trigger guard. Jessop . . .

. . . Jessop glowered back up at the Chinese colonel,
standing impassively in the cabin doorway. Chinky
bastard . . . He turned slowly in the air as the wire was paid
out by the winchman. The pagoda came into view – Hyde
was armed and alive. The gunship could reduce the whole
place to rubble in minutes but the Chinky colonel
wouldn't risk a border incident with any more air attacks.
*If you want him, and wish to be certain of his death, join
my troops on the ground.* Just like that . . . Radio traffic
from somewhere on the border had alarmed the Chink.
No more gunship activity.

The cable was lowering him so *slowly* on the winch!
Come on, Hyde's out there, armed—!

His feet touched leaves, branches. His legs were
swallowed by vegetation. Sweating and thankful, he lost
sight of the pagoda . . .

Hyde lowered the AK-47. Jessop had even sent Cobb
down first, just in case.

'If I'd have fired, the ground troops would have known
our exact position,' he murmured.

Ros offered him chocolate, eating some herself. He bit
and swallowed, shaking off the lethargy and tiredness
that even the momentary stillness had caused. He ate
more chocolate. Ros seemed less illuminated by the drug,
less fervid. He listened to her stomach rumbling, watched
her eyes grow duller. Listened to the noises in the jungle,
filtering them from the mush of the rotor noise,
distinguished the movements and nocturnal grumblings
of animals from the human sounds . . . Bushes being bent
aside, twigs snapping, the clink of metal.

Seventeen minutes to go—

He fired over her shoulder at a new shadow where the

jungle spilt creepers on to the terrace. Something stumbled back into the undergrowth – he swung the gun and fired three more shots. The soldier slipped into the shadow of a rock below the terrace. Then he heard something through the air; it bounced on the paving from a different direction, and rolled towards the pagoda—

'Down!'

Hyde covered her body with his own as the grenade exploded. Fragments embedded themselves in his hair, clothing, skin; chips of stone stung him. He rolled away from her immediately. He rose above the balustrade and caught the grenade thrower, thirty yards away, with his arm raised. Two shots. The man tumbled backwards into the bushes. Hyde thumbed the change lever to automatic and swept the trees until the box magazine was empty. Unclipped it and fitted the spare he had snatched from the dead Chinese. Thirty more rounds before the AK-47 was useless.

Silence. Momentary—

—the rocket-propelled grenade blew one of the mythical stone beasts away from the central stupa of the pagoda. It shattered, tumbling down, as he dragged Ros and the pack thirty yards along the terrace. A second grenade shattered the balustrade only yards from where they had been crouched. *Fifteen minutes.* It had to be the man who'd slipped into the rocks' shadow. Hyde remembered the loading sequence – he'd have to raise the launcher, raise his body . . . *There.*

The soldier popped up like a target and Hyde fired twice. The body slid back out of sight. Coughing with dust gouged from the terrace, he squashed himself flat against the cracked, uneven stones as crossfire raked above him.

Slow silence . . . He gestured Ros to move another ten yards. She crawled after him on her stomach, uncertain.

Thirteen minutes ... By now, the Cheetah's moonlit shadow would be flicking along the river gorge they'd be using for radar cover ... He looked up at the gunship. Twelve minutes – the MiL's radar and IR would pick up the dot of the Cheetah and wait, just wait ... It hovered, as if possessed of infinite patience and certain knowledge. The AK-47 wouldn't bring it down, it was out of range ... He needed a SAM launcher – *launcher*.

The dead soldier and the RPG were almost a hundred yards away ... Already he was using the pocketscope, sliding it across the immediate landscape. Small, flimsy shadows, boulders, bushes, chalk-white rocks ...

He'd have to leave Ros here alone, for five minutes, maybe longer. He checked the bushes, shadows, rocks again. He slung the Heckler across his chest after removing the sight.

'Ros, I have to go down there – get the grenade launcher. Use it on the gunship.'

'Christ, you'll kill yourself!'

'There's no other way.' She wouldn't be able to use the AK-47 to cover him. 'Couple of minutes—'

'We're buggered, Hyde, aren't we?' He looked at his watch. Ten minutes, a bit more. No more than six or seven before the MiL picked up the Cheetah on radar.

'Not yet ...'

He skittered in a crouch along the terrace and scrabbled through the gap in the balustrade the second grenade had made. No firing ... Eighty yards now ... He located the rock that was his next cover. Crouched, then ran again, stones slipping away from his boots, his progress jagged and weaving—

Flung himself behind the rock as bullets chipped at it and the earth around it. He was shivering with effort and adrenalin.

Ran again, along a narrow channel cut by countless monsoons. Was knocked off his feet. Hit.

'Christ—!' The impact, then the ground, winded him. Arm? It hurt hugely, throughout his body. His arm was useless.

The dead soldier's pale face, close to his own, stared at the sky and told him it was futile. The pain in his arm and shoulder kept blowing across his consciousness like a huge black curtain. He heard shouts, orders. A voice was yelling in English. Jessop—

He struggled off the dead soldier and propped himself against the side of the narrow trench below the rock. The RPG launcher aided him like a crutch. The grenades were still in their harness on the dead man's chest.

Five or six minutes – too late. The Cheetah was already on radar, coming blindly on. Cass was about to die, like himself . . . *Blank*—

Jessop saw the stupid fat tart clambering down the slope towards Hyde. Ros could watch, he thought, as he blew the bastard away.

'Hello, Hyde,' he announced, kneeling and pulling the Heckler easily out of Hyde's grip. The Australian looked dazed. His sleeve was darkly sodden, his arm hung uselessly. 'Mission accomplished, you Aussie bastard—' He raised the Smith & Wesson semi-automatic. Forehead shot, lovely. Hyde stared at him—

Ros saw Jessop kneeling in a parody of prayer on the edge of the trench as she staggered against a boulder, sitting heavily. Jessop looked up at her, as if disappointed she was still at a slight distance. Two hands, aim, squeeze . . . The pistol bucked, again and again. She couldn't see Jessop for tears . . . Thirteen rounds. The hammer clicked emptily, over and over. She was still squeezing the trigger convulsively as she lumbered the last few yards to the trench.

Hyde stared at her, one arm hanging by his side.

'Where is he?' she asked.

Jessop was a few yards away, lying on his back, his breath bubbling in his throat. She turned away, as if to disclaim all responsibility, then she lowered herself into the trench.

'Let me look—'

'No time for that.' He pointed at the launcher. 'Quick, pick it up, give it to me!' He hefted the narrow tube in his hand and tried to rest it on his shoulder, unable to move his wounded arm. He realised how quickly he was losing blood. He was dizzy and on the verge of unconsciousness. *He had to stay awake, look after her* . . . The scene blurred again, all detail vanishing into a sheen of moonlight.

'Hyde!' he heard distantly. 'Let me look at that arm!'

'No!' he growled. ' *You*'ll have to do it . . . Get one of the grenades – yes, off his body. Come *on*, doll—' She picked up the projectile. 'Now, screw that there . . .' He had regained the Heckler, and squashed it against his side, holding it stiffly at an elevated angle, the selector lever pushed to three-round burst. One hand was slippery, the other numb.

'What next?'

The pain of his arm and shoulder, the loss of blood, were bringing him close to unconsciousness again . . . He shook his head violently.

'Into the tube,' he answered muzzily. *He must stay awake—*

'Yes.'

'Nosecap – pull it off.' *Awake—*

'Yes.'

'Pull out the pin . . .' *Blank.* He felt her shake him awake. Pain shrieked through him.

'Yes . . . ?'

'Up to your eye,' he managed. Then, his voice a long way away from him, 'Adjust the focus on the—'

'Helicopter, right?'

'Right. Clear, is it?' Unlike his own vision. He stared at the blurred gunship, blinking again and again to bring it into focus.

'Yes.'

'Aim for the middle, then squeeze the trigger.'

Ros fired. The tiny rocket motor ignited ten yards away. The grenade moved towards the MiL at three hundred yards a second. One, two, three ... It detonated in self-destruction well beyond the MiL like an inadequate, disappointing firework—

Hyde fired. The soldier fell away from the lip of the trench. Vaguely, he heard shouted orders a long way off ...

'Again!' he yelled. Last grenade, last chance.

Head out of the trench, Hyde could see fuzzy, ghostly shapes running – saw the gunship turning slowly to face them, its interest aroused by the flealike missile fired at it. Ros fumbled the rocket into the tube as the gunship, affronted by their presumption, moved slowly towards them.

He squeezed off another three rounds at shadows he might have imagined. He caught the navigation lights of another helicopter, not the troop carrier. Illusion—?

'Fire it, Ros, for Christ's—!'

The MiL was turning again, its interest reawakened by the Cheetah. The rocket motor of the grenade ignited and the missile flashed towards the gunship. The Cheetah's lights were on as it approached the pagoda, then flicked off.

The gunship exploded. The fuel tank at the rear of the cabin gouted flame. It staggered in the air, two hundred feet up, as the explosions pulled it to pieces. Then the burning wreckage lurched sideways, rotors flailing like tortured limbs, before ploughing into the hillside jungle. Flame roared up.

He pushed Ros ahead of him, as they staggered towards the terrace. He and Ros and the Cheetah were the only moving things in the scene that was hideously lit by fuel-soaked trees burning like dry grass.

Cass—

Cass pulled him up the slope, through the gap in the balustrade on to the terrace. An Indian helped Cass to half carry him to the barely landed helicopter.

He saw Ros dimly, her relieved features close to his, as if listening to his breathing.

As they bundled him into the rear of the cramped cabin of the Cheetah, he was grateful for unconsciousness—

POSTLUDE

We are the Furies still, yes,
but now our rage that patrolled the crimes of men,
that stalked their rage, dissolves . . .
Aeschylus, *The Eumenides*, 11.514-16

As she opened the door of his room, Colin Evans' sense of comfort, his pleasant tiredness, immediately disappeared. Marian's strain was as apparent as the stains beneath her eyes. Rest, a bath, pills had had no effect on her. She remained the haunted, driven figure she had appeared in the night-glasses.

Her eyes darted towards him. A nurse's heels clicked along the corridor, but the sounds of the hospital's routine no longer lulled him. She had come for the bloody photographs...

When he'd told her earlier that Patrick and Ros were safe, she'd been pleased, but somehow impassive.

She perched on the bed in a borrowed silk dressing gown, ominously violent with golden dragons. He attempted to pat her hand but she snatched it away.

Behind her eyes, she was having the horrors. The

endless loop of film that had captured the past days continued to play to an audience of one. Alder, what had happened to her, the dead Burmese boy who'd helped to save her – they were all there, like ballast constantly moving in her head. He felt sorry for her. She was still out there, in the Rangoon night, alone.

Beyond the window, the noon sun blanketed Rangoon, the city once more innocent behind its heat haze. Except to her.

'Who was that who came to see me this morning?' she asked peremptorily, her fingers plucking at the counterpane.

'Who – Braxton? Bill's the military attaché here. He's all right—'

'Did you give him the photographs?' she demanded, her manner distraught, almost hysterical. She was barely in control of herself.

'All copies to Alex Davenhill,' he reminded her. 'The price of your safety.'

'I don't give a damn about Davenhill—' She faltered, her arms waving a distressed semaphore, her eyes suddenly filled with tears. 'What about Robbie, Kumar, Zeya, all those people at Tripitaka – *you*, almost . . .' Her face was shiny with the snail-tracks of her tears as she stared blindly at the window. 'They're all *dead* – all of them . . .'

Evans reached into the drawer of the bedside cabinet and placed the photographs, in a buff envelope, on the counterpane. Perhaps her naked emotions were irresistible; perhaps he just wanted her out of his room. Eventually, he said:

'What will you do?'

She got to her feet, the envelope clutched against her breasts. One of the dragons seemed poised to devour it. Her body was shivering as if the halo of light from the

A DIFFERENT WAR

Craig Thomas

On its final test flight, a new American airliner crashes
mysteriously in the Arizona desert. An accident, or
something more sinister? Mitchell Gant, the hero of
Firefox, and now an expert on aviation accidents, must
risk his life by repeating the test flight in every detail
to discover the truth.

In Britain, Marian Pyott, MP, finds evidence of a massive
fraud involving hundreds of millions of pounds ... and
implicating an ailing UK aircraft manufacturer seeking a
market for its latest commercial airliner. Behind Aero UK is
the conglomerate headed by Marian's childhood friend,
David Winterborne, a man ruthlessly determined to
prevent the collapse of his worldwide business empire
whatever the cost.

When a second airliner crashes off the coast of Finland, is it
coincidence or design? Is there a conspiracy that involves
business, politics and the global marketplace?

Gant survived Vietnam, the Cold War and the Gulf. Now,
he finds himself fighting a different – and far more
dangerous – war.

Other bestselling Warner titles available by mail: